Rumours
&
Recklessness

A Pride & Prejudice Variation

Nicole Clarkston

Dedication

To my mother and my grandmother, who both always told me I ought to write a book.

And to Mrs Gerhardt, who introduced me to the great ones.

Nicole Clarkston

Contents

Acknowledgements

My heartiest appreciation to Jane Austen for crafting such unforgettable characters and rich narratives. They have lived long in the imaginations of two centuries worth of readers, and will continue to do so for much longer than that. I must also thank those who have gone before, continuing to examine our favourite characters from fresh new angles.

One

Thomas Bennet had not slept a wink. He tossed fitfully in his bed, the sheets now a hopeless tangle about his legs. Indigestion, he told himself. The observant reader might perhaps infer that all of his tossing and turning could be attributed to Mrs Bennet's hysterical reenacting of every scene at the prior night's ball at Netherfield. Additionally, one might expect that his changeful mind wavered between amusement and hope at his neighbour's burgeoning attachment to his eldest daughter. It was also possible, perhaps, that his discomfort may have been aggravated by the nagging worry that his unwelcome house guest had an eye on his second daughter as a fitting mistress of the Hunsford parsonage.

Likely as any of these possibilities were, Mr Bennet did not consider them as influential to his agitated night as the over-abundance of fine victuals in which he had indulged the previous evening. He groaned, rolling out of the bed he had only a short while ago occupied.

Peering out the small window, he could see only the first warning streaks of dawn marking the horizon. Mr Bennet always slept near an eastern window if he could help it. It was a habit he had passed on to his second daughter, who shared his youthful love of the early sunrise. He doubted Elizabeth would be up so early, after dancing so long and so often last night.

There was nothing else for it- he was well and truly awake, and would find neither rest nor companionship for hours. He considered retreating to his library as was his wont, but he felt unusually restless. He noted that the sky was relatively clear; the typical early winter rains had held off for at least

1

one more day. He resolved to do something he had not done in many years- an early morning ride over the frosty fields.

He dressed quietly and crept down the hall, careful to avoid the squeak on the third stair. The household staff were already awake. Mrs Hill glanced up in mild surprise from where she crouched to light her kitchen fire. "Good morning, sir!" she greeted him.

The Hills had been with the Bennets since the days of his grandfather, and always treated him with friendliness bordering on diffidence, but still properly tempered with respect. He had come to value the current Mrs Hill even more highly after his own marriage, when his wife had proven a flighty, distractible sort. Mrs Hill was perfectly capable not only of managing the household, but of managing her mistress. A smooth operator, she was able to make sound, reasoned decisions and then let her mistress feel as though the choice had been her own.

"Well, well, thank you Mrs Hill. Though, I doubt you will find a willing audience for your delicious fare this morning. They will all be abed a long while yet. You may as well skip the morning repast and go back to bed yourself until tea time!" he chortled.

Hill, well acquainted with the master's pithy humour, simply nodded. Her practiced hands coaxed the sparks to life. "Did the young Misses have a fine evening then, sir?"

"Aye, I suppose if you count flirting with the officers and displaying their talents on the pianoforte, I would say all the younger girls enjoyed themselves well enough. Jane I believe spoke to no-one but Mr Bingley, so I suspect she may have found the company rather monotonous. And Lizzy! Lizzy got to savour a lovely dance with our distinguished Mr Collins, but her toes may be rather bruised this morning. She may not be taking her morning walk today." He walked off, chuckling to himself.

Mrs Hill made a face as she continued to tend her fire. That foolish Collins would someday be Master at Longbourn, and thereby her employer. She did not look forward to it one bit. As much as she would regret losing any of her young misses to either marriage or banishment due to the entail, she would regret even more seeing one of the lively Bennet girls tied here to that ridiculous man. But there, a servant had her place. Still, if she were ever called upon to shield one of her girls or the estate from the interfering, bumbling presence of a pompous fool, she would do all she could.

Mr Bennet had long ago given up keeping a dedicated hunter in his stable. The estate could ill afford the upkeep on a horse for which he had little use. He kept a pair for work on the farm which doubled as their carriage horses, and one saddle horse for road use. He was occasionally ridden by the family and often put into a low cart for any servant sent on an errand. The older gelding had been a sprightly hunter in former days, and his good breeding showed in the lines of his neck and shoulder.

An unfortunate hock injury three years earlier had forced one of Mr Bennet's neighbours to look elsewhere for a sporting mount, and the gelding had been retired to more sedate use. Mr Bennet had thought the bay a fine bargain, since he never rode hard, and in fact seldom rode at all. Jane had instantly loved the old gentleman, for gentlemen the gelding was- at least when she rode. She had been the only one of his daughters to show any interest in riding, and the horse had been as much hers as his.

He swung up into the saddle and set off for the furthest field at a brisk trot. In the gray light, only a heavy mist could be seen. The cool smell of the fresh grass and crisp autumn air was an instant balm to his soul. *Why did I ever give this up?* he wondered to himself. He jogged over the cool fields and for once remembered the days of his youth at this house.

There was one particular path of which he had always been fond. Lizzy, he knew, walked that way frequently, but it had been years since he had taken the route himself. Turning toward it, he slowed his horse to a walk after a bit. The poor fellow was not conditioned for long bouts, and he had no desire to aggravate the horse's old injury.

He had ridden just over a quarter of an hour when distant hoofbeats from the opposite direction caught his attention. The mist had begun to clear in the last few minutes, but he still could not make out the rider. A tall black horse galloped toward him at breakneck speed, the rider pushing him relentlessly.

Mr Bennet could see even from a distance that this was no express messenger on a post nag, but a well-to-do gentleman on a finely bred hunter. Either the man was fond of vigourous morning exercise or there was some emergency in the neighbourhood- or the man had some demons to exorcise and his poor horse bore the brunt of his frustrations.

A moment more, and Mr Bennet could make out the stern features of Mr Darcy, who still had not noticed him. Even in the damp chill he wore no coat, only a white lawn shirt which clung to him. The horse was lathered with sweat. Evidently they had been riding hard for a while.

Horse and rider cleared a low hedge, and Darcy, who carried no whip, skillfully used his hands and seat to land on the opposite lead and then urge the horse yet faster. Rounding a bend in the lane, the newcomer gave a start when he detected his observer. He pulled up sharply, breathing hard.

"Mr Bennet!" Darcy was surprised in the extreme. He reined in his restless mount, willing him to settle between his knees. He presented a fair sight, he knew. He was drenched in sweat, his hat gone, his shirt open and sleeves rolled up despite the biting cold. "Forgive me, sir, I did not expect to encounter anyone so early this morning."

Bennet raised an eyebrow, a curious smile playing at his mouth. "So I see. May I ask, sir, has Netherfield caught flame in the night? Or perhaps has Miss Bingley taken ill from all the dancing last evening? I am afraid you are going the wrong way for the doctor."

Darcy looked entirely discomfited. He pressed his lips together and his gaze darted from side to side, grasping for a proper response. Mr Bennet could well imagine the man was not used to such casual humour. He had witnessed the fellow's lack of ease in social settings and had taken great amusement in watching Darcy awkwardly rebuff the hopeful- and sometimes mercenary- advances of others.

He remembered that a few weeks ago Darcy had spent several days locked in the same house with his Lizzy. With perverse delight, he wondered how the austere Darcy had fared under her playful jabs. Lizzy held him in no awe, he was certain of that, and this stiff fellow would have been prime fodder for her drollery.

The tall man adjusted his seat in the saddle and cleared his throat. "I was just out for some exercise, sir."

"After so late a night of dancing, sir? You must indeed have an iron constitution! I believe I saw you stand up at least twice last evening. Once was even with my Lizzy- now *that* would wear out a lesser man for at least a se'nnight!"

Darcy bridled at Mr Bennet's merciless quips. He answered in clipped tones, his teeth clenched. "I could not sleep, sir. I have often found that a brisk morning ride helps to clear my head." He did not wish to defend his motives in dancing only twice, rude as some might perceive him, any more than he wished to discuss his one dance with this gentleman's daughter. It was, in fact, that one dance which had driven him out this morning to punish his body rather than his mind.

The older gentleman relented somewhat. "I confess, I did not rest well myself. There is nothing like fresh air and a little exercise to revive the soul. It is lovely scenery, is it not?" he asked, tactfully turning the subject.

Darcy finally took a deep breath, catching up on all the air his body demanded. His horse panted hard and fast under him, filling him with guilt for his treatment of the creature. "It is, sir. It is very different from the Derbyshire country, but I have come to enjoy the rolling fields of Hertfordshire a great deal," he admitted.

Mr Bennet smiled appreciatively. He loved his home, and enjoyed the pleasure of hearing so distinguished a man as Mr Darcy of Pemberley expressing his admiration. Mr Bennet was a fine reader of characters when he gave himself the trouble. There was something under this man's commanding presence which seemed… disquieted.

He could imagine that such a young man, thrust early into the heavy responsibilities which Darcy reportedly had been, would have more than his share of struggles. Mr Bennet's natural inclination to amuse himself at another's expense yielded to the vulnerability he sensed in the other man's manner.

Mr Bennet had not been born heir to Longbourn. That honour had fallen to him when his older brother, while still a very young man, died in some skirmish on American soil. Like many other second born sons too young for conscription, Thomas Bennet had studied for the church. His heartbroken father had required his return home to manage his affairs, and the young heir had at length secured a wife.

The father had not long outlived the older brother, thus Thomas Bennet had ultimately inherited Longbourn at such a young age that he had spent little time in the service of his fellow man. Still, his counseling instincts had been honed, if forgotten these many years. "If you do not mind me saying, sir," he ventured cautiously, "your horse could use a breather, and I might add that you look wrung out yourself. Come, keep an old man company for a bit."

Darcy hesitated to reply. He had only ever spoken just enough for propriety to the man, and had actively tried to avoid spending unnecessary time among the Bennet family. They were all wildly improper at times. Aside from the two eldest sisters, Mr Bennet was certainly the most respectable of the lot, but Darcy had steered clear of him as well. It had quickly become apparent to him that the enchanting Elizabeth Bennet shared her father's capricious humour. He was uncertain about the wisdom of spending much time around the father of the woman he was trying desperately to forget. The older gentleman had been correct, though- his horse needed a break badly, and he could not politely excuse himself.

He turned to match his mount's strides to Mr Bennet's bay. His practiced eye touched briefly over the horse, correctly guessing the former hunter's history and the reason for his current reduced circumstances. It was all too common a history, and the wonder was that this particular horse had escaped serious injury well enough to remain useful.

Again he felt remorse for his punishment of his own favourite mount. Pluto was the pride of Pemberley's breeding operation, the result of four generations of patient planning and the hope of the future. Already his foals were showing tremendous promise. To have so carelessly endangered his soundness this morning for the sake of a bad night's sleep was inexcusable.

The two men spoke uncomfortably of the unseasonably fine break in the otherwise wintery weather. Darcy made an offhanded observation regarding the slickness of the path- which, though damp with a heavy rain a few days before was still hard with frost beneath, a treacherous combination. Such talk of the elements led naturally to the plenitude of fowl and successful shooting season the younger man had had. Finally, they hit upon the topics of crop rotation and land management.

Darcy found that his usually flippant companion had a great deal of insight into the subjects. Save for his uncle, Darcy had seldom had opportunity to speak with a more experienced landlord. Owing to his status in society he more frequently found himself advising others, such as Bingley, when his own lack of experience occasionally worried him. Although Mr Bennet's holdings were by no means on a par with Pemberley, he was surprisingly knowledgeable and, Darcy sensed, an equitable and compassionate landlord to his tenants.

They passed nearly a half hour in this way, slowly walking the narrow lane together. Darcy would ask pointed questions, which to a casual observer would not appear to be those of a student to a master. Mr Bennet was not fooled, but he tactfully refrained from teasing his younger counterpart. He even found several frank questions he could ask in reply, which would cause his companion to consider slowly, then expound upon his opinions. Darcy expressed himself well, with earnest intelligence and pragmatic respect. Mr Bennet found it difficult to reconcile this very agreeable fellow with the recalcitrant wallflower he had known previously.

Mr Bennet began to sense that Mr Darcy's arrogant pride was, in a small way at least, a cover up for his own innate shyness and discomfort. Some part of his own jocular being wished to be of some material good to the younger man. He had never had a son. It was Elizabeth who had gained most of the fatherly attention which would have been due his heir. She knew more about running an estate than most young ladies, as he had found her quick mind to be the perfect sounding board for his management plans about the property. He now discovered in this young man, whose wealth dwarfed his own, an apt and willing pupil.

They crested a small knoll, and as the hillside fell away it revealed a breathtaking view beyond the small rocks. The rising sun had fully crested the distant horizon, spreading pink hues through the remaining gray of pre-dawn. Drawing their mounts up, Darcy allowed that the vantage point was, indeed, a remarkable sight. Glancing down, he saw that his horse was almost fully cooled. He patted the stallion's crested neck affectionately.

"Yes, this used to be a favourite spot of mine, but I have not visited in years. It is called Oakham Mount. Elizabeth, I believe, walks here regularly." He watched Darcy stiffen out of the corner of his eye.

The curious father had wondered what had caused Darcy to single out Elizabeth last night for a dance. The man could hardly have escaped dancing with his eager hostess, but the Master of Pemberley had quickly developed a reputation in the region for avoiding dancing, and women altogether, whenever possible. Either his favourite daughter had caught

Darcy's eye, or the man had simply wished to oblige his friendly host by appearing once again on the floor. Perhaps he was the sort of man who enjoyed a little verbal sparring with his partner during an otherwise tedious half hour, and for that Mr Bennet could not have faulted him. Whichever was the case, the father in Mr Bennet had watched the scene with interest and observed that neither partner had left the floor satisfied nor in good humour.

Darcy pressed his lips together and sought to make a diplomatic reply. "Miss Elizabeth seems to enjoy walking a great deal," he supplied neutrally, then lapsed into stony silence. He continued smoothing his horse's ruffled mane without looking back up.

Mr Bennet eyed him carefully. Most, including himself until this moment, assumed Darcy never looked at a woman but to disapprove of her. With a sly glance at his companion, Mr Bennet decided that, perhaps, Darcy did not quite disapprove of *every* woman. Of all the women in Hertfordshire, Elizabeth was probably the most unlike the reserved gentleman in demeanour. In most cases, it would be easy to assume that the dissimilarity in their temperaments would dispel any attraction. Darcy, however, would not be the first taciturn man of Mr Bennet's acquaintance to find himself fascinated by a spirited woman.

Mr Bennet continued to regard Mr Darcy's granite expression from the corner of his eye. *A man who felt nothing surely would not have to work so hard to affect a casual air!* he chuckled to himself. *Why, the fellow practically turned green.* If his guess was correct, Darcy did admire his daughter to a certain degree, but a man of his status could surely never form any serious design on her.

He considered Darcy's sudden stoicism for another moment, and decided that Elizabeth's loudly proclaimed dislike of the man would prevent any harm. He certainly did not see in Darcy the rash, foolish mind of a love-struck rake. No, young as he was, Darcy was bound by responsibility and duty. He seemed an honourable enough man as well, despite Elizabeth's report of some wrong done to that Wickham fellow. He was certain that, even if the young Master of Pemberley were intrigued by Elizabeth as he suspected, Darcy would not dally with his dearest girl. Much good it would have done him to try! The swine in his stockyard would sprout wings before Elizabeth would tolerate the attentions of such a man.

He cleared his throat, hoping to bring to light the younger man's intentions. "If I may, Mr Darcy, how long do you propose to remain at Netherfield? I should have thought the duties of your estate and the allure of Town would have called you away to more interesting events by now."

Darcy looked up quickly. Did he detect a note of warning behind the friendly tone? He could not tell if Mr Bennet had purposely dropped Elizabeth's name earlier, waiting for a reaction. It seemed improbable; likelier indeed was the possibility that his own guilty thoughts stimulated his imagination in that regard... but if the father were anything like the daughter, anything was possible. Knowing her puckish humour as he did, he did not want to give her father any morsels of insight into his private thoughts. He hoped he had maintained adequate control of his expression and that Mr Bennet had perceived nothing.

"I return today, sir," he replied, trying to keep the stiffness out of his voice. Whoever this man's daughter was, he had enjoyed the past half hour more than he could have expected. He did not wish to take offence with the one agreeable companion he had met in the region. "Mr Bingley returns with me to attend some matters with his solicitor. I expect we may be in London some duration."

Mr Bennet quirked an eyebrow. "If that be the case, sir, I suggest you give your good horse a few hours of rest before setting out! I presume you do not intend to leave him here, nor plan to return for him. Though, I daresay, there will be bitter disappointment in my home this morning at your party's departure."

Darcy clamped his lips into a thin line. The exquisite torment of being near Elizabeth Bennet and unable to call her his own was beyond what he could bear any longer. In four years at Cambridge and five seasons in London as a highly eligible bachelor, he had never encountered a single woman of her caliber. She was of a class apart, somehow so far above them in quality that she had squelched the hope of ever finding a love match in anyone else.

Perhaps it was the very fact that she did not seem to care for his good opinion that intrigued him. She had his admiration, he was certain she knew it, and yet she played cat and mouse with him. Rather than overtly trying to impress him or fawn over him as others did, she baited and teased. She cleverly jousted with him, causing him to rethink some of his opinions with her delightful intellect. Thrilling, provocative woman! He could see himself happily spending the rest of his days puzzling her out.

Exhilarating as she was, he knew he could not offer for her. It was unthinkable! The shame of a connection to her family was too much. Though an indolent parent, the father seemed respectable enough, as did the eldest sister, but the rest of the family were utterly ridiculous! It was more than that, though. Her station was decidedly beneath his notice! His circles in London may never actually meet the outrageous family, but the meanness of the lady's upbringing would be apparent. She had not been brought up to his level of society and could not hope to be found acceptable... could she?

Though he conceded it as likely that Elizabeth Bennet would shine in whatever circumstances she found herself, she would meet with ridicule and he with scorn among those of the *ton*. No, it was impossible. His early morning ride had been about ridding his mind and heart of her once and for all. If he wrung himself out completely, perhaps he would be able to endure the long carriage ride which would take him away from her forever.

Resolutely, he picked up the reins, turning from the glowing sunrise, a promise of hope, back to the somber grey which yet lingered over Netherfield- over everything his life represented. "You are perfectly right, sir. I should return to complete my preparations. I thank you for your company, it has been a most agreeable visit. Good day, sir."

"Good day, Mr Darcy, and Godspeed on your journey," Mr Bennet smiled warmly. He received a most civil salute in reply, and Darcy galloped off.

Mr Bennet chuckled to himself. Darcy had altered quite rapidly from the interested fellow landowner back to the rigid proud gentleman he had first known when he had brought up Elizabeth's name. Much as he had enjoyed his morning chat with the younger man, he could not rid himself of the delight he found in amusing himself at another's expense. It seemed to him highly possible that his lively daughter *had* piqued the austere man's interest, much to the other's chagrin. *Well, what else do we live for, but to make sport of our neighbours, and laugh at them in our turn?*

He studied the rosy skyline a few moments more, then decided to return home himself. Darcy's early morning vigour reminded him of the heady days of his own youth. How he had once loved a brisk morning gallop! Decisively, he wheeled his once well-schooled mount and dashed toward home at a spanking canter. The gelding responded smoothly, seemingly enjoying the speed as much as his rider.

Only five minutes from his home, a grouse started from the brush by the path. Mr Bennet would not normally have been unseated by his horse's shy, but the gelding's old weakness, combined with a slick part of the path, proved too much. The horse stumbled hard, his hind legs slipping out from under him as his forelegs paddled for solid purchase. Mr Bennet's last coherent thought was to desperately grab for his horse's mane before terrifying weightlessness claimed him. An instant later, all was blackness.

Two

Elizabeth fought against the first pinpricks of wakefulness niggling their way through her veil of sleep. She rolled over, noting even through her closed eyes that it must be well past dawn. She flipped the covers over her head and buried herself within their soft cocoon, if only for a few moments more.

Her traitorous body was warming up and tingling, as it always did when alertness finally jolted her out of bed. She knew she would soon become restless, and unwillingly disturb Jane who still slumbered peacefully beside her. After her wondrous but exhausting evening, Jane deserved her sleep. They had only been abed a few hours.

With a sigh, Elizabeth threw back the covers on her own side and slipped out of the bed. She cringed at the first touch of the cold floor on her bare toes, and hurriedly pulled on her clothing. She chose a simple day dress, thinking it would not yet be too late for a short morning walk. Pinning her hair into a plain knot, she closed the door behind herself as quietly as possible.

Elizabeth tiptoed down the hall, taking special care to make no noise that could possibly wake the odious Mr Collins. He had so far shown no inclination toward being an early riser, but he had taken to hounding her every move of late. *An hour's peace, that is all I ask*! she thought to herself.

She crept down the stairs, glancing toward her father's study. She would have expected to see the door closed with light pouring beneath already this morning, but it stood ajar. What she could see of the room beyond looked cold and empty. After so late an evening, perhaps even her father found his bed's appeal outweighed the delights of his library.

Elizabeth hugged herself and rubbed her hands vigourously on her upper arms. The drawing room fire had not yet been lit, which she found odd, but she knew that Hill's kitchen would already be toasty and comfortable. She pushed the door open and began to help herself to a fresh pastry when the housekeeper herself bustled through the back door of the house, her face red and lined.

"Good morning, Mrs Hill…. what is it?" Elizabeth interrupted her greeting when she saw the look of concern written on the woman's face. Just behind Mrs Hill came her husband, and he was bending to speak words to her in a low voice when he noticed his young mistress. His face froze and he straightened.

Elizabeth's eyes darted between the two in growing alarm. It was not like the Hills to be secretive or anxious, and their hesitation fueled the nervous fist balling in her stomach. "Has something happened?" she demanded, her voice wavering slightly.

"Oh, well, it's probably nothing, Miss," Mr Hill stammered. "Only that the Master went out for a ride this morning, and the horse has lately returned without a rider."

Elizabeth sucked in her breath and her face turned pure white. "*What?* Probably nothing, how can you think so?" Her voice rose perilously in pitch. "Father never rides in the morning! Has there been some emergency in the village?"

"No, Miss, it was nothing like that," Hill assured her. "He said he wanted some exercise, that was all. I'm sure he'll be back soon; you know he could easily have dismounted to read a book for a bit and the horse wandered off. Young Jim Hayes from the stable has gone to look for him."

"Do you know which way he went?" she trembled, irrational fear for her father's safety beginning to take hold.

"No, Miss, I did not see. But Jim…." He did not get a chance to finish, as Miss Elizabeth had flown out the door without even bothering to find a coat or hat. Shaking his head, he resolutely kissed his wife on the cheek and followed after his young mistress.

Elizabeth powered down the path toward Oakham mount, her instincts telling her that in the absence of some emergency, her father may have bent his steps in that direction. Mr Hill had to jog to keep up with her. In a short way, they spotted a muddy patch of trail which clearly showed fresh hoof prints. A horse had come that way only this morning. With a strangled cry, Elizabeth hurried on even more quickly.

Hill panted behind her, trying to talk some reason into the young lady. Then, as they turned a subtle fork in the path, they saw Mr Bennet's crumpled form lying among the browned grass by the side of the road. Elizabeth sobbed and ran to him. Together they turned him face up and she pressed her ear to his chest. She gasped in infinite relief when she heard his steady heartbeat, but he did not open his eyes. Without a word, Hill stood and, old as he was, ran back toward the house as quickly as his stubby legs could carry him to alert his wife. Elizabeth was left to cradle her father's muddied face, praying for him to wake up.

~

The shrieks from Mrs Bennet's room could have wakened the dead. Unfortunately, they only woke Mr Collins. The round-faced parson emerged from his room, shoddily dressed and with a countenance of stern disapproval. Jane happened to quit her mother's room just in time to pass by him, and he readied himself for a firm reproof against the matron's behaviour. "Ah, Miss Bennet, I…." He was cut off quickly when Jane simply brushed past him without even a backward glance. She hurried down the stairs and burst through the door of the family's kitchen, leaving his gaping mouth in her wake. "Well!" he huffed to himself. He would chastise his young cousin for her rudeness later, but first he would get to the bottom of the unruly disturbance in the household.

With great dignity, he squared his shoulders and descended the stairs in as stately a manner as he could muster. He would require Mr Bennet to answer for his family's uproarious behaviour! After all, as a future son-in-law, it was within his rights to insist the family of his dearest Cousin Elizabeth behave in a manner befitting the relatives of a clergyman. Of course, he had not yet tendered his proposal, but in the course of the morning he fully expected all would be settled to his satisfaction.

Without regard for the sanctity of his host's private library, he gave a brief knock and entered, not waiting for a reply. Instead of Mr Bennet, as he expected, he found a tear-streaked Elizabeth cloistered with a middle-aged man in a grey overcoat. The man had placed a familiar hand on her shoulder as she muffled her tears in a handkerchief. A surge of indignant jealousy bubbled up. Without much grace, he demanded an introduction to the man who would dare impose himself on a young lady in her own father's library.

The man stood gravely, not entirely masking his irritation. Though he spoke to Collins with an iron in his voice, his eyes turned frequently with gentle concern toward Miss Elizabeth. "My name is Jones. I am the apothecary in Meryton, and I have known Miss Elizabeth since her birth. May I ask your name and the nature of your intrusion?"

The apothecary's tone was even less cordial than his words. Clearly he was posing himself between the young lady and this interloper. Collins bristled, but as a clergyman, he remembered that he ought to consider it incumbent upon himself to arbitrate peace among those connected to him. "Of course, Mr Jones, do forgive me. I feared you might be distressing my young cousin," he smiled winningly at her. She gave no indication that she saw it, for surely if she had, she would not have turned suddenly away with a renewal of her sobbing. He drew breath for a speech of introduction, but the apothecary interrupted.

"I am afraid, Mr Collins, there has been an accident this morning. Mr Bennet took a fall and is currently unconscious. I will thank you not to disturb Miss Elizabeth at the moment, as she and I are working out what must be done for him." Jones returned a comforting hand to Miss Elizabeth's shoulder and she took a deep shuddering breath.

Collins' eyes went wide, and Elizabeth was sure she detected a mercenary gleam in them. "Oh, my dearest cousin! Allow me to offer my condolences for the indisposition of your esteemed father! Please do not fear for any of the arrangements. I feel it is my duty as a clergyman, and, dare I say it," he smiled charmingly at her, "a very *close* connection of the family to supervise these affairs. I feel certain that, when I have explained all to my noble patroness Lady Catherine de Bourgh, she will sanction my excellent intentions to…."

"*Thank you*, Mr Collins!" Elizabeth stood bolt upright, clenching her handkerchief in her small fist. "My sisters and I are perfectly capable of caring for my father while he recovers. I assure you, he is not in any danger, and only wants time and rest."

Collins smiled condescendingly, directing his next comments to the apothecary. "My dearest cousins are quite accustomed to having to make do without the comfort of a decisive man to settle things for them! Their natural modesty becomes them, but I am quite persuaded that when the full import of the circumstances shall be revealed, they will be greatly in need of my services. If you please, sir, I insist you direct any information or inquiries through myself, and I will be flattered to be of assistance."

Jones's jaw dropped at this audacious speech. It was no secret that Collins stood to inherit Longbourn. Word around Meryton was that he was silly and self-important. Jones settled with himself that Collins was also a worthless fool. He did not like leaving the Misses Bennet to his mercy. Caring for their injured father and hysterical mother would be strain enough, but to have this pompous vulture living right under their own roof could mean leaving them vulnerable.

He had no doubt of Miss Elizabeth's indomitable spirit, or of Miss Jane Bennet's wise discretion, but there were the younger girls to consider as well. There was the additional concern that he as yet had no indication whether his old friend would recover, or if he would be in his right mind when he did so. He resolved to have a word with Mrs Hill to see what could be done toward the family's protection.

They finished the short conference in the library, both Elizabeth and Jones purposely interrupting Collins whenever he spoke. Had they not, the discussion might have lasted another hour. Jones took his leave of Miss Elizabeth while Collins profusely assured him of his devoted condescension toward his lovely young cousins. He could not make his way out the door without being delayed three full minutes while the red-faced oaf thanked him artfully for his assistance. He shut the front door firmly behind himself and made his way around to the back door of the house, where he hoped to find the family's servants.

He knocked on the door and found Mr and Mrs Hill in close conversation over the servants' breakfast table. They welcomed him like the old friends they were, and Mrs Hill asked Clara, the house maid, to fetch him a cup of coffee. When she had gone, he brought his concerns to the couple.

They all agreed that Collins should not be trusted with the care of a dog-let alone a house full of spirited girls, a distressed Mistress, and a seriously injured Mr Bennet. No one was ready to accuse him of malicious intent, though he could certainly be found guilty of avarice every time he toured through the house. His appraising study of his future inheritance had been inappropriately bold from the first day of his residence there. There was little to be done about that, as it was well within his rights as legal heir to know of the property, but they did not have to allow him authority over Mr Bennet's private affairs while he yet lived.

Then there was the concern for the girls. Suspicions had been aroused as to his intentions regarding them, thanks to Mrs Bennet's boisterous glee and general approval of his plans toward marriage. It would be Mr Bennet's place to either sanction or forbid such a match, but as he was indisposed, no one wanted to see any undue pressure placed on the girls to secure their future.

"Miss Jane sent an express to their uncle in London, but I expect it will be a day or two at least before he can arrive. I wonder, should we send word to Netherfield?" Mrs Hill suggested.

Jones arched his eyebrows. "On what grounds?"

She settled her cup between her hands, pursing her lips. "Certainly the serious injury of a neighbour warrants the news being shared. I wonder if Mr Bingley could be prevailed upon to offer any assistance with the estate, as they are the nearest neighbours...." She left unspoken what they were all really thinking.

There was a general expectation that Mr Bingley might soon offer for Jane, thus securing her future and making the family's circumstances somewhat less precarious. Even should he not make Jane an offer immediately, the current Master at Netherfield Hall was known to everyone as a kind, generous soul who would compassionately exert himself for a neighbour.

The men nodded, agreeing that her reasoning was sound and would not be overstepping their bounds. Jones stood, thanking them for the hot coffee. "It is a little out of my way, but I can detour to Netherfield on my way back to Meryton. Good day Mr Hill, Mrs Hill."

~

"Jane, he is a monster!" Elizabeth slammed the door of their shared bedroom, her cheeks flushed scarlet. She plopped down heavily on the bed, snatching up her pillow and crushing it to her chest. Jane- dear, ever-faithful Jane- came comfortingly to her side. She pressed a cup of tea into Elizabeth's hand and stroked her sister's hair.

"Dearest Lizzy, I am sure he is only trying to help. Our cousin is not a clever man, but I do not believe he means any harm."

"Oh, Jane, you did not see his face when he heard about Papa. He is probably taking measurements of the master bedroom as we speak!"

Jane's charming, bell-like laugh bubbled forth. "Oh, Lizzy, surely not! I cannot believe even he would be so callous. Besides, we have only to avoid him for a few days, which we can easily do while caring for Mama and Papa. You will see, Papa will wake soon and all your fears can be put to rest."

Elizabeth grunted her disbelief. Only Jane could attribute disinterested motives to their vulgar houseguest. "You are too good, Sister. But you are right, there is little else we can do, and Mama and Papa need us. Will Mama rise today, do you think?"

Jane shook her head. "You know Mama. Mrs Hill was downstairs while I sat with her, but since then Mama has kept her close and has demanded constant attention. We should go relieve her so she can tend to other matters. Mary is still sitting with Papa."

"What of Kitty and Lydia?"

Jane shrugged vaguely. "I do not know if they are even dressed. I spoke with them earlier, but I have not seen them out yet."

Elizabeth's lips thinned. She would see to their younger sisters. "Jane, you go to Mama, I will find out what needs to be done about the house." They rose, and went to set about their separate duties.

Elizabeth stormed into Lydia and Kitty's room, interrupting a fit of giggles. They still tittered but sobered quickly under her fiery gaze. Her eyes narrowed at her younger sisters. Their lives had been careless and unstructured for far too long, in her opinion. That was the doing of their mother's enabling and their father's indolence. *Well*, decided she, *that is at an end for now. While Jane and I are managing things, they will pull their own weight!*

"*How dare you* remain here gossiping while your own father lies unconscious down the hall?" she roared. The girls' eyes rounded. They knew Lizzy to have a temper when goaded, but it had been years since any such display had been witnessed from her. She usually preferred to turn the tables with her considerable wit, and for a moment they were shocked at her departure from her normal behaviour. It was noisy, heedless Lydia who recovered first.

"Oh, listen to you, Lizzy. Anyone would think that Papa will wake up this afternoon and catch us still in bed. What matter if Kitty and I remain here? It is not like we can rouse him."

Elizabeth's face purpled in rage. "Would you disrespect your own father so? And Mama needs our help! You both need to dress and find something constructive to do. Mary has been sitting with Papa and needs a rest, and Mrs Hill has too much to do. I insist you dress and go downstairs at once to help her!"

"Help in the kitchen?" Kitty's face clouded in dismay. "But we've already dried all the herbs, and I *won't* help make candles. Last time I burned myself, you know." Inspired by her giggling younger sister, she pulled a face at her furious sibling.

Elizabeth stood speechless for an instant. A string of biting retorts came to mind, but the mortifying evidence of her own sisters' insensitivity stung her. With sudden fierceness, she snatched the bedcovers they still hid behind, bundled them into her arms, and heaved them through the second floor window onto the wet ground below. Kitty screeched in horror, but Lydia just crossed her arms, staring right back in challenge.

When Elizabeth slammed the door shut, Lydia turned to her sister. "I know, Kitty, let's walk into Meryton. We shall wait for Maria Lucas, you know she said she would call this morning. I want to see if Wickham has come back!" The girls squealed in delight and hastened to dress.

~

Darcy emerged from his rooms, refreshed after a hot bath and a shave. Wilson, his valet, was busily packing the remainder of his personal effects for a morning departure. He and Bingley had settled between them the previous evening that they would leave shortly after the morning meal. As he struck up his long stride down the corridor, an unwelcome voice arrested his progress.

"Mr Darcy!" Miss Bingley oiled her way toward him. Clearly she had been lying in wait for his arrival, contriving for him to escort her to breakfast. With an inaudible sigh, he bowed and offered his arm. A debilitating waft of her powerful musk perfume assaulted him, but he was long practiced at ignoring it.

"I imagine you are well pleased to be leaving this country!" Miss Bingley sidled comfortably up to him, incidentally brushing his arm with more bits of her anatomy than was strictly necessary. "Such insipid company! Why, the conduct last evening! Louisa and I were agreeing that we could not fathom such behaviour." She batted her eyelashes at him, to no avail, since he refused to look her direction. Neither would he be baited into a reply. She tried harder.

"I noticed that Miss Eliza's fine eyes were rather bright last night during her family's performance. Her mother so well spoken! Such accomplished dancers they all are, and so popular with all the officers! And the middle sister with such *ex*quisite talent on the pianoforte! You really must introduce them all to Miss Georgiana. How de*light*ed she would be to meet such distinguished company!"

Darcy only clenched his jaw, a subtle mannerism that the oblivious Caroline was unlikely to observe. As they stepped into the breakfast room together, he noted Bingley's downcast attitude. *Reluctant to leave Miss Jane Bennet,* Darcy mused. *This is one time when I actually agree with Miss Bingley. Better to get him far away from temptation, as well as myself!*

Caroline released his arm and blithely helped herself- or rather, forced the maid to help her- to the sideboard; generously laden with imported fruits, hot meats and fresh pastries. Mr Hurst was busily tucking into his plate, while his wife surveyed her fingertips and toyed with her coffee. Bingley stirred his tea dejectedly, his uneaten food scattered on his plate.

Caroline pouted and picked at the young maid she had required to fill her plate. First it was too full, making her look slovenly and ill-bred. Another attempt revealed it to be too lightly furnished, and Caroline knew for a fact that Mr Darcy disdained the unhealthful habit of fine ladies who ate too little. After a third try, she scolded the poor girl for forgetting any sort of meats to round out her selection. At last she was satisfied. Caroline dismissed the relieved girl, then proceeded to ignore the offering set before her.

Darcy cannily waited until Caroline had settled herself in a seat before taking one himself- as far from hers as possible. Her mouth crinkled in disappointment, but she said nothing. The gathering around the table was shrouded in unnatural quiet after the gaiety of the previous evening. At length, Caroline and her sister began trading their mirthful observations from the ball.

Darcy tried not to listen, as most of their spiteful jabs involved the Bennets. It was impossible to ignore, however. The one woman to ever catch his interest had the most absurd family! Their behaviour in public was utterly shameful. Then again… he narrowed his eyes. At least the Bennets were genuine. He knew almost positively they were not sitting around their breakfast table abusing their staff or belittling their hosts of the previous evening. *When did Bingley's sisters become so mendacious?*

He found their vindictive conversation positively turned his stomach. *Do other women behave so?* He knew Georgiana did not, nor would he have tolerated such attitudes from her. There were others, though. Caroline Bingley was far from the first ambitious woman to pursue him, and certainly not the only one to resort to snidely maligning anyone who could be perceived as competition.

It was not only the competition, he corrected himself, but anyone she perceived as less important than herself. She had been mocking the Bennet family from their very first introduction, before he had ever verbally made note of Elizabeth's appeal.

Again, the playful, enigmatic smile that would forever be burned into his heart came to his thoughts. Miss Elizabeth Bennet may traipse the dirty country paths and speak a little too pertly for fashion, but in every way that mattered she was far more the lady of the two. Even with her skirts doused in mud and that challenging lilt to her voice, that genuine tender heart of hers shone through. She brimmed with confidence, more so than he had ever thought should become a woman, but because of her bold assurance she was not afraid to humble herself in the service of another.

That, he decided, was the true quality an accomplished woman should possess to begin with. Lacking a gentle spirit, everything else was just a cheap veneer, doomed to crack and fade. He frowned unconsciously toward Caroline. He had once thought her a fine enough lady, though never fine enough to interest him. Now that he had met with the real thing, the ideal combination of womanly grace and hearty goodness, he saw that everything else, every other woman he had ever known save his mother and sister, was just a poor imitation. *And yet, I must learn to live without her!*

The week following Elizabeth's departure from Netherfield with her sister, while riding through the tiny village of Longbourn, he had spied the luscious beauty bringing a basket to one of their tenants. He had stayed well back, not wishing to attract her notice. He watched three small, ragged children embrace her with glee, and admired the easy camaraderie she shared with them. There was no condescension or haughtiness in her manner. Instead, he believed he saw true affection as she greeted each one.

To his utter astonishment, after gently paying her respects to the lady of the house, the oldest of the children coaxed Elizabeth to play a short round of stick ball in the street with him. He tried to feel disapproval at her conduct as he watched her throwing, hitting, and running like any street urchin. *What would London society say of this little scene!*

Instead, he only felt his admiration swell. With an enchanting mixture of elegance and enthusiasm, she could have been playing Graces rather than a rough pauper child's game. *What a Mistress she would make!* Though playful as a child, she still looked and acted every inch the lady he believed her to be. He was more than certain that the tenant family adored her as they did no other. She did not remain long, but Darcy had lingered a good while after, perplexed at the enigma that was this bewitching woman.

Never since his mother had Darcy encountered a lady of such genuine worth, who treated others with dignity and gentleness regardless of their station. Most women of his acquaintance would be afraid of dirtying themselves by such an association. Elizabeth Bennet flaunted it, and to his admiring eyes only looked the more refined for it.

He himself had been brought up in the finest circles, to every privilege. Though his mother was lavishly generous and considerate to all, it was his father who had trained him from the earliest age in his future duties as Master. He learned to accord respect to the people around him, but never to treat those of lower rank as equals to himself. That behaviour automatically branded oneself as also of low class, and was unpardonable in the heir to Pemberley.

Elizabeth Bennet's peculiar manners stretched and challenged him. There was nothing base or unladylike about her, yet she blithely thwarted every stricture his father had drilled into him. Still... He mused briefly that his mother might well have been delighted to make Miss Elizabeth's acquaintance.

As another brittle remark about the younger Bennet sisters reached his ears, he began to honestly ponder his own manners. He never would possess Charles' ease in company, but he believed he never behaved insultingly as his sisters did, either to a person's face or behind their back. He knew he was not good at carrying on stimulating conversation, but neither did he think he gave offence. *If I had* her *by my side, with her bright eyes and teasing manner that never seems to be intimidated, I might even find it possible to please in company!*

He frowned. *Had* he offended her? She had seemed rather put out with him last night. He doubted it could be simply over the matter of George Wickham, that reprobate who did not deserve even to be in the same room with her. Truly though, she had been irritated by something. He could well imagine Wickham had told her any number of fanciful tales, but he would not allow himself to set matters straight in that regard- much as he longed to! The satisfaction of seeing himself vindicated in her eyes was mightily tempting, but if she could never be his anyway, taking such a risk with Georgiana's future was merely vanity. The truth was too dangerous, and to simply respond in kind was unthinkable. It would not do to stoop to the same behaviours he found so disgusting in others.

His manners were certainly not perfect, he admitted at last. It was a subject which required some serious introspection, but not now. He would never see her again in any case, so he put the matter aside for the moment. The long carriage ride ahead would provide a perfect opportunity. He expected he would have to feign sleep to avoid conversation with Miss Bingley.

"You are very quiet this morning, Mr Darcy!" His head jerked around as that very lady's affected tones reached him.

"What?" He reacted with uncharacteristic brusqueness.

Caroline preened a little. "I hope you are not pining for the loss of Eliza Bennet's pert opinions and fine eyes."

He stiffened. "Not at all. Quite the reverse." *I am glad, truly I am! I must get away from her so I can stop comparing every other woman I have ever known to her and finding them wanting!*

Perhaps if he punished himself by spending the foreseeable future in Miss Bingley's company, he may someday find another woman more pleasing by comparison. This time he would take care that her connections were suitable. *Yes, for certainly that is all this present attraction is. I have been stuck in this house with Caroline for too long, and am naturally drawn to one who is quite her opposite. It serves me right for allowing this to happen!*

He sighed, unaware that he drew Caroline's calculating attentions as he did so. Every fiber of his being rebelled against his determined course, but he would not be shaken. His will *would* triumph and he would be the better for the misery he was about to force upon himself. He cast another grimace toward Miss Bingley. *Then again, if I had exerted some simple self-control this morning and not exhausted my horse, I could have ridden Pluto to London. Fair weather or foul, the scenery would have been preferable.*

Hoofbeats outside attracted everyone's notice. Straining his neck to see who was calling, Bingley recognized the Meryton apothecary who had attended Miss Bennet during her illness. "Why, it's Jones. What could have brought him, I wonder?" He rose and bounded like a puppy out of the room to the front door, delighted for the distraction. He reached the door quickly, opening it before the butler could. Darcy stayed put. Caroline rolled her eyes for her sister's benefit in response to her brother's undignified behaviour. Mr Hurst only continued to reduce the pile of sausage on his plate.

Bingley returned to the room immediately, motioning Darcy to follow him. Curious, he set down his coffee cup and went after Bingley and Jones as they disappeared into the study. Bingley offered them each a seat.

"Well, Jones, what is it, man?" Bingley could not contain his interest.

The balding apothecary cleared his throat. "You gentlemen are quite well acquainted with the Bennet family, I understand?"

Bingley's face fell, and Darcy felt his own pulse quicken. "Has something happened?" Bingley asked tremulously.

"Mr Bennet had a rather serious accident this morning. It seems he was riding and his horse took a fall."

Darcy started in shock. "I saw him only this morning, not far from here. This could not have happened long ago?"

The older man nodded. "Only a short while ago. It was rather close to his home, I gather. When I arrived he had already been carried into the house by his butler and Miss Elizabeth."

Darcy quirked an eyebrow. Somehow he could imagine Elizabeth hefting her father up the stairs, and coolly commanding the situation as she did so. "How seriously is he injured?"

Jones shook his head. "It is too early to tell. He is unconscious and shows no signs of waking, but he is breathing well. I cannot detect any other injury. I am calling back into town for more supplies and checking back later today. I am not a doctor, and the nearest one I know of is in Hatfield. We have to try to coax him to swallow so he can take nourishment, but I expect we will be able to do so. The immediate concern now is the management of Mr Bennet's affairs. I was wondering if I might impose upon you gentlemen, as his nearest neighbours, to lend some assistance?"

Bingley hesitated, glancing uncertainly at Darcy. "We were bound for London this morning. We both had some pressing affairs to attend to in Town. Why can his staff not manage while he is indisposed?"

Jones steepled his fingers. With a sigh, he admitted his true concerns. "It is Mr Collins. He is heir, as you must know. If anything were to happen to Mr Bennet, the entire Longbourn estate falls to him."

Bingley was aghast. "You cannot mean to imply...."

Jones held up a hand. "I do not imply anything. I only suggest that he is not the most tactful of men, and under the present circumstances, the Bennet ladies are quite distressed. I was hoping to find them an ally while their father's situation remains unknown. They do have an uncle in London, whom I would expect within a few days. I only thought... well, if you are bound for London yourselves, there is nothing else for it. They will have to wait for their uncle. I am sorry to have troubled you gentlemen."

He began to rise. Bingley, who had been stroking his chin thoughtfully, spoke up. "Wait...." He turned to Darcy, who had been watching his friend's reactions carefully. Darcy knew what Bingley would say before the words were out of his mouth. "We can delay our departure for a few days, can we not?" His face was full of eager concern for his "angel," as he had taken to calling Miss Bennet.

With a sigh and a small nod, Darcy acquiesced. He was torn between his prior resolve to put as much distance between himself and Elizabeth Bennet as possible, and his concern for her well-being. Whether she could be his or not, he did not like to think of her in affliction, and he did pity her for the necessity of bearing with an unpleasant houseguest at such a time. What could a couple more days hurt?

Perhaps he would even have his fill of her, if he were called upon to spend hours each day around her family. With that vague hope, he resigned himself to staying a while longer in Hertfordshire.

Three

After making a few hasty arrangements, the two men mounted their horses directly and covered the three miles to Longbourn at a brisk pace. They said little, except to note Caroline's extreme disappointment with the change in travel plans. They had told her as little as possible, but she had still managed to make one or two uncivil remarks regarding the selfishness of a neighbour who would get himself injured at such an inconvenient time.

As they approached, they noted a bundle of blankets tossed carelessly by the front walk. Darcy regarded it quizzically. Could they have been used to assist with Mr Bennet's removal to the house? He shook his head, wondering at the incompetence of the staff who would leave them as they lay.

They dismounted and handed their reins to a stable boy who ran out to meet them. Bingley was first through the door, scarcely waiting for it to be opened to them. They were met by the greasy, smiling face of Mr Collins as the man bowed profusely. "Ah, Mr Darcy, and Mr Bingley, so good of you to call with your condolences on our dear Mr Bennet! I assure you, every detail has been attended to in his care, and I have personally seen to him myself. I flatter myself, I can guarantee that he is in the best of hands.

"Why I spoke with the apothecary myself, and he assured me, 'Mr Collins' he said, 'Our dear Mr Bennet will recover very soon.' Those were his very words, and so during his convalescence I feel it incumbent upon myself, as the nearest relation, to see to all of the family's concerns. My dear young cousins have no cause for worry, thanks to Providence- and dare I say it, the great foresight of Lady Catherine de Bourgh, which guided me here at such a time when I might be of *most* use to my dearest cousins."

He had not stopped his insistent bobbing during the entire speech, and it was evident he would have gone on but for the arrival of Miss Elizabeth. The lady greeted them in a more dignified manner. She looked somewhat harried, but had composed herself rather well, under the circumstances.

Darcy helplessly admired the curls falling loosely around her temples. She had apparently taken little care for her toilette this day, but her native beauty had always held him entranced. He imagined the stubborn ringlets to be the remains of her elaborate coiffure from the previous evening, and the notion of seeing her hair tousled after sleep held him spellbound. His lips parted unconsciously as mute admiration seized him- just as it always did when she was around. *Idiotic wretch!* he chastised himself.

She curtseyed very properly to her guests, and Bingley at least returned the compliments with proper decorum. Then she whirled and eyed Collins archly, her lips pursed into the most delicate bow. Darcy found his eyes riveted on them. *What would it be like to kiss those lips until she smiled that bewitching smile at me?* He shook his head to clear the unbidden thoughts. *Get hold of yourself, man! This cannot continue without consequence!*

Elizabeth glared at her cousin. Her irritated look silenced the obsequious little man, but he did not manage to refrain from smiling ingratiatingly at her. Darcy felt a pang. Whether it was pity for her forced proximity to this eel, or jealousy at Collins' ready access to her, he did not give himself the trouble to discern.

"Miss Elizabeth, how is your father?" Bingley inquired most graciously.

"He is resting, thank you Mr Bingley. My sister Mary and I have been taking turns sitting with him." Her eyes shifted unhappily to Mr Collins. It was apparent that she did not want to reveal more of her father's condition or her true concerns in his company.

Bingley was astute enough to take the hint "And may I ask how Miss Bennet does this morning?" he asked politely, intentionally addressing himself directly to Miss Elizabeth so Mr Collins could not reply for her.

"She is with our mother, sir. Mama finds herself unwell this morning, I am afraid. I was about to take them both some tea sir… if you care to wait, I may sit with Mama in her stead. May I offer you…."

"Of course, by all means, my dear sirs!" Mr Collins interrupted her. With an expansive wave, he ushered his unwilling guests into the sitting room. "Come, make yourselves easy! The entry way here, I flatter myself, is eminently serviceable but I daresay you will find the sitting room more comfortable! The furniture, while not as fine as that of Rosings Park, of course, is perfectly suitable for an estate of this station…."

Arching a brow, Elizabeth saw an opportunity to make good her escape. Mr Collins's queer mixture of pomposity and subservience grated on everyone. She was sorry Mr Bingley would be exposed to the man's ridiculous fawning until Jane came down. While she could not likewise pity

Mr Darcy for leaving him thus, she did feel the sting of shame for her relations every time he looked at her.

What could he have meant by just staring, without saying a word? *He never comes near but to find a fault! He always makes people uneasy in company. Why could he not have simply remained at Netherfield? I am sure Miss Bingley would have kept him well entertained!* At that last thought, a mischievous smile curved her lips. She clattered up the stairs, entirely forgetting her mother's tea in her haste to escape Mr Collins. Wickedly, she felt herself almost enjoying Mr Darcy's imagined discomfiture at being left with such an irritating companion.

Below, the two guests settled uneasily in the sitting room. Mr Collins seemed to feel no compunctions against playing host in a home which was not yet lawfully his own. Darcy schooled his expression carefully into his typical stoic mask. Bingley, not as practiced at hiding his disdain, found his eyes widening in shock at the man's brazen attitude. Mr Bennet was merely unconscious, not deceased, but Collins could scarcely contain his exuberance. Magnanimously, he sought to entertain his distinguished guests with his fancied wit and charm.

"Mr Darcy, have I told you what Lady Catherine de Bourgh advised me before I departed?" Darcy groaned inwardly. He hated how people courted him for his connections and his wealth. Some were well-mannered enough to try to hide it, but subtlety was lost on this fool.

Collins smiled broadly, bursting with desire to share his glad tidings. "She said to me, 'Mr Collins, you *must* marry! Choose properly,' she said. 'Choose a gentlewoman for my sake, but for your own, let her be an active, useful sort of person, not brought up too high, nor too low. Find such a wife, and bring her to Rosings, and *I will visit her!*' There, you see how kind and affable she is! Nothing is beneath her notice. Why, she is all condescension. I myself have dined at Rosings twice, and Lady Catherine promises to show the highest consideration for my wife!"

Darcy made no reply but a simple nod, hoping it would be sufficient to encourage Collins to move on to another topic. He could not pity enough the woman who would find herself tied to this ridiculous man. He wondered distantly who the unfortunate woman was.

"I hope you gentlemen are warm enough. This fireplace is quite adequate, I daresay, but not nearly so fine as the fireplaces at Rosings Park! I have it on all authority that the chimney piece alone cost…." Darcy stood abruptly, striding to the window. He was abandoning Bingley and he knew it, but he could bear no more of Mr Collins' worship of Lady Catherine.

He blocked out the droning noise of the sycophant's voice as he gazed out the window. He saw the housemaid, obviously recently chastised, hurrying to the front of the house to collect the pile of bedding. She gazed up at the window above for a moment in wonder, then scurried away with her burden.

~

"Jane, Mr Bingley and Mr Darcy are here." Elizabeth's voice was soft, hoping she would not wake her apparently sleeping mother. She eased herself into the chair opposite Jane's.

Mrs Bennet was not sleeping, however. At the mention of Mr Bingley's name, her eyes snapped open. "Oh, Jane, he has come! He has come! Oh, I knew it, we are saved! I knew you could not be so beautiful for nothing! Oh, my dearest Jane! And you are so sly, not to tell me he was coming!"

Jane was horrified. "Mama! I am sure he has only come to inquire after Papa!"

Mrs Bennet was out of bed now, hurrying to put on her things. "Nonsense, girl!" she waved airily. "Hill! Oh, where is Hill! I must go meet our guest! Jane, do you go down and see to him. That's a good girl. But promise me you will not say anything important until I come down! Lizzy! Help me with my gown!"

Mrs Bennet trembled and fluttered, so excited she made Elizabeth's task doubly complicated as she tried to secure her mother's gown. Primping her unruly curls beneath her lace cap, Mrs Bennet flew out of her room, her second daughter following reluctantly behind. Elizabeth prayed her mother would do nothing to embarrass Jane or Mr Bingley… especially in front of Mr Darcy.

~

"Mr Bingley! We are *so* glad you have come to see us today!" Mrs Bennet was all smiles as she greeted her favourite guest. She cast a dark look in Mr Darcy's direction, but he did not notice. Mr Collins was busily regaling his esteemed one-man audience with his patronizing concerns at the Parsonage at Rosings Park.

Darcy's head came up finally when Elizabeth entered the room again behind her mother. He stared in mute concern when he saw her downcast visage, her eyes devoid of her usual impish sparkle. She was biting her lower lip, her gaze meeting his and sliding away with a humiliated blush. He was beginning to feel it would be worth enduring Mr Collins' company all day just to see her smile at him. The mother, on the other hand….

Bingley had seated himself next to Jane, but he rose to greet Mrs Bennet. "Madam, I am very sorry to hear of Mr Bennet's accident. Is there any assistance we could offer during his convalescence?"

"Oh, my dear, *dear* Mr Bingley! It is so good of you to call! Why, we are all so distressed by Mr Bennet's mishap. I have warned him again and again against the dangers of riding, but he would not listen to me! No one ever does, you know. Oh, my poor nerves, he cannot know what I suffer! And now here we are, with Mr Bennet on his death bed and five girls without a roof over their heads! But they are the most *beautiful* girls, are they not, Mr Bingley?" She batted her eyelashes at the hapless Bingley, who had shrunk somewhat closer to Jane during her speech.

Elizabeth's cheeks were burning. When she finally dared to raise her eyes, she found Mr Darcy's gaze on her with an expression she could not read. She groaned, her every sensibility cringing. She could not let him see any more of her family's humiliation than necessary! Steeling her courage, she tried to undo the damage from her mother's callousness. "Mama, you know Papa is not on his death bed! He will recover very well, Mr Jones said so."

"Oh, that Lizzy, she thinks nothing for the future! What does Mr Jones know, I ask you? Never any thought for what I must suffer. Mark my words, young lady, you'll be starving in the hedgerows by the end of the month!" Mrs Bennet waved her handkerchief flamboyantly for emphasis.

"Ah, on that point, Mrs Bennet, allow me to set your mind at ease." Collins stepped dramatically to the center of the room. A chill of foreboding swept through Elizabeth.

"Mrs Bennet, you know it was my intention to try to remedy the wrong that I unwittingly inflict upon your amiable daughters by the iniquitous crime of inheriting Longbourn estate. To that end, I have had it in my mind to seek an acceptable means of securing your daughters' future well-being. I came here because I had heard much of the beauty of your daughters, and I wished to see for myself. I am now quite certain, and I know you will sanction my excellent intentions to make… a suitable arrangement."

He grinned broadly. "I have, at long last, selected the lovely Miss Elizabeth as the companion of my future life. Cousin Elizabeth, you have made me the happiest of men!" He drew near to the astonished young lady and put out his hand familiarly to touch her forearm.

The room erupted. Mrs Bennet leaped up in immediate joy, coming to embrace her future son-in-law with the favoured Bingley now quite forgotten. Jane and Mr Bingley immediately turned to each other with scandalized whispers.

A burst of uproarious giggling behind Mr Collins alerted everyone to the presence of Lydia and Kitty, who, along with Maria Lucas, had been passing by the open door of the room on their way out to Meryton. They would not leave now, this was too juicy to pass up! The three girls huddled near the doorway, hiding peals of laughter behind their gloved hands.

Only Elizabeth and Mr Darcy were silent. The faces of both were a startling white, two pairs of dark eyes glittering dangerously. Elizabeth's mouth fell open in outraged consternation, while Darcy's welded shut in barely suppressed rage. *Elizabeth, my Elizabeth, married to that arrogant toad? Impossible!*

His eyes fixed on her as her face turned from white to flaming scarlet. *The cretin is touching her!* Fury began to blind his eyes and quiver through his limbs. He lunged at the shoddy parson, grasping his little parochial collar and throttling his empty head back and forth until Collins' teeth rattled and his feet left the floor, then listened as the man's lumpy shape made a satisfying *plop* as he slithered to the carpet.

Darcy blinked when he found himself still seated. Gratifying as that particular fantasy was, he yet continued in his task of holding the cushions down to the sofa- civilized and detached, just as a gentleman ought to be… doing absolutely nothing about any of it. His hands clenched as his mind cursed and stormed in a flurry of verbiage not fit for mixed company.

Elizabeth balled her fists. *She* was not constrained by any such ingrained notions of propriety. She shot to her feet, causing Collins to jump backward in preservation of his toes. Stunned silent no longer, Elizabeth stalked closer to the supercilious oaf who would dare to announce an engagement without even asking her permission. "You forget, Mr Collins, *I have made no answer!*" she hissed. Had he addressed her privately, she could have found it within her to attempt to spare his feelings. Instead, he had humiliated her and attempted to manipulate her publicly. She could not bring herself to show a speck of remorse, and in fact felt it imperative to immediately dismiss the notion with all the more vehemence. "It is *impossible* for me to accept your proposal, my feelings in every respect *forbid* it!"

"What are you talking about, Lizzy? Of course you will marry him!" Mrs Bennet turned from the object of her salvation only long enough to chide her daughter. "Miss Lizzy will be very honoured, Mr Collins! And I must say, you are very sly to have waited until now to surprise us all!"

"Out of the question, Mama! I *cannot* marry him, and I *will* not!" she cried. "You cannot make me Mama!" Elizabeth began to feel a sense of panic. She felt reasonably certain that her father would have supported her, but here, in this moment, she had no one to defend her. Even loyal Jane had felt it best to remain silent. Elizabeth glared at her sister, but Jane only covered her face with white fingers.

If this went too far… if word got out in Meryton that Collins had proposed before so many witnesses and her mother insisted upon her acceptance, while her father was bedridden, his fate uncertain…. She began to feel sick. With her father ill, anyone of sense would consider it her duty to secure the family's future! A vision of herself bonded for life to this perspiring, hateful clod made her shudder visibly. Better to sully her reputation and become an unmarriageable spinster, endangering her entire family, than be stuck forever with him! Forced to tolerate his attentions! She commenced to tremble all over, her palms cramping and beginning to sweat.

Darcy was having similar thoughts. Everything he admired about Elizabeth Bennet would be squelched and crushed under the bonds of the sniveling Collins. Her independent spirit would wilt, her fire and wit would crumble with no one but this simpleton to pass her life. A complete and utter waste of such a brilliant treasure! Collins, buffoon that he was, could not even fathom how far above him she was! What hideous twist of fate would have placed her, his beautiful Elizabeth, beneath his own notice and within reach of the likes of Collins?

Darcy's mind was suddenly filled with the worst idea, the most unimaginable…. Collins would demand everything of her, owning all her days and even her midnight hours. Elizabeth to bear *his* children? Unthinkable! He would never escape the haunting agony either; the humiliated shell of the former Miss Elizabeth Bennet would greet him every spring at his aunt's estate. A nauseating image of his precious Elizabeth, diminished by her husband's insipid banality and beleaguered by hordes of homely, red-faced children came to mind. Bile surged into his throat.

"Elizabeth Bennet!" her mother snapped. "You *will* marry Mr Collins, or I shall never speak to you again! Now, come right over here this instant and say you will marry him!"

Elizabeth lifted her chin, tears beginning to glisten in her eyes. "I *cannnot*!" she declared heatedly.

Without a thought, Darcy was by her side, clasping her nearest hand in his own. "No, indeed, Miss Elizabeth cannot agree to marry you, Mr Collins," he agreed.

Elizabeth flicked her eyes gratefully to his. She had no idea what objection he intended to raise, but for once she was thankful for his presence. No one else seemed inclined to defend her.

Collins tilted his head in confusion. "Ah, of course, Mr Darcy, I understand I must speak with her father. Not to worry, if… *when* he wakes, I will petition him directly. You can see that Mrs Bennet is quite delighted with the match, and I am certain my eminently wise and far-seeing uncle would be more than honoured to sanction such a suitable alliance. I have within my power to offer intimacy at Rosings Park, and, I flatter myself, that is something any father would be delighted to welcome! That is, of course, providing he does wake."

Collins beamed hugely, letting the implied warning behind his reasoning linger. He was not a vicious man, but he had no qualms about making certain his intended knew her place and that she owed him everything.

Darcy felt Elizabeth shiver again and he squeezed her hand reassuringly. *I will protect you, my Elizabeth!* The thought flashed through his mind before he could stop it. Where his next words came from, he would never know, but he found himself uttering, "Miss Elizabeth cannot agree to marry you, Mr Collins, for the simple reason that she has already done me that honour." He could only hope she would forgive his impulsive presumption.

Elizabeth's gasp of horror was lost in the general upheaval. She jerked her hand away from him and glared furiously. He offered her an apologetic shrug, but there was no time for explanations. Everyone was speaking at once. Kitty, Lydia and Maria burst into gales of laughter and ran for the door, no doubt to share the news with anyone they could find in Meryton.

Mrs Bennet nearly fainted. "Oh, my, Mr Darcy! Oh, my sweetest Lizzy! Only think! Ten thousand a year! A house in Town, everything charming! Oh, what jewels, what pin money you will have! Oh, Mr Darcy, please forgive me for my mistake. Oh, Jane! My smelling salts! Oh!"

Jane's expression was utterly stupefied. She knew very well that Elizabeth had not, and probably never would have, agreed to marry Mr Darcy. What, then, had made him say so? Was he trying to protect her from Collins? Of course, that must be it. But why? Whatever his reasons, she decided that her esteem for him had just risen.

Lizzy would be justifiably angry, but Jane knew her sister well. If forced into a choice between a fool and a snob, Lizzy should take the latter. Mr Darcy might be softened by Lizzy's playful ways, but Jane doubted anything could be done to make Mr Collins a more pleasing partner. With a commiserating glance at her sister, she strove to propel her effusive mother from the room. The continued presence of the hysterical Mrs Bennet could do nothing to improve matters.

Mr Collins' mouth was moving, but no words were coming out. Elizabeth gave Darcy one final scowl, then crossed her arms to glower at Collins. Men! How had she found herself in this position? She was too angry to cry, too furious for scornful barbs. She merely stood silently fuming, her teeth set, her eyes burning holes into each man by turn.

Collins finally found his voice. "Mr Darcy! Of course, forgive me sir, but I had no idea you were so humourous! I know it is the usual manner of elegant females to at first reject the man they secretly intend to accept, but I did not expect such jollity from our guests! Now, quite seriously, *my dear* Cousin Elizabeth," he smiled patronizingly and approached, tugging free Elizabeth's unwilling hand and kneeling before her. "I wait on you; simply say the word and we will set the date that will make me the happiest of men!"

She snatched her hand away in contempt and nearly shouted, "I was perfectly serious in my refusal! You could not make me happy and I am convinced I am the last woman who could make you so!" She could not resist the urge which compelled her to wipe her defiled hand on her skirts. With a stinging backward glance at the second object of her ire, she stalked out of the room. The three remaining occupants jumped at the two succeeding door slams announcing her incensed departure from the house.

With an embarrassed smile, Collins rose and bowed to Mr Darcy. "Forgive my fiancée sir, I beg you. I am afraid she is a bit out of sorts this morning. You find us at a very unsettled time. I do hope you will return tomorrow to wish us joy!"

His jaw clenched grimly, Darcy took an intimidating step toward Collins, towering over his aunt's parson. "Mr Collins, Miss Elizabeth Bennet is engaged to *me*! She will not marry you. I will thank you to refrain from distressing *my* fiancée at such a time, with her father injured and in need of her care."

Mr Collins' eyes bulged. "But… but Miss Anne de Bourgh! You are engaged to marry the daughter of Lady Catherine! Surely, Mr Darcy, Miss Elizabeth is charming, but you have the honour of an alliance with one of the most noble families in the land! Lady Catherine…."

"… Is *my* concern, Mr Collins. I insist you leave off meddling in my affairs at once!" Darcy's face was darkened with anger, his eyes narrowed and glittering.

Collins gulped and gasped. "Lady Catherine will be most seriously displeased!" He fled the room, and they could hear his ponderous weight taking the stairs above the outer hall perhaps more quickly than he had ever moved.

Bingley had sat frozen during the entire scene. His bright blue eyes were rounded in awe, his mouth hung open. Finally he rose, and clapped a hesitant hand on his friend's shoulder. "Congratulations, old boy! I had no idea, but Miss Elizabeth is a lovely girl! A fine choice, I daresay."

Darcy sank down heavily with a sigh and buried his face in his hands. What had he done? "Bingley, I am not engaged to Miss Elizabeth. I was only trying to make that dolt leave her alone."

Bingley laughed outright. "I say, you could have found another way, old chap! And yes, you *are* engaged to her." With a jerk of his head, he gestured to the doorway. "By now, half of Meryton will already know about it. You had a fair number of witnesses, you know! You have no choice, my friend, unless you wish to ruin the lady's reputation."

Darcy groaned. Bingley was right. He had acted impulsively and now would pay the price. "What do I do now?" The novelty of himself, Fitzwilliam Darcy of Pemberley, asking Charles Bingley for advice was not lost on him.

"Well," mused Bingley, "you will have to talk to her, I suppose. And the sooner the better, I say."

Darcy gave a bitter laugh. To Bingley's uncomplicated soul, everything could be solved with a simple apology. Shrug and move on, that was Bingley's style. He doubted the unpredictable Elizabeth Bennet would see things the same way. He had not been able to forget the look of betrayal in her eyes before she stormed out of the house. And how could *he* accept the current state of affairs? Had he not just assiduously resolved *not* to seek such an alliance because of her situation, so decidedly beneath his own?

Jane Bennet chose that moment to step serenely back into the drawing room. Bingley's eyes went immediately to her and he smiled warmly. "Miss Bennet, Darcy and I were admiring that little wilderness garden. Could I persuade you to take a turn with me?" She willingly took his extended arm, and the couple stepped outside.

Darcy remained a moment longer. For perhaps the hundredth time in the last five minutes, he wondered *What was I thinking?* In truth, he really barely knew the woman. After so many years of thwarting the most carefully laid plans of the best connected daughters of the *ton,* what impetuousness had seized him to make him speak for a virtual stranger?

What he did know of her was in parts beguiling and in other parts perfectly shocking. Her family, he had already settled with himself, was abominably mortifying. What of the woman herself? Any prospective groom's thoughts naturally dwelt less on the family and first on the woman who would be the mother of his children.

A very private man, Darcy had long dreaded such a level of intimacy and partnership with any woman of his acquaintance. To invite such a woman as any of the others he had known into his home, into his thoughts- into his bed? To join with one of those shallow, mindless puppets in raising his own heir? The very notion was insupportable. He had never been able to even imagine such closeness with any woman… until Elizabeth Bennet flashed him those marvelous eyes and that glorious smile.

After such a short acquaintance, he knew little enough of Elizabeth Bennet's tastes and habits… oh, who was he kidding? Had he not hungrily devoured every morsel of information he could glean about her ways during her stay at Netherfield? Was not her name the only one he listened for when visiting the town of Meryton? He had memorized her favourite dishes, knew what time she habitually arose for the day, and deliberately marked each book which caught her interest. And her birthday- the twenty-second of May. He had overheard Caroline's coarse inquiry of when Elizabeth should reach her majority. Not that the subject had been one to interest him at the time, of course. He simply had an outstanding memory… especially for anything concerning *her.*

He also knew for a certain fact that she could boast a sterling character. There was goodness in the way she had cared so diligently for her sister, there was honour in her bearing and comportment, so thoroughly graceful even in unpleasant circumstances. He had witnessed her compassion and her spirit, and he knew her to be intelligent and well informed.

Already with those few superlative qualities she stood out as the most remarkable woman he had ever known. To all of these she added a striking- if unconventional- beauty, and an enchanting impertinence which, in spite of himself, utterly captivated him. For the first time in his life he had found himself wishing to know more of a woman. *It would be far from a burden*, he decided, *to take Elizabeth Bennet to my home and heart.*

The lady might perhaps take a little more convincing. She had been righteously infuriated by his presumption. Though he fully expected she would extract a contrite apology for his lack of discretion, as was her due, in little time she would feel the full honour he had bestowed. He, the scion of one of England's greatest families, direct descendant of William the Conqueror and at the moment one of the most sought-after bachelors in the country, was delivering up his hand and heart to none but her.

Surely, there was no other option at this point. No doubt the younger Bennet girls, silly Miss Lucas and that ridiculous matron of the family were already gleefully spreading the report abroad that he had engaged himself to Miss Elizabeth.

Though he did not relish furthering his acquaintance with *them*, he could find joy in at last giving in to his heart's desire. *Elizabeth will be mine!* No longer would he be alone! No longer would he have to fend off the grasping, pretentious ambitions of hopeful debutantes and their manipulative mothers. He would be armed Elizabeth's charm and wit wherever he went with her. He would have her brilliant mind to partner with him in all things- surely an intelligent, lively woman such as she would take an active role as Mistress of his sprawling estate.

His expression warmed when he realized that Georgiana would at last have a generous, loving sister. He felt certain that the entire staff of Pemberley and all his tenants would adore her, just as everyone in Meryton, Longbourn, and even Netherfield seemed to. Bestowed with his tender care and ample worldly blessings, he comforted himself that Elizabeth would blossom into her full potential as a captivating, graceful woman of means.

With her sparkling, vivacious personality to keep him company, the gray of his days would at last vanish. And the nights! What passion lurked behind those sparkling eyes? Darcy trembled with delight at the very idea, then harshly chided himself. There would be time enough for such thoughts.

With a bracing deep breath, Darcy rose and left the house to find his fiancée.

Four

Elizabeth ran as hard as she could down to the stream behind the house. Since she was a little girl, this place had been a solace and a refuge for all her childish hurts and cares. When she had grown old enough to walk out on her own, she had discovered the joys of other places, more distant. Still, this retreat, so close to her own home, had retained its place as first in her heart. Throwing herself down on the bank, she gave way to her sobs.

Why did things have to become so complicated? Had it only been Mr Collins, Elizabeth felt certain she could have stood up to him in her refusal. He was thick-headed, but eventually she would have made her point. But to have assumed her cooperation, in front of so many witnesses- including their neighbours! It could not have been more ill timed. Elizabeth angrily flung a stone into the creek. It landed with a satisfying splash.

Inspired, she stood to her feet and found a larger rock. She heaved it into the deepest part of the stream and waited for the deep *Thunk!* it made. She found three or four other palm-sized stones, and one after another they too found their way into the stream bed. Her frustrations abated somewhat, she felt simply drained and depressed.

Once again she dropped onto the bank, this time a little more properly seating herself on a great flat rock rather than the muddy shore. The tears flowed freely then, tumbling through her fingers as she covered her face. What had possessed Mr Darcy to claim they were engaged? The insolence of the man! He was no better than Mr Collins, simply announcing what she was to do and expecting her compliance! The conceited arrogance of his actions was beyond even what she could have thought him capable of. *Does he try to run* everyone's *life? Of course, the powerful Mr Darcy, he expects everyone to kowtow to his wishes because of his ten thousand a year and his wonderful Pemberley! Well, I will not, and he cannot make me!*

Elizabeth's fierce anger melted into dejected self-pity. She was no fool. She knew that her reputation would be in irreparable tatters by the end of the day if she refused. Was it worth it? Taking a deep gasping breath, she tried to calm herself enough to think. *If only I could talk to Papa!* Yet... what if her papa never recovered? Had she any right to fling away any chance to save her family? Fear trembled in her breast and her sobs racked her body.

Her piteous thoughts were interrupted by a fine white handkerchief materializing over her shoulder. Without even glancing up, she knew that the hand holding it belonged to Mr Darcy. She tried to ignore it, but he sat down rather indecorously on the rock next to her and pressed it into her unwilling fingers.

"I do not wish for company at present, *sir.*" She kept her voice from wavering quite admirably.

"Miss Bennet," his normally clipped tones were softened with sympathy. "We must talk. I humbly apologize for having offended you. I only wished to be of help."

Her sharp eyes turned on him. "*Help?*" she sputtered incredulously. "You fabricated an engagement! Without ever considering my sentiments, you announced to my entire family that we... that you... that I had accepted a proposal! One which you had never uttered, and certainly never gave any prior indication of!" She turned her face back toward the stream, clamping her mouth shut before she could hurl the insulting and unbecoming words that she longed to express. "How could you do it, sir?" The anguish quavered in her voice.

There was silence between them for a long moment. Risking a glance sideways, she could plainly see his face wreathed in turmoil. *Let him suffer a little longer,* she thought smugly. Knowing him to be a man of few words, she savagely decided she was going to enjoy watching him try to talk his way out of this one.

At length his voice came, the words forming slowly at first, then building in fervency. "In vain I have struggled, and it will not do. My feelings compelled me to speak. Miss Bennet, you must allow me to tell you how ardently I admire and love you! I know that in declaring myself as I have done, I have gone against the express wishes of my family and my own original intentions, but it is done and I do not regret it. Almost from the first moments of our acquaintance, I have come to feel for you a- a *passionate* admiration and regard. You know of course, that the relative positions of our families make such an alliance a highly reprehensible connection. I have regarded it so myself- your family's want of propriety and low status I had considered insurmountable obstacles to my forming any serious designs upon you, much as I might have desired otherwise. I confess that I cannot rejoice in the inferiority of your connections, but under the present circumstances it cannot be helped. I beg you, please, to relieve my suffering and agree to become my wife."

Elizabeth had received so many shocks in one day that this final blow absolutely took her breath away. Her outraged fury was checked only by her stunned incredulity. She searched his expression and found no evidence of this alleged internal struggle. Indeed, he seemed quite assured. She shook her head slowly in disbelief. How far was he going to take this insulting charade?

Darcy watched her carefully, his hope buoyed on the rising tide of his own passionate feelings. He had done it, he satisfied himself. Since his rash words had necessitated the confession of his love, he finally allowed himself to thrill in the thought of her. He put his misgivings behind himself. His family might expect a fashionable woman of the *ton*, with fortune and standing, but he had been fooling himself for years to think he could ever find the kind of love match he desired there. There was only one Elizabeth. *Hang it all, I will be happy!*

But why would the eloquent Elizabeth Bennet be finally struck speechless? Her dark eyes flew wide, her delicate lips parted in amazement. *Certainly*, he thought, *I must have entirely surprised her with the honour of my proposal. Of course, modest as she is, perhaps she was not expecting it after all! Surely she must have felt my regard for her, but her estimable good sense would not allow false hope. Wise, discreet woman!*

Overcome with tenderness, he wished to reassure her of the sincerity of his feelings. Darcy leaned toward her and at last claimed those luscious lips as his own. Cupping his hand behind her deliciously unruly curls, he melded his mouth to hers, shivering with the sublime contact. Elizabeth was his at last.

A firm hand pushed violently against his chest, and he found himself propelled roughly away from her lovely face. Her other hand raised and she slapped him soundly across the left cheek.

"Miss Bennet, what is the meaning of this?" He put his own hand to his throbbing face. As a sporting man, Darcy had been punched by men and slashed by sabers, but never slapped by a woman. He could scarcely credit her petite frame with the kind of strength she clearly possessed.

She bolted to her feet, trembling with rage. He followed, more uncertainly. "How *dare* you, sir?" she cried.

He took his hand away from his face, instinctively glancing to see if she had drawn blood. Fortunately she had not, but the insistent sting of her strike would take some time to fade. "Pardon me? May I remind you, Miss Bennet, we are engaged! There was nothing improper!"

"We are most certainly *not* engaged, Mr Darcy!"

"Miss Elizabeth, please, be reasonable. I know I took liberties. I beg you would forgive me, but under the circumstances there is no call to take such offence. I might wonder why you would treat me with such incivility," he returned, a little stiffly.

Her eyes began to fill with tears again. "And I might wonder why you would choose to tell me you loved me against your will? Is that not some excuse? But I have other reasons to dislike you, you know I have!"

"Reasons? What reasons?" he demanded, his anger growing.

She took a gulp of air, fighting for composure. "Do you think any consideration could tempt me to marry a man who would declare an engagement without my consent? Who would presumptuously demand I cooperate, regardless of my own wishes, simply because I have not at present the protection of my father to tender my refusal?"

"Refusal? You cannot be serious!"

She gritted her teeth and took a threatening step closer. "I am *quite* serious, Mr Darcy. From our earliest acquaintance I was impressed by your arrogance, your conceit, and your selfish disdain for the feelings of others!"

Darcy was reeling with shock. Elizabeth was… refusing him? And she thought him selfish and conceited? He stared, open mouthed, as she continued her litany against him.

"In our every meeting, you have shown yourself to be the most ungentlemanly of men! I have long believed you to be the most prideful man of my acquaintance, and you have certainly proved it today with your callous disregard for my sentiments! You bully and you insult, and *this* is the behaviour of a gentleman? Yet even before today's events, my opinion of your character was decided when I heard Mr Wickham's tale of your dealings with him!"

Wickham! Again! Blast that reprobate! "You take an eager interest in that man's concerns!" he snarled.

"Who that has heard his misfortunes could not take an interest?" Elizabeth resented Darcy's insinuation. She was not in love with Wickham, but at present the latter man's company would have been a great relief.

"His *misfortunes*! Yes, they are *great* indeed!" Darcy's voice wrung with sarcasm.

"And of *your* infliction!" she cried back, affronted that Darcy could even yet deny his infidelity regarding a man of his father's affections. "You have deprived him of the advantages which were designed for him, disregarding the will of your own father and leaving him destitute!"

His eyes narrowed menacingly. "What could you possibly know of my father?"

Her face sparkled with righteous indignation. "I know that his son is the *last* man in the world I could *ever* be prevailed upon to marry!" With that, she turned on her heel and sped back to the house.

~

Jane and Mr Bingley had indeed toured the garden together, but as it happened the garden was rather small. Feeling they ought to act as chaperones for the newly "engaged" couple, they bent their steps toward the stream when the audible splashing of stones revealed Elizabeth's location. They remained a discreet distance away, but they were near enough to see everything, had their own inclinations tended toward such a vicarious amusement.

Jane cautiously revealed to Mr Bingley that Elizabeth was unlikely to take this engagement talk with equanimity. Without actually admitting that her sister stoutly disliked his friend, she tried to prepare the man she favoured for what was likely to be a very turbulent period in her family.

Bingley laughed. "I admire Miss Elizabeth's spirit. She will need it in spades to stand up to Darcy! He has long needed someone to set him down. Darcy is the finest man of my acquaintance, Miss Bennet, but he is not entirely without fault, as none of us are. Miss Elizabeth possesses every virtue that he lacks, I believe. I am surprised I had not seen it before, but Miss Elizabeth may well be the perfect match for him. I confess, I look forward to seeing how things will play out!"

Jane was not so certain. She was quite sure that her sister would fight the marriage kicking and screaming, but she knew as well as everyone else that by now there was little else to be done. Even should their father wake this hour, he would not be able to undo the reports already spread abroad, some even by his own wife. She only hoped that Lizzy had been entirely wrong in her opinion of Mr Darcy, and that she might come to see that… very soon.

A sudden shout from the direction of the stream diverted their attention. Darcy and Elizabeth were both standing up now, the gentleman holding his face. It was obvious they were exchanging heated words. They could not make out much of what was said, but they could hear the fevered pitch of Elizabeth's anger, and the restrained fury in Darcy's voice. Jane groaned. *Oh, Lizzy, must you make this so difficult?*

She dared a glance at Bingley, but instead of reflecting horror, his face was showered in unbridled delight. "Indeed, Miss Bennet, your sister is a marvel! I say, no one *ever* tells him what-for! I've feared for years he would fall prey to some simple-minded woman of fashion who will agree with everything he says. Miss Elizabeth will keep him on his toes! What a fearsome thing it will be to behold!"

They watched in helpless wonder the grand finale, when Elizabeth delivered her blistering valedictory riposte. Her voice was raised clearly enough for them to hear every word she said. Jane sighed painfully. "Oh, Lizzy…."

She looked up to Mr Bingley, her face apologetic. He smiled encouragingly back at her. "Do not worry, Miss Bennet. I will collect my friend and we will call tomorrow, or perhaps yet again this evening. Please send word if there is any change in your father's condition, or…" he glanced toward the house, "… any other developments." He smilingly raised her fingers to his lips and daringly brushed a gentle kiss on her knuckles. Jane blushed prettily as he took his leave.

~

Elizabeth flounced up the stairs, angrily making as much noise as she could. Her mother's door stood ajar. *Perfect… she is gone to Meryton to brag about my conquest. It is too late to stop her- I will have to set her right when she returns!* Elizabeth sought refuge in the only place which made sense.

Mary looked up from her book when Elizabeth softly opened the door. She clenched her fists and locked her arms by her sides, struggling to calm herself for her father's sake. "How is he?" Hope shone in her eyes.

Mary stood with perfect equanimity. "He is the same. Mrs Hill brought some broth, and we got him to drink some. Mr Jones has not yet returned."

Elizabeth sat hard in the chair next to Mary's, blocking Mary's exit from the room and forcing her younger sister to sit back down. Mary was not often the most observant of people. She could see that her sister was upset, but she did not trouble herself to investigate. The assumption that their father's condition accounted for all of Elizabeth's irritability sufficed for her.

Mary resumed her reading while Elizabeth stared hopefully at her father's rising chest. *Please, Papa, wake up! I need your help! We all need you.* She closed her eyes and tears began to tumble down her cheeks.

"Why do you not use your handkerchief? There is no sense in making your eyes puffy, or spoiling your gown with the drips," Mary observed practically.

Elizabeth looked down at Mr Darcy's handkerchief, still clutched between her fingers. She had forgotten about it. Her eyes blurred and she acquiesced. Once she could see clearly, she began to examine the cloth. It was very fine, and embroidered simply with his initials in brilliant blue. *FD*

Elizabeth ran her fingers over the stitching, wondering vaguely if Mr

Darcy's mysterious younger sister had worked this for him. She felt sorry for the girl, stuck with such a proud, disagreeable older brother as her only relation. Well, almost her only relation. Elizabeth's lip curled when she remembered there was evidently a noble aunt and cousin. Then again, according to Mr Wickham, Miss Darcy was just as arrogant and unpleasant as her brother, and doubtlessly did not want or need her pity. Another Miss Bingley, no doubt.

Her thoughts rumbled turbulently between the two most offensive men she had ever met. Complete opposites that they were, both had tried to claim her in marriage that very morning, without the warning of a courtship or even the courtesy of a private audience. She still felt certain that she could have eventually rebuffed Mr Collins, even without the support of her father and heartily against her mother's wishes.

Mr Darcy, on the other hand, was not a man to be gainsaid. He was certainly used to having his way. *What, then, would have possessed him to propose to me?* she silently demanded again. *We cannot stand each other! He barely speaks to me, and I have been anything but deferential to him. Surely he should have been looking for that perfect woman of accomplishment of whom I have heard him speak. I should have expected him to marry one who is just as proud as he is, and who would never trouble him with disagreement!*

Elizabeth grimaced. She hated to think of having to be in company with whatever woman Mr Darcy deemed worthy of himself. He had been quite clear that *she* was not that woman, with her low connections and lack of sophistication! And what else was it? Her family he despised, and *she*- why, she was barely tolerable!

Anger seethed through her very pores. She could almost spitefully accept his proposal with the single intention of making his life miserable, but the thought of spending the rest of her days with the staid and silent Darcy was a depressing one. *What would Miss Bingley give to be in my shoes!* Even the temptation of teasing Miss Bingley lost all its lustre. *What am I to do?*

~

"It seems we have worn out our welcome, old friend!" Bingley's jovial tones caused Darcy to turn. "We had best be... Darce?" Bingley studied his closest friend's face. He would have expected outraged anger, or silent boiling resentfulness. Instead, Darcy looked utterly stricken. His face was ashen, his eyes stark and staring.

"Forgive me, Bingley..." Darcy's voice was hushed, his words uncertain.

"I am afraid I am not fit company at present. Excuse me." He brushed past his friend, his purposeful strides eating the distance to the stables.

Bingley's eyebrows shot up in surprise. Apparently Miss Elizabeth's rebukes had completely rattled Darcy's usual composure. He watched Darcy gallop away without a backward glance. He did not go in the direction of Netherfield, but off in what appeared to be a random path.

Charles Bingley was faced with a dilemma. He had convinced himself that the morning's developments really were for the best. If marriage were more than a convenient business arrangement- if the characters of the individuals involved should be considered to be compatible and complimentary, Miss Elizabeth was everything Darcy should be looking for.

Certainly she had almost no dowry, no moneyed connections, but what was that to a man who already possessed fortune and status in abundance? She was sprightly and vibrant, and she might do much to enliven his dour friend. He, on the other hand, could provide her with all the security and dignity a woman could desire, and Darcy was not the kind of man who would mistreat his wife. She was clever- intimidatingly so- but so was Darcy. Certainly, with their equally active minds, they could learn to respect one another.

He frowned. Respect could not develop when they could not overcome their mutual stubbornness. He could understand why Miss Elizabeth would be angry at the morning's events, but it seemed Darcy had done little to assuage her fury. From all appearances, they had only succeeded in baiting each other until an explosion finished all discourse.

Heaving a discouraged sigh, Bingley called for his own horse and began a slow jog back to Netherfield. Darcy was affronted and obstinate, but Elizabeth was perhaps even more so! Bingley, who detested conflict, did not wish to see Miss Jane's sister end in disgrace. He predicted woefully that the very thing would surely occur if they did not settle their differences. All of Meryton must be abuzz with the news of their "engagement," thanks to the wagging tongues of Elizabeth's own family.

Mulling over his options, Charles Bingley made an unaccustomed bold decision- the first of many over the next few days. He resolved to save this engagement. It would most assuredly require him to involve another party, as the present troubles seemed beyond his meagre skills. Who could sway the implacable Darcy to overlook his indignation and apologize? Who possessed the diplomacy and sweetness which would surely be required to convince Miss Elizabeth of Darcy's worth? He had no doubt of an ally in Jane, but Jane could not honestly claim to know Darcy any better than Elizabeth herself. Bingley smiled as he hit upon the perfect solution. Miss Georgiana!

Darcy would be furious at him for overstepping his authority and involving his sister, but perhaps it would be enough to distract his anger from Miss Elizabeth. Their enduring friendship could weather that storm. Bingley knew she was staying at Darcy's London house. It would be improper to write her directly, but he also knew Darcy would not leave Georgiana completely alone. Colonel Fitzwilliam would be near at hand. He determined to write the colonel with his regiment in London at once.

~

A soft knock on the door brought Jane's sweet face into their father's room. Elizabeth sighed gratefully. While sitting with Mary, she had tried to pretend nothing was out of the ordinary. Mary was blissfully unaware of the morning's happenings, and Elizabeth would be the last to admit to them. Still, she needed a sympathetic ear, and outside their father, there was no one dearer to her than Jane.

Mary appeared relieved to be able to escape Elizabeth's glowering presence. She took up her book and hastily retreated, leaving Jane to claim her seat. They sat in silence for a few moments, each waiting for the other to break the stillness.

Jane noted the handkerchief Elizabeth was twisting between her fingers. She wrung it viciously, as though wishing to inflict the same punishment on the owner as on the article. With a desperate silent prayer, she ventured a beginning. "Lizzy, I am so sorry about... well, you know."

Elizabeth laughed bitterly. "Why, Jane, there is no need to pity me. Did you not know, I have suitors falling all over me today! What woman would not be delighted? You ought instead to be petitioning me for the privilege of visiting the great Pemberley! Mama is doubtlessly already planning my first ball for me. Do you know, I will now be able to throw our younger sisters into the way of other rich men!"

"Dearest Lizzy, Mr Darcy did not mean to hurt you. Really, would you prefer that right now our mother were announcing your engagement to Mr Collins?"

Elizabeth groaned. "I could prefer a mother and sisters who could claim some measure of discretion! To not have my private affairs bandied about as vulgar gossip to entertain our silly acquaintances, that would be ideal. But as that is not to be my lot... Oh, Jane!" she sobbed.

Jane placed a comforting arm around her sister as Elizabeth gave way to tears. "Darling Lizzy, I am sure Mr Darcy is not so unpleasant as you have believed. You know Mr Bingley thinks very highly of him, and they have been close friends for many years. He could not be so deceived in his friend's temperament. Surely there has been some great misunderstanding! I believe your Mr Darcy will in time be shown to be a very amiable gentleman."

"He is not *my* Mr Darcy, Jane," Elizabeth lashed out. "I will *not* marry him! How could I? You did not hear how arrogant he was! Oh, yes, he was very clear that *I* was unworthy of his lofty status. He claimed to have feelings for me, but Jane, how could such a conceited man truly care for anyone but himself? He is only trying to salve his guilt at interfering in my affairs. Egotistical, stubborn man! How could he claim the right to meddle in my life, and demand I accede to his wishes? I would rather remain an old maid!"

Jane laughed lightly. "Lizzy, you say so now. Pray, remember that you almost were stuck with our cousin! At least Mr Darcy's person is pleasing, and he is intelligent. I know you delight in teasing him. Surely you could find sources of amusement as the wife of Mr Darcy."

"Oh, Jane, I tease him because I cannot do otherwise! He deserves to be shaken up a little. Everyone treats him with such unmerited deference! He is so smug, so certain of his superiority. Truly, I cannot imagine having to converse with him for the rest of my life. He scarcely opens his lips! He is so insufferably dull and aggravating!"

Jane's brow furrowed thoughtfully. "Lizzy, I think Mr Darcy may like your teasing. I have never thought him so very arrogant, you know. I think rather that he may be just shy. Mr Bingley does not think him prideful, and he knows him better than anyone else here. You know that Miss Bingley likes to distract him when he does speak, I am sure he does not enjoy it. I think he does not like so much attention as he gets."

"That is the most uncharitable thing I have ever heard you say about Miss Bingley, Jane. Brava! I am sure you are wrong about Mr Darcy though. I believe he thinks very highly of himself, and of no one else. I have told you how he wronged Mr Wickham, and he did not deny it when I tasked him with the facts today!"

"Oh, Lizzy, you did not!" Jane gasped, appalled.

"Indeed, I did. I needed to know," Elizabeth shrugged practically. "I could never marry a man who would behave so dishonourably! If it is not true, let him deny it! Until then, I believe the virtue is all Mr Wickham's."

"Lizzy, do be careful," Jane enjoined seriously. "You are determined to convict a man whom many others believe to be honourable based on the testimony of one person, whose credibility it seems is only in his pleasing countenance. We do not know the particulars."

"Indeed we do, or enough to cast a shadow of doubt on the impeccable Mr Darcy's reputation. Besides, even without Mr Wickham's testimony, I know Mr Darcy to be vain and egotistical. Why else would he simply announce before everyone that I had agreed to marry him? The impudence of the man!"

Jane shook her head. The conversation was going in circles. It was hopeless to talk sense into her sister when she was so justly riled. Perhaps when she had time to cool down, she would be more reasonable. In the meanwhile, there was nothing to do but tend to their father, attempt to control the excitement of their mother, and at all costs avoid Mr Collins.

Five

George Wickham strolled contentedly down the main street in Meryton. Despite having denied himself the pleasure of a ball full of beautiful women and another man's table the night before, he had no cause to repine. He had the esteem of his fellow officers, the cards had fallen favourably for him the night before, and so far nearly every drawing room in town was open to him. The one exception was a place he did not wish to visit anyway.

Denny and Carter had joined him and the trio canvassed the town, amusing themselves in talking to pretty girls and listening to the morning's gossip. Wickham's sharp ears caught the name of his youthful rival, and out of curiosity he stopped. What had the old man gotten himself into?

Several young ladies stood giggling nearby. Wickham smiled ingratiatingly at the red-headed Miss King, who blushed and cast her eyes downward. If the rumours he had heard were true, he should be getting to know this young lady a little better. The girls chattered incessantly about the Netherfield ball. Listening with an affected carelessness, he learned that the reserved and unlikeable Darcy had finally been persuaded to dance with someone other than his hostess, entirely against his wont when not in Town. Darcy allowing himself to become sociable in a backwater place like this? The event was remarkable enough in itself, but his partner's name was on everyone's lips. Miss Elizabeth Bennet?

Wickham smirked. He knew that particular lady held no kind thoughts for the gentleman. He cherished a private laugh as he imagined the verbal darts Miss Elizabeth might have lobbed at his former patron's heir. *What could have brought that about?* he wondered to himself.

Perhaps old Darcy was trying to escape some of the other gold-diggers, but Miss Elizabeth was a peculiar choice. Proud Darcy stooping to dance with the daughter of a modest country gentleman? A lovely one, to be sure, but not one inclined to the blind flattery he was used to. His imagination wandered pleasantly, picturing a scene where Darcy was enamored with a woman he could not afford to have. What a change that would be!

A noisy commotion down the street heralded the arrival in town of the two youngest Bennet sisters, as well as the youngest Lucas girl. That buxom strumpet Lydia Bennet led the charge. When her eyes lit upon him, she bustled up directly. "Oh, Mr Wickham! How we missed you last night! Me and Kitty were determined to dance with you, but as it was, there were plenty of officers and we danced every dance anyway!" She artlessly fluttered her eyelashes at him, then coyly bestowed the same look on both Denny and Carter.

"Miss Lydia," he greeted her suavely. He knew he would get an unvarnished recounting of last night's ball from this source, if he were only patient enough to wade through the twaddle of her gossip.

Lydia Bennet did not disappoint. She began to regale him with the number of partners she and her sisters each had, the names of the officers present, and the disappointed looks of some of the girls who had to sit out. She also mentioned "that dull Mr Darcy" asking her unhappy sister for a set, but only as an aside.

"Oh, and then, this morning! Mr Wickham, you'll never guess! Tell him, Lydia," her older sister urged.

Lydia's eyes brightened more, as if she had just remembered the most interesting morsel of gossip. "It's too much fun! Only think, Mr Darcy is engaged to my sister!" The girls squealed in glee.

"E-excuse me?" he stammered. "Darcy! Engaged to… Miss Elizabeth, I presume?"

"Oh, yes, but he is so dull. The fun of it was that our cousin, Mr Collins tried to propose to Lizzy first, but Mr Darcy came up and announced his engagement to her instead, and so Mr Collins could not marry her after all. I suppose Mr Darcy wanted to talk to Papa this morning, but Papa fell off his horse, you see, and would not get out of bed."

"Lydia, he is unconscious!" Kitty at least had the decency to be scandalized at Lydia's cavalier treatment of their father's condition.

"Oh, bother, Kitty!" Lydia waved dismissively. "Mama was just in at Mrs Long's, and they say that Mr Darcy is sure to bore Lizzy to death, but that she will be practically the richest woman in England. I do not know that Mr Darcy is so very rich, after all, he brought but one servant with him when he came to Netherfield, so says Aunt Phillips. But Mrs Long says his estate is so very vast, and that he even has a house in London near Grosvenor Square. I shall ask her to take me shopping after she is married!"

Why, only think of the gowns I shall have! Oh and the balls I shall attend in London, cannot you *just* picture it?"

The wheels were spinning in Wickham's mind. This turn of events could present a brilliant opportunity. He needed to find out more. Smoothly, he offered his arm to Lydia and asked permission to see her home.

~

Darcy galloped out of sight of Longbourn as hastily as four legs could carry him, then settled his mount into a dejected walk. The burst of humiliated energy faded, leaving only morose gloom. She hated him! How could he have missed it?

His mind replayed every event, beginning with her arrival at Netherfield to tend her sister a month ago. She had toyed with him, baited him, flirted even. His eyebrows creased. Or was it flirting? Had she, even then, despised him? Could her capricious humour, bent only on amusing herself and provoking him, be misinterpreted?

Why? What could she find so offensive about his person that she would set out with so violent a dislike? He thought darkly of Wickham. That scoundrel's lies could have contained anything, twisted and contorted to suit his fancy. He could well imagine what sordid version of events he might have relayed to a willing audience.

Still, Wickham had only been in town less than a fortnight, and it seemed likely that her disapproval of himself had its foundations before then. He would have hoped that a woman of Miss Elizabeth's caliber should know better than to believe unflattering gossip about an honourable man without some foundation. Wickham, however, had found a favourably disposed listener in her. That could only occur if she had already believed him to be essentially flawed.

Angrily he dismissed the errant notion. How could she find him lacking? He had shown her every courtesy! He had tried to discourage Miss Bingley's sarcastic attentions to her, he had shown interest in her sister's welfare, confound it he had even asked her to dance- more than once! The idea that her reticence to stand up with him traced to profound dislike rather than the coy flirtatiousness he had assumed stung him more than he liked to admit.

His good sense told him he ought to turn tail and run, now while he had a chance. Fitzwilliam Darcy of Pemberley need not cater to the whims of a woman who did not want him! Goodness knew, there were plenty of others who would only too gladly take her place!

His reputation would not suffer unduly- after all, it was she who had denied the engagement, not he. No one would press a breach of contract suit under such circumstances. In this situation, he thought wryly, there was no one even to speak up for the lady at all, save perhaps the unknown London uncle.

Thinking of her, alone and defenceless, his heart began to ache. Despise him though she might, he loved her still. He had allowed himself to glimpse a future with her in it, and he could not, would not abandon her with her reputation in tatters. Because of him she would be ruined, and then what would her fate be? Married off to some tradesman? The second wife to a third rate gentleman with four unruly children? Or worse yet, a poor relation, a ward of that fop Collins, who was such a little minded man that he would not treat the woman who had refused him graciously. No. He had embroiled her in the precarious situation in which she now found herself, he would see her to a respectable end of it. A desolate sigh wrung from his lips. *Elizabeth!*

He clenched his eyes shut, then set his mouth into a rigid line. The only thing to be done was to somehow convince her of the truth. One way or another, he had to convey to her the depth of Wickham's depravity, to let her know that he was not a man to be trusted. For what if she did trust him, turn to him even now? He shuddered to think what else could befall her, vulnerable as she was.

She was an intelligent woman, she would value sensible discussion. He was confident that she could be brought to reason, if he were only given the chance to plead his case. Unhappily, he doubted she would be willing to speak with him again anytime soon. He had done quite a thorough job of blasting that bridge. What could be done? She would likely not listen to Bingley as a character witness- would she have, she had ample opportunity to have already done so. Nothing less than full disclosure would do.

He groaned. Could he trust her fiery temperament with Georgiana's history? He had been willing to trust her with his own future. He had left himself no other choice. He wandered the twisting paths of Hertfordshire until at length he came to a crossroads. With a soul-stirring exhale, he turned his horse reluctantly back toward Netherfield.

~

Bingley trotted up to his front gate and dismounted, passing his reins to a stable boy. He hoped his sisters were otherwise occupied- he did not look forward to satisfying their curiosity about their neighbours at this moment. Caroline especially would be discomposed, to put it lightly. Glancing surreptitiously toward the dining parlor where he had left her, he stepped softly toward his study.

"Brother! You have returned!" He cringed and turned around as his sister's overly welcoming tones bubbled down the corridor. She had not been in the dining parlor, of course, but the drawing room. Caroline looked about her in dismay. "Where is Mr Darcy?"

"Darcy had… some business to attend to I believe. I expect we shall be seeing him shortly."

Caroline cocked her head in chagrin. "But what business could he possibly have? Really, Charles, I thought we were all set to leave for London. I cannot bear another day in this dreary place! What could possibly have called him out, and why do you not assist him so that we may leave sooner?"

Bingley turned his back, unwilling to disclose the morning's events just yet. "It was a private matter, Caroline. Please excuse me, I have urgent business myself." He firmly closed the door of the study, leaving her pouting outside.

He composed his letter to Colonel Fitzwilliam quickly, grimacing at his own barely legible scrawl. Well, it would have to do for now. He sealed the missive and called for his butler to have it sent express to London.

Ten minutes later when he emerged, he spotted two of the housemaids in close whispers. Their eyes widened when they noticed him, and they scurried off to their duties. *So,* he thought, *it's already begun. The entire house knows.* How was it that the servants always managed to spread word even faster than the post?

A sudden slamming door from above stairs alerted him to another fact. *Oh, no. Caroline knows too.* Swallowing hard, he braced himself for the explanation she was surely about to demand. Suddenly, inspiration struck. He had taken one wild risk, but was not yet equal to a second. As he watched her clambering distractedly down the stairs, her face red and seething, he snatched his hat from a footman and slipped back out the front door.

~

Elizabeth fled the house when her mother returned home. She could not bear the boisterous gushing of her mother's every maternal feeling. Try as she might, she could not dissuade her mother from attempting to begin the wedding plans. She sought refuge again in her solitary retreat by the stream. Even there, Mr Darcy would intrude.

His indignant anger returned to her memory. She felt at least satisfied that she had discomposed him as greatly as he had her. Helpless frustration burned at her. Would she really be forced to marry that arrogant man? Not if he had given credit to any of her words by the stream! Darcy, however, was trapped as neatly as she by the entire town's gossip. *At least,* she thought grimly, *if my name is to be linked with a man's, the man has some attractions and is not repugnant like Mr Collins!*

She had to admit that he was very easy to look at. Had he refrained from insulting her at every turn, she felt she could have once found him devastatingly handsome. He was tall and strongly built, as an active man full of vigour ought to be. He owned dark rich hair that had just a hint of curl, which she knew to fall low and unruly over his brow when he was just returned from riding- not that she had noticed, or anything. His eyes were also soft and dark, and kindled with fine intelligence. That was another mercy, she supposed. Though she did not like him, at least she could respect his intellect and discourse. He was far less annoying to talk to than her cousin- when he *did* talk.

Elizabeth was not an avaricious woman, but an income such as Mr Darcy claimed *would* allow his wife many luxuries. Perhaps Mr Darcy's estate was even large enough to allow her to avoid him for days at a time. A rueful smirk curled her mouth. *That is hardly likely, as we would no doubt squabble over exclusive rights to the famous Pemberley Library!* In spite of herself, she gave a short little chuckle. Perhaps she and Mr Darcy did have one thing in common, after all.

Soft footsteps behind her and a comforting hand on her shoulder turned her bitterness to a relieved smile. "Hello, Charlotte."

Her friend greeted her warmly. "Dear Lizzy, I heard the news. I am so sorry."

Elizabeth gave a broken little laugh, then sniffed back her tears. "Pray, what news have you heard? We have an abundance of it this morning."

Charlotte's face broke into an easy grin. "Everything, I believe. Maria stopped by the house on her way toward Meryton. I came as soon as I could get away. Oh, Lizzy… are you well? It must have come as such a shock to you!"

"Indeed!" Elizabeth wiped her cheeks- belatedly she realized she was still using Darcy's handkerchief. She shoved it down the inside of her sleeve, hoping Charlotte had not had a chance to inspect its initials. "I am recovering from the shock now. It has been a very trying day! First, poor Papa…" She choked back a sob, then reached again for the unfortunate handkerchief.

Charlotte was the kindest and wisest of friends, next only to Jane in Elizabeth's heart. She wrapped an arm around her dear friend without requiring more words of explanation. Elizabeth wept shamelessly on her shoulder.

After a short time, Elizabeth calmed herself again. "I still cannot believe that both Mr Collins *and* Mr Darcy would speak so; without warning, and in front of so many!" Elizabeth tried to lighten her own mood with a forced laugh.

Charlotte pursed her lips, deep in thought. "How do matters stand now? I assume you have accepted Mr Darcy in lieu of Mr Collins?"

"Heavens, no!" Elizabeth retorted. "You know how ill I think of him, and I know he truly feels the same for me. Surely he will want nothing to do with me after this morning. Besides, I do not believe I could be happy with such a man, Charlotte."

"Why ever not, Lizzy? In one day you've had two eligible men, one of them *very* eligible, offer you a respectable home, security and protection. You should be thankful. Many are not so fortunate." Charlotte finished with a soft wistfulness

Immediately Elizabeth felt guilty. As justified as she felt she was in her anger, before her was her friend who would have been most appreciative of either of the two offers Elizabeth had spurned. Well, perhaps not Mr Collins' offer, but Charlotte would be too practical to turn down any other eligible match. Charlotte was not romantic, which was fortunate, for neither was she beautiful. Charlotte was a warm, caring woman of sense who deserved a wonderful husband, but at the age of seven and twenty her odds of finding such were slim to none.

"I am sorry, Charlotte," Elizabeth answered miserably. "You must think me the most wretchedly ungrateful woman alive!"

"Indeed, I do not, Lizzy! I understand why you were upset. As things are though… what do you intend to do? You cannot refuse to marry Mr Darcy now!"

Elizabeth sighed hopelessly. "I believe I already have! As for what is to come next... I do not know, Charlotte. I just do not know. Would it be very much talked of, do you think?"

Charlotte gave a short chuckle. "Oh, no more than usual, considering the richest, most eligible bachelor around has engaged himself to the most celebrated beauty in Hertfordshire! What do you think, Lizzy?" Charlotte's eyes twinkled teasingly.

Elizabeth groaned and dropped her head back onto her friend's shoulder. "I feared it would be so." She sniffed into her handkerchief again. "You are wrong about one thing, though, you know. Jane is so much more beautiful than I," she teased back halfheartedly.

Charlotte became serious. "Lizzy, you say so because your mother tells you that. Jane is striking, but anyone looking twice would prefer you. Do not underrate yourself so. I say this as Jane's friend as well. She is everything that is wonderful, but you have such beautiful eyes, and your hair is so lovely the way it curls over your forehead! You are not a conventional beauty perhaps, but you are so lively and endearing, you are the one I would pick, were I a gentleman," she finished with a wink.

Elizabeth smiled with genuine gratitude at her dear friend. "What a pity for us both that you are not, then! Such a handsome gentleman you would make, and with such a genial address!" Charlotte laughed and Elizabeth squeezed her hand. "What would I do without you, dearest Charlotte? You always know exactly how to cheer me up!"

"What would you do? Oh, let me see… well, certainly you would offend a good many more gentlemen. Also, how would you ever determine how to make over your bonnets after Lydia has torn them apart? You certainly would never have learned my trick for tying herbs, or the best way to get the mud out of your hems to avoid angering Mrs Hill…." Charlotte's list was cut short when Lizzy playfully jabbed her in the ribs, giggling.

The two sat companionably for a bit. After a while, Charlotte began to make her excuses, as she was wanted at home. "Lizzy, before I go, I must implore you- consider carefully what you must do. Do not let your opinions of Mr Darcy sway you away from a most prudent match. To refuse now could ruin your reputation, to say nothing of your family! Do try to find out the facts and be certain of him before you take such a drastic step. Mr Wickham is amiable enough, and he seems to have been very wronged by Mr Darcy, but remember we do not know all the particulars. Please, Lizzy. I do not want to see you hurt for no good reason."

Elizabeth blew out a frustrated breath. "You begin to sound like Jane! But for you, Charlotte, I will try to act prudently. I have difficulty believing I could be wrong about Mr Darcy. His actions have always led me to a single conclusion about his character, but if the damage to myself is potentially as serious as you say, I will take care that I act with discretion. Let it not be said that I was foolhardy. I expect you will find, however," here Elizabeth heaved a weary sigh, "that after the way I spoke to him, Mr Darcy will not return and all such worry will be for naught."

Charlotte pursed her lips, studying her friend. "Perhaps," she murmured slowly. They squeezed hands chummily, and Charlotte turned to go. Remembering something, she turned back. "Oh, Lizzy? Do you think I ought to invite Mr Collins to our house for dinner? It would get him out of your way for a while."

Elizabeth nodded vigourously, her eyes widening in recognition of her friend's genius. "Do, please! With my thanks!" Charlotte left her friend in a much better mood than she had found her. Elizabeth put her arms stiffly out behind her and reclined on her rock, her attitude reflective. She blew deliberate little puffs of steamy breath into the air, finding the pursuit calming to her nerves.

After a time, the din of cheerful giggles slowly approached. Elizabeth tried to ignore it for as long as was possible. Lydia and Kitty had returned. She was not insensitive to the fact that had they not run off to Meryton, the entire affair of the morning might yet have been hushed up. Irked that her sisters' uncontrolled gossip and dissolute ways had worsened her situation, she resolved to disregard them until she felt she could confront them coolly.

A smooth masculine voice caused her to jump. "May I join you, Miss Elizabeth?" Mr Wickham's welcome tones inquired.

Composing herself as best she could, she replied, "Of course, sir. Please, make yourself comfortable."

"I hear congratulations are in order, Miss Bennet," he smiled amicably as he sat beside her. "May I wish you every joy?"

"Your wishes would fall on deaf ears, I am afraid Mr Wickham," she retorted scornfully.

He arched his eyebrows in conciliatory surprise. "Really? Pray, tell me the matter. We are good friends, are we not? Are you not pleased with the engagement?"

She bit her lip. Caution whispered to her to keep her confidences close for the moment. Her situation at present was delicate, as Charlotte had so prudently reminded her. She found herself by all appearances betrothed to a man she did not like, an opinion shared by the gentleman before her. What did she dare relate to him?

She wished to openly confide in him, depending on his mutual disdain of Mr Darcy to ease her conscience for treating him so scandalously. However, it would not do to fan the flames of the present situation, no matter how sympathetic the listener. There would be nothing that Wickham could realistically do to help her out of the predicament, and careless talk had done enough harm for one day. The less said, the better.

"Only that it has all come as something of a shock," she supplied hesitantly.

"I can well believe it!" he laughed. "Imagine my surprise at hearing your news this morning! Why, only a few days ago you abused Darcy rather roundly, did you not?" His eyes challenged her to agree with him. In fact, Wickham was quite delighted with this turn of events. He intended to prod her for weakness, wondering if his own circumstances stood to gain somehow.

"I… I believe Mr Darcy has his flaws," she admitted carefully. "Do not most men?"

"Aye, that is true, but Mr Darcy has more than his share of pride! Along with it though, he has ample blessings which could more than make up for a lack of sterling character, does he not?"

Elizabeth bridled at his implication. "Do you mean to suggest, sir, that I would accept Mr Darcy merely for his wealth?" she snapped, with more irritation than she had expected. "That I would count a man's character and address of no consequence, and blindly accede to the unscrupulous quest for material possessions?"

"Well," he nodded disarmingly, "did not you? And who can blame you? Darcy is favoured by the fortunes of birth, and why would any sensible woman not wish to ally herself with such a one? For where, Miss Bennet, does prudence end and avarice begin?"

She narrowed her eyes cautiously and considered her words. "I concede the point, Mr Wickham, that we do not all have the luxury of marrying without regard for fortune. Handsome or plain, it is true we all must have something to live on. I have, however, long believed that nothing but the deepest love could persuade me to matrimony."

"Oh! Is that so? Well, then, Miss Bennet, I must beg your pardon. I had been under the impression you did not much like my old friend, but I see I was mistaken. I am glad you can love and still see the faults of a man, for a blind love is a foolish one. You might do much good, you know, as Mistress of Pemberley. Perhaps you can alleviate the concerns of others that Darcy has neglected. I am not the only one with grievances, you must know."

Elizabeth straightened, her gaze turning curiously upon her companion. What could he possibly mean? Wickham smiled genially and went on.

"Perhaps you may even help select a suitable husband for Georgiana. Mark my words, Miss Bennet, she will need a firm hand to make her a tolerable member of society, and Darcy spoils her, you know. He will consider none but the best connected, most fashionable young men for her. You ought already to be aware of the Darcy temperament though, as it will take a lively, capable woman such as yourself to keep the old man in check. Take heart, Miss Bennet, I am sure the love of such a spirited woman as yourself will transform him into a most pleasing fellow indeed."

Elizabeth felt her cheeks burning. What on earth was Wickham insinuating? The assumption that she was in love with Mr Darcy was humiliating enough, but to hear that others would assume she meant to manipulate him, and that a domineering wife would perhaps even be necessary for such a man! Should she be frightened of Mr and Miss Darcy? Wickham painted them as an imposing pair, too fond of their own way to be amiable. Elizabeth didn't know what to think, but that she could not imagine being other than miserable in a marriage with a dictatorial spouse. She liked her autonomy far too well to yield easily.

Her tumbling thoughts were arrested by another voice calling her name. "Hullo? Miss Elizabeth? Ah, there you are, I was looking for you." Mr Jones rode around the corner of the house, near the stables. He dismounted his horse and began to rummage in his saddle bags.

Elizabeth was grateful for the interruption. She liked Mr Wickham, but she was not yet ready to talk to him- or anyone else, for that matter- about Mr Darcy. His suggestions had unnerved her and she needed time to think. Rising and brushing off her skirts, she flicked her eyes to Wickham as he gallantly offered his arm. She took it, smiling rigidly, and began to make her way to Mr Jones.

"Miss Elizabeth, how does your father? Is there any change?"

"Not at present, thank you. I was sitting with him just above an hour ago. My sister Jane is with him now."

Jones nodded and came forward, carrying a small jar with a wired lid. Elizabeth cocked her head curiously. He noticed her look, and held the jar up with a shy smile. "Leeches," he informed them. "As near as we know, he has an ascendancy of blood to the head, so these ought to be of some help."

Elizabeth shuddered. She hated looking at the vile creatures, but she trusted Mr Jones's advice. Mr Jones also carried his familiar satchel, which she knew to contain any number of his mysterious concoctions. "May I offer you some tea before you go up?"

"No, thank you, Miss Elizabeth. I would like a private word with you though, if it is not too much trouble."

"Of course." She smiled at Mr Wickham. "I thank you, sir, for your company. Do please call again soon? I am afraid I must see to my father."

He nodded graciously. "Until tomorrow then, Miss Elizabeth." He gave a deep bow and departed.

Six

Elizabeth followed Mr Jones into the house then opened the door for him into her father's library. "Can I help you, sir?"

He frowned uncomfortably. "Miss Elizabeth, I do not mean to intrude where I have no right, but I have just come from Meryton. There is... much talk this morning." He paused, studying her reaction.

Elizabeth's face fell. She knew exactly what sort of talk he must have heard, but she had hoped this conversation would have less to do with her and more to do with a treatment plan for her father. "Is there?" she asked nonchalantly, attempting to keep the edge from her voice.

He cleared his throat nervously. "Yes, well, it would seem that... that Mr Collins and Mr Darcy had both taken an interest in you?"

Her faced flushed crimson. That seemed to be her lot today, to find herself perpetually embarrassed and the situation spiraling out of control. "Yes, sir, that is true," she replied, her voice barely above a whisper.

Mr Jones patted her shoulder kindly. "Child, I have known you all your life. I have tended your ailments and mended your skinned knees. I knew you were not happy to have Mr Collins' company at such a time, as he is such a tactless fellow and you had enough to concern you. I feared Mr Collins would have something of this sort in mind, but I had no idea that you and Mr Darcy...."

Elizabeth laughed at this. "Neither did I! I assure you, Mr Jones, what he said this morning came as much as a shock to myself as everyone else. What could have brought that man here, I wonder? If he fancied that he was helping me, he could not have been more mistaken. Arrogant, headstrong man! Had we not been in company when Mr Collins spoke, it might all have been forgotten and I would not now appear to be engaged to Mr Darcy!"

He smiled sheepishly. "I am afraid, Miss Elizabeth, that you have me to thank for the gentlemen's interference. I spoke with Mr Bingley this morning after I left you, hoping he could simply check in on your family, and of course Mr Darcy was with him. I wished you and your sisters not to be alone and friendless with Mr Collins making himself comfortable here. I knew he was not entirely welcomed by you, and we feared he might become somewhat overbearing while your father is incapacitated."

"'We?' Tell, me, Mr Jones, are there others conspiring to come to my aid? I do hope not, as I really do not think I can bear any more assistance from my neighbours."

"No, my dear, no," he chuckled self-deprecatingly. "I spoke with Mr and Mrs Hill. I should not have, I know, and I beg you would not be put out with them on my account, but they shared my concerns for your family's protection. I am truly sorry, Miss Elizabeth, if my actions have caused you further distress. I did not mean any such result." His kindly graying face drooped with remorse.

She sighed in resignation. She knew her father's old friend had spoken the truth, and that he had involved Mr Bingley, and by extension Mr Darcy with the very best of intentions. She could not blame him for having done what he could. She was too emotionally exhausted at this point for anger or tears. What she needed most was some time alone to reflect, and of course for her father to waken. She did not want to talk about Mr Darcy or Mr Collins any more at present. "What are we to do for Papa?"

His expression cleared, replaced by his professional mien. "Yes, well, I will go place the leeches. I also have a compound I would like to try, one I normally administer for headaches, but I hope it will relieve the abundance of swelling to the head. I, uh… yes, if you will excuse me, Miss Elizabeth." Jones gathered his collection of items and awkwardly stepped around her to the door.

Elizabeth began to follow him up the stairs when the front bell rang. Shrugging apologetically to Mr Jones, she changed direction to the drawing room to receive their caller.

Mrs Hill came in a moment later with a stout-looking woman, somewhere past middle age, with a perfectly starched work dress and a friendly weather-worn face. She dropped a deferential curtsey, then introduced herself boldly. "My name is Mrs Cooper. My husband is the doctor in Hatfield. He's away at present, attending courses in London. We're not expecting him back for a few days yet, but I'm to understand you need an experienced nurse."

"Uhm…" Elizabeth stammered. "Yes, indeed, perhaps we could use a nurse, but… how did you come to know of it?"

"Oh, the gentleman from Netherfield sent word first thing this morning," she replied tidily.

"Mr Bingley? That was very thoughtful. He must have sent for you before he even came to us?" Elizabeth was grateful for her neighbour's consideration, but she was not certain the estate could comfortably pay for the potentially indefinite hire of a nurse. She and her sisters had intended to take on the burden themselves.

"No, Miss, the name on the note was not Bingley. I have it..." the woman's brow furrowed as she peered into her reticule. "Here it is," she presented the pressed paper into Elizabeth's hand.

Elizabeth unfolded the note and read. Her eyebrows rose precipitously. The note was from Mr Darcy. She had never before seen his crisp, precise handwriting, once so admired by Miss Bingley. He had written for the assistance of a doctor as well as a trained nurse, and the note mentioned enclosed payment for their services. Furthermore, it promised that the writer of the note would guarantee generous remuneration for whatever treatment was necessary until the patient should recover. *What could have induced him to take such trouble on himself?* She wavered between gratitude for his consideration and resentment for his officiousness.

"I see," she murmured, handing the note back. For the space of a heartbeat, she considered sending the woman away, then thought better of it. Though she did not like indebting herself to Mr Darcy, it was her father's health at stake. For him, she would brave anything and anyone. "Follow me, please. The apothecary is here, perhaps he can help you settle in. May I offer you any refreshment?"

Mrs Cooper shone a motherly smile back at her. "No, thank ye, Miss. I'll be comfortable enough for now, I brought my own little tidbits."

Elizabeth started up the stairs with Mrs Cooper in tow when the bell rang again. She groaned in exasperation. *Does everyone want to visit today?* Becoming testy, she resolutely completed her climb toward her father's room, intending to let someone else receive the next caller. At the top of the stairs her mother pressed by her, fluttering back down the stairs behind them.

"Jane! Oh, Jane, dear, he is come back! Oh, where is that girl? Lizzy, find Jane and send her down! Oh, Mr Bingley, how pleased we are to see you again so soon!"

Elizabeth shook her head as her mother's voice drifted up from the direction of the open drawing room doors. Her mother must have been lurking by her upstairs window like some powdered vulture in a lace cap.

Showing Mrs Cooper into her father's room, she made the necessary introductions and asked Jane to come down, at her mother's request. When all was done, she retreated behind her own locked door for some desperately needed time to herself.

~

Bingley remained with the Bennet family as long as he decently could that day. His dear Jane seemed well pleased with his companionship, as Miss Elizabeth had made herself scarce for the rest of the afternoon. He had hoped to have a chance to speak with the latter, but she studiously avoided any chance at more than the most perfunctory of greetings.

When he finally did take his leave, the early winter sunset was aflame in the sky. He was grateful the weather had remained tolerable for the day, and he absolutely reveled in the beauty of the Hertfordshire countryside as his horse ambled casually homeward. His thoughts were with the sweetest blonde-haired angel he had ever laid eyes upon. His heart and mind were firmly and finally made up. Miss Jane Bennet was the only woman for him.

He handed his horse off to his coachman and stopped apprehensively before his own door. He doffed his hat and ran his fingers nervously through his unruly mop of hair. Caroline would be watching for his return. Dear heavens, what sort of scene awaited him?

He sighed and resigned himself to his fate. Darcy ought to have come back; perhaps she had exhausted her grievances upon him already. In a way, he hoped so- Darcy was a grown man, and rightfully should defend his own actions. The way his friend had looked at Longbourn though… Bingley had never seen him appear so fragile.

"Charles! Where have you been, I have waited tea for hours!" Caroline's harried visage greeted him with his first steps into the house. "Come! Sit down," she ordered. She led him to the family sitting room, where Louisa and Mr Hurst lounged idly, the latter just beginning to snore.

Caroline virtually pushed him into a chair and with a stern expression commanded a frightened maid to serve him his tea. He smiled gratefully, relieving some of the maid's jitters, but the girl was clearly terrified of Caroline.

"Where is Mr Darcy?" Caroline wondered aloud. "Charles, did you neglect to tell him you were returning? I do hope some harm has not befallen him!"

Bingley frowned. Darcy had not returned? He was his own man, perfectly capable of looking after himself, not to mention a splendid horseman, but Bingley worried. His friend had not been himself when they last spoke. Clearly his conversation with Miss Elizabeth had shaken him. He would have to ask at the stables if any word had been had.

At the moment, however, Darcy was not his first problem. He sipped his tea silently, waiting for the storm to break. As soon as the servers had vanished, which was as quickly as they possibly could, Caroline drew her seat closer to his. She leaned forward and whispered conspiratorially. "Everyone is spreading the vilest rumours about Mr Darcy! Have you heard? You cannot have! Of course, it is the most scandalous falsehood. Why, they are circulating the report that he has engaged himself to Eliza Bennet, of all people! Charles, you must have these rumours uniformly contradicted!"

He purposely nursed his tea cup, snatching for himself a few precious seconds more before he was forced to make reply. When he had drained the entire contents, he set it down gingerly and slowly composed himself. "Caroline, it is quite true. I was there when Darcy made the announcement."

Her face drained of all colour. "There must be some mistake! He could not… no! He disdains the Bennet family as much as we all do! Why, if you had only seen his face last night when they all put on such a scene!"

Charles Bingley was by no means done with his sudden decisiveness for the day. He jerked to his feet angrily, throwing his heavy chair backward several inches. His voice lowered with a brand new threatening tone he had just discovered. "Caroline Bingley, you *will* cease your mockery of the Bennet family. I will not tolerate another word from you on the subject! Miss Jane and Miss Elizabeth are enchanting girls. As for the younger girls, they only want time and guidance. Who among your fashionable London friends does not have relatives for whom they must occasionally blush? Their father is a *gentleman*, Caroline. Do not forget our own father was in trade, and as such we ought to be grateful for their society! The family is in considerable distress at the moment, and I insist you refrain from attempting to taunt or humiliate them." He threw his napkin in the chair and made to stalk out of the room.

She leaped from her seat and pressed placating hands on his chest. Biting his lip, he held his temper back. "Charles, you have never spoken to me in that way! Why, I have never seen you so angry! It is this country, the uncouth company we keep here! Please, Charles," she sobbed, "let us leave at once, at the earliest opportunity tomorrow! Surely Mr Darcy will be only too grateful to join us. He cannot have been thinking clearly, surely! We will all go back to London for Christmas, and all will be forgotten! Truly, you will see how much happier we all will be!"

Louisa chose this moment to speak up. "We all so long to return to London, Charles! Only think of the winter balls we are missing! Mrs Spencer wrote me just last week to tell us of all the news. Her daughter Amelia came out only this last Season, I know you thought her quite a lovely girl. All our friends are in Town now, and I do declare, Charles, we are all quite miserable here!"

His teeth clenched, he faced his sisters as they stood unified against him.

"Go, then. Darcy and I must remain here yet a while." Louisa's dismayed gasps were lost in Caroline's devastated sobs as he quit the room.

Bingley bounded up the steps to his private room and began uncomfortably tugging at his cravat. He only managed to make a more tightly snarled knot of it before his valet appeared. The man seemed to materialize out of nowhere. He sighed gratefully. "Thank you, Jenkins. I know it is early, but I intend to retire for the night."

"Very good, sir. Shall I have a tray brought up?" The short, balding man was a perfect professional, never batting an eye at his young master's whims.

"Thank you, yes. No, never mind. Wait, has Darcy returned? Would you send down to the stables for any word?"

Jenkins' face twitched slightly. "Mr Darcy returned several hours ago, sir."

"Really?" Bingley was relieved. "How can the house not know of it?"

"He used the staff entrance, sir," was the cryptic reply. "I believe you will find him in his room."

The staff entrance! Clever dog, I should have thought of that years ago! Bingley thanked his valet and dismissed him. Peering cautiously into the corridor, he determined that it was safe to slip unobserved to his friend's door.

A knock produced no response. Bingley knocked softly again, afraid to create too much noise in case Caroline had retreated to her own rooms nearby. Still there was no answer.

Concern for his oldest friend outweighed his manners. Bingley slowly pushed the door open. The room was dimly lit, with only a dwindling fire in the hearth. Several burned-out candles littered Darcy's writing desk, and he could just make out some blotched pages, the pen knife, and half a dozen stubs in the shadows. The man had been up working, but where was he now?

Scanning the room, his eyes finally lit on Darcy's form. He sat forlornly on the floor, his waistcoat and cravat gone, his expensively tailored shirt half open and untucked. He was staring dazedly into the fire, his hand curled around a bottle of Bingley's best Scotch. Polished and sophisticated Darcy was downing the fine spirits without even the encumbrance of a glass, which shocked Bingley as much as anything else. From the looks of things, he had been sitting there quite some while.

"Darcy! Darcy, are you well?" Bingley came around for a better look. It would seem Darcy's other hand held a bottle as well... an empty one. "Good heavens, man! Whatever is the matter?" Bingley impatiently threw more wood on the fire, stoking it so he at least would have better light to assess his friend's condition.

Darcy's bleary eyes slowly made their way to his face. "Chrlesss? Verry glad you're 'turned. Didjou have good sport-t t'day?"

Bingley squinted, trying to make out his friend's slurred speech. "We had no shooting today, you know that."

Darcy snorted derisively, his head rolling to the side just a bit to better look at his friend without having to move his aching eyes very much. "You wurr always-s a turrible shot-t."

"Well, now, if you're going to insult me, as well as drink all my best Scotch…." Bingley frowned and made as if to go, but Darcy went on as though he had not heard.

"Nevur-r did *hick* any good to c-coach you!" he waved an arm expressively. "'St-steady pull on the t-trigger,' I say, 'Don't j-j-urrk the m-muzzle,' I say, but-t therr you go, half-f-f c-cocked ag-again. *hick* Damned w-wayst-t of powdurr! What the devil-l-l makes you so 'mpulsive, man?" Darcy grunted, lifting the bottle to his lips.

Bingley reached to snatch it from him, but Darcy only jerked away, glowering. He swilled the expensive liquid without even bothering to savour it and dropped the bottle again, heaving out a caustic sigh. Bingley observed him with a raised brow. "It seems to me that *I* am not the impulsive one today. What is this all about? Miss Elizabeth?"

Darcy huffed. "Therrr, you have hit a f-fine id'y'a. Pur-h-haps *she* could t-teach you to sh-shoot burrds-s. *hick* Sh-she sh-shoots ev'r'thing else down. *hick* Fearf'lly angrrry though, s-stay well back. She may well sh-shoot you r-rath-urrr than the groussse."

"Shoot me? What the blazes are you talking about, man?"

"…then therrr is that r-river nearest the house where she throws rocks-s-s. Can you s-s-swim, Charles-s?"

"Swim? Darcy, you're completely foxed! I don't understand what you're going on about."

He groaned and fell flat backward, the half full bottle of Scotch tipping precariously in his slack hand. Only Bingley's quick action saved it from being dumped. He spirited it out of his friend's reach. "Liz'beth. I think she wants-s to k-killll me."

"Oh, Darcy, be reasonable. I am sure Miss Elizabeth could not hurt a fly! She is a perfectly lovely girl."

Darcy craned his neck, his drunken features suffused with an earnest light. "She is, iz-she not?" he whispered. His head dropped back. "And no, *hick* I know she could most def-definitely hurrt a fl-fly." He closed his eyes with a ridiculous half-smile. "She c-can pack quite a wal-wallop when you try to kissss hurr. Don't do that," he admonished, wagging a finger seriously at Bingley.

"You… you did not! Darcy! I never would have imagined you, of all men…."

Darcy's arm dropped over his face. His muffled voice came from under his elbow. "Don'n wurrry Ch'rlesss, her s- *hick* ssissssturr is surrrre to be much eas-ssiurrr tempered. She lets you dance with hurrr. Sm- *hick*s- smiles too much. Wait, where is my horrrssse? I d'not think she likes dan- dans-sing."

Bingley shook his head. Darcy's erratic speech had him entirely lost. He needed to get the man to bed and away from the bottle. He made a grab for Darcy's arm to help him up, but his intoxicated friend writhed away. "Merciful heavens... Darcy, for your own sake I hope that first bottle was not full when you began! Was it the one we were drinking two nights ago?"

"Mmmmffff... not... No," his expression turned mournful once again."It is Fis-william Darcy she doesn'n like. She ssays he-sss..." his eyes fixed on an imaginary Elizabeth Bennet across the room and he waved his arm, extending an accusatory finger in emulation of the non-existent young lady. He stiffened, quoting the image's words verbatim. "Arrr'gant and self- fisssh and cons-seeted, and..." his face clouded. "What else was it? I was only trying to keep hurrr from mar-marr'ing Caroline... wait... no it was... what is that r'diculous oaf's name? Bingley," he brightened suddenly, straining up a little, "maybe you should mar- *hick* m-marry her. She's-s nice to you."

"You forget, old friend, you claimed her yourself! I think I had best not get involved!" Bingley could not help chuckling a little. He had never seen Darcy show the least effect from drink since they very first met. Darcy never lost control, never wavered in his solemn propriety. Even as a young fellow at school, the future Master of Pemberley had looked and acted every inch the proper gentleman at all times. Now here he was, dead drunk and raving like a fool after clashing with a mere country miss. The man must be thoroughly besotted! But no, not Darcy, that was impossible.

Darcy grumbled and rolled to his side. Carefully, he put his hands on the floor and tried to push to a sitting position. With a deep groan, he paused to clutch his head, then took a breath and heaved himself up. Immediately he shielded his eyes. "Eg-gad, what happened to my f-fi-urrre!"

"What fire? You had let it die. Now, tell me what all of this is about. Miss Elizabeth is angry with you, I understand?"

Darcy made a scornful noise, then hiccoughed. "Angr-ry? Angry would have been s-something like, 'Missturrr Dar-Darcy, you were somewhat pres-sumpchuous in the-there. You must promise to w-warn me before pro-pr'posing in public ag-again.'" He mimicked a high falsetto voice, setting off another hiccough and drawing a helpless snicker from Bingley. "Not my Liz-Lizzbeth. She does nothing in half m-measures."

"What did she say? Exactly." Bingley spoke slowly so his friend's muddled brain could keep up.

With haunted eyes, he gazed at his companion dully and repeated with careful enunciation, "That I was the last man in the wurrrllld she would evurrr marry. Did you know sh-she likes to throw rocks? No, I already mentioned that. Did I?" Darcy rubbed his furrowed brow, either trying to clear his thoughts or ease the growing headache.

Bingley covered his mouth, hiding his merciless smirk. He was dying to laugh out loud at how little Miss Elizabeth Bennet had dressed down the great Fitzwilliam Darcy of Pemberley, but it would be too cruel to taunt his friend quite so heartlessly. Still, he itched to snicker just a little.

"The last man in the world? Even ranked behind Collins, eh? I say, Darce, that is some achievement! You have finally found a woman who wants nothing to do with you. You ought to be pleased! Why, you will never have to dance again!"

Darcy glowered at him beneath his tousle of dark hair, anger causing him to sober somewhat. "I would get more sympathy from Aunt C-Catherine! *hick* Charles, I am ser-serious, she hates m-me!" Darcy's heartbroken tone was palpable, so much so that he was beginning to sound almost lucid. Even then, it was difficult to take him seriously when he could not even manage a complete sentence.

Bingley sighed, pity for his friend finally forcing him to put aside his amusement. "I am sorry, Darce. Look, Miss Elizabeth will calm down. The poor girl is just shocked. You did give her quite the surprise, declaring you were engaged in front of everyone like that. Whatever made you do it?"

Darcy stilled, gazing vacantly into the fire. He sighed, his breath escaping softly, and on it the words, "I love hurrr, Charles."

Bingley sobered. Of all the men he had known, Fitzwilliam Darcy had seemed the least vulnerable, the least disposed to romantic folly. Had not this same man, on more than one occasion, even pulled him back from unfortunate entanglements of his own? Was it possible that the impervious Darcy had a chink in his armor after all?

He drew closer to his friend, resting a comradely hand on his shoulder. "See here, Darce, we will call tomorrow… when you are fit to be about," he eyed his friend's face sceptically, "and we will have a chat with the ladies. If you think it will help, I will talk to Miss Elizabeth myself. You are in too deep now, old chap, we have to find a way to work this out. She is an intelligent woman, and you are… well, you are normally a very agreeable fellow," he paused as Darcy interjected another hiccough, followed by a loud belch. "We will get this all straightened out."

Darcy shook his head emphatically, earning a pounding between his eyes and a wave of dizziness as a result. "She hates me. She said she didn'n like me before, and then sh-she got an earf-ful from W-Wickham. He-'s the pride of the r-reg'ment, you know. Has all the town fawning over him. Blast, where did the man g- *hick* get all his ch'rm? I'm j'st 's' ch'rming, right Charles?"

"It would be better if I do not answer that just now. Come on, Fitz," Bingley had not called him such since their days at Cambridge. "Up with you, you need sleep, old friend. Let's get you into your nice, comfortable bed."

"S-staying right here." Darcy pouted, childishly shoving his hand away and flopping back onto the floor. "Do not feel like r-riding to Long- *hick* Longbourn."

"Darcy, *your* bed is precisely eight feet away. It is not at Longbourn."

"Eh? Oh." Chagrined, Darcy let Bingley help him to his feet. "Ch'rles-s?" he asked uncertainly, turning his face close to his friend's.

Bingley coughed and gasped. "Have a care Darcy! Do face that way! Yes, what is it?"

"'Liz'beth is a gr-great reader."

"Mmm-hmm. Here you go," he hefted the taller man's frame haphazardly into his elegant bed.

Darcy rolled awkwardly onto the mattress, holding his head but turning to look back up at his friend. "You are wr-rong, you know. She is much lov-loveliurr than her sis-sisturr."

Bingley stiffened his neck, helplessly compelled to defend his lady despite his companion's unreasonable state. "I cannot agree with you there, man. Jane Bennet does not have her equal, but I will allow that her sister is far from plain."

Darcy lay back on his pillow and waved his hand dismissively. His words- coherent, for a change- came out as a soft breath. "You have not seen her with the wind in her hair and a flush on her cheeks. Ch'rles-s?" Darcy craned his neck again toward Bingley. "Think she w-would like Pemburrrley? Sh-she likes to walk in the m-mud." Puzzled, he turned back to Bingley, who ducked quickly out of range. "Does Pemburrrley have mud in the libr'y? Hope she will read my letturrr."

Bingley shook his head. There was no making sense of the man's ramblings. "Good night, Darcy. I will send Wilson in to look after you." He threw the counterpane over his old friend, still fully dressed, and took himself to bed.

Seven

Elizabeth rose stiffly after a miserable night's sleep, or rather lack thereof. She could not cease her restless anger or her stunned musings. She and Jane had talked deep into the night, but Elizabeth was still no nearer forgetting Mr Collins or forgiving Mr Darcy.

Dragging her dressing gown over her night clothes, she crept down the hall to her father's room, rousing Mrs Cooper who had been dozing comfortably. "Has he shown any signs of waking?" she whispered.

Mrs Cooper shook her head. "Nay, Miss, but it's still early. Let the body have time to heal."

Elizabeth sagged with disappointment. "I know. He *will* wake though, will he not?" Her eyes implored the older woman to answer in the affirmative, but Mrs Cooper was too experienced to make an attempt at false hope.

"I cannot say, my dear," she placed a motherly hand on Elizabeth's. "We can only do so much. He has everything in his favour, and we can find no other injuries. Cheer up, love," she smiled in encouragement. "I've seen it happen, and more than once."

Elizabeth sighed and nodded dejectedly. The pair sat in silence for some time. At length, she offered to dress then return to allow Mrs Cooper a break, intending to sit with her father through the morning. One by one, as the morning began to ripen, her mother and two oldest sisters came to pay their respects.

Jane's deep compassion and care was welcome to Elizabeth, as was the offer of a hot cup of coffee and a scone. Less welcome were Mary's practical observations, and her pointed assumption that Elizabeth's prudent engagement to Mr Darcy alleviated their worry of homelessness, in case their father should not improve. Entirely disagreeable was her mother's visit. Elizabeth's nerves grated raw, but there was little she could do to silence Mrs Bennet's excited planning.

"Lizzy, do find out what Mr Darcy's favourite meal is! I intend to serve it tomorrow. I invited Mr Bingley to dinner tomorrow, you know, and he promised to bring your Mr Darcy."

Elizabeth grunted inarticulately. What did she care what the man liked to eat? "One of Hill's ragouts will surely suffice, Mama," she fibbed at last. Truthfully, she had already observed at Netherfield he preferred plain dishes as she did, but she had no intention of dangling that morsel of information before her ravenous mother.

"Oh, and Lizzy, you must see what you can do to encourage Mr Bingley to offer for Jane! He so clearly admires her, and he must be very shy, I think, not to have said something yesterday when there was so much talk of marriage! It is only a matter of time, you know, but you must do what you can to help her secure him! After all, your dearest father may not wake and that horrid Mr Collins may turn us out before he is cold in his grave!"

"Oh, Mama," ashamed, Elizabeth buried her face in her palm. "Papa will be fine, Mama. Only give him time to recover. Please do not go on so, it is most unseemly!"

"Oh, you do not think what I must suffer, you careless girl! But Lizzy, you were so clever to ensnare Mr Darcy! Oh, how sly you are! How very fine you will be! Only think, a house in Town, everything charming! We need have no fear now, do we? Let that horrible man do his worst!" she giggled confidently.

Elizabeth wryly noted that Mr Collins had suddenly fallen out of Mrs Bennet's favour as quickly as he had found it. And this the man her mother would have had her marry only yesterday! Disgusted, she adopted the tactic of silence to put off further conversation. She returned deliberately to her book. Mrs Bennet, rather than taking the pointed hint, soon grew bored with her silent daughter. She bustled off, in search of more willing listeners.

Mr Collins' imperious tones drifted through the half-closed door. Elizabeth tucked herself more firmly into the corner near her father's bed while she eavesdropped on his affronted monologue- directed at anyone within earshot. He loudly announced his intentions to return to Lucas Lodge for the whole of the day, where he had been the entire afternoon previous. *Good riddance,* she thought spitefully. *One less overbearing man to deal with today.*

That still left Mr Darcy, who would be publicly expected to call at some point, if he had a shred of decency about him. Elizabeth testily resolved to spend the entire day in her father's room. Let him come find her if he dared!

~

Bingley woke at his usual time, but lingered above stairs as long as he felt he was able. He did not relish facing Caroline or Louisa this morning. He had asked to be kept apprised of Darcy's activities, and so far yet this morning the man snored in a dazed stupor.

Through delicately veiled comments, Darcy's valet suggested that his master had been sick a good part of the night. Bingley was only surprised it had not occurred while he had been yet in the room. His old friend had downed a considerable amount of alcohol. With some relief, he had been able to discover that Darcy had begun on the bottle that had been nearly empty, but still, to consume that quantity of stout drink, and then make as much headway as the man had on the second bottle was quite incredible. That had been a particularly strong- and expensive- vintage. It would be a wonder if Darcy were not still entirely drunk.

Eventually Bingley resigned himself to face the onslaught and made his reluctant way downstairs. He expected a repeat of the prior night's scene. Instead, he found the breakfast room curiously quiet. Only Hurst was there, and his brother barely spared time for a greeting before returning to his meal.

Bingley thanked the maid who brought him his paper, and sat down to his breakfast. Louisa joined them a few moments later. Her silent pout told him that she had not yet given up the scheme of departing for London immediately. He sighed inwardly. He really did have business which needed his attention. He had sent a letter delaying his attorney's appointment, but he would need to go to town soon, unless his man could come to him instead. He felt that before he could go anywhere, he needed to see how things developed with Mr Bennet... and with Darcy and Miss Elizabeth.

A fresh idea came to him. No harm in helping the situation along a little! Calling for his butler, he scribbled a quick note to the Bennet family. He asked after Mr Bennet, and then requested permission to call later in the day. One way or another, he would have to make sure Darcy went with him, and it would be some while yet before he could be made presentable. Giving the note back to his butler, he asked that it be delivered at once and a reply requested.

He turned his attention back to his meal and ate the rest undisturbed. Quietly he retreated to his study, more to escape Louisa's sulking demeanour than to do any real work. Unlike Darcy, Bingley was perfectly satisfied to remain idle for a time, when had little to do. He contented himself by toying with the fire and daydreaming of Jane Bennet's beautiful blue eyes.

His reverie was disturbed when his valet burst through the door, thoroughly flustered. Concerned, Bingley ignored his man's breach of protocol. "Is something the matter with Darcy?" he started from his position. The gentlemen's pair of valets were thick as thieves, a fact for which Bingley was most grateful.

"Yes, sir. It seems Miss Bingley had been waiting for him to come down to breakfast, and she is losing patience. She is demanding entrance to Mr Darcy's rooms! Mr Wilson asks if you can come."

"What? Good heavens!" Bingley fairly ran upstairs. He found Caroline loudly berating Wilson, calling him any number of unflattering names. Wilson stood embarrassed but resolute, guarding his master's door with his hands locked behind his back on the latch.

"Caroline! What is the meaning of this!" With a nod, he dismissed Darcy's valet. The poor fellow gratefully escaped back into his master's room. Wishing to defuse the scene his sister was causing, he gripped her elbow, dragged her back into her own room and slammed the door.

"Charles! Let go! Ouch! How dare you abuse your own sister in this way! Unhand me!" Caroline ripped her arm out of his grasp. Brother and sister stood toe to toe, fuming.

"Caroline, what were you thinking, setting up such a fuss outside Mr Darcy's door? Demanding to enter his rooms? I am appalled! Do you know what the servants will be saying?"

Caroline straightened herself, assuming a serene dignity. "Charles, how you do go on. You know very well I would not engage in such vulgar behaviour! I only wished to tend to him! His valet said he was quite ill this morning and I know he would wish for me to care for him in his indisposition. It is my duty, as your hostess, to see to our guests!" She sniffed, turning her face away.

"Of course, this explains everything," she went on, picking at the lace of her sleeves to arrange the cuffs as she liked. "This misunderstanding with Miss Elizabeth Bennet must have been some misapprehension due to his sudden ailment. A doctor must be called at once to ascertain that it is not serious and to testify that he had not his senses about him yesterday." She finished and leveled a perfectly tranquil gaze at him, as if daring him to believe her mistaken.

Bingley shook his head in astonishment. One moment she was as coarse and ill-bred as a sailor, abusing the staff and making both a nuisance and a spectacle of herself. The next she was placid as any fine gentlewoman, while at the same time asserting the most preposterous notions. "Caroline," he rubbed the bridge between his eyes, "for the last time, Mr Darcy has never shown the faintest interest in you. I am sorry to disappoint my own sister, but it is the truth. Do stop preoccupying yourself with the idea."

Caroline huffed, tossing her head airily. "Mr Darcy thinks very highly of me! We have been on intimate terms for years, and I know he admires how I dote on dear Georgiana. The issue, Charles, is whether *you* will be a kind friend to him. You cannot allow him to debase himself by an alliance with such a family! Why, it is simply not done! Their uncle is in *trade*, Charles. He would make himself the laughingstock of London!

"You yourself would be tainted by such an unfashionable connection, which our family can ill afford! You would simply have to give him up, Charles, and I know you would be loath to do so. This 'engagement' is a sham, Charles, a deplorable trickery wrought upon an estimable gentleman! Miss Elizabeth Bennet is a country chit, not worthy of a man of his standing! She must be made to know her place and to relinquish any claim upon him."

"I cannot believe I have allowed this to go on," he turned away, aggrieved. "Caroline, you have just proven to me in a few words why I have never cared for many of the *ton*. If the profession of one's uncle is a significant enough indictment against them to discredit such lovely girls as Miss Elizabeth *and* Miss Jane Bennet, then you and I must have an entirely different way of looking at the world.

"Do you forget, Caroline, that our own fortune comes from the woolen mills? We are no further away from this disagreeable taint of trade than the Bennets, yet you act as if you are infinitely better than they! What basis do you have for this assumption of superiority? Furthermore, what does it matter? I have met many a person whose company I find delightful, regardless of their low station, and many more I cannot abide who claim fashionable connections."

Caroline made a crude noise and glowered in disgust. "I might have known you could not be made to see reason. You never did show discretion in your associations, Charles! I had hoped that Mr Darcy could have brought you to some sense, but I see now that it is you who have influenced him for the worse! If it were not for my good instincts and all the connections I have made, why, we would have no standing at all in society! You know that your poor taste will affect my chances!" Her voice rose to a spine-shivering screech.

He turned back to her, grinning recklessly. "I would not despair so, Caroline! Indeed, I am quite sure that Miss Bennet's uncle in Cheapside will know of some charming young solicitors or office assistants with whom he would be glad to acquaint you- after I have offered for Miss Jane."

Her mouth flew open in outrage, but for once she was speechless. Bingley's smile widened as he stepped back into the corridor, a merry whistle upon his lips. The door slammed violently behind him.

~

It was nearing midday when Bingley's attention was again diverted so forcefully. He had been attempting to read one of the books Darcy had left in the drawing room, the *Journals* of John Wesley. Try as he might, he could not retain more than a paragraph or two before he found his eyes skimming the page uncomprehendingly.

The wheels of a carriage grated roughly on the gravel outside, causing him to jump up in relief. Not one to stand on ceremony when it seemed unnecessary, he moved quickly to the foyer to greet his unexpected guest. Great was his surprise when he found Colonel Fitzwilliam himself stepping out of the carriage. The colonel reached back inside to hand down a timid Georgiana Darcy, followed by her silent maid.

"Colonel! I daresay I am glad you are come, but I did not expect you so soon!"

The colonel turned his smiling face away from the young lady to greet his host. "Bingley!" he returned jovially, "It is good to see you again. Your note was most… intriguing," he flashed a roguish grin.

Bingley bowed to Miss Darcy, then offered her his arm. "You are looking well, Miss Georgiana," he welcomed her gently. "You must be tired from your journey. Would you like to take a rest?"

She thanked him bashfully, but replied, "I am not tired, but I would like to see Fitzwilliam."

"Yes, where is the old man?" the colonel rejoined. "Off calling on this mysterious Miss Bennet? I confess, Bingley, when I got your note I was completely stunned. Fancy Darcy finally succumbing, and to a country girl! He has always been an impenetrable fortress. She must indeed be something charming to turn his head. I had to meet this young woman for myself!"

"Colonel… Miss Darcy… perhaps we should speak more privately." Bingley showed them into the house and gestured to his study. Fitzwilliam's eyebrows shot up, his curiosity now at a fever pitch. Miss Georgiana, ever astute, hesitantly followed the gentlemen.

Bingley offered them seats and refreshments, the latter of which were politely declined. Both parties were burning with interest at the novelty of Fitzwilliam Darcy's recent actions. Bingley seated himself, and after some initial hesitation, began to relate their history with the Bennet family. His listeners sat quietly, without interrupting.

He began with their initial acquaintance, and how Darcy had scoffed at the notion of even standing up with the young woman. A moment later, he was describing the few days- marvelous, they were to Bingley, but perhaps rather uncomfortable to Darcy- when the eldest Bennet sisters had taken refuge under his roof. Darcy had never in that time shown any signs of warming to the young woman, certainly!

Progressing to more recent events, and still shaking his head in wonder, he told of the ball two days ago, and how Darcy had singled Miss Elizabeth out for an unaccustomed dance. Miss Georgiana did not appear so surprised, but Fitzwilliam let out a low whistle. Lastly of all, he told of Mr Bennet's accident, and the unwelcome houseguest who stood to inherit the family's home should the gentleman not recover.

"...And so, yesterday when Mr Collins tried to insist upon Miss Elizabeth marrying him, Darcy stepped in. I know now why he did it, but at the time…. well, I was just as shocked as Miss Bennet," he finished.

"Pray tell, what could his reason be?" Fitzwilliam queried, his eyebrow arched teasingly. "Do not tell me that the dreary chap has finally given over to a pretty face? I cannot believe it."

"I think for that you had best speak to him. I warn you, however, he may not yet be fit to receive company."

"What is the matter? Is he unwell?" A sister's concern pouring from her eyes, Georgiana leaned forward urgently.

"Nothing a little time and perhaps some hot coffee would not mend. You see," he glanced uncertainly between the two, "Miss Elizabeth did not take Darcy's interference well yesterday. They had words… well, Colonel, I have not seen him this morning, but he was somewhat the worse for wear last night. I am very glad you have come."

Comprehension began to dawn in the colonel's eyes. He turned gently to the fair-haired girl and suggested, "Georgiana, why do you not allow a maid to see you to your room? You can take some refreshment there, and we will join you in the drawing room later."

Unwillingly she acquiesced, and Bingley rang for a maid. Nancy, one of the younger maids, came smartly, but her eyes shifted nervously to her charge as Bingley gave instructions. Caroline had terrorized most of the staff, he realized with a sinking feeling. At least the polite and sweet Georgiana would give the young maid no reason to fear. She would not even be required to have chief charge of the girl, as Georgiana's own ladies' maid had accompanied her. Still, it was only proper to assign Nancy as well, who was familiar with the house. Georgiana smiled a little at the equally nervous Nancy, and the two departed.

"Colonel, if you will kindly follow me," Bingley showed Fitzwilliam upstairs.

~

Darcy had finally lurched upright, his head throbbing. He sat for a few minutes, his pounding eyes shielded in his fists. Dimly he perceived Wilson making preparations for his morning shave, but the sounds which were usually so welcome in the morning only aggravated his suffering.

Darcy could not remember ever having been the worse for drink. What had he done last night? Shadowy memories flitted through his mind, spinning and dissolving and then finally coalescing to one single point-*Elizabeth*.

Good heavens, what had he done? His muddled mind struggled to piece together the events of the day before. Had he really...? And she.... He groaned, flopping back down on the bed. It hurt his head to think about it.

He struggled to a sitting position again when he heard muffled voices approaching from the corridor. Bingley's clear, happy tones were joined by another voice, deeper and heartier... *Dash it. That is all I need.*

"... *Two* bottles of Scotch! We cannot be talking about the same Darcy!"

"Indeed, it is the truth. I have never seen him so..." there was a brief rap on the door, and then it opened abruptly. Bingley still stood with his knuckles in the air, but Richard Fitzwilliam strode confidently into the room and accosted him as he still sat in his bed.

"William!" his cousin grinned as he slapped him mercilessly on the back.

"Go away, Richard," Darcy growled.

"Oh-ho, my boy, is that any way to greet your favourite relative?" Fitzwilliam's voice was much, much louder than normal. Was it his imagination, or was his cousin deliberately trying to increase his agony?

"You are most decidedly *not* my favourite relative," was the cross retort.

"No, I suppose not, but I brought her with me. Best clean up, Laddy, we cannot let Georgiana think you are less than a paragon. Here we go!" Richard shouldered his younger and taller cousin and hoisted him to his feet.

Darcy's head reeled with the sudden change in posture. His stomach rebelled and he tried to grip both aching body parts to still the overpowering queasiness. "Richard, curse you, let go of me!" Immediately he regretted his words. Fitzwilliam yielded with an exaggerated flourish, and Darcy nearly crumpled to the floor. He had to let go of his stomach to grasp the post of the bed.

Finally Richard's words clarified in his head. "You brought Georgiana? Whatever for? And what are you doing here, you blackguard?"

"Temper, temper, Darce. I say, Bingley, he is in fine form today, is he not? Here you are," Richard braced him again and with Bingley's assistance the pair helped him to walk over to the chair where Wilson waited to shave him.

Out of consideration for the man with the hangover, Bingley and Fitzwilliam stood quietly while Darcy received his shave. Bingley decided a bath ought to be drawn to revive his friend, but seeing Darcy's continued lack of coordination, the two men were obliged to help. Fitzwilliam dunked his cousin into the bath with a little more exuberance than was strictly necessary, but the job was at last done.

Bingley and Fitzwilliam retreated to the bedroom while Darcy dressed and was made presentable. Wilson once again earned his rather lavish pay, for Darcy looked nearly respectable when he emerged. His steps were still short, his movements painfully slow in regard for his aching head. He greeted them with a slow nod. Bingley wordlessly handed him a cup of black coffee and encouraged him to sit at his writing desk.

"So," the colonel began, drawing a chair near. "Tell me about this Miss Elizabeth Bennet, who I hear is so enchanting."

Darcy moaned, rolled out of his chair, and stumbled toward his bed. Behind the screen, they could hear him retching into the chamber pot.

"Wrong subject, I suspect, Colonel," Bingley whispered.

Fitzwilliam's eyes were round in wonder. "I never would have imagined it," he replied, his voice low. "He is utterly besotted, is he not? And she refused him, you say? Indeed, I must meet this singular woman!"

Bingley nodded in agreement, but said nothing. Darcy was tremblingly emerging from behind the screen, wiping his mouth. He dubiously regarded his companions, who both sat in nervous silence while he gingerly resumed his seat and his coffee. A soft knock at the door brought a note from Bingley's housekeeper and provided him an escape, which he gratefully took. Colonel Fitzwilliam remained, eyeing his cousin's condition sceptically.

"Well, Cousin," he recommenced, more gently this time. "Tell good old Richard what the matter is."

Darcy scowled. "Your patronizing is not necessary."

"That's more like it, Cuz. So, I understand I am to wish you joy?" He watched carefully, wondering if his return to the previous subject would precipitate another run on the chamber pot. Darcy held himself in admirably, but did not make a proper reply. A groan and a deep sigh was his only response for a moment.

Half a cup of coffee later, Darcy looked up. "Did you say you brought Georgiana? What the devil for?"

Richard handled his surly cousin with aplomb. He would get the full story when Darcy was good and ready. "She was concerned about her brother, naturally. Bingley sent me an express yesterday which he intended as an invitation for her to come to you. He indicated that you might be in need of a little support from your dearest sister. Had I *chosen* to hold her back I would have been unsuccessful. I have absolutely *no* idea where she learned to be so stubborn," he innocently suggested. "She insisted upon leaving at first light this morning. Something about traveling post-chaise alone if I did not present myself at the door by the proper hour...."

"Richard," Darcy's expression was deadly serious, his voice a harsh whisper, "Wickham is here."

The colonel's face paled. "What, here in Meryton?"

Darcy nodded, sickening again. "Bingley could not have known when he wrote for her to come... Wickham has joined the regiment stationed there. It seems also that he has been merrily spreading reports about myself, which you and I both know to be false, but she...." his voice trailed off as he fought back another wave of nausea.

"Oh..." Richard breathed. "I see." He sat contemplatively, brushing his chin with his forefinger. "How do we keep her away from him?" His eyes narrowed, focusing on his cousin. "Or was it Georgie you were talking about just now?"

"Yes, and no." Darcy sighed. "We cannot let him anywhere near Georgiana, but the rascal has done plenty of damage already."

"Aye, that it would seem. So," he leaned forward, the seasoned battlefield commander replacing the worried guardian. "Wickham has been sowing seeds of discord with your lovely lady, and she heartily dislikes you. The problem is," he looked up, verifying his facts, "now the entire town of Meryton believes you both to be engaged, and given your decided lack of finesse with the ladies, I am guessing your 'betrothed' will not speak to you. Yet you seem inordinately fond of her. Does that about sum it up?"

Darcy nodded wearily, his head throbbing. "Remind me never to try to keep a secret from you. It is not worth the effort."

Fitzwilliam grinned rakishly. "What would be the point of being older and wiser if I could not weasel a confession out of you every time? Now," he clapped his hands together and rubbed them briskly, as though he were planning a grand entertainment rather than counseling a heartbroken cousin. "First things first. Bingley has you fooled, by the way Cousin."

At Darcy's startled questioning glance, Fitzwilliam smirked and continued. "He is not quite as oblivious as some might think. The fellow is a genius, you could learn a thing or two. He wrote for Georgiana's help, hoping that her presence would help this lovely Elizabeth, of whom you are so enamored, to possibly see your good side. You do have one, if I remember correctly."

Darcy looked daggers at him. "If you think I will place Georgiana in the company of... of some of the local populace here, trotting her out as if she were some peace offering, you had better get back in your coach and return to London!" he snarled.

"Very well, but it was your coach I brought. As for Georgie, good luck getting her to return with me. She was very insistent upon meeting this Miss

Elizabeth Bennet. She said you had previously written about her, and you were even very complimentary? My word, Darcy, I believe I must meet her as well!"

"Is it your intention to uselessly aggravate me, Richard?" Darcy grumbled.

"Well, you must admit, I have never had such a golden opportunity to do so. Now, quite seriously, once you have made yourself human again with your coffee, Georgiana is waiting most anxiously to speak to you. I believe," he gestured with his chin over his shoulder, "she was going to try to remain in her private room, unless Miss Bingley has already forced her out." Richard suppressed a shudder.

Darcy sighed, nodded, and picked his nearly empty cup back up. It was useless to argue when he was still so muddled, and Richard was enjoying himself far too much.

Richard propped his chin on his hand meditatively, waiting for his cousin to finish. "What of this other fellow, Collins, Bingley wrote about? Who is he? The heir, he said it was?"

"A cousin. Unpleasant, as most cousins are," Darcy shot him a sardonic look over the rim of his cup.

"Touché. Perhaps you are not so impaired as I thought. But from where does he come? Why would he be staying with the Bennets just now?"

"He is… Oh…" Darcy reddened and swore. "He is our aunt Catherine's new rector at Rosings." Darcy jumped from his chair and began to pace, for the moment ignoring the clamoring of his head.

"You don't say! Well, this is rich!" The colonel began laughing, shaking his head.

"You do not understand, Richard," Darcy breezed by him, suddenly energized by his frustration. His words came in bursts as he pounded the carpet. "He panders to Aunt Catherine utterly- you would not believe it. I can easily see why she offered him the preferment. He considers it his duty to compliment her unceasingly. Surely he wrote to her immediately. He was not only offended because Elizabeth refused him, but also because he has been listening a little too much to Aunt Catherine. You know her expectations." He ground his teeth, scowling.

Fitzwilliam held up his hands. "I am a step or two ahead of you, Cousin." Darcy stopped and regarded him expectantly. The colonel smiled, relishing his moment of cleverness. "I expected if word of your engagement got out, there might be repercussions in certain branches of the family. I happened to mention to your coachman and butler in London that perhaps a relative or two might be expected to be passing through within the next few days.

"I thought someone might show up, for example, demanding to see you or Georgie. Should anyone pay a call, they will be *persuaded,* rather firmly, to take accommodations for the night. You know how cogent old Drake can be, I imagine he is up to the task. In addition, I recommended their coach should be *thoroughly* gone over. It would not do for any safety issues to go undetected, putting any of our family at risk, would it? As I have taken your last coach from the London house, there are no others available. You know how some of our relations feel about a hired carriage. I expect any needed repairs, you know, if any issues are discovered, may take at least a day, perhaps two."

Darcy smiled weakly, his first of the day. "You are devious, you know." He began pacing again, more slowly. "Surely, she would not give herself the trouble of traveling so far, but I can imagine some rather strongly worded letters- both to myself and to your father."

"I am a soldier, I take precautions." Richard stood. "Go see Georgie, you have kept her waiting long enough."

Eight

"William!" Georgiana rushed into her brother's arms with relief.

Darcy pressed his baby sister close. It had been nearly two months since he had last seen her. He had been a fool to leave her alone so long, but the alternative would have been to bring her along. He knew she would have been uncomfortable spending so much time with Caroline, and she had truly begged him to go as Bingley had asked.

"Georgie... why, I believe you have grown!" He held her back at arm's length to inspect her. She blushed, smiling shyly up at the brother who was more like a father.

"Bingley said you were ill. What is the matter?" He looked away, trying to evade her penetrating gaze, but did not have the heart to try very hard. She cocked her head, inspecting his bloodshot eyes and weary face. "William?"

"I am well. Truly, Georgie," he replied gently but firmly, taking her small hands in his own. "I want to hear about you. How are you finding your new painting master?"

She narrowed her eyes sceptically, a perfect imitation of himself. "William," she spoke softly, "will you not tell me how it is with Miss Elizabeth? You wrote so well of her. I was so hoping to meet her. Bingley's letter said... well, I was worried." Georgiana cast her eyes down bashfully.

"Georgie..." he sighed, pulling her to the small sofa in her dressing room. "I cannot say what will happen with Miss Elizabeth. I have offended her greatly, you must know."

"How could you possibly? You are the kindest and most wonderful of men, William! Can she not see that?" Georgiana's lip quivered slightly. In

78

her innocent mind, there was no better man than her brother, who had been everything to her for nearly as long as she could remember. Even before their father's death, William had been her companion, advisor, and protector. It was impossible for her to fathom that any woman could fail to see his worth.

"Georgie, it is more complicated than that. I put her in a most unforgivable position yesterday."

"You were a only trying to help! Mr Bingley said that a man she did not like tried to force her into an engagement in public, and that she was finding it difficult to maintain her refusal. I think what you did was wonderful and noble. She did not?"

He gave a short bitter laugh. "Far from it. Collins is not the only man who is not high in her graces. I have been completely wrong about her, Georgie. She informed me yesterday that she has never cared for me, and she believes... well, some things do not bear repeating. It is enough to say that she has heard unsavoury rumours of me, and I fear my behaviour to her has not been such as would cause her to overlook them as false."

"Rumours? But what rumours could there be of you? You are always just and upright."

"Sweetling," he sighed, grasping her hand gently, "you know that not everyone in this world speaks the truth. In our position, you must realize there are many who would seek their own aggrandizement at our expense." She began to colour, but he touched her cheek in encouragement, raising her eyes back to his.

"Georgie, the trouble is not what Miss Elizabeth heard, but what she has believed. Had I somehow earned her good opinion prior, she might have been less willing to believe me capable of the things of which I am accused. The fault is mine, not hers." He spoke softly, the truth of his own words seeping into his heart.

Georgiana's eyes clouded with stinging moisture. Her lonely girlish heart longed desperately for a sister, and her hopes for Miss Elizabeth had been high. William never wrote approvingly of any other young woman of his acquaintance, and he certainly had never been inspired to shield any others from gentlemen they did not like- and at such a cost to himself!

She blinked rapidly, a few errant tears spilling on her cheeks. With a sympathetic smile, her brother tugged her close to his chest, tucking her under his arm as he had when they were children. Georgiana burrowed her face into his dark morning coat.

They sat, comforting each other in silence. Georgiana gazed devotedly up at him as he stared vacantly across the room. William was always so kind to her. He deserved a woman he could love, and who could love him in return, but most only courted his wealth and position. Most cared little enough whether he were kind or honourable, and certainly none would have dreamed of turning down the heir to the Darcy fortune because he had offended them.

Hope began to breathe again in her breast. If Miss Elizabeth had tried to refuse him, then it meant she was *not* the kind of woman who relentlessly pursued him solely to become Mistress of Pemberley. She must have a heart. Perhaps....

"William?" Georgiana fingered the rumpled collar of his jacket hesitantly.

"Yes, Dearest?" He was looking better already, the effects of the previous night gradually giving way to the light of day and his pleasure at his sister's comradeship.

"Do you think I could meet her? I mean… would she talk to me?"

He peered down into her earnest face. His heart longed for exactly that, despite what he had told Richard. He had ruminated in endless frustration on how Georgiana would love Elizabeth since the first day the latter had stayed at Netherfield.

In truth, Georgiana needed someone like Elizabeth. Her easy playfulness would go far toward cheering and encouraging shy Georgiana. Since her narrow escape from Wickham's clutches, she had been increasingly unsure of herself and nervous in company. He did not wish her to follow in his own footsteps, despising social settings because of his awkwardness in conversation. If anyone could brighten his dearest sister and set her at her ease, it was Elizabeth Bennet.

"I do not know," he answered slowly. "Her father is injured, and the family is rather troubled just now. I am certain she is expending most of her time and energy caring for him, as well as her mother and younger sisters. I must speak with her, however. The entire town believes us to be engaged and it could prove disastrous for her if it is broken off. We will certainly be expected to call, but whether she will be in a mood to receive me, I cannot say."

Georgiana rose suddenly, unsettling him. "Then let us go now!" she smiled girlishly. She tugged at his unwilling hands, pleading with him to rise and join her. "Come, William, you must eat something, and then you will feel better. May we call on her today, do you think?"

A reluctant smile forced itself upon his lips. "We shall see, Georgie. Though a square meal does sound very appealing right now." He followed her and, arm in arm, they strolled down to the family dining room for a belated luncheon.

~

"Why *dear* Georgiana!" Caroline Bingley greeted them exuberantly, spreading her arms in magnanimous salutations. She strode toward Georgiana, but her eyes were on Darcy. He stood stoically, ready to intervene if Georgiana appeared overwhelmed. He completely sympathized; anyone would be ill at ease in the presence of Bingley's sister.

"And dear Mr Darcy, I was in such distress when I heard you were ill this morning. Just look now, you are so well recovered! I am certain we owe that to the arrival of our dearest Georgiana." She patted Georgiana's hand in a great display of affection. He proved resolutely non-committal.

Undaunted, she rattled on, this time addressing herself to Georgiana. "I was *so* surprised and delighted to hear you had come to us! I was just saying to your brother the other day how I admired your newest sketches, was I not Darcy?" Caroline beamed at him. He remained silent, refusing to relinquish Georgiana's arm lest she be seized by Caroline. "I was simply in *raptures*, how you captured the beauty of Pemberley's lake! Why, I never saw the like, were we not saying so Louisa?" Louisa nodded and smiled obligingly across the table, but Caroline paid her little attention. "Come, darling, sit by me. What a merry party we shall be! We have so much catching up to do!"

Georgiana cast a braver glance than she truly felt toward her brother, and only then did he turn loose of her elbow. With some trepidation, she followed Caroline to a seat at the opposite end of the table from her brother. She never knew what to say to Caroline Bingley. She always felt like the woman was a gale force of gossip and chatter, the likes of which it was impossible for her to follow. There was little substance to her conversation, and little opportunity to contribute to a dialogue.

"How lovely it is to settle in the country for the holidays, is it not dear Georgiana? So much pleasanter than Town, I always say." Georgiana managed a wan smile. On the brighter side, if she allowed Caroline to prattle on, she would not be required to speak herself.

There had been a brief time, a few years ago, when she had feared William might marry this woman. Caroline Bingley's first visit to Pemberley had very nearly been her last, when she had tried to assume hostess duties at their Michaelmas feast. William had been scandalized! He had not very kindly set her in her place... as it happened, that place had been as far from himself as possible. Georgiana fought to suppress a wholly inappropriate smirk at the memory. Caroline, meanwhile, had forgotten her love of the country, and she droned on about the dullness of Hertfordshire and her plans once they reached Town.

At the other end of the table, Darcy helped himself to a heaping pile of smoked meats, cheeses, and scones. He topped them with a tantalizing cranberry sauce and cream, then a second plate full of fruits from the hothouse joined the first. Bingley's eyebrows raised dubiously, but whatever he considered saying was drowned in his cup.

Fitzwilliam sat nearby with an empty plate, already leaning back from the table somewhat further than was proper. Darcy tucked into his luncheon with as much zeal as Hurst ever had, finding relief even in the first few bites from the lightheadedness which still plagued him.

Bingley waited for the beast to finish wolfing down his victuals before broaching the subject of the Bennets. Once he felt safe, he began. "Darcy, I sent a note to Longbourn this morning to ask after Mr Bennet."

Darcy paused, very properly setting down his fork and wiping his mouth before replying. "Has there been any improvement?"

"None so far, but he is no worse. Miss Jane Bennet wishes to thank us- by which I assume she means you- for arranging a nurse for him." Bingley stared pointedly at him.

Darcy reddened, feeling Richard's questioning gaze on him as well. "Go on," he urged.

With a surreptitious glance down the table, Bingley went on in a lower voice. "I also asked permission to call on the family this afternoon, and the reply was favourable. We are invited to stay through tea. I intended to go directly after luncheon." Bingley stared at him briefly, clearly demanding for Darcy to agree to join him.

Darcy nodded without enthusiasm. He would have expected an arrangement of the kind, though he did not yet feel ready to face Elizabeth. He returned to the remains of his scone with less zest than before.

His eyes wandered to the end of the table to see how Georgiana was faring with her companions. He hoped they would be able to avoid Caroline Bingley's company while they paid the call. It would be difficult to extract his own sister without inviting Charles' sister as well, but this day would be trying enough without Caroline's unwelcome moodiness and excessive attention to himself.

Looking long at Georgiana's stretched features, he knew it would *not* be acceptable to leave her alone at Caroline's mercy while he went alone. Georgiana would have to come to pay the call, and he would just have to leave Caroline to her brother to manage.

Fortunately, he was not alone in those sentiments. The three men excused themselves to make ready for their departure and found themselves unanimous in their desire to encourage Caroline to remain at Netherfield. "I brought your smallest coach, Darcy. I am afraid it can only seat four comfortably," Fitzwilliam winked at him.

"Well, Colonel, how fortunate that we have one larger to suit us all!" Caroline breezed into the entryway where the gentlemen were receiving their outer coats from the footmen. She already wore her muff and coat and she sidled comfortably up to Darcy as he settled his scarf over his collar.

She had no intention of relinquishing her prize without a fight, and she would not sit idly by while Darcy visited Elizabeth without her. Only look what kind of misunderstanding had happened when she did not go the day before!

Darcy forced a neutral expression, looking down to his buttons to avoid acknowledging her. Bingley cleared his throat. "I am afraid, Caroline, that Mrs Nicholls wished to discuss preparations for the reception I planned to hold for the tenant farmers in a fortnight. Had she not mentioned it to you?"

Caroline turned, her face betraying her outrage. "Charles! A tenant reception? You never mentioned that to me! Only yesterday we were quitting this country for good, and now you want to host a party for the farmers?"

His eyes shifted nervously to the other two gentlemen, who both resolutely avoided his gaze. Bingley was on his own for the moment. "Y-yes, well..." he stammered. "We are still invested in the estate, and it is the proper thing to do for our tenants. I will not be planning to return to Town for any duration in the immediate future, and I think this scheme will do very well."

Her mortified stare drifted disbelievingly between the three men, settling on Darcy. "Surely, Charles, the housekeeper can manage sufficiently, it is only the farmers you are receiving! My hostessing skills are not required," she attempted to recover smoothly.

Bingley bit his lip. Caroline *would* deepen her humiliation by refusing to accept the situation with grace. Why could he not have had a sister with some measure of taste and decorum, more like Georgiana? *She* never did anything wrong. To his relief, Darcy and Fitzwilliam tactfully excused themselves out of doors, leaving him to handle his sister in privacy.

"Caroline, we must not leave this to the housekeeper. As the present lady of the house, it is your place to plan these events. It matters not whether we are hosting the farmers or the local gentry or our friends from London. I must insist you heed my wishes on this point, for I will not yield!"

"Charles! These Bennets have been a poor influence on you, I fear. You are entirely forgetting your place! We should have been in Town, not dallying further with these mean country folk. We owe nothing to the farmers here!"

Charles Bingley was fed up, enough so that his impulsive decisiveness from the previous day made a reappearance. He set his jaw, much as Darcy might have, and made unshakable reply. "Caroline, you forget that *you* were in favour of my forming an establishment in the country. I have made a commitment to this place for the term of my lease, and I will honour it! If you find your duties as hostess so distasteful, take heart. I intend to relieve you of those duties as soon as may be."

Her eyes flashing her wrath, Caroline screwed her mouth into an outraged scowl. She turned on her heel and marched toward the stairs in a fit of pique. Deflated, he watched her go. How he hated confronting her! It was not in his nature to be so firm and it was very uncomfortable to him. His life would be so much easier with more amiable relatives!

His eyes followed her hastily retreating figure and were caught by Georgiana. The girl was peeking guiltily around the corner from the sitting room. Apparently she had witnessed much, if not the whole of the scene. She could scarcely have avoided it! With a sigh and a contrite smile, he encouraged her to follow him by offering his arm. Together they joined Darcy and Fitzwilliam in the carriage.

"So, Darcy," Fitzwilliam settled himself next to Bingley, leaving Georgiana to sit with her brother, "do you have a plan of how you may win the fair lady's affections?"

Darcy clamped his teeth. He was not best pleased to discuss his plans regarding Elizabeth in company, even as trusted as each person in the small compartment was to him. Seeing the expectant stares of all the parties in the coach, he finally gave way. "I wrote her a letter," he replied stiffly.

"A *letter?*" the colonel sputtered. "You cannot simply hand the lady a letter! Trust me in this, Darce! You have to talk to her! Egad, man! Bingley, am I not right? Criminy, it is little wonder you are still unmarried. Ladies appreciate a little romance! Invite her for a pleasant stroll, bring her small gifts, tell her how lovely she is… I presume the lady in question *is* lovely?" He looked to Bingley for confirmation, who gave an agreeable nod of the head. To him, no other lady could compare to his angel, but her sister *was* most pleasant to look upon.

"Aha!" Richard put a finger to his lips, then traced it in the air, fabricating a mental picture. "She must be tall, fair… blonde, I should think. Blue eyes?"

Georgiana giggled. "Miss Elizabeth is not quite my height, Cousin Richard. She has dark hair and curls, and very fine dark eyes!"

Richard roared a great guffaw. "You described her to Georgie! In a letter no doubt." Darcy tried unsuccessfully shrink his tall frame, his ears reddening. "Oh, Cousin, you are dead gone. Indeed, she does sound quite fetching, I cannot wait to make her acquaintance!"

"Your description could fit her sister quite nicely though, Fitzwilliam! You shall see, Darcy and I are quite in disagreement over which sister is the loveliest. You must help us settle the dispute!" Bingley put in laughingly.

"Oh, Darcy!" Richard wiped his eyes, still chuckling. "Tell me seriously, you cannot truly be planning to just hand the lady a letter and return to Netherfield whilst she reads it? No, it is unthinkable. You must secure a private audience, and I hope you have something worthwhile to say."

Darcy shifted uncomfortably in his seat. Talk to Elizabeth? He would be lucky to untie his tongue while in her presence. She, who never seemed to lack for a clever repartee, would utterly demolish any plea for reason and forgiveness he might try to present in person. He had never doubted that if they should reach a good understanding, he would quickly be completely at his ease with her. He knew he would trust her utterly, and she would tease him in that delightful, intimate way he had seen her reserve for those she loved. Until then, he had much he truly needed her to know, and dared not chance the important communication to his uncertain conversation skills.

He opened his mouth to defend himself, but his rescue instead came from an unexpected source. Georgiana looked approvingly to him and squeezed his arm. "William says Miss Elizabeth is very intelligent. I think he must know best how he can tell her what he needs to clear any misunderstandings. Surely a clever woman of sense would value sincere communication, no matter what form it takes. Do you not agree, Mr Bingley?"

Bingley stared for a moment, gathering his thoughts. Miss Elizabeth was perhaps unique among the women of his acquaintance. It was true that Darcy had rarely maintained a conversation with her without falling victim to her playful wit. To be fair, most of the time the gentleman seemed rather to enjoy his loss, but with so much at stake he feared his friend would be at a disadvantage.

Still, he felt the colonel had the right of it. "Surely, Darcy, if her family considers you engaged to her, you will be granted some little time to speak privately if you wish. There can be nothing improper in that. Does not the lady deserve to hear you speak your case and make reply?"

"That, Charles, is the material point. I do not have reason to believe she will consent to another private conference, no matter how favourably her mother might view such an arrangement. Miss Elizabeth vehemently denied the engagement, and with good reason, for I regret that I surprised and offended her in the extreme. I have the greatest doubt that she will lend ear to what I must say."

Glancing down at Georgiana's trusting blue eyes, he froze with a sudden fear. There was much in the letter which concerned her directly. Though he had written the letter with the sincere hope that Elizabeth and Georgiana would meet one day, he had not anticipated the meeting would come so soon. He had expected and hoped that a conversation, perhaps several, would follow before Georgiana was introduced to her acquaintance. Had he shared too much? Would Georgie be hurt?

He closed his eyes, heart hammering in his breast. Vainly he tried to calm that willful organ, knowing that for the first time in his life it was becoming increasingly impossible.

"I say, William, at least *try* talking to her. A compliment or two would not be unwarranted either. You would be amazed how smooth words can tame ruffled feathers. If you still feel you must give her that infernal letter of yours, do so as a last resort." Richard straightened his red coat for emphasis, craning his neck to look out the window. Just around the corner, a homey estate dotted with barren trees began to come into view.

Nine

Elizabeth had held true to her resolution to remain with her father that day. She sat curled by the window, a double-knitted blanket thrown over her lap and a book in her hands. Mrs Cooper had proven to be a wise, experienced nurse as well as a cheerful presence to keep her company in her sentry. She sat on the other side of the window opposite Elizabeth, comfortably crocheting a small cap.

"For my youngest daughter, Jenny, who was married this past spring," she had confided with a secretive smile. Elizabeth watched her from the corner of her eye, admiring the woman's dignified anticipation- so unlike her own mother's unseemly excitement.

Jane knocked softly as she opened the door, carrying a tea tray. Elizabeth looked up with a welcoming half-smile. "How is Papa?" Elizabeth held her tongue, knowing Mrs Cooper's more experienced opinion was what Jane sought.

"He has more colour, would you not agree? I have seen his eyes flutter a time or two, that is a good sign. Miss Elizabeth here has been reading aloud to him a bit, I think she ought to keep it up. I believe he likes it."

Jane looked puzzled. "Can he hear us, do you think?"

Mrs Cooper made a small shrug. "Dr. Cooper tends to think so, in these cases. It is difficult to say, really, but he has seen one or two people brought round in such a way. He gives credit to the voices of their families, comforting them and giving courage."

Elizabeth's eyes sparkled. "In that case, we ought to keep Mama at bay, do you not agree Jane?"

Jane shook her head with a gentle laugh. "Mama is quite occupied enough, as you know Lizzy. She has plenty of diversions with which to busy herself at present." She flashed her sister a sly smile.

Elizabeth rolled her eyes. "I take it she has been abroad again this morning, boasting of my 'conquest'?"

"You did not know? No, she remained within. Apparently the distinction of having a daughter well engaged meant, once the news had been shared, that many of our neighbours were obliged to call to wish you joy."

Elizabeth glowered, her stomach churning. "And of course, Mama was not to be denied *that* satisfaction. What a pity to have missed it! Tell me, has she selected my wedding date yet?"

"Take care, Lizzy, that statement savours strongly of bitterness!"

"Bitter? Why not at all, Jane. I adore how supportive Mama is, and how helpful. You know, she brought me a sample of wedding lace to try on this morning. She is of the opinion that ivory matches my skin tone and wished to verify it. Tragically, I lost my footing as I moved about this cramped room- dangerous with all of these books in here, you know! Such a shame, I sloshed some of Papa's broth all over it. Poor, dear Mama, it must be trying to have such a clumsy daughter, but she bears it the best she can."

Jane gagged on her tea, desperately covering her mouth to forestall a most unbecoming reaction to her sister's gallows humour. Gasping and making good use of a napkin, she cleared her throat delicately. When she dared to speak again, she was more serious.

"Lizzy, we have had a letter from our Aunt Gardiner. She says our uncle is in Portsmouth, on some matter of shipping to his warehouses in London."

Elizabeth tensed. "He cannot come at all, then?" Her heart began to sink.

"She does not know. She wrote him directly, and she believes he shall come as soon as he is able- in a few days perhaps. Meanwhile, she intends to come herself to lend us whatever support she can. It is difficult, you know, with the children, and she has just hired a new governess. She hopes she can be here by tomorrow evening."

Elizabeth swallowed. She had not counted on her uncle being detained by business. It made sense, of course, that he would be settling any necessary matters before their Christmas travels. The tenuous hope that he could arrive soon, possibly by that very evening, had virtually sustained her. She had a fleeting notion that when he arrived, perhaps as acting head of the family he could put to rest once and for all the rumours about herself and Mr Darcy. The longer his delay, the dimmer the hope that it could be done quietly.

A long, racking sigh shook her. She was fooling herself. There could be nothing "quiet" about ending her supposed engagement. She expected half of Meryton had graced the Bennet sitting room only that morning. She was well and truly stuck.

"Do not forget that Mr Bingley and Mr Darcy are expected to call this afternoon," Jane reminded her. As if she could forget. "Do you not wish to change?" Jane dubiously eyed her sister's simple, old work gown.

"No," Elizabeth replied smugly, hugging her knees to her chest and sinking more deeply into her chair. She had no intention of scrambling to make herself agreeable for *his* sake. Jane blew air through her lips, but wisely dropped the subject. She would do all she could, but Darcy would have to earn his own way into her sister's good graces. With an affectionate glance at her stubborn sister, Jane hoped fervently that the gentleman was both willing and able to do so, for Lizzy's sake.

Only a moment later, a flurry from the next room alerted them to some sudden excitement on the part of their mother. Elizabeth groaned. It could mean only one thing. The two girls peeped out the window, Mrs Cooper helpfully making way for Jane.

Drawing up to the front of the house was a glistening black carriage they had not seen before. Elizabeth squinted. The crest on the side was unfamiliar to her, but it had to belong to Mr Darcy. The matched foursome of chestnuts pulling it were splendid, much finer than she had seen outside the boundaries of London. As the coach drew to a halt, their mother burst into the room behind them.

"Oh, my dearest Lizzy! Only look, that is the Darcy carriage! Mrs Long said she saw it drive through Meryton this morning, but she could not see who was inside. He must have had it sent from Town! Is it not magnificent! This is a great honour to you, my dear, though I daresay you've done little enough to deserve it. Oh, look at you, girl! Hurry up and change, the gentlemen are calling! Mrs Cooper, tell Lizzy to leave at once!" With a nervous flick of her lace handkerchief, she turned about and pranced down the stairs to greet her guests.

Elizabeth was chagrined at her mother's apparent lack of concern for her husband. She had not even glanced his direction whilst in the room. With a grim sigh, she met Jane's eyes. "Do be patient with her, Lizzy. You know she truly is worried for Papa. She is only... distracted."

"Jane, only you can truly speak the best of people and still contrive to be honest. I shall never know how you manage it." Elizabeth reached to squeeze her sister's hand.

A flash of movement diverted their eyes once again to the window. They were just in time to see a handsome gentleman in a red coat disembark to stand by Mr Bingley. "Who could he be, I wonder?" Jane's breath fogged the glass.

Elizabeth gestured flippantly. "Whoever he is, he would be wise to avoid Kitty and Lydia," she quipped. Flopping back into her cushiony chair, she stubbornly returned to her book.

"Lizzy, look," Jane waved her hand, beckoning her back. Elizabeth complied unhappily. Mr Darcy was out of the coach now, his arm reaching inside to help out a willowy blonde beauty. "Do you think she could be the sister we have heard of?" Jane studied the girl down below. She took small, uncertain steps and leaned timidly on Mr Darcy's arm.

Elizabeth pursed her lips. The famous Miss Darcy; constantly idolized by Caroline Bingley, assiduously praised by her brother, and repeatedly maligned by George Wickham. If her judgment of the character of the witnesses should be accounted, Elizabeth felt she would lean toward Wickham's appraisal of the young girl. "Splendid," she replied in a deadpan.

Jane turned to look her fully in the face. "Lizzy, please do try to remain calm and polite. I know very well that you are angry, but please… for my sake, if nothing else." Jane took her hands hopefully.

Elizabeth narrowed her eyes critically. "Why, Jane Bennet, I do believe you are trying to hoodwink me! If you think you can convince me that my affairs with Mr Darcy can possibly distract Mr Bingley from your beauty, you are quite mistaken. He is entirely smitten with you, you know. I never saw the like. You need not fear for yourself," she winked.

Jane responded with a slow, calculating smile. "Well, then Lizzy, think what a pleasure it would be for us to be married to such close friends!" Pleased with herself for her clever retort, she beamed back at her sister's flustered face. "Come, Lizzy, we will be wanted downstairs. I suppose… well, that gown will have to do, there is no time to change now."

Elizabeth tossed her head with a mutinous spirit and held it yet higher. Together they politely took their leave of Mrs Cooper and began the long march downstairs.

~

Elizabeth's first impression of Georgiana Darcy was lukewarm, at best. The girl stood half hidden by her brother's shoulder. She was tall and fair, with a light but womanly figure. She was well grown for her years, but clearly not as comfortable in company as Kitty, who was near to her in age. Elizabeth decided that was not wholly a bad thing, and resolved to withhold judgment until she knew the girl better.

Georgiana smiled politely but only offered the barest of civilities when they were introduced. She cast her eyes to the floor, her cheeks red. Elizabeth had little time to ponder whether the girl's reticence could be attributed to extreme vanity or painful shyness. She was busy herself, trying to duck Darcy's steady gaze and thwart her mother's overly officious attentions to their guests.

The gentleman in the red coat proved to be another cousin, a colonel in the Regulars. Kitty and Lydia tittered shamelessly over how handsome he was in his regimentals. He was wonderfully gentlemanly with them, even going so far as to tease the younger girls a little as he took his seat, but he seemed intensely interested in herself. Elizabeth could only wonder what the man had heard.

Thanks to her mother's machinations, Elizabeth found herself situated between Darcy and the colonel, who occupied her father's favourite wing-back chair. Miss Darcy sat silently on the sofa, on the other side of her brother. The only relief to be found was in Bingley cleverly taking a seat on the other side of the room between Mrs Bennet and Jane. Mary sat not far from Jane, frowning over her book.

With her mother so occupied, the only present sources of mortification were Kitty and Lydia, who were noisily remaking their bonnets just to the colonel's right. Lydia did not miss an opportunity to smile or even wink boldly at him whenever he looked her direction. As it was, Elizabeth felt her humiliation was complete.

Elizabeth was seated on the same sofa as Darcy and his sister. Each uncomfortably kept their distance, a nervous tension filling the space between them. Fitzwilliam arched a brow as he took in the awkwardness of the pair. They never looked each other in the eye, the faces of both were flushed. Darcy stiltedly but politely asked after Mr Bennet.

"He has not yet awakened, sir, but we have a good deal of hope. It was very kind of you to send for a skilled nurse." Elizabeth trained her eyes steadily on the tea tray, her voice everything that was mannerly and insincere. "Mrs Cooper has been most welcome, but I must insist that we be allowed to repay you for your trouble."

"There is no need, Miss Elizabeth. I am pleased to be of some service to your father. I beg you would think no more of it."

"I am afraid I must, sir, for my father would not wish to be in your debt." Her eyes flashed warningly to his, only for a second. "It is not seemly to neglect one's obligations, would you not agree Colonel?"

Darcy bit back a retort. Was she implying that he had attempted to ingratiate himself to her father and family with his purse? Or was there a more subtle barb? She still believed him dishonourable and remiss in his management of his affairs. He grit his teeth.

Fitzwilliam was lighter on his feet. "Indeed not, Miss Bennet. As a man sworn to duty myself, I regard attendance to my personal obligations as my highest order of business. It is the mark of a man, or woman, for that matter."

"I could not agree more, Colonel." She cast a sweetly arch expression toward Darcy, who paled a little. "May I ask, Colonel; do you regard your duty to king and country- the pride of your rank- more or less highly than your obligations to family and friends, the companions of your youth?"

"Well, I am uncertain what you can mean. In my mind they are one and the same. Serving my country keeps my family in safety. By fulfilling my official commitments with distinction, I bring honour to my family name in my small way. As for my friends, why most of them serve alongside me. I believe, Miss Bennet, that some of the finest, most noble men I have ever had the honour of knowing wore regimentals." Kitty and Lydia twittered their agreement from his far side, breaking into giddy laughter.

Darcy made a strangled sound. They had been seated under five minutes and already Fitzwilliam was digging a deeper hole by the second, falling right into Elizabeth's trap. His cousin reluctantly tore his eyes from the lady's face to observe Darcy's frantic expression, the minuscule shake of his head. Fitzwilliam's eyes widened in sudden understanding.

Elizabeth followed Fitzwilliam's gaze, turning to Darcy questioningly. Darcy snapped his eyes back to hers with a deliberate nonchalance. His body tensed with the effort of locking his wavering gaze to her flinty expression.

A rebellious dark tendril fell low over her forehead, and, momentarily distracted, he absolutely stared. He held her eyes for a long beat, his mouth opening despite his lack of words. How was it that the more time he spent in her company, the more like a knobby-kneed colt he became? Should he not be gaining confidence as his reward for continued effort? Fitzwilliam cleared his throat, forcing him to start from his reverie.

"I… Er... That is... You are looking very well today, Miss Elizabeth."

Her lips parted. Once again, he had taken her by surprise. Her eyes took in her own appearance; the gown which should long ago have been retired, the worn shoes, the splash of broth on her sleeve from her "mishap" that morning.

Cynically she raised her eyes back to meet and share a mischievous smile over Darcy's shoulder. The girl's eyes twinkled in camaraderie as she grinned between Elizabeth and her brother. Perhaps Georgiana Darcy had potential, after all.

"I thank you, sir," she managed, most civilly if she did say so herself. "I fear you have caught me while I was not prepared to receive company."

Darcy took a deep breath, steadying himself. Out of the corner of his eye, Richard gave an encouraging nod. Was the old sod smirking at his blunder? Bravely he forged on. "Surely, Miss Elizabeth, caring for your father has consumed much of your time. I remember how devotedly you cared for Miss Bennet when she was ill."

Elizabeth smiled a little. She *had* been primarily motivated by concern for Jane, but her desire to avoid the rest of the party downstairs had added incentive to her devotion. Slyly she replied, "No one could have done less for her. Jane is all that is sweet and fine."

She favoured him with an impish smile and continued. "I believe there is none other with her goodness. I fear I have not her talent for always seeing the amiable qualities in people and honestly speaking well of everyone. It has been my experience that not everyone has such a fine character as she often detects, or at least it is not always apparent to me." A slight stirring to her right brought her eyes back to the Colonel, who was rubbing his upper lip with his forefinger and quickly looking away.

Darcy took advantage of the diversion to recover. He leaned forward slightly. "You are a student of characters, I know. You praise your sister's generous nature, but I have long believed that a more analytical philosophy can be greatly advantageous. It serves to discern what is wise from what is foolish, and truth from untruth. Would you not agree?"

Elizabeth arched her eyebrows. "I cannot dispute that conjecture. I wonder, however, is it possible for truth to be always readily distinguished? I suspect it is a not always a fixed notion. Is it possible for a man to think he has done right when, in fact, he is greatly in the wrong?"

He gaped for a moment. Tension wrung his gut, but he was as a moth to the flame. The challenging lilt in her voice could not be ignored. For a brief second, she looked to Colonel Fitzwilliam for a response, but he only gazed expectantly at Darcy. *A fine time to decide to be silent,* he thought sourly.

Slowly he answered her. "I agree that is a possibility, Miss Elizabeth. I believe that is where honour begins. An upright man, with worthy intentions, should at least be due the benefit of the doubt in such cases. He should be able to depend upon his peers for a favourable opinion of his intentions, at the very minimum. A man of true virtue makes it his business to have considered all the information available before embarking upon a course potentially injurious to others."

"And if he finds he was mistaken? Would it be more admirable decisively to stay his course, or humbly to make amends?"

"The latter, of course, is preferable. We ought to right our wrongs as best we can. However, there have been times in my experience, for example with my tenants, where a reversal of judgement would have caused even greater harm. So you see, it is not always possible to undo an error. That is why it is prudent, and indeed absolutely necessary to be sure of wise judgement in the first place."

Her eyes sparkled and a mysterious smile curled her lips. He was not certain by her expression whether he had passed or failed her little test. The one thing of which he was not in doubt was the certainty that she had indeed been testing him. She studied him briefly, as if trying to decide whether to press the matter further.

Apparently she decided to drop it for the present, as her eyes shifted to Georgiana. "Miss Darcy, I have heard much of your skill on the pianoforte. Miss Bingley praises your abilities most frequently. May I ask your favourite composer?"

Darcy let out a breath of relief as her scrutiny transferred away from him. Fitzwilliam caught his eye with a look of incredulity. He was clearly impressed. The gentlemen listened in rapt appreciation as the ladies left them behind with a discussion on the merits of the various German composers. The topic could not have been more considerately chosen for Georgiana's comfort, and Darcy silently added another virtue to the growing list of Elizabeth Bennet's charms. She seemed to captivate Georgiana instantly.

Darcy listened proudly as Georgiana's shy expertise revealed itself to her inquisitor. Elizabeth was obviously well informed, but she freely admitted possessing only marginal skills on the pianoforte. Darcy, who had heard her play with much pleasure, countered warmly. Elizabeth thanked him primly, then turned her attention back to Georgiana.

Elizabeth's tone was easy and gentle, not at all like Miss Bingley's imperious style of discourse- or monologue, as so often occurred. They talked of their favourite performances in London, and Richard found a few entertaining anecdotes to add to their conversation there. Elizabeth bantered with him pleasantly, but always she returned to Georgiana.

For her part, Georgiana was slowly letting down her guard, like a morning glory discreetly unfurling its petals to the soft dew. Darcy breathed more easily as well, reveling at the sight of the two dearest to him getting to know one another. Elizabeth did not disappoint. Abrasive as she could be when properly riled, she was all warmth and sincerity for his little sister.

"I should dearly love to hear you play one day, Miss Darcy," Elizabeth encouraged humbly. "Do you often play to an audience?"

Georgiana blushed. It was a frequent request made of her in family gatherings, but one she disliked in the extreme. "Oh, no, Miss Elizabeth. I do practice a great deal, but I normally prefer to play only for Fitzwilliam."

Elizabeth looked puzzledly between the gentlemen. She had never heard anyone call Darcy by his first name, and suddenly found it amusing that he should share his cousin's surname.

Picking up on her reflections, Colonel Fitzwilliam laughed lightly. "My father was not only brother to Darcy's mother, Lady Anne, but also very good friends with his father, George Darcy. Our families are friends for five generations, at least, with many intermarriages. There are a number of us who share a name. My older brother was named George also, in honour of my uncle."

"I see." As much as she normally tried to ignore everything Mr Collins said, something came back to her. "Then your father... is the Earl of Matlock?" She kept her voice a little hushed, fearing her mother might overhear that they had the privilege of hosting the son of a peer.

"Correct, Miss Elizabeth, but as the 'spare', such a title does me little good." He gestured self-deprecatingly to his uniform. "I have little to complain of, though. I do not believe I should have liked my brother's lot in life, or Darcy's for that matter. Dealing with their responsibilities is no easy matter. Certainly it is not as clear-cut as life in the army. Despite its hardships, I do not have the cares and worries of a landlord with three hundred or more souls in his keeping to trouble me."

Elizabeth's eyes widened at the figure. She glanced quickly to Darcy, who modestly dropped his gaze to the floor. She had not considered the awesome responsibilities which must be his, but he clearly did not wish to discuss it at the moment.

Turning back to the colonel, she probed gently, "I think you undervalue your position. As a colonel, you must have a good many men under your command. Is not your duty one of sacrifice and hardship? You have the responsibility of sending men off to war. Is not war terrible? I have heard stories." Elizabeth shuddered. She had heard more than stories, as had anyone with a heart. The horror of the battlefield was fresh in the country's mind, with a scattering of bitter wars overseas only recently concluded in their parents' generation, and more looming in their own.

His eyes softened, his easy humour receding somewhat. "It is, Miss Elizabeth. The men of my regiment, we live and work together, and tragically I have more than once been forced to issue the final command in a man's life. Ultimately, however, my command is not my own. I answer to my general, who answers to the war office. I am never left entirely to my own devices, thus the success or failure of my regiment does not rest absolutely on my own shoulders.

"I do my best, as my men deserve nothing less, but others have a role they must play as well. I do not say my lot is an entirely easy one, only that the cares of others make me understand that I am by no means the only man with the burden of heavy responsibilities. I daresay, Miss Elizabeth, every man has his struggles and each has his gifts. Sometimes it is best to content ourselves with the lot handed us, is that not so?"

Elizabeth felt suddenly they were not talking of military life any longer. Surmising she was the victim of a two-pronged assault, she gave a small nod, acknowledging the hit. Her eyes shifted suspiciously to Darcy, but there was no trace of smugness in his face.

"Do you not all find the weather today unusually fine?" Bingley was saying from across the room. He raised his voice just loudly enough to divert attention to himself from the party on the sofa. "Miss Bennet, might I persuade you to a short walk before tea?" He rose and invited Jane to take his arm. A subtle look toward the others encouraged them to break up their cozy group. Lydia, rolling her eyes at the dull couples in the room, announced her intention to walk to Lucas Lodge, seconded by Kitty.

Darcy's breath caught. He knew very well that Bingley and Fitzwilliam were conspiring to purchase him a few minutes with Elizabeth in private conversation. His body tingled in anticipation, but his heart froze in fear. She had been civil to him, but barely. He could well imagine the litany she might unleash on him when he was without the protection of others, before whom she had decided to remain polite.

He rose on nerveless legs, but when he turned to her he found that Richard had beaten him. His cousin proffered his arm gallantly, and with a teasing smile, Elizabeth took it. Her eyes flicked provocatively to his, taking in his disappointment and winking at it.

Chagrined, he turned to Georgiana and helped her to her feet. She read his vexation and snuggled comfortingly to him. "I do like her very much, William," she confided as he helped her on with her pelisse. "She is kind and honest. I do not feel embarrassed talking to her. I think we might become good friends," she whispered shyly.

With a relieved smile, he squeezed her small hand and rested it on his elbow. He was glad to hear of Georgiana's comfort with Elizabeth, but he burned with annoyance that Richard was at this very moment sweeping ahead of him with that lovely lady on his arm.

They followed Bingley and Jane Bennet on the same path Darcy had taken from the house the day before. The stinging memory of his turmoil of yesterday made the colour in his face rise. Elizabeth walked blithely before him, her lilting voice drifting back on the breeze. Something she said made Richard laugh gaily, and he placed his off hand on the small feminine one nestled in the crook of his elbow. Darcy fairly seethed. She had never walked with *him* so! What was Richard up to, strolling so cozily with *his* Elizabeth?

The path came to a minor divergence, with a lower path proceeding through a muddier place and the higher rounding a small bend. Bingley took the higher path, darting a quick but significant glance at the walkers behind. Elizabeth and Darcy both noticed, if the others did not. Elizabeth tactfully suggested that as the path was not yet impassable, her party might appreciate the small bubbling creek that lay just ahead on the lower road.

As they approached a low bending oak tree just before the creek, Elizabeth released the colonel's arm and turned to Georgiana with an infectious grin. "Miss Darcy, may I show you something?" Hesitantly, but with a pleased little smile to her brother, she placed her hand in Elizabeth's. The two young ladies traipsed out of view over a small grassy patch to a grove of trees beyond, heedless of the mud and grass tugging at their skirts. As they vanished from sight, the gentlemen could hear the musical sound of their distant laughter.

Fitzwilliam turned to his cousin with an arched brow. Darcy regarded him darkly. "Unhappy, Cousin?" Fitzwilliam smirked.

"Why would I be?" he growled. "You and Elizabeth seem to be getting on famously."

"Yes, *Elizabeth*, if we are calling her such, is quite charming. She promised to sing for me some day, you know. You said she had an enchanting voice, I should like to find out for myself." Richard affected an air of nonchalance, but he secretly loved goading his brooding relative. Never since eleven-year-old Richard had picked the best puppy- the one seven-year-old William had wanted- from George Darcy's favourite pointer had it been so easily done.

His cousin took the bait admirably. He stalked closer, glowering. "*Be careful, Richard!*" he hissed.

Richard laughed lightly. "Oh, come on William, do not be that way. You know I only wished to put in a few good words for you. She had you completely at her mercy in there. Have to admit it must not be entirely unpleasant." He gave a low whistle. "You did not exaggerate, Cousin, she is impressive. Lovely and clever, and she talks about more than bonnets and dancing."

Darcy sighed heavily, leaning against the oak tree. "Georgiana likes her," he murmured.

Richard nodded. "She would be good for her. There is something genuine and sincere about her. I believe she would be kind to Georgie for her own sake, not yours."

Darcy made a wry face. "Not very optimistic about my prospects, are you?"

"You know what I mean, William. More than one lady has tried to worm her way into your affections by ostentatious attentions to Georgie. Surely you have noticed. I can promise you, Georgie has too, and she does not care for it. Miss Elizabeth is quite the opposite. Truly, she is a remarkable young woman."

"Is she not?" Darcy gazed longingly in the direction the ladies had taken.

Richard was still incredulous at the easy way this country miss had thoroughly bewitched his staid and cautious cousin. Now that he had met the lady he could see exactly why the secretive and close Darcy had found her zest appealing, but he had never expected the man to be so wholly given over to his feelings.

"Father will give you a bad time, I fear. At least he will rant and storm until he gets to know her, but I wager she will have him eating out of her hand before dessert is served. Mother will love her immediately, but there is still Aunt Catherine."

Darcy was still, his voice quiet. "She was going to be made unhappy in whatever choice I made. You know as well as I, there was no future in that."

"True, but be prepared for unpleasantness all the same. She will not attempt to spare your lady's feelings. I only hope that whatever form her disapproval takes, you will be able to shield Miss Elizabeth at least until the lady becomes resigned to the match. You do not need Aunt Catherine discouraging your Miss Elizabeth just now."

Darcy snorted to himself. "She would stand in no awe of Aunt Catherine. In fact, if she did not dislike me so strongly, I would wager that the surest way to obtain her acceptance would be to have our aunt forbid the marriage."

"You have a point," Richard chuckled. "Aunt Catherine will not be the only one who disapproves, you realize. Enchanting as Miss Elizabeth is, she is nothing like the women of the *ton*. I mean that in the best possible way, but do you think she will fit in with your circles in Society?"

"Better than I do," Darcy grunted. "She is not easily intimidated."

"Yes… so I see." Fitzwilliam eyed his cousin thoughtfully. "She is not very happy with you, that much is obvious, but neither is she frightened of you. If you can somehow earn her regard, she could be just the ally you need against those gussied-up cats." He finished with a playful wink.

Darcy turned to look his cousin full in the face, his eyes deeply serious. "Richard… I *must* win her affections." His voice wavered somewhat. "I have only ever met women who want Pemberley and my wealth more than they want me. I do not mean to sound vain, but you cannot know what it is like, to know that everyone who approaches me sees only my pocketbook and my position. Elizabeth is blind to all of that. If nothing else, her refusal proves that. There is no one like her. Do you think she can ever be brought round?"

Richard blew out a long breath. "If things truly stand as you say they do, she has little enough choice. She will have to marry you eventually. Give it time, Cousin. You are as fine a man as any I know. She will learn to like you well enough, I daresay."

Darcy rubbed a hand over his eyes. "I fear that is no longer enough for me."

Ten

Elizabeth had initially reached out to Georgiana as a relief from speaking to her brother and cousin. The colonel was certainly charming enough, and she felt that under different circumstances she could have thoroughly enjoyed his company. Within a short while, though, she had become convinced of the unnerving certainty that he had more than one ulterior motive.

The timing of his arrival was too strong of a coincidence. She suspected that he had been summoned from London after the events of yesterday morning. Elizabeth felt more than sure that he was seeking to determine an opinion of herself on behalf of the rest of Darcy's family. She haughtily determined that she did not fear his disapproval, having not sought the connection in the first place. The more unsettling prospect was that he also seemed unusually interested in praising his cousin to her. One of His Majesty's soldiers as an ambassador of peace; it was a strange emissary to choose.

With little expectation of pleasure, she had tried to cultivate conversation with the sister. Her initial feelings about the girl had proven ungenerous. Within a very few minutes, Elizabeth became convinced that what George Wickham had described as extreme pride was instead profound bashfulness. It was an easy enough mistake, she reasoned. A young woman possessed both of great wealth and painful shyness could easily be called overly proud. Anyone could have thought so, had they not spent enough time around the girl. Perhaps Wickham's youthful connection to the family had occurred when Georgiana was too young to be known well to him.

Now, as they plundered toward a well-loved grove of trees, the girl's demeanour underwent a dramatic shift. She giggled lightheartedly and had no fear of either mud puddles or brambles. There was nothing prideful about Georgiana Darcy. Instead, she seemed like a young girl desperately in need of a friend.

Talkative people love good listeners, and Georgiana was one of the best Elizabeth had ever known. She intuitively picked up on any nuances in Elizabeth's words and discovered the more subtle humourous references which usually only her father could detect. Georgiana's smile grew broader by the moment and by the time they reached the trees, an easy fellowship had begun to develop between the two.

"Look here," Elizabeth reached up to one of the lower branches to pluck a fruit.

"It is beautiful! What is it? I have never seen one like it."

"It is called a persimmon, I believe," replied Elizabeth. "We are just on the border of Longbourn, so this is my father's grove. My grandfather was somewhat peculiar, father tells me. As one of his hobbies, he imported a few exotic trees. This one came from the American continent. My grandmother was very traditional, and she thought an orchard full of such strange trees was not decent. Hence, the orchard's location far from the house." Elizabeth gave the odd-looking fruit into Georgiana's hand.

"Is it sweet?" she asked dubiously. "It looks something like the tomatoes William keeps in the hothouse."

"When they are fully ripe, as these are. It is strange that they are such a late fruit. Jane and I often sneak out here through the early winter and they are good on the branches for a long while, even after the leaves are gone. Mrs Hill does not like using them in her kitchen, so we always eat them just like this." Elizabeth took a large bite of a second fruit, just as if it were an apple.

Georgiana hesitantly lifted the fruit to her lips and took a timid taste. The texture was firm and smooth, but not crunchy or juicy like an apple. The flavor was mildly sweet. She smiled in pleasant surprise and eagerly took another bite.

"That tree there," Elizabeth gestured between bites, "is a pomegranate. I do not know where Grandfather obtained it, but you have probably heard of it from the ancient tale of Persephone. Unfortunately, I believe it is too cold here for the tree to do well. We are in a warm little gulley here, protected from winter winds, but it is really a Mediterranean tree. The flowers are lovely, but the tree rarely produces much fruit. Sometimes, if we have had a good summer like we had this year and you look sharp, you can find some before the birds do."

Georgiana dutifully looked. "Is that one? It looks something like a dark pear, or a very large apple from here."

Elizabeth's eyes followed her hand. "Why, yes it is! Oh and there are two more. Shall we try to reach them?" Georgiana's eyes were bright with agreement. They spent a highly undignified ten minutes shinnying up the trunk a short way and helping bend the branches for each other. In the end they had proudly collected five of the curious fruits. Elizabeth taught her how to tap the fruit and listen to the tinny sound it made to make sure it was ripe.

"William will be so excited to taste these!" the girl enthused. Georgiana cupped three of them in a makeshift apron, using the front of her exotic cream coloured pelisse, which was now grown quite muddy. Her gaze flashed to Elizabeth's face and found it suddenly subdued. "Miss Elizabeth... is something wrong?"

Elizabeth's eyes snapped back to her new friend's. "No! I..." she stopped, searching for words.

Georgiana came a hesitant step closer, shifting her hands on her fruit to place one uncertainly on Elizabeth's arm. "Miss Elizabeth, do you... do you care for my brother?"

Shocked at the girl's uncharacteristic audacity, Elizabeth answered with breathless silence. She met Georgiana's eyes unwillingly. Her lips parted as if she were about to speak, but could not manage it.

Georgiana's hopeful face fell. "I see." She hung her head and sighed deeply, her lip quivering.

Seeing the girl's acute disappointment, Elizabeth felt dreadfully guilty. "Miss Darcy, I am so sorry! I did not mean to hurt you. With Mr Darcy and myself, well, things are... complicated." Elizabeth placed a hand over Georgiana's, trying to soothe her.

Georgiana looked carefully into Elizabeth's face, the fear of losing the friend and sister she had longed for plainly written across her features. "I like you, Miss Elizabeth," she stammered. Her eyes bashfully dropped to the grass. "I was hoping that... well, you know." Her voice was scarcely above a whisper.

Elizabeth felt her heart twist. Colonel Fitzwilliam may have been jovially attempting to drop positive comments about his cousin, but it was Georgiana Darcy's sincere faith in her that would likely prove her undoing. "Surely, Miss Darcy, we can be friends in any case, can we not?"

The girl blinked rapidly, raising her eyes again. "Do you think so?" Surprised pleasure fluttered in her gaze. Few had ever desired her companionship at the exclusion of her brother's. "Would you please call me Georgiana? I would so much like that."

Elizabeth relaxed into a smile. "Of course, and you must call me Elizabeth, or Lizzy if you prefer. It is what my sisters call me," she explained with a light chuckle.

The wistful look returned to Georgiana's face. "I like calling you Lizzy, if I may. Sometimes people call me Georgie, since my name is so dreadfully long. You may as well, if you like." She looked bashfully to Elizabeth, who nodded in cheerful reassurance. Georgiana sighed. "I should have liked to have had a sister."

Elizabeth laughed. "Perhaps you are fortunate, as I have an abundance of sisters, but no brother. Had I, our family would have had considerably fewer concerns! I find myself somewhat envious," she comforted cheerfully.

"William truly is the best and kindest brother to me. He treats me so gently, and is forever doing little things just to please me. I am so lucky to have him, he is always so good!" she whispered daringly, hope trembling in her voice.

"It is no more than you deserve, I am sure," Elizabeth smiled encouragingly.

Georgiana's eyes widened in denial. "Oh, no, Lizzy!" she gasped. "If you only knew! I have done such terrible things, such dangerous, foolish things! If not for William, I would be…" her mouth kept moving but it was as if she did not have the heart to put voice to her words. She shook her head ever so slightly. "I know I do not deserve William's kindness… or even yours." She glued her eyes to her feet, shuffling them uncomfortably.

Had the words come from anyone of whose sincerity she was less convinced, Elizabeth would have found that speech highly manipulative. The pain in Georgiana's voice was too real, her conviction of her own shame genuine. *What has happened to this poor girl?*

Elizabeth wrapped an arm around the girl's shoulders. "Georgie, whatever you think you have done, you are wrong to think yourself undeserving. You are so young and innocent! There could not possibly be anything you could have done that could be so grievous that you should believe such of yourself. It is only right that your brother should take care to be kind to you. Surely you cannot believe yourself unworthy!" Georgiana's head was still bowed, her shoulders trembling ever so gently. She was not crying, but she was very near it.

Elizabeth tried a different tactic. "Georgie, please look at me." The girl complied slowly, her eyes misty and her mouth drawn into a quivering line. Elizabeth thought fleetingly that the sister looked today very much like the brother had yesterday, but she dismissed the notion quickly. She touched the tip of Georgiana's chin to hold her gaze, and stated her words slowly and firmly, like a mantra. "You are a remarkable girl. You are beautiful, and sweet, and terribly charming. I am so pleased you came here today, and I am glad to call you my friend. I should like to spend a good deal more time with you. Please believe me Georgiana Darcy, when I say you are one of the most delightful people I have ever met."

Georgiana's eyelashes fluttered, her gaze darting unbelievingly around the periphery of Elizabeth's countenance until the latter spoke of continued friendship. The craving in her soul anchored to Elizabeth's words and she could not hold back a grateful sob. Not caring one whit for propriety, she dropped the pomegranates and flung herself into Elizabeth's arms. Shocked beyond reason, there was nothing for Elizabeth to do but to draw the girl close and murmur comforting words to her. Georgiana was like a frightened child, quaking in her embrace.

Elizabeth held her with sincere concern until the girl's shivers slowed. When Georgiana's fervour had abated somewhat, Elizabeth drew back enough to look at the girl's face and smooth her hair beneath the edges of her bonnet. "You must think me a little fool!" Georgiana dabbed her eyes with her bare fingertips.

Elizabeth's heartfelt smile was firmly in place. "Not at all, dear Georgie. Sometimes we all need some reassurance. Tell me, have you many friends in Derbyshire, or in London?"

The girl shook her head mournfully. "So very few. I have a companion, Mrs Annesley. William hired her this fall, after…" her voice broke curiously again, but she forged ahead. "She is a widow with two grown children- in fact, she asked leave to visit her son in Mitcham now, while I came to be here with my brother and Richard. She is kind to me, but she is older, and she is paid to endure my company. She cannot be like a friend of my own… or a sister."

She looked hesitantly to Elizabeth again, who nodded her encouragement to continue. Summoning a new kind of boldness, she went on. "I have had others try to make friends with me, but normally they only ask me about William, and try to put themselves in his way. I used to fall for it, but not anymore." Her shoulders drooped dejectedly.

Elizabeth closed her eyes briefly. There was clearly more to Georgiana's secret pain than simple loneliness, but she found herself outraged that this sweet girl would be used as a pawn in others' matrimonial schemes. To be picked up with false intimacy and dropped on a whim- that alone would be enough to shake the confidence of a shy girl like Georgiana Darcy- and she was not even out yet! She could only imagine how this quiet, sensitive soul would suffer when subjected to the ambitions of women like Caroline Bingley.

She resolved to speak with this allegedly kind and attentive brother. If Georgiana were troubled by hopeful debutantes trying to garner the attention of her eligible brother, then Mr Darcy would simply have to keep them at bay himself. Though, she admitted to herself wryly, he already appeared to do a creditable job of rebuffing the advances of others. How anyone ever warmed to him was a wonder, rich and eligible or no.

Her thoughts froze when reality jolted her. As far as everyone else was concerned, Darcy was no longer eligible, and *she* was the bride elect. Her eyes narrowed briefly as an uncomfortable thought rose. Darcy had not brought Georgiana to her notice to work through the girl in the same way... had he? No... She doubted that proud Darcy would stoop to such. When had he ever cared what her opinion might be? He was used to getting what he wanted without need for resorting to subterfuge. Georgiana on the other hand....

Her jaw had dropped as those ideas flew through her mind, but she recovered before Georgiana noticed. The girl had clearly been hoping that *she* would be that constant sister and companion that she had so lacked. In her willful dislike of Darcy and dogged determination not to bend to his will, she had nearly overlooked the fragile heart before her. Circumstances between herself and the gentleman in question were bound to become yet more complicated, but she instantly set her mind and heart to be the truest friend she could be to the man's sister.

With a fearsome swipe at her eyes, Georgiana bent to gather her lost pomegranates. As she did so, Elizabeth added a few persimmons to her makeshift apron, offering a playful smile.

The trembling sorrow gradually dissipated from the girl's face as Elizabeth kept adding more and more fruit. Her pelisse, stained and sagging, began to slip out of her fingers with the weight. Laughingly Georgiana begged her to stop, but Elizabeth pursed her lips and made a measured pitch, tossing the last persimmon into her lap. They both began to squeal with laughter as Georgiana nearly lost her precious cargo and Elizabeth almost slipped in the mud trying to steady her.

The sound of slow clapping and a cheerful "Brava!" drew their attention from each other. Darcy and Colonel Fitzwilliam waded through the tall yellowed grass toward them, then carefully down the short bank into the hollow of the orchard. Apparently they had grown weary of waiting for the ladies to return in safety. The former bore an expression of relieved worry, the latter one of lively amusement.

Cheered and feeling saucy, Elizabeth met them with an arch smile. "Have you gentlemen lost your way? I believe you will find nothing of interest in these parts. You ought to try further up on the higher road, I believe there may be some worthwhile sightseeing there."

Near her shoulder, Georgiana stifled a giggle. Elizabeth had nearly forgotten about Jane and Bingley until that moment. Her heart lifted when she considered the likelihood that her dearest sister's happiness was on the cusp of being secured.

Darcy's countenance warmed as he drew near. He stood an arm's length from Elizabeth, his searching gaze taking in the joy on his sister's face and the relaxed happiness on Elizabeth's. "What have you there, Sweetling?"

Georgiana arched her shoulders proudly, the closest she could come to lifting her burden for his inspection. "Pomegranates, Brother! And... What did you call these others, Lizzy?"

Darcy's eyebrows shot up and his face split into a wide grin when he heard Georgiana's casual use of the nickname. His wondering gaze hovered on Elizabeth. The woman was a miracle worker! Never had he seen Georgiana so enraptured and comfortable with a new acquaintance. Had he not known better, he would have taken the pair before him as the oldest and dearest of chums.

"They are called persimmons, Georgie. Here, Colonel, have you ever tried one?" Elizabeth took one from Georgiana and offered it to Fitzwilliam. He took it suspiciously, turning it over as though she were handing him a snake.

Darcy had drawn one of each type of fruit from the folds of Georgiana's pelisse and held them up to his delighted eyes. "I have never seen a persimmon. I did order a pair of pomegranate trees planted at Pemberley last year, but it will be some years before we have any fruit of them. We are so much further north, my gardener had his doubts that they would even survive the shipping. We put them in the orangery, and I have high hopes they will thrive. It was a great deal of trouble getting them, I can tell you, but now I see how wonderful the fruit is, and I am glad." He turned the persimmon over in his hand, wondering how difficult it would be to start his own trees from the seeds of that very fruit. He might have better luck, he decided, in taking a cutting from the tree.

Elizabeth watched him curiously, never having witnessed Darcy in the natural elements. His fascination with the fruits was highly out of character with the man she thought she knew. "Have either of you gentlemen a pocket knife?" she ventured. Elizabeth expected a negative from both, but Darcy procured a fine silver one. She cocked her head inquisitively.

He offered her the same bashful smile that she now recognized as belonging to his sister. "One learns to carry a pocket knife at all times when tending the estate. It has proven amazingly useful." Removing his gloves, he drew the blade out for her and gently gave it into her hand. The way the corner of Elizabeth's mouth tugged as she reappraised him made his heart beat a quick thud.

Elizabeth herself was slow to recover. Mr Darcy, the prim and proper, evaluating horticulture and walking around at all times with a practical tool on his person? She was more than a little surprised.

Recollecting herself, she carefully sliced through the persimmon in her hand. *It would be just my luck to accidentally nick myself now. No doubt Mr Darcy has another handkerchief as well, and he would be able to play the gallant again!* Despite her mind's dire predictions, she made the cut safely and handed back the knife. Her bared fingers tingled slightly where the tips of his brushed against them. Quickly she looked back to the fruit.

"My grandfather told me this tale when I was quite young, just before he died. The native peoples in America had a legend about these trees. When the seed is shaped like a fork, as this one is, we should expect a light winter. A spoon-shaped seed means we should expect to shovel a heavy snow, and one shaped like a knife means cutting winds."

Colonel Fitzwilliam laughed. "And do you believe the legend, Miss Elizabeth?"

She surveyed him with mock gravity. "Never argue with a tree, Colonel. I daresay if you do, one of you will prove to be the fool, and it will not be the tree."

Even Darcy laughed at this. Curiously she regarded him closely again. She did not recall him ever laughing aloud in her presence. Shifting her eyes to Georgiana, she lifted her brow questioningly. Georgiana's matter-of-fact expression was her only reply- as if to say, *See, I told you.*

A light tapping sound alerted the entire party to a turn in the weather. They all tipped their heads to observe the small drops pattering on the bare branches of the trees. "We had best turn back. Let me help you with those, Georgie." The colonel stuffed the pockets of his overcoat until they bulged. Darcy did the same, and soon the girl's hands were free.

With a daring little grin in Elizabeth's direction, Georgiana deliberately stepped closer to her cousin and took his elbow. The older man smiled affectionately down at the young girl and led her carefully out of the slippery hollow, leaving the others to catch up.

Elizabeth felt her throat constrict. Darcy was nervously twitching his gloved fingers, looking between her face and the sodden earth. Politeness dictated that he should offer to escort her over the slick ground, and that she should accept. Wordlessly, he gave a short bow and proffered his arm for her to take. Gingerly, she slid her fingertips around the curve of his coat sleeve, holding herself as aloofly as she possibly could.

As they mounted the short incline together, Elizabeth's worn shoe slipped in the mud and she faltered, trying to catch herself. Reacting quickly, Darcy steadied her, turning and grasping her shoulders so that she could regain her footing. Her hand had instinctively clutched the lapels of his coat. Their eyes met and both quickly looked away, shivering from the awkwardness of their posture. He held her firmly until she indicated with a curt nod that she was ready to walk ahead, then released her. Elizabeth resumed her tenuous possession of his elbow and fastened her eyes to the ground.

They walked silently together several paces in the sprinkling rain. Elizabeth's face was pensive, her mouth resolutely closed. Darcy glanced at her uncertainly, hoping she would break the stillness. Anything would be better than this stalwart silence. She was clearly leaving it to him to speak first.

Summoning his courage, Darcy took a deep breath, hoping he had chosen a safe topic. "Miss Elizabeth, I would like to thank you most sincerely for your kindness to my sister."

Her eyes darted to his briefly, then straight forward. "She is a delightful girl, Mr Darcy. I was very glad to make her acquaintance."

"She was most eager to meet you," he added warmly. At this, the lady's eyes flashed uncertainly to him again, but she did not reply. "She has made few friends. I cannot tell you how relieved I am that she seemed so happy just now."

"Do you choose her friends for her then, Mr Darcy? I seem to recall your tendency to make decisions for others. I cannot fathom why such a charming girl should have no friends, other than she has had no opportunities to do so for herself."

Her words stung. He stiffened, schooling his offended feelings before making reply. It would not do to take her bait just now, when he needed to gain her good opinion. Tight lipped, he attempted to avoid the obvious reference to their quarrel from the day before and focus on her concerns for Georgiana. "Miss Bennet, not everyone is as articulate as you are, nor as comfortable making conversation with strangers. She does not prefer a great deal of company. You must have found that Georgiana is rather shy."

Elizabeth dropped her arm and turned to him, stopping them. "She has been left too much alone, Mr Darcy. The ability to make friends comes with practice, which one cannot gain with only a hired companion. I cannot pretend to know all on such a short acquaintance, but anyone with eyes can see the girl is desperately lonely and unsure of herself. She is barely sixteen! One might wonder why such a 'kind and caring' brother as she describes would choose to leave her so often to her own devices?"

Darcy bristled. "Do you mean to imply that I neglect my duties to my sister? Miss Bennet, nothing could be further from the truth! Would you prefer instead that she be allowed to run freely, largely unchaperoned, without suitable guidance and protection? Do you think it preferable that a young lady who is *too young to be out* should be allowed improper liberties for her age?"

Elizabeth gasped, her eyes now full of fire. He so clearly held her father's neglect and her mother's mismanagement of her younger sisters in contempt. The words may not have provoked her so greatly had they not exposed her own shame at her sisters' wild behaviour. Indignant, she harshly repressed her own feelings and rushed to attack the words which her own sensibilities confirmed as so true.

"At least, Mr Darcy, *my* sisters know affection and the pleasure of one another's company! Do you truly care enough for this dear sister of yours to make your sentiments known to her and to spend time with her? Or do you find it more convenient to shuffle your responsibilities to those in your employ?"

"Miss Bennet, you overstep your bounds!" Her narrowed eyes declared to him that she did not care for his reproof and would stand her ground. His blood boiling, he flung all caution to the wind. "How *dare* you accuse me of negligence and callousness with regards to my own sister! Georgiana has my very heart. I care for her to the best of my abilities! She wants for nothing!"

Elizabeth tilted her chin brazenly, meeting his searing gaze without flinching. "Nothing but a friend!" she cried. "The child has only false companions who would exploit her position! There is no one in whom she can confide, no genuine attachments to brighten her existence. Why is that, Mr Darcy? Why should you keep her sequestered away from others her own age, exposing her only to the frivolous attentions of those who have more interest in yourself than in her?"

He ground his teeth, clenching and unclenching his fists to control his temper. He had desperately wanted to avoid another scathing argument with Elizabeth, but it was too late and her accusations were too much to bear. "I *protect* her! Miss Bennet, you have no idea of what you speak. Why do you think I did not bring her to Netherfield before? Do you think I do not wish for her company?"

"She certainly wishes for yours!" she lashed back. "Tell me, Mr Darcy, are you such a poor protector that you cannot defend her from the grasping attentions of others when you come away to stay with your own friends? You do not bring her with you, so what has she when she is alone in London? Are you so afraid for her that you would not welcome to your home other young women her own age who *would* be true friends?"

"Miss Bennet, I did not *choose* my situation!" he hissed. "I am well aware of my inadequacies as both guardian and brother to Georgiana. I have done my best, but some things have proven beyond my control. Trustworthy companions, the like of which you speak, are more rare than you can know. I had hoped that *you* might be the sort of companion she so desperately needs! Is it your intention, Miss Bennet, to simply lecture me regarding my failings, or will *you* be a friend to my sister?"

She slanted a grimace at him. "I *will* be her friend, but it is for *her* sake alone, Mr Darcy, not yours!" Elizabeth turned and marched homeward, blinking tears of frustration which mixed with the stinging rain.

Darcy sagged. He stood alone, his head drooping and arms hanging uselessly at his sides. His hopes had begun to rise, only to be blasted again. She and his sister had shown every propitious sign of the blossoming closeness he had desired to foster between the two women dearest to him. Skillfully and gently, she had drawn Georgiana out of her shell, infusing the girl with her liveliness and sparkle. She had even drawn sword to vehemently defend his precious sister- unfortunately she imagined she was defending Georgiana from himself. Elizabeth Bennet had proven once again that she was everything he had ever dreamed she could be... except in love with him.

Slowly he trudged toward Longbourn, heedless of the now steady drizzle dripping from his hat brim and soaking through his woolen coat. They had not walked far from the house before Elizabeth had diverted them to the grove, and he found himself at the doorstep sooner than he could have wished.

Fitzwilliam was looking out for him and held the door. The colonel clapped him comfortingly on the shoulder, and in a low voice suggested, "Better give her that letter, after all...."

Eleven

W hen Elizabeth stepped into the drawing room, her eyes flew immediately to Jane's face. Her sister's flushed and happy smile told her all she needed to know. Elizabeth's joy for her sibling was reinforced by the proud satisfaction written across Bingley's features. Elizabeth concluded they had not yet informed her mother of their understanding, since that lady was chattering contentedly to Miss Darcy. Mrs Bennet had seated the quiet girl near herself, hoping to work her way into the brother's good graces.

Elizabeth winked at her sister, respecting the new couple's present silence on the matter. Surely Bingley and Jane would wish to speak to either her father or Uncle Gardiner before making any kind of announcement. She glanced round the room and saw the colonel rise from his seat and walk toward the door to greet his cousin. With quick decision, she excused herself and bolted upstairs.

She stepped softly into her father's room and looked expectantly, desperately to Mrs Cooper. "How is he?"

The woman shrugged. "No change, Miss. He swallowed some broth from Mrs Hill a short while ago, but little else."

Elizabeth heaved a sorrowful sigh. Nodding her understanding, she closed the door softly and walked down to the room she shared with Jane. She closed her own door and leaned against it, wishing to burrow under the covers of her bed and remain there until the next day.

The soft hum of voices below drifted through the thin walls and through the door. She knew she owed it to Jane, to Georgiana, to make her

110

appearance for tea. Their guests would be leaving soon enough, and surely she could survive another quarter hour in the same room as Mr Darcy. A glance across the room at her bedraggled appearance in the mirror made her frown. Resignedly, she began tugging at her old gown, now splattered with mud. The least she could do was to clean up a little.

~

Darcy sat uncomfortably next to Georgiana, and nearer than he liked to Mrs Bennet. He did not even have to try to ignore the matron's giddy ridiculousness. His mind was solely occupied with his latest argument with Elizabeth. Georgiana could not miss his saddened expression, and placed a hand gently on his arm. He acknowledged her with a tight, grateful smile, then his thoughts turned inward again. How was it that every conversation with such an intelligent, reasonable woman devolved into accusations and misunderstandings?

Elizabeth stepped softly into the room. He looked immediately to her, noting the sage green gown he remembered from Netherfield. Her hair had been neatly rearranged and as she moved by him he caught the scent of lavender. The most readily available seat in the room was opposite him, allowing him to command a full view of her downcast countenance. She would not look at him. She half-heartedly followed the conversation between her mother and Colonel Fitzwilliam, who rallied valiantly to the cause. She said as little as possible, while he said nothing at all.

When the tea was brought, Mrs Bennet insisted that Elizabeth should serve the guests, in particular Mr Darcy, forcing her to draw near. Darcy looked at her steadily until she met and held his gaze, hoping the contrition in his eyes would be apparent to her. She blinked, pursed her lips, and moved on to serve Fitzwilliam.

Just as she had resumed her seat, hot cup in hand, Lydia and Kitty burst into the room, late for tea and trailing a fit of giggles. Elizabeth blushed, glancing furtively at Darcy. The girls plopped on the sofa near Elizabeth.

Noisy, boisterous Lydia banged her spoon against her cup heedlessly as she stirred a lump of sugar. "Lizzy, guess what! You'll never guess! Mr Collins is engaged to Charlotte Lucas!" the girl bubbled over her cup.

Elizabeth paled, setting her cup on the saucer with a clatter. Darcy straightened, his feet finding their place on the floor in preparation to step to her side. Chiding himself, he stilled. She had made it abundantly clear that she did not care for his interference. Elizabeth's face was a mask of disappointment and disbelief. "Lydia... it cannot be true. Charlotte? It is not possible!"

"Aye, but… Oh dear! I wasn't to tell you! She wanted to make him wait so she could tell you herself, but Mr Collins was so dull, it was all he would talk of, even if me and Kitty were there- that and the fireplaces at Rosings Park. It is so plain that Charlotte could not give two straws about him, but she is quite satisfied, I daresay, for she will live here at Longbourn one day!" Lydia chortled giddily.

Mrs Bennet gave a cry of dismay, fluttering her laced handkerchief before her face. "Oh, do not speak of that odious man! Charlotte Lucas to live here! To think that I shall have to make way for the likes of her. Those Lucases are all out for what they can get! Thank heavens, dear Lizzy, you are so well settled, or I should not know what would become of us all!"

Elizabeth hid her face in shame, unable to stop herself from peeking through her fingers at Darcy's reddened face. She could never marry him, and after such arguments as they had had, he surely felt the same about her! What was she to do?

"Oh la, she will have to put up with Mr Collins first, Mama. He is so tiresome! He would prattle on all day but we were so bored we decided to come home, though we were invited to stay to tea. There was nothing interesting to be had, except Mr Wickham came by, and he wanted to see us home, but we told him that Mr Darcy was here, and he said he oughtn't come by… Oh, I wasn't to tell you that either! What did I tell you Kitty, she is speechless. Why- Miss Darcy!"

Oblivious as Lydia was, no one could miss Georgiana's sudden shock. She paled, shook, and her cup rattled off the saucer to the floor. Desperate eyes sought her brother, trembling hands took his and she began to sob.

Mrs Bennet wailed, fearful her distinguished guest had suffered a fit of apoplexy. "Hill! The smelling salts, quickly!" She ruffled her shawl, waving her hands in distress.

Heedless of the splattered tea, Elizabeth dropped on the floor before Georgiana. She met Darcy's eyes, and for a moment a mutual understanding passed between them. Their argument faded in the light of the girl's white face. "I must take her for some air," whispered Darcy urgently.

Elizabeth nodded, numb. What could have shaken her young friend so? Glancing through the drenched windowpane at the steady downpour out of doors, she looked back to Darcy. "Follow me, I will show you somewhere private."

Ignoring her mother's dramatic reactions to both the news of Charlotte's engagement and Georgiana's "case of the vapours," Elizabeth stood quickly. Helping the girl to her feet, Elizabeth led them to the library with Georgiana supported on her shoulder. Darcy had his arm around his sister, lending his strength. Elizabeth blushed fiercely when she realized their arms were laced together, forming a web of comfort for the forlorn girl. She glanced quickly to Darcy, but his concern at the moment was all for Georgiana.

Colonel Fitzwilliam, who had jumped to his feet at Georgiana's initial reaction, shrewdly resumed his seat. He sat poised at the edge of the chair, but his well-practiced command regained control of his limbs. Best to let Darcy and Elizabeth find some common ground in comforting Georgiana. Meanwhile, he saw no harm in pumping the youngest loudmouthed Bennet girl for some information about Wickham.

~

Elizabeth closed the door to her father's library while Darcy eased Georgiana into a chair. Helplessly, she watched brother try to comfort sister, wondering if she should remain or go. He looked to her then with pleading eyes, and she nodded her understanding. She took her place to the girl's other side. Blonde curls tangled wetly on her cheeks. Darcy took Georgiana's hands in his own while Elizabeth soothingly stroked her hair and cradled the girl's head against her shoulder.

"William," she trembled, "is it true? Is… that man… really here?" Georgiana bit her quivering lips. Elizabeth looked questioningly to Darcy.

He glanced to her, then looked back to Georgiana. "I am afraid so, Sweetling. He will not come near you, I promise. I am here. He cannot hurt you."

Georgiana began to heave, great racking breaths, turning her face into Elizabeth's shoulder. "I th-th-thought he w-w-was g-g-gone!" she wailed.

Elizabeth and Darcy held a silent communication. She was utterly shocked, but ready to do anything to help her young friend. Darcy's face betrayed his regret and begged her assistance. Wordlessly he conveyed his need to simply console Georgiana, without further discussion about the man in question. They sat with her, Elizabeth rocking her comfortingly while she clung to her brother's hands.

Gradually her tears gave out, and she sagged exhausted against Elizabeth. She put her hand to her forehead, a sign recognizable to Elizabeth as the onset of a headache. Elizabeth turned the girl's face gently to her. "Georgie, do you want to rest a while? I will take you to my room and you can lie down." Georgiana miserably nodded her assent.

Elizabeth glanced to Darcy- another soundless understanding passed between them. He would wait for her in the library. There was much explaining to be done.

~

Darcy paced the small library anxiously. The next conversation with Elizabeth could well clinch her pronounced dislike of him, or it could be the turning point toward a better understanding. He prayed fervently for the latter.

This most recent demonstration of Elizabeth's loyalty had only intensified his need to win her affections. If she would so staunchly stand by a girl of a mere afternoon's acquaintance, what a faithful, devoted heart could belong to the man bestowed with such a gift! She so fiercely defended a worthless scoundrel because she believed him to be wronged; how much more would she unwaveringly support a just man if she knew him to be such? His fingers fisted and flexed impatiently. He closed his eyes and soothed himself with an old proverb taught to him in boyhood. *A gentle answer turneth away wrath.*

With a barely audible click, she entered the room behind him. Her face was sober, her hands clasped lightly in front of her. Elizabeth recognized for the first time that day the pronounced fatigue lining his eyes and felt compassion. "Will you sit?" she offered softly.

He nodded, relieved. Elizabeth chose her father's padded chair, and he drew another near. Elizabeth leveled her gaze at him, but this time without rancour. "Tell me," she asked with open frankness, "what happened to Georgiana with Mr Wickham."

He had not expected her to be so forthright, or so meek. He let out a long breath, many of his fears assuaged. Expecting her to lead with bitter accusations, he took a moment to defuse the defences he had rallied and gather his thoughts. Reflecting on the letter still secreted in his waistcoat, he slowly pieced together events as he had related them there, leaving out the resentfulness of his hurts from the day before. If she could speak gently, he could as well.

"Mr Wickham was the son of my late father's steward, a Mr James Wickham. Mr Wickham senior was a capable, honourable man, and my father trusted in him. My own father was fond of the son, and as boys we grew up together."

Elizabeth acknowledged this information with a small nod. This much she had heard from Wickham himself.

Darcy slowly went on. "My father was the very best of men, Miss Bennet. He pledged on his honour his support of George Wickham to his friend. Though a year older than myself, George came to Cambridge the same year as I. He became popular with many very quickly, as his manners were always engaging. Unfortunately, once away from the guiding influence of both our fathers, George's habits quickly became dissolute. I shall not share the details- there are many things a lady ought not hear." His eyes darted to hers self-consciously, but her gaze remained locked on his face in earnest attendance. His lips tightened as he sought what to relate next.

"Mr Wickham senior passed away the year we finished school, not long at all before my own father. Thus, within a relatively short span of time, we both found ourselves orphans. This all occurred nearly five years ago, Miss Bennet. My father had provided for George in his will by making the living of Kympton available to him upon the decease of the rector at the time, a Mr Tate.

"The living, however, was contingent upon George Wickham proving himself willing to take orders and show himself worthy of the post. You must know," he said with a brief sigh, "that the choice of a rector for the parish is one of the most important ones an estate owner must make. A good man can inspire the entire being of the parishioners, bringing light and salt to a whole village, whereas a poor one can increase the misery of all." Elizabeth was reminded ruefully of her cousin. How unfortunate the souls dependent upon *that* man for guidance!

"I knew that Wickham ought not to enter the church," Darcy continued, "but I would have been honour bound to provide such a living, had he shown himself willing. Much to my relief, he did not. He announced to me his intentions of never taking orders, and rather to enter the study of law. He requested instead the value of his allotted inheritance, which was equivalent to approximately three thousand pounds. The money was paid at once, and Mr Wickham went to London. I did not follow his activities there, however I can state with authority that he never entered law school."

Elizabeth shifted uncomfortably in her seat. Darcy's story agreed too closely with Wickham's for either to be an outright lie, but Wickham had left out some crucial details. Darcy's earnest manner, his serious eyes which steadily held her own without jest or lightness, made her deeply question her previous assessment of the man.

"I did not hear from Mr Wickham for over three years. Upon the decease of Mr Tate, I assigned the living to a Mr Silva, an excellent man with a sterling record and a highly estimable character. Mr Wickham came to me then, demanding I honour the terms of my father's will and divert the living to him. As a reminder that all between us was settled, I had my solicitor in London surrender to Mr Wickham a copy of our previous agreement, settling upon the three thousand pounds. Mr Wickham was outraged, and I can well imagine his anger was proportionate to his financial distress at the time."

Elizabeth closed her eyes in shame. The conviction of the truth of his words was dawning on her, flooding her with humiliation. Mr Darcy's version of the events filled in the holes she had never detected in Mr Wickham's retelling. For a woman who prided herself on seeing people as they really were, discerning their flaws and foibles, she had been utterly blinded to the gaping faults in Mr Wickham's character.

Darcy paused. What he had to say next was the most vital piece, as well as the most harmful. Georgiana's reputation hung in the balance, her very future at stake if the wrong ears heard. He studied the young woman in front of him. Her sweet face was wreathed in remorse, her chin tipped low, her being exuded gentleness and humility. As she waited for him to continue, her eyes slowly came up to his. Intelligent understanding shone back to him. He took a bracing draught of air and continued.

"Georgiana was only eleven when my father died. I was young myself, and at two and twenty was ill equipped to raise her alone, as well as take over all of my father's responsibilities. Colonel Fitzwilliam, who is four years my senior, was named in my father's will as a co-guardian. My father had great faith in both Richard's abilities and his affections for Georgiana, as do I.

"We have watched over a tender young girl as well as any two bachelors could, I daresay, though I know she has longed for what I could not give her. Wishing to provide opportunities for more varied society, this past summer we took her from school and sent her for three months at Ramsgate to enjoy the sights and make new acquaintances. We carefully chose a companion to stay with her, a Mrs Younge. She came highly recommended, but we were sadly deceived in her allegiances.

"I decided to visit her as a surprise, and I thank God to this day that I did. I found Mr Wickham in the drawing room alone with her... Mrs Younge nowhere to be found... he was...." Darcy's voice broke. He brought his hand to his mouth, blinking rapidly. Elizabeth leaned closer, concern and fear for her new friend beating in her breast. "He was taking liberties a gentleman would never take, Miss Bennet. He intended to shame her, should she attempt to change her mind." He looked to her, begging her to understand without saying more. Elizabeth swallowed hard and made a grim nod, signaling her comprehension.

"He had convinced her that he was in love with her, and Georgiana was persuaded to agree to an elopement. Wickham had made arrangements for a private coach to take them to Gretna Green on the very next day. He intended, I suppose, to pay for the journey out of her rather ample pin money, as we found he was at the time rather destitute. His object, of course was Georgiana's dowry, which is thirty thousand pounds."

Elizabeth gasped at the figure. She and her sisters had at best only a thousand each after their mother's death, paid in an annuity, and nothing at all from their father due to the entail. The sense of the differences of their status pressed on her, but weightier was her conviction that she had been entirely unjust in her outraged defence of a wicked man. George Wickham was everything that was pleasing in conversation and delightful in company, but this evidence of his iniquity forced her to acknowledge that she had been deceived. Her eyes sought the ground, unable to face Mr Darcy. "What of Georgiana?" she murmured.

With a deep sigh, Darcy rubbed his temples and continued. "I made it clear to Wickham that I would not release her dowry under any circumstances to him. The conditions of my father's will and her young age give me some leeway to administer her settlement as I see fitting, and, Miss Bennet, I can be very inventive. He sought, of course, to blackmail me by either marrying her or ruining her. She was but fifteen, Miss Bennet.

"She remembered his association with our family from happier days, but I had perhaps unwisely shielded her from his less honourable deeds. She paid the price for my error. She believed herself in love, and you must know by now that Georgiana was an easy target to someone who knew the right words to say. A young girl such as herself, deprived as she has been of a mother's love and a father's care, is... very vulnerable, Miss Bennet. Mr Wickham left Ramsgate without even attempting a farewell to her- of course I would not have permitted it in any case, but his interest in her was purely selfish. To say she was broken-hearted is to put it lightly."

He stopped. Elizabeth had said almost nothing during his entire recounting. Her eyes were on the carpet at her feet, tears glistening on her cheeks. "Miss Bennet?" he inquired softly. "Are you well?"

Her gaze slowly met his. "I did not know. Poor Georgie... no wonder she was so troubled!"

A deep sigh of relief escaped him. She believed him. He watched her tenderly as her whitened face flushed bright crimson at the cheeks. She bit her lip and dropped her eyes again. Hesitantly, he leaned closer to her, reaching for her hand. "Miss Bennet?"

Her eyes fluttered back to his, shame and remorse written across her features. Moistened lips parted, but she did not speak. She let him hold her hand- her fingers slack and lifeless in his, but this time she did not pull away.

Encouraged, he spoke from his heart. "Miss Elizabeth, please forgive me if I speak too boldly, but you must not blame yourself, as I fear you do. Mr Wickham is a practiced deceiver, and you are not by nature a cynical person. You had no reference, no other source of information by which to detect the truth. Any blame must be mine for failing to check him, or to warn others."

"I-I should have known," she whispered miserably. "It was improper for him to say the things to me that he has said! He flattered my vanity and I *wanted* to believe him. I cannot believe I was so easily taken in." She looked steadily into his drawn countenance. "I was far too ready to believe ill of you."

He gave her a tight little smile. "Clearly your opinion of me was already poor. Miss Bennet, I know I have given you offence. I do not know where my first error lies, but you spoke of arrogance. I had never thought of myself as such, but my trust in your judgement is such that I must allow it to be true, at least in appearance. I have always believed that pride in my family, in my conduct and in my responsibilities to be well and good. I have striven to remove myself from foolishness, iniquity and slackness of character. Coupled with the fact that I find it difficult to mingle easily in company and awkward to make new acquaintances, perhaps I do appear... forbidding."

She gave a short bitter laugh then sniffled a little, wiping her eyes with the bared fingers of her other hand. "Mr Darcy, I believe I have never heard you speak so much as you have just now! You ought to make a practice of it, you know, as the more you speak the better a person can finally understand you. Had I a more accurate notion of your purposes, I might not have made it a point to amuse myself to your disadvantage at every opportunity. In my defence, you do provide ample fodder for my rather unfortunate sport." She arched an eyebrow, a pitiful return to her accustomed playfulness.

His breath loosened a little and he began to smile timidly. If she was attempting again to tease him, it had to be a positive sign. He gave a gentle squeeze to the hand he still clasped, then released it before she could grow uncomfortable and pull away. He fumbled for words, not knowing what to say next.

Despite her jesting comment, her shoulders slumped and she fixed her eyes at her feet, her cheeks still stained a dusky pink. At this point, he could not be certain whether it would be best to press for more conversation or back away, granting her some time to consider all she had heard and its implications.

His answer came in a soft knock at the door. Beckoned to enter by Elizabeth, Colonel Fitzwilliam poked his head into the room, speaking to his cousin in a low voice. "Darcy, I think it best we take our leave. Georgie would like to return to Netherfield to rest, and a Mr Jones is just arrived to tend to Mr Bennet. He is asking for Miss Elizabeth." The colonel's gaze shifted to Elizabeth and he acknowledged her politely before removing himself and closing the door.

The pair stood, awkwardly trying to decide what to say to one another to gracefully end their tête-à-tête. Rather than speak, he gave her a nervous bow and she quickly returned the courtesy, avoiding his eyes. She felt his gaze steadfastly following her as he held the door for her to precede him out of the room.

The party in the drawing room had already broken up. Bingley was still in the doorway of the drawing room, taking his reluctant leave of Miss Bennet and creditably ignoring Mrs Bennet. Colonel Fitzwilliam was helping Georgiana into her pelisse in the foyer. The girl's pale face brightened when they came into view, and she took Elizabeth's hands. "Thank you so much for your kindness, Elizabeth," she murmured with a return to her shyness.

"Georgiana, I am so glad to have made your acquaintance today," Elizabeth met her blue eyes with a sincere smile. "Will you come tomorrow for dinner? My mother tells me she has invited your party." Curiously, Elizabeth found she did not dread the event as she had before.

Georgiana's eyes turned to her brother doubtfully. Knowing the question before it could be asked, Elizabeth quickly added, "I understand it will be a small gathering. Only your party and my own family will be in attendance. We are in hopes that by tomorrow evening my aunt will have arrived from London, and I believe you will like her very much." Elizabeth felt a little swell of smug satisfaction at her intention of introducing Mr Darcy's fashionable sister to her aunt, whose husband was known to him to be in trade. She glanced to him to witness his reaction, but his face revealed neither revulsion nor interest. Instead, he seemed to be focused only on Georgiana.

The girl smiled and nodded her acceptance, and she was duly escorted to her waiting carriage by her cousin. Darcy gave another quick bow to Elizabeth, joined by a hopeful little tightening about the mouth, then departed himself without waiting for words.

The carriage ride back to Netherfield would have been a very silent one, had Bingley not decided to share his joy. While he waxed romantic about Miss Bennet's beautiful face and sweet disposition to Fitzwilliam, two of his listeners were focused instead on another sister.

Twelve

George Wickham laid down his losing Whist hand, shrugging apologetically to his partner across the table. Denney made a disgusted noise and tossed his own cards back into the pile to be reshuffled.

"That's the rubber," Captain Carter grinned and gathered up the cards, as well as his winnings. His partner, young Saunderson, grinned boyishly. It was the best luck the fellow had ever had. "Another?" Carter's hand poised over the deck, his questioning glance hovering on each man's face.

"Not for me, I'm out," Denny grumbled and rose from the table.

Wickham was torn. He fingered the small quantity of coins still lining his pockets- the last of the week's pay. It wouldn't go far. A hot meal, perhaps a drink. It was just enough to bid for another rubber and hope his luck turned, but not without a fourth player.

"May I join your table?" a familiar voice rumbled over his shoulder. With a sinking feeling, Wickham turned slowly. His old boyhood companion stood behind him. Well, perhaps "companion" was too charitable a term.

Colonel Fitzwilliam bowed politely to the assembled party, giving no particular sign of recognition to Wickham. His quivers of apprehension grew more intense. Fitzwilliam could have only one reason for seeking him out and then pretending not to know him.

Carter signaled his agreeability and the colonel drew up a chair. The officers around the table each regarded the senior officer from the Regulars with deference and curiosity. Fitzwilliam's expression was perfectly relaxed as Carter dealt the hand, turning up spades as trump. Wickham watched the colonel narrowly as he picked up his cards, but Fitzwilliam never showed a flicker of interest in his partner beyond what the game required.

They took the first trick, then a second, but Carter took the third and fourth. Wickham frowned. His hand was full of low ranking cards. Fitzwilliam did not seem to have such poor luck. With a few strategic plays, very soon they were in the lead. Saunderson gleefully took a few, but in the end Fitzwilliam's pile of tricks taken was the largest.

Carter dealt again, the faintest trace of a frown on his face. Wickham allowed himself an inward smirk. Carter and Denney were perhaps his best friends these days, but he had never yet been able to best either of them at cards for more than a hand or two. He knew from long experience that Fitzwilliam was nearly a wizard at the game, and for once, the man was on his side.

A third hand went to Fitzwilliam and Wickham, and the latter, examining his pockets, found that he had regained what he had lost this night. With a significant glance at the back door of the ale house, the colonel rose to excuse himself. Carter and Saunderson saluted him properly, but were not sorry to see him go. A man too lucky or too skilled at cards wore out his welcome rather quickly.

Wickham waited a full minute, pretending to deliberate on another hand, before he, too, stood. He lingered over a mug of ale at the counter, then slowly sauntered out the front door. He considered darting quickly into the shadows, disappearing into the night, but he had no ability to leave town on such a short notice. Fitzwilliam would surely find him. The man was too resourceful. He had apparently already gone to the trouble of tracking him down once, and would do so again in a far less mannerly fashion.

With a sigh, he jingled the winnings in his pocket then tiptoed around to the back of the ale house. Grimacing, he stepped around rotting crates of vegetables and stinking puddles made up of more than mud. He did not see Fitzwilliam. He stood a moment, looking about him.

"I see you're broke again," a chuckle came from the shadows. "It's comforting, don't you think, that some things never change."

Wickham spun, pulse thudding. "What are you doing here, Fitzwilliam? I've done nothing wrong, you've no reason to be harassing me!"

"Oh, dear me George, you sound so very guilty! By the way, that's *Colonel* to you now, *Lieutenant.*" Fitzwilliam tipped a two-fingered salute with a pointed gleam in his eye. "Looks to me like you're one of His Majesty's finest these days, and… well, well, I outrank you."

Wickham adopted a cocky stance, chin lifted. "You didn't come here to talk about my commission. What do you want?"

Fitzwilliam smiled broadly, acknowledging the truth with a cheery gesture of an ale mug clutched in his left hand. "Why, to catch up on old times, of course! You know, George, it's been far too long. Let me see, when was the last time we bumped into each other? Oh, yes! I remember now…." His face waxed reminiscent as he let his words hang.

Wickham paled a little. Fitzwilliam had always been protective of Georgiana Darcy, with a vehemence that was second only to her own brother and not nearly so tightly controlled. Darcy might be powerful, but Fitzwilliam was dangerous, and he had incurred the wrath of both. That, however, was six months ago, and he had not been near the coddled little heiress since. What could the colonel want with him now?

He stiffened, going on the offensive. "Still Darcy's lapdog, I see. I never did figure out why a clever, gifted fellow like you would be at the beck and call of a spoiled puppy like him. Do you ever think it unfair that he landed with all the money, while men like us must labor and struggle in deprivation and danger?"

"Oh, believe me friend, I have had my share of thoughts."

Still wary, but growing a little less apprehensive, Wickham wondered if there was a chink in the colonel's normally impervious armor. Was there some glimmer of malcontent with the favoured cousin, the poor second son of an earl? "Have you never wished for a tenth of his income?" he tested. "What a man like you could do with a living such as that! No more need to suffer the hardships of military life. Do you not deserve it? You're twice the man he is!"

"Don't I know it!" Fitzwilliam's eyes twinkled strangely. "Yet there is that pesky matter of inheritance, and the next of kin is fairly set in stone."

Wickham drew himself straighter, suddenly suspicious.

"I hear," Fitzwilliam changed the subject, "that there is a considerable fortune to be made in America, if a man should have it in him to go. Much opportunity, they say. Fur, gold, tobacco...."

Wickham set his jaw, beginning to understand. "You're threatening me?"

"Oh, George, how black and white of you. I speak of opportunity! You may take it as you wish. Of course, passage is a problem. I understand it is not inexpensive to travel so far, and berths on the better vessels are not to be had cheaply. You could resign from the militia... indeed, you would have to do so and disengage properly, as we are at war currently and I would hate to see you before a tribunal as a deserter."

Richard shook his head, chuckling, but fixing Wickham with a piercing gaze. "Odd, those Americans. They've no love lost for the Crown, but they'll turn in a deserter in a heartbeat. Ah, well. Do you know, I would go to America myself, but my poor dear mother has not been well of late, and I must be a dutiful son. However, a man with no ties to bind him...."

"I won't go to America just to please Darcy! He'll just have to deal with me. I've steered clear of him, and that chit of a sister. He may own others, but he does not own *me!*"

Fitzwilliam bristled at the insults against both himself and Georgiana. It took every ounce of his well-rehearsed self-control not to beat Wickham senseless where he stood. As it was, he simply shrugged, hoping his façade did not slip before the practiced eyes of Wickham.

"Oh, well, a good chance lost, I say. I am afraid I haven't time to dally any longer, I am due for drinks with a dear old friend. Let us have no more unpleasantness, shall we? Here, would you care to finish this ale? It's practically full yet, but it would be rude to show up half in my cups already. Bad form, and all of that. As Colonel Forster offered to buy the first round, I expect I'll have to buy a second, and so on. Cheerio."

The colonel passed his foaming mug to Wickham, who only took it in utter astonishment. Fitzwilliam and his own commanding officer old friends? He had not considered that danger. Frowning down into the froth, his hackles rose. What could Fitzwilliam have secreted in that ale? Poison was not the man's style, but there was no sense in taking chances for a drink given only in patronizing jest. Disgusted, he flung the liquid out on the ground.

Instead of a gentle splash, he heard the heavy clinking sound of coins. *What the devil….* Dropping to a squat, his questing fingers searched out the cold metal. Even in the darkness the faces glinted brightly at him in the light of the moon. He had no trouble being certain that he had collected them all. Squinting, he held one up to examine it in the dim light. *A guinea! Twelve of them!*

What could the colonel be about? Twelve guineas? More than a month's salary. His lips thinned. *Enough for passage to America.*

Pocketing the coins, he jingled them in his pocket as he strode to his barrack. He had no intention of sailing for America, but for a clever man, twelve guineas could be parlayed into a much greater figure.

~

Elizabeth did not come down to dinner that evening. Nor did she accept the plate which Jane brought her. Jane made as if to stay with her, but after one look at Elizabeth's deflated expression, the eyes which uncharacteristically avoided hers, she decided to withdraw. She would give Lizzy a little space, then try to gently draw out- as only a sister could- what was troubling her when they retired for the evening.

Elizabeth sat in gloomy silence, watching her father's breathing and Mrs Cooper's steady knitting. Her lax fingers lightly cradled the red-bound book she had carried in from her father's library, but as yet she had not found the energy to open it. Mrs Cooper had encouraged her to find one of her father's favourite light novels and to read it aloud to him in her own beloved voice, but her spirits flagged.

Mrs Cooper sagely continued on with her work, silently appraising the young lady's morose countenance. She had taken an instant liking to Miss Elizabeth. As a nurse and a doctor's wife, she had often had occasion to witness families of patients. Loved ones exhibited behaviour running the gamut of human feeling. Most were concerned and involved in the recovery of their dear ones. Occasionally, and always to her surprise, she encountered relatives who were careless and flighty, like the younger Bennet girls appeared to be.

In her years of experience, only a precious few shared Miss Elizabeth's determination to singlehandedly will her father back to sound health. Miss Jane was a good sort of girl too, truly concerned, but her attentions were necessarily divided between her ailing father and the demands of her mother. Mrs Cooper felt less familiar with the older sister, but she sensed Miss Elizabeth would welcome some encouragement.

"Do not fret so, Miss Bennet," she sweetly admonished. The young woman's glistening eyes flashed to hers in surprise.

"Pardon me, Mrs Cooper?"

"You needn't worry your dear heart out, is all. I have been watching your father very closely, and I believe he shows every sign of waking soon."

Relief washed over the girl's features, but the weight bearing her down remained. "Thank you, Mrs Cooper," she whispered, her gaze dropping to the floor.

A little puzzled, Mrs Cooper frowned. "Is there something else troubling you, my dear? You seem rather down this evening, most unlike yourself I daresay." The question was improperly bold, but her assessment of Miss Elizabeth's character had been rather quick. This was a young woman who valued outright honesty and would not be offended by bluntness.

Elizabeth blinked a few times in rapid succession. She shook her head, and with a little face of resignation, Mrs Cooper returned to her knitting. After a moment, Elizabeth's soft voice brought her attention back. "Mrs Cooper, have you ever found that you misjudged someone?"

With a contemplative breath, she shifted the little blanket she knitted off her knees and studied Miss Elizabeth carefully. "I have, a time or two. It is a mistake we all make, I am afraid. I take it you have done so?"

Elizabeth nodded. She seemed reluctant to elaborate, though she clearly yearned to pour out her feelings. Mrs Cooper wisely decided not to pry further. If the girl needed to unburden herself, she would let her. A moment later, she did.

"I was wrong about… about two men, to be truthful. One I thought truly amiable and the victim of unfortunate circumstances, now appears to me to be an utter reprobate and a deceiver. Another, whom I had judged to be arrogant and conceited proves to be… quite the opposite."

"Well, one cannot always judge by first impressions, so my husband says."

Elizabeth roused herself a little. She had not intended to slip so in the company of a virtual stranger. She really ought to talk to Jane. She was aching for the morrow, which would hopefully bring her aunt Madeline. Mrs Gardiner's advice was always welcome to her nieces. The shame of her error burned and gnawed at her. How could she forgive herself for her gross misapprehension, for her stubborn blindness? She could not.

Not wishing to remain an ill-tempered companion to Mrs Cooper, she forced herself to turn to another subject, if even for a few moments. "Dr. Cooper seems a very wise man," she murmured.

"Aye, that he is, that he is, Love," Mrs Cooper rocked a little, picking her little blanket back up. "The very best of men, if I do say so. Though, I did not always know him for that, I can tell you! I was not so impressed with him when he first came to court." She chuckled a little, and Elizabeth almost expected to see a girlish blush staining her cheeks.

"Will you tell me, please?" Elizabeth felt a smile growing, despite her gloom.

"Oh, we were childhood mates, he and I. I had only brothers, you see, no sisters with whom to play properly as a little girl ought. His family lived close by, and they had no girls either. We spent the summers wading the creeks, making mud pies, riding his pony. I caught many a frog with Daniel! When we were older, of course, he went off to school and I only saw him on holiday. For some time, it was just the same when we saw each other.

"Then the year I turned fifteen, here he shows up in fancy clothes with a bouquet of flowers. Well, I tell you, I would have none of it at first. I had all these fine notions of what manner of man I should marry, and a little boy who made mud pies and caught frogs would not suit! Of course, in a very short time I saw he was not that little boy I had remembered, but neither was he the dashing sort of fellow I had imagined. He was just… Daniel. He still is, my dear, and I love him the better for it." Mrs Cooper suddenly looked bashful. "I suppose you did not wish to hear my entire tale."

Elizabeth was smiling broadly now. "Yes, in fact, I did. I enjoyed your story very much. Thank you."

Mrs Cooper nodded and smiled. "It's a good life we've had, my dear. There may have been handsomer men, and certainly there were lovelier ladies, but Daniel and I suit. A doctor's life is not a glamourous one, but we have made do, and now our son wishes to take it on." Her face beamed with pride as she glanced to Elizabeth to see if her listener were still engaged.

"Robert got his studies done last year and has been working with Daniel. They heard there was a famous surgeon lecturing in London. He thinks someday we will be able to perform surgery on the heart, if you can only imagine! It will never happen, I said! But poor Robert, after losing his

Maggie, he has had a rough time of it. Daniel mostly took him to London to get his mind off his troubles." Here she looked up to Elizabeth again. "They may be both wonderful doctors, Miss, but sometimes there is nothing you can do for a woman and a child when delivery goes wrong. The poor lass was never strong, but my Robert still blames himself."

Elizabeth closed her eyes and blew out a breath in pity. Every woman understood the risks of childbirth. That risk would likely be hers someday as well. How bitter to face that danger for the sake of a man she could not love! Could she? An unaccountable tightness seized her breast and she began breathing in short little gasps. Her mind began to turn over sudden new ideas. With merciless good sense, she reminded herself that not only was she strong and healthy, but her mother had always experienced smooth deliveries.

But what of the intimacy required of her? Heat flushed her cheeks as she began to contemplate the matter more deeply. Mrs Bennet had kept her daughters occupied with the necessity of marriage, but they had little idea of what went on after the vows were said. Still, Elizabeth had grown up on a farm, and was probably better acquainted with the physics of the matter than a lady ought to be. Her whole body flushed in a mixture of mortification and wonder. Would Mr Darcy... and she...?

Desperately she sought to quell her scandalous thoughts before she either died of embarrassment or began to laugh outright. If Mrs Cooper noted Elizabeth's shift in demeanour, she gave no indication. Softly Elizabeth raised her voice again, hoping her tones belied the swirling emotions inside her. "Mrs Cooper, should I read a little?"

The older woman peered sceptically at Elizabeth over the rim of her glasses and adopted her best nurse's tone. "You look like you need rest instead. Your Papa is not going anywhere. Off to bed with you, Dearie. You can relieve me in the morning. I think your father would very much like to hear that book you brought up once you are rested."

Elizabeth glanced to the book she held. "Oh. Yes, I... I will see you in the morning. Good night, Mrs Cooper." She rose, carefully placing the book on a small table by the window. "Oh, and Mrs Cooper?" The woman looked back up with a warm smile. "Thank you."

Elizabeth slipped quietly into her own room. Jane was already tucked neatly into their shared bed, the candle snuffed. Tiptoeing so as not to disturb her, Elizabeth crept to the corner of the room where there shone just enough moonlight through the window to undress by. Through the window she could see the creek, and just out of sight lurked her favourite rock. Remorse sank her heart.

Her dress forgotten, she leaned her elbows on the window frame, visualizing clearly with her mind what could not be seen in the darkness. She was at the rock, where she had so horrifically abused Mr Darcy to his face. She imagined herself facing him down, heartlessly berating a just man because he had wounded her pride. With a groan, she forced herself to remember all.

She saw herself slapping him, blasting him verbally, exposing her own ignorance and her own mortifying lack of decorum. *And I thought Lydia and Kitty ill mannered!* Worse yet, this very day she had accused him of negligence to his own sister! The poor man had tried to protest his good intentions, had alluded to the difficulties he faced in raising a young girl on his own, but she had stubbornly refused to listen. A small sob escaped and she covered her face with her hands.

Gentle hands on her shoulders snapped her to attention. She jumped, startled, and let out a squeak of surprise. "Oh, Jane! You mustn't frighten me so! I thought you were asleep!"

"I am sorry, dear Lizzy. You were standing there so long, I thought something might be dreadfully wrong!"

"Was I? It did not seem so very long. Truly?"

"Ten minutes, at least. Oh, your hands are freezing! Let me help you. Off with this gown, and into bed to warm up!" Jane's nimble fingers had Elizabeth draped in her night clothes and her hair plaited in a matter of moments.

By the time she was finished, Elizabeth was grateful to climb under the covers, and even more grateful to share her sister's warmth. Jane snuggled close, taking Elizabeth's hands under the covers and placing them between her own to warm them. Elizabeth murmured her thanks, shivering slightly and wrapping the coverlet tightly around herself with her ankles.

Jane waited until Elizabeth's shivers ceased and her hands were no longer icicles. Then, with every sisterly affection, she tipped her chin closer to her sister's ear. "All right, Lizzy, come out with it. What has troubled you so this afternoon? You have been terribly distressed since your long talk with Mr Darcy."

"What if I should not wish to tell you?" came the somewhat defiant retort.

Jane smiled in the darkness, pleased to hear again a saucy reply. Perhaps Lizzy's anger was fading. "Then I shall tickle you until you confess. Right... there!" Jane needled her slim fingers beneath her sister's arms to her sensitive ribs, triggering a peal of panicked laughter.

Elizabeth wormed away, writhing under the covers, but Jane was not to be deterred. With one hand locked under her sister's arm, she reached with the other for the ticklish hollow just above Lizzy's knee. Since girlhood, she had known her sister's greatest weakness. She had employed her advantage only at moments of great need, but always with perfect success. Tonight her goal was two-fold. Not only was she after information, but she also wanted to help lift her sister's uncharacteristically low spirits.

Elizabeth howled and bucked under the covers. Twisting and squealing, she grasped and brushed at Jane's hands, but Jane had the advantage of surprise on her side and had taken care to secure her hold. "I confess, I confess! I will tell you all!" Elizabeth caught her breath.

Jane ceased her attack and waited. Instead of making good on her deal, Elizabeth grinned in the darkness and flopped over, stealing all the covers and shielding herself with them. Proper little Jane squealed in challenge and fell upon her sister. Elbows flying, they vied for leverage until Elizabeth hooked her knee under Jane's and gave a great jerk. Girls and counterpane tumbled to the floor, snarled in a knot.

They lay tangled and gasping, still laughing, when an insistent thumping sounded at their door. Mr Collins' muffled voice creaked through the slit. "Miss Bennet! Miss Elizabeth! I demand you desist from this outrageous behaviour! It is *most* unseemly for young ladies to conduct themselves after such a fashion! Young ladies of good family would never comport themselves in such an uproarious manner!"

Elizabeth hid behind her hand and snickered. "I forgot all about him! I did not even know he had returned this evening!"

Jane choked back a giggle. "Oh, yes, and he insisted upon reading Fordyce's Sermons to Lydia and Kitty after dinner. He tried, anyway, but they just talked over him until he stormed out in a great huff!" The girls burst into a new fit of laughter, which only drew greater protests from Mr Collins.

"Miss Elizabeth! It is incumbent upon me to inform you that the family of the clergyman of Hunsford is expected to behave at all times with the utmost propriety! What will Lady Catherine say when she hears such an indecorous young lady has tried to ensnare Mr Darcy himself? I insist you leave off this commotion!"

With a wicked little "Hmmf," Elizabeth swiftly disentangled herself and jumped to her feet.

"Lizzy, no!" Jane's shocking premonition proved true. Elizabeth, in all her nocturnal glory, leaped to the door and jerked it open to a flabbergasted Mr Collins. The man's mouth gaped like a fish.

"Excuse me, what was that, Mr Collins? We had too much trouble hearing you. You see, we were far too occupied in our scandalous behaviour, we could not be troubled to listen."

"Miss Elizabeth!" Mr Collins' hands flew over his face, but he peeked helplessly between his fingers. The light was dim, but he could just make out the hazy lines of her form through the thin gown, thanks to a sliver of moonlight beaming from the window at just the right angle. Behind her, Jane scrambled to her feet, modestly wrapping herself in the counterpane and ducking out of sight.

"Yes, Mr Collins?" Elizabeth crossed her arms nonchalantly, just as though she were not clad in only a nightgown.

"You- Miss Elizabeth, you are not properly attired to be addressing a gentleman in the dark of the night!"

She cocked an eyebrow, letting her frame fall carelessly against the door. "So you say, but you are still here. By this I accept your admission that you must not be a gentleman, Mr Collins. Am I to report, sir, that you would harass young ladies in their own bedrooms, in their own homes, in the middle of the night? Terribly shocking, Mr Collins. Lady Catherine would be most seriously displeased!"

He gulped, his fingers spasmodically moving to cover his eyes one moment and afford him a better view the next. He knew he ought to turn and flee to his room, but he could not tear himself away. "Miss Elizabeth Bennet, I shall speak to your mother about your serious lack of modesty!"

"Oh, do, please." A sardonic smile tugged her lips. "I am quite certain she and all her friends will enjoy hearing how the clergyman of Hunsford came by such knowledge."

With a strained little cry, Collins spun and fairly ran back to his room. Elizabeth chuckled to herself and closed the door casually, strolling back to join Jane in the bed.

"*Lizzy!*" Jane admonished, still pale from the encounter. "I cannot believe you could be so bold! Lydia would not even behave so dreadfully!"

"I think Jane, I can answer you with every confidence that she would do as much, and more." Elizabeth felt uneasily certain of that.

"Lizzy! Do be serious!"

"Oh, Jane, I know you think me awful. You must know, after the two days I have had, it felt wonderfully freeing to defy the rules so. I confess, I have longed to properly shock our esteemed cousin! Do not fear, Jane, he would not dare spread an ill report of me. He cannot do so without damaging his own *sterling reputation as a clergyman*." Elizabeth made a dour face and mimicked his pompous tone.

"But Lizzy, he is not very well disposed toward us just now! He considers himself greatly wronged by you, and even by Mr Darcy. He said as much at dinner. You know yourself, we can ill afford more rumours at present!"

Elizabeth sighed, then nodded her acquiescence. "Fear not, Dearest Jane, no one could speak ill of you. Your Mr Bingley knows that you are a paragon of virtue, utterly untainted as the rest of us are by any wanton or wicked notions." Her mischievous smile in the moonlight prodded her sister. "That reminds me… It is not only I who have much to share this evening, is it?"

Jane dipped her head, hiding what would surely have been a most becoming blush if there were enough light to appreciate it by. "That is true," she confessed softly.

"Well?" demanded Elizabeth playfully.

"We… have an understanding. He asked for my hand, but we must speak to Father, or Uncle, before we can consider it an engagement."

Elizabeth could tell from Jane's inflections how truly pleased her sister was. Jane was far too modest to allow strong feeling to show, and one less acquainted with her might not detect the depth of her joy.

Elizabeth would not be fooled. "Oh, dear Jane!" she hugged her sister enthusiastically. "I am so happy for you! He is a fine man, and he will suit you well."

Jane sighed contentedly, nestling her head onto Elizabeth's shoulder. "I believe so. He is everything I had hoped to find- amiable and pleasant, and I believe his temper is much like my own."

"Yes, save that where you are reserved, he is demonstrative. Have you found some way to assure him of your regard? You know that not everyone is as well acquainted with you as I, and it would not do for Mr Bingley to be in any way uncertain of your feelings."

Jane cringed, but a tiny embarrassed giggle escaped. Elizabeth pushed her back a little. "Tell me all," she commanded firmly.

Jane took a moment to gird up her courage. Modest as she was, a confession of her intimate conversation with her intended, even to her dearest sister, pushed the furthest boundaries of her comfort. Finally she began in a small voice, "He told me he loved me."

Elizabeth waited for more, but nothing was forthcoming. "And?" Jane hesitated sheepishly, covering her mouth with her fingertips. "If that is all you had to tell, I will go to sleep, for I already knew as much," Elizabeth chided her.

"He… he got down on one knee and asked for my hand."

"To which, I assume, you replied that you would have to consider a while? Or did you refuse him outright?" Elizabeth playfully pinched her sister's cheek and found it warm with embarrassment. "What else?"

"Well… then he- he kissed my hand. After that, he…. Oh, I cannot!"

Elizabeth's fingers crept menacingly toward her sister's ribs, threatening Jane with her own tactics.

"No!" Jane jumped, then hurriedly squelched her outburst, fearful of yet another visit from Mr Collins. Elizabeth cocked her head insistently. "Oh, very well." Jane blew out a puff of tension, then dared a low whisper. "He kissed me… and I confess, I- I believe I kissed him back." Jane could scarcely believe she had given voice to her secret. She hunched her shoulders self-consciously.

"Capital!" crowed Elizabeth. "Good girl, I am glad you left him in no doubt of your feelings."

Jane's mouth gaped. "You do not think me immodest? *I* am shocked at my behaviour, when I recollect it."

"Immodest to encourage the honourable attentions of a gentleman, to whom you have just become engaged? No, I do not believe anyone could accuse you of impropriety. If anything, they might say just the opposite." Jane tilted her head questioningly, forcing Elizabeth to explain.

"Charlotte first attracted my attention to it, and I disagreed with her at the time. I believe now she may be right, at least a little. Your natural modesty becomes you, but a less secure suitor than Mr Bingley might not perceive your regard for him and might leave off the pursuit unless he were given some assurance that his feelings would be returned. I am glad he did not. It is clear to anyone with eyes that he loves you Jane, despite the lack of encouragement he received from his companions."

"Does that include Mr Darcy?" Jane's voice was softly challenging.

Elizabeth closed her eyes. She had forced Jane to confess all, now it was her turn. "That it does. I do not believe he was at all in favour of Mr Bingley's preference for you." Elizabeth's tone took on a forced lightness. "I suppose the one good thing to come of recent events is that Mr Darcy had no longer the power to discourage your Mr Bingley from making you an offer. Mr Bingley has now done no more than Mr Darcy had already done himself." She swallowed. "He kissed me as well, you know."

Jane gasped. "He did not! When?"

"Yesterday, when I was at the creek. He came to apologize, or console me, or some other nonsense. Can you believe the cheek of the man, to presume an understanding when I had not given my consent? And then to take such a liberty! I slapped him soundly for his boldness."

"Lizzy!"

Elizabeth turned an arch expression on her sister. "Would you have me acquiesce so easily when I had *not* agreed to an engagement? Of course I had to act to rebuff such an advance! What would you say had I not done so?"

Jane sighed, admitting that Elizabeth had a point. "But surely, he did not mistreat you, did he? I cannot think that Mr Darcy would force such an intimacy...."

"No, he did not exactly *force* me- in fact, in all justice, he was very gentle. He did, however, surprise me so thoroughly that I had not the time to react." Elizabeth's voice was full of irritation, but not anger. It seemed her indignant animosity toward Mr Darcy had dissipated, but she refused to entirely reconcile herself to her present situation.

Jane was silent a moment. If she were not mistaken, her sister was

---

showing signs of softening toward Mr Darcy, unwillingly or not. Perhaps some revelation of what she had learned from Mr Bingley could help matters. "Lizzy, I believe Mr Darcy was truly hurt after your conversation yesterday."

Elizabeth's head snapped up. "Why would you think so?"

Jane bit her lip. "Mr Bingley told me that Mr Darcy was very much not himself yesterday evening. He did not share many details, but he did lead me to understand that… that Mr Darcy awoke somewhat ill this morning." Jane's tones were hushed. It mortified her to so much as imply that a gentleman would indulge in intemperance, to the degree that his condition would suffer the following day.

Elizabeth was silent for several seconds, then gave a short laugh. "That could account for a few things, I suppose. Still," she stiffened slightly, "I am at least gratified to know I am not the only one who passed a miserable evening! If you ask me, the man deserves to be made a little uncomfortable after acting as he did."

Jane had not spent twenty years in close relationship with her sister without learning her disposition well. "Lizzy," her tone carried a hint of admonishment, "I do not believe it is Mr Darcy with whom you are angry tonight. You sound as if you are trying to justify something. Will you not tell me of what you two spoke this afternoon?"

Elizabeth sighed reluctantly, then resigned herself to the inevitable. Slowly she spoke, her tones broken. "Jane… I have been so wrong about him, so blinded by my own folly!"

"Mr Darcy?" Jane's voice sounded relieved.

"And Mr Wickham." Elizabeth faltered. Blinking uncomfortably, she began to share the whole of what she had learned. Jane listened with great patience, squeezing Elizabeth's hand consolingly. By the time she had finished, tears glistened in the moonlight and dripped on the blankets.

Jane gasped as Elizabeth ended her tale. "Poor Miss Darcy! Little wonder she was so distressed when she heard Mr Wickham's name today! But are we certain there was not some misunderstanding? I cannot believe he could be so cruel, he seems such an amiable young man. Surely he could not mean harm to an innocent girl, the daughter of his patron! No, there must be some mistake."

Elizabeth tried to laugh lightly, but it came out as more of a sob. "Oh, believe it Jane, it is true! They both have the same story, they agree in all the particulars but those which matter the most. Not even you cannot make them *both* good. No, one man has all the goodness and the other has all the appearance of it. There is only enough goodness between them to make one good sort of man. It pains me to admit it, but I believe the virtue must be all Mr Darcy's."

Jane pondered to herself a moment. "I suppose it is well to find that, of the two, Mr Darcy is the honourable man, in light of your present circumstances."

Elizabeth hung her head wearily. "Jane, what am I to do? I am so ashamed! I let my vanity lead me astray. I, who have prided myself on my discernment of the characters of others, have been so grievously and dangerously wrong! I have exposed myself for the most ignorant and prejudiced of people. What must he think of me?"

"I do believe that is a first, Lizzy. You have never before cared what Mr Darcy thought."

"Please do not tease me, Jane! You know my situation at present. Mother has made sure everyone believes I am to marry him! I still have no desire to, for I do not care for him, but he must truly despise *me*. I suppose it is just as well I do not wish to marry him, for surely after how I have treated him he will desire to call off the 'engagement'."

"Lizzy, I do not think he will do so. Mr Bingley told me something else. I hesitated to tell you before, for fear it would only make you disdain him all the more…."

"Well, do not keep me in suspense, Jane. What is it?"

"That… Mr Darcy seems truly to love you… very much, in fact."

She laughed out loud, wishing to deny the possibility. "I cannot believe it. No, it is impossible! Your Mr Bingley is reading his own sentiments into the matter, surely."

"Mr Bingley said he had it from Mr Darcy himself."

Elizabeth sucked in her breath, entirely astonished. "But how, Jane? Why? The very notion is absurd! We have never once sat in the same room together without some argument, unless he determines to ignore me entirely. We never get along, we have nothing at all in common! For him to actually love me, it is inconceivable! More credible is the notion that he thought to exploit my position of weakness."

"Think, Lizzy," Jane admonished gently. "Why do you suppose he spoke yesterday to stop Mr Collins' proposal? I agree with you that he is not overtly demonstrative of his feelings, and I do think it likely he intended never to have spoken for you. It is true that he is proud and we are not of his circles in society, but I do believe he truly cares for you. He could not bear to see you engaged to another before his very eyes. Mr Darcy could see you did not wish to marry Mr Collins, and he could not restrain himself." Jane presented her thoughts as the most perfectly reasonable explanation.

Elizabeth shook her head doubtfully. "I do not know if I believe that, Jane. Mr Darcy is nothing if not always in command of himself- and others," she added wryly. "I have trouble crediting your understanding of his actions."

"That, dear Lizzy, is precisely why I believed Mr Bingley when he told me of his friend's feelings for you. He *has* always been in control, until now.

You are most certainly the first woman to inspire such sentiments, and he does not quite know what to do with them. Did you not tell me that he confessed his feelings himself yesterday?"

Elizabeth narrowed her eyes introspectively, reexamining the words he had spoken. "He did speak of a regard for me. I did not think he truly meant it; I thought he intended only to justify his actions. I told you that he expressed his pride and his belief in my unworthiness just as eloquently as he pronounced any sentiment for me."

"Do you not think, Lizzy," Jane replied slowly, "that he really did suffer some struggle in confessing his feelings? Surely a man in his position is expected to marry from better circles than those in which we are able to move. Perhaps he has already been pressured by family to marry advantageously. Did not Mr Collins mention some expectations on the part of his aunt? Surely he has known of these plans for himself since his youth. Mr Darcy has the reputation of a very responsible man, you know. It cannot have been easy for him to reject his family's expectations in favour of his own wishes."

Elizabeth sighed, a deep shuddering breath. Ashamed as she was of her own misjudgments, she no longer felt equal to the examination of each of Mr Darcy's motives and actions. The proof of her own error had blasted her confidence in her own perceptions. Her head wagged. "Jane, I just do not know. I wish I could talk to Papa!" A few tears leaked down her cheeks and she wiped them tiredly.

Jane pulled her closer. "I know, Lizzy. I know. Aunt Madeline will be here tomorrow. Perhaps she can help. You know she is so wise and discreet. For now," Jane stroked her little sister's cheek affectionately, "I think we should get some rest. We both need it, I daresay."

Elizabeth nodded, sniffing. She allowed Jane to bundle her in her arms as she had when they were children. Cuddling her chin over Jane's shoulder, she finally drifted into a fitful slumber.

Thirteen

Three miles away at Netherfield, Darcy bid his own sister a tender good night. Georgiana had remained timidly by his side the entire evening, resolutely denying even Miss Bingley's determined attempts at separating her from her brother. In a way, she had demonstrated a rare fortitude- it was not like her to have such success at thwarting the manipulations of others upon her. It worried him, however, that she was still so shaken that she would not leave his side.

Later, he had pulled her under his arm in the privacy of her rooms. "Georgie, you are not well. Is there something I can do to offer you some comfort? Would you like a glass of wine?"

She had smiled gently. "Brother, you must be truly concerned to be offering me wine. You do not often do so."

"Diluted, of course," he admonished with a raised finger, drawing a small silent chuckle from her. He crooked his finger and touched her chin. "It must have come as a shock to you to hear about Mr Wickham being so near. The fault is mine, Georgie. I should have told you before. I did not think…."

She shook her head. "You must stop blaming yourself, Fitzwilliam! You cannot always be responsible for the actions of others. It was my own foolishness that led me into danger, not yours."

"I had not warned you…."

"William, please stop!" Her eyes flashed with a new spirit. "I was taught the same principles as you, I ought to have known what he asked me to do was wrong. He knew my weaknesses, and I fell for his lies."

She took a breath, set her jaw, and met his gaze with a gravity out of character for her sixteen years. "You cannot know how fortunate I feel to have had you looking out for me! I know very well that many brothers or fathers would not have treated me so gently as you have. Many would behave with contempt, or would have let me suffer in my folly. You have cared for me far better than I deserve, and yet you continue to blame yourself!"

He allowed himself a reluctant smile, admiring the fire which warmed her features. "You have done a good deal of thinking during your time in London. This is a new Georgie I see before me!"

She blushed. "I have been, but it was Miss Elizabeth who reminded me… showed me that there is more to me than my mistakes. You have been good enough to allow me to start over, without shaming me, and I intend to do just that."

"Georgie!" He clasped both her hands, struck dumb with delight. Blinking furiously, a trembling smile on his lips, he felt his heart swell. "You cannot know how pleased I am to hear you speak so!" He paused, peering carefully into her eyes. "Did you really like her so well?"

"Oh, yes, William!" she gushed. "Ever so much! Miss Elizabeth is truly kind. I so much wish to further my acquaintance with her. Do you think," she breathed hopefully, "that she and you…?"

He swallowed. "I do not know, Georgie. Perhaps she does not dislike me so much as she did yesterday. Georgie- I told her everything."

The girl stiffened. "She knows about me? Even… everything?"

"Yes, Dearest, she does. I am sorry, but after today, an explanation was required. It was not only your reaction," he stopped her before she could protest her guilt again, "I had intended to speak to her today anyway, hoping we could clear up some misapprehensions. Miss Elizabeth had also been misled by Mr Wickham's pretty words."

"Even she!" Georgiana's face betrayed her shock. "I would not have thought he could fool her, she is so clever!"

"You know how convincing he can sound, Georgie. He knows how to make himself agreeable and to cast others in a bad light. Without proper facts to counter his assertions, he is capable of fooling many."

Her face lit with sudden comprehension. "So that is why she disliked you? The things she heard about you which angered her so, they were from him?" She paused in wonder. If even Elizabeth could be deceived, her own guilt seemed not quite so convicting.

He nodded. "In part, but as I told you before, I had not behaved as well as I ought toward her- or anyone else in the area, truly. She had no reason to disbelieve what she heard."

Georgiana's face brightened more. "But she knows the truth now! Did you think she believed you?"

"Yes, Sweetling, she did," he answered, relief palpable in his voice.

A shadow passed over Georgiana's features. "Does she think ill of me, now that she knows everything?"

He gave a wry little laugh. "If anything, it made her the more sympathetic toward you. *You* at least have won her good opinion. I should think you have made a true friend."

She smiled shyly, with genuine pleasure. "And what of you? Does she think better of you now?"

He sighed. "I think she understands me better. Perhaps I could say she no longer retains some of her former reasons to despise me. Remember that she did not think highly of me before she met Mr Wickham. Whether she will improve her opinion of me in the future, I cannot say, but I believe I yet have some mending to do."

Georgiana beamed confidently. "I know she will change her mind! When she comes to know you for your true self, she will love you!" He interrupted her with a quiet laugh, shaking his head modestly. "I am serious, William! Perhaps neither of you realize it, but I think you are much alike. You are both thoughtful and kind, you both are well read, and she is adventurous and loves being out of doors, like you. She cares little for people's outward appearances, I can tell, and you know how you grow weary of people affecting wealth and status. There is nothing pretentious about *her*. I also noticed," she batted her eyelashes at him playfully, "that she takes her tea exactly the same as you! No cream, one lump of sugar."

"Oh, well, then that is surely a basis for an enduring attachment." He chuckled at her good humour, allowing her hopeful spirits to buoy his. He visited with her a few moments longer, then left her to her maid to prepare for bed.

~

Darcy was too restless to retire for the evening himself. He found Bingley in a similar state of agitation, and challenged his friend to a game of billiards. Bingley accepted with alacrity.

"Where the devil is Fitzwilliam?" Darcy asked, looking about. "I have not seen him since just after dinner."

Bingley answered with a shrug. "Hiding in his rooms, I should think. I believe he is afraid of Caroline." Bingley lowered his cue and took aim, sending the first ball into the side pocket with a sharp clatter.

Darcy made a face. "*He* has nothing to fear from her, he is a second son." With a start he remembered himself. "I am sorry, Bingley. I should not have spoken so of your sister."

Bingley held up a hand, shaking his head. "No, Darcy, I should apologize. I know Caroline has made a nuisance of herself, pursuing you as she has. I wish to heaven she would listen to me, but she hears nothing I have said."

Darcy heaved a sigh. "I should have been more forthright, I suppose. She is not one to take a hint." Darcy considered his play, then pocketed the next ball. "I beg you would not trouble yourself further. It is no more than I have endured from many others, some even more determined than she."

Bingley pursed his lips, wondering how much of the morning's ruckus Darcy was aware of. Certainly his sister was not yet ready to relinquish her quarry, but rather soon she would be forced to admit the futility of her efforts. Seizing that thought, Bingley brightened. "It seems we shall be brothers one way or another, eh old friend?" Bingley made his shot, hoping Darcy would drop some revealing comment. When his friend only silently lined up his next move, he tried again. "I can only assume that today went somewhat better with Miss Elizabeth, as you are not in your cups this evening."

Goaded, Darcy missed his shot. He straightened, eyeing Bingley cautiously. "Only somewhat, you might say. It seems I am capable of effectively making a woman despise me after all."

"She appeared to be speaking to you when we left. I say, that is progress, old man! Well, I mean, after yesterday, I would call it progress," Bingley stammered. He reddened a little, wondering if he had overstepped. Darcy had never before spoken of women, save to express his dissatisfaction. Now that he had irretrievably committed both his honour and his heart to a woman who claimed to want little to do with him, Darcy's introverted nature was even less inclined to pour forth his feelings.

Darcy's mouth twitched, and a kind of sadness shone in his eyes. Blinking, he lowered his cue for another attempt, not really caring that he should have relinquished the table to Bingley after his failed shot. In his estimation, Bingley's tactic of employing Elizabeth's name was foul play.

Bingley cringed. Sensing that nothing he could say would improve matters, he clamped his lips shut. He determined to simply play his game and watch Darcy win… again.

~

The morning fog hung drowsily over the fields. A light rain threatened, but he needed to be out. Darcy pulled his hat down a little more tightly on his head, hunching his shoulders against the chill. A brisk ride would warm him soon enough.

Walking into the barn, he startled the young stable boy, already up and about his duties. The boy offered to saddle his horse for him, but Darcy waved him off. It had been some while since he had allowed himself this pleasure. The rich familiar smells of the fresh stable, the supple leather beneath his hands, the warmth of Pluto's breath as the animal caught his master's scent were all a balm to his soul. The black put his nose trustingly to his chest, communicating in his own way that he was glad for the attention and eager for a ride.

Affectionately he stroked the stallion's neck. Growing up with horses as he had, Darcy knew to be cautious with such a creature. So much raw power and native beauty existed in the form of a friend, yet even as trusted as his favourite mount was, he was still a stallion- still a virile animal in the prime of his life, and as such the horse was not wholly predictable, not wholly his own. Never would he be. Darcy could respect that. Still, something deep within him ached for a heart he really could possess.

He swung into the saddle, striking a gallop immediately after leaving the courtyard area. Only one destination called to his restless spirits, and somehow he knew she would be waiting for him. The dry, hard path clapped under his horse's hooves as he made his way toward the short hill where he had last spoken with Mr Bennet.

A flutter of green shawl caught the mild breeze as he neared the place called Oakham Mount. Dark hair shone in the sun and a hatless young woman turned toward him, expectant. Elizabeth's bright eyes smiled at him as he dismounted, with a gentleness that fairly radiated from her lovely face. It was so right coming to her in this place, with the glow of the sunrise warming her features and the whole of the new day before them. Somewhere in the distance he heard a dove calling to his mate, and it filled him with a natural peace. He came wordlessly to her, claiming his right to be near her. Somehow she found her way into his arms, resting her soft cheek on his chest.

Breathing deeply, he pressed his face into the swirling mound of her windswept hair and inhaled the fresh scent of her. She melded to him, fitting neatly under his chin as he curled his arms protectively around her waist. Then words- "I am sorry." The same words tumbled from both their lips. She looked up, he down, surprise and amusement lighting her face. He brought trembling fingers to her cheeks, aching to share with her all his tender affections, but never daring to offend or frighten her.

A slight softening of the corners of her mouth, a barely perceptible crinkle around her sparkling eyes, and then she tipped her chin up to the beckoning of his hand. His head lowered, draping over hers to shield her from a sudden rivulet of water trickling off his hat brim. She arched away from the drenching, but snuggled her shoulder closely under the protection of his arm. Undeterred, those marvelous eyes held him and drew him closer again.

He crooked two fingers under her chin, boldly this time reaching for her. His hand became instantly slippery and cold. She lifted her face from his fingers and straightened. She shook her head ever so slightly. "I cannot love a conceited man," she murmured. She turned and vanished in a sudden fog.

With a strangled cry, Darcy's long arms swept the cool air before his face. His hand crashed into a water pitcher which had been left by his bed, sending it splashing over his sleeves, the sheets, and the floor. Gone was the glowing vision of Elizabeth standing in the warm sunrise, favouring him with her inviting smile. He jolted out of bed to the cold reality of a bitterly chill morning. A glance out the window revealed a pummeling rain falling. No doubt the sound had filtered into his dreams.

Groggily he sat up, scrubbing his face with his hands to clear his vision. There would be no riding today, badly as he longed for an escape over the rolling fields. It was yet very early, and he doubted even Bingley's staff were up and about.

Wilson, jarred from his sleep in the adjacent dressing room by the crash of the pitcher, opened the door and peered carefully into the room. "Mr Darcy? Is there something I can do?" His eyes widened when he took in the drenched person of his master. "Some dry clothes? Do you wish to dress for the day?"

Heaving a sigh, Darcy looked about him at the carnage wrought by his disappointed dream. "No, not as yet. Just a housecoat and a dry shirt, please. You may return to bed."

Wilson quickly procured the garments his master requested, but was dismissed before he could help him change.

Darcy looked askance at the sopping blankets. Even should he desire it, he could not return to his bed without rousing the housemaids. The fire had gone out too, leaving the room frigid. He ought to re-light it himself, he thought. Instead, he moved to the window. It was almost entirely fogged over, but even through the milky haze he could see there was no light at all yet.

He began to pace restlessly, his thoughts on his last conversation with Elizabeth. Had she hinted at the end that she might come to view him in a more agreeable light? It had pained him to see her so broken, so miserable. She had believed him, of that he was certain. Would she blame him still? What was it she had accused him of after his disastrous proposal? Conceit, arrogance?

He spun around. Without a second thought, he jerked open the door to his room and made his way down the hall. So long and purposeful were his strides that he nearly collided with a sleepy housemaid, creeping through the corridor lighting candles for the morning staff.

She leapt back with a little squeak of surprise. "So sorry Sir! T'was my fault, I were not watchin'." She held her eyes down in contrition, afraid to displease so distinguished a guest. He could well understand why. Caroline Bingley had bullied the staff into a sullen fear, threatening them all with immediate dismissal on more than one occasion. He was not certain that fact had become apparent to her brother. He decided to speak to Bingley about that later.

He began to apologize, but saw the girl's face redden even further. He stopped, allowing her to speak. "Were there... somethin' in partic'lar Sir was wishing for?" She shuffled uncomfortably, not daring to meet his eyes.

He cocked his head quizzically. "I do not understand you, miss...?"

"My name is Sarah, Sir." She lifted her face and swallowed nervously. "Mr Benson, th'old Master here, he....." she trailed off, dropping her eyes again.

Mortified, Darcy gasped. "Heavens, no! I regret you should have thought so, Sarah. No, and I am sorry you previously had such a disgraceful master. Have you been treated unkindly since?" He would not believe Bingley capable of imposing himself upon his servant girls, but he wanted to confirm it from her own lips.

She shook her head, her eyes still glued to the floor. "No Sir, but Nancy... t'is not your concern, Sir. F'rgive me for d'sturbin' you."

"You do not disturb me. I should like to know. Your friend, Nancy, has she some trouble?"

She was clearly reluctant to speak. He was fairly certain there was a Nancy who was still in Bingley's employ- was that the girl who had been helping tend to Georgiana? Of course, any shame attached to her would naturally result in her immediate dismissal. Little wonder Sarah was afraid to speak.

"Sarah, please trust me. Has someone disgraced your friend Nancy? I would like to try to right any wrong done to her." He spoke gently, hoping to encourage her to confide fully in him.

A tear began to tremble at the corner of the girl's eye. When she spoke, her voice was barely above a whisper. "There's a bairn, sir, born last year. Nancy has to pay a woman in the village to watch him and to stay quiet."

Darcy pressed his lips together. "Thank you, Sarah. I will see to it that Nancy has the provision she requires. You need have no fear for her." The girl stared wide-eyed at him in shock. In sudden inspiration, he thought to ask, "Are there any others who have suffered under your old master?"

Beginning to relax somewhat, she nodded, hesitantly. "T'is not in that way... my brother. My father was one o'the farmers, but he took sick a couple of years ago. Mr Benson 'victed us when my father could not pay the rent. My brother tried to pay him back, rent the farm again, but then Papa died and Mr Benson would not heed...."

"So your family is without an income? How many are there?"

"Mama died just after Papa. John- my brother, Sir- he works some odd jobs for other farmers to keep my two sisters fed, but they're not old 'nough for work. I were lucky to be handsome enough for Mr Benson to take me on here, though I were young. I've been able to help a little." The girl bit her lip, her embarrassment at her circumstances painfully apparent.

Darcy was filled with disgust. He had heard little of Bingley's lessor, but the more he knew the more revolted he was. He had always been ashamed of masters, members of his own class, who dallied with their servants; little more than girls, mostly, bullied into compliance. Hearing a firsthand account of one man's ignominious ways made him feel a new contempt. Was this how the landed gentry were perceived in much of the kingdom? Heartless, profligate libertines who used and discarded people for their pleasure? The French gentry had been accused of such offences, and the result had been brutally cataclysmic. He wondered suddenly if Elizabeth lumped him in with that lot as well.

Gulping down his sudden ire, he forced his fingers to unclench. "Sarah, I am sorry to hear of your family's distress. I will look in to the matter. Please, have no fear that any harm will befall them because of your revelation. I have kept you long enough, please excuse me."

She nodded, surprise and doubt still written across her features. She picked up the snuffer that she had dropped when he nearly collided with her and scrambled away. Darcy sighed and resumed his trek down the hall, missing the creak of the nearest bedroom door as it closed softly.

Caroline Bingley crossed her arms and huffed in amazement. Always a light sleeper, she had been awakened by the voices outside her door. What she overheard made her head spin. What would cause Mr Darcy to take such a burden upon himself, to attend the cares of the servant class? It was far below his notice, shameful even that he should dabble in such concerns.

She feared the same influences she found alarming upon her brother were now swaying her own Mr Darcy. *It's those Bennet sisters! They flutter their lovely eyes and the men swarm to them!* What was it about Jane and Elizabeth that made men forget their place?

Caroline began to worry the notion about in her head. They were fair, it was true, but so coarse and vulgar! Had they been brought up in good society, they may have made passable ladies, but they could claim no elegance or refinement that she could discern. Then there was the insipid mother! And the younger girls, so insufferably wild! Caroline wondered at the father who had not troubled himself to control his family.

She sneered a little, remembering how at the ball, the haughty Miss Elizabeth had tried to champion that knave Wickham. She knew little of the man herself, only that Darcy disdained him. That was enough to satisfy her. It was proof enough of Elizabeth's ill-guided notions that she would concern herself with a soldier of no account and no good family. She did not doubt that Miss Elizabeth would even associate among the farmers and tradesmen, as the girl obviously had no taste or discretion. To think that Darcy would be brought to such lowness should he marry her!

A pit of yawning dismay gnawed at her stomach. Elizabeth's influence may already be too strong! Only moments ago, Darcy appeared concerned that someone would mistreat a servant girl… a *servant girl!* Why should he care what happened to a mere chit of a servant? And had she heard properly that Nancy had a child? Well! She must be dismissed immediately! To think such a girl should be tending Miss Darcy of Pemberley, right under her own roof, was shocking. What if word got out among their friends?

Caroline glided back to her bed; even in the privacy of her own rooms, she always practiced the correct poise and comportment that should be expected of the future Mistress of Pemberley. It was surely only a matter of time, she comforted herself. Only one obstacle stood in her way, and she was confident that with a very little more effort, she could puncture the veil of Eliza Bennet's allure.

Fourteen

Darcy did not even bother knocking when he barged into Colonel Fitzwilliam's bedchamber in the frosty gloom of morning. It was only fair, he thought in justification. It was no more than Richard had done to him the day before- though, perhaps, a bit earlier in the morning.

Grousing, Richard rolled over and tugged the pillow over his head. "Have a care, Foster! I had watch last night! Out, and do not wake me before seven hundred!"

Darcy snatched the pillow. "I'm not Foster, and you're not with the Regiment. Wake up Richard, I need to talk to you."

Richard groaned, sat up, and stretched. "Cannot this wait? I am barely human before two stiff cups of coffee, you know that."

"That matters little, I don't need a human. I am accustomed to dealing with an orangutan. Richard- do you think me arrogant?"

Richard smirked wryly. "You march in here at an unholy hour and proceed to insult me? No, Darcy you haven't an arrogant bone in your body," he growled sarcastically. "Now, can I get back to sleep?"

Darcy forestalled his cousin from flopping back on the pillow by sitting down on the bed beside him. "I am serious, Richard! Elizabeth told me I was arrogant and conceited. Is she right?"

"Of course she is. Did you not know? Now, get off my bed." Richard sleepily gave an ineffectual shove on Darcy's shoulder. When it didn't budge his cousin, he resigned himself to the lost sleep and sat up fully, rubbing his eyes.

Darcy felt as though he had been stabbed. "How?" he demanded. "I am fair and generous, I treat others honourably, I have never disgraced a woman, I am indebted to no one! How can she claim I am arrogant?"

Richard rolled his eyes dramatically, slumping forward with comic flare. "Oh, Darcy, you cannot really think that is all there is to it? When was the last time you willingly conversed with someone beneath your station- someone who did *not* possess an enchanting wit and lovely chocolate brown eyes?"

Darcy looked pensive. "Only a moment ago, as a matter of fact. That is neither here nor there, though. What has it to do with my question?"

"Everything," Richard sighed, peering back in his memory. "I remember Uncle George used to worry that you would be taken in by gold-diggers and flatterers. You were younger than I, you may not have been aware of it, but I remember him speaking to my father more than once about his concerns for you. I think," he supplied softly, "he knew you would be Master at a very young age."

Darcy wiped his eyes with his hand until they were blurry. He had been ill prepared at this moment to have Richard bring up his father's memory. "What can you mean by that?"

"Auntie Anne- sorry, I still think of her by that name- she was always so gentle with you and Georgie. I remember how she would encourage you to speak to anyone and everyone, just to help you overcome your shyness. You took her advice a little too much to heart for Uncle's comfort. Do you remember how you used to play with the shopkeepers' boys from Lambton?"

Darcy nodded slowly. "Father eventually declared an end to that. He felt it beneath me." He had been devastated at the time, although too proud to let his father see it. His playmates had been his primary diversion after losing his mother. After losing their fellowship as well, he had retreated to the stables and his books, and of course, to little Georgiana.

"You must not blame Uncle for that," Richard continued. "He genuinely feared you would be taken in by anyone who would try to use you for his own advantage. He wanted to prepare you for your responsibilities, and he knew no better way to do it. Father advised him to limit your acquaintance to only those who stood little to gain from using you. Only Wickham was allowed to continue with you, and that was because he was your father's namesake and his own father was respectable."

Darcy chewed thoughtfully on his lower lip. "Are you saying that I was purposely taught to be prideful and conceited to protect me from being taken advantage of? That makes no sense."

"Well, perhaps not in hindsight, no. You were far too softhearted though, and Uncle knew it. Remember the robin's nest?

Darcy laughed lowly at this. "I had forgotten about that! I cried about those broken eggs the entire afternoon until Father returned home. Little did I know the empty shells actually meant the chicks had hatched and were well!"

"I remember," Richard chuckled. "Uncle thought you were being ridiculous! And what happened that time you had to destroy that dying broodmare in the field?"

Darcy shuddered. It was the first time he had had to put an animal out of its misery, but unfortunately not the last. Hunting was different. This had been his father's finest broodmare, a horse he had ridden himself as a toddler. To this day she appeared on his pedigrees as one of the granddams of his own stock, including Pluto. "It was horrible. I will never forget that dreadful shriek, and then the dead foal… that perfect white diamond, such a promising colt…."

"See what I mean? You wouldn't go back to the stables for days. Uncle felt you needed to learn a little distance, a little coldness even, for your own good. Even then you were naïve, blind to Wickham's ways until you were at school together and were daily confronted with his notoriety. You refused to believe any one of your good friends could be such a rogue. It was while you were at school that you truly began to change. Then later, when you first entered the *ton* as an eligible bachelor…."

"When I was relentlessly pursued by lackluster debutantes and their scheming mamas? Yes, I suppose that did pull the wool from my eyes rather quickly. In very little time I was fed up with most people's society"

"Of course, your one close acquaintance who *had* been truly beneath your status ended up betraying you, no doubt reinforcing your father's lessons to not mingle below your station. You never were an easy one to know, but you became even more distant and forbidding after that. Bingley has been good for you, I think, but amiable and friendly as he is, even he has not been able to quite chip off that calloused exterior you worked so hard to build up."

"You would have me make myself vulnerable again? The way you describe it, I have done nothing more than to protect myself."

"You are ten years the wiser now," Richard pointed out. "I cannot tell you how delighted I was to hear you had found a woman you truly esteemed- and not even of the *ton*! When I first heard of it, I supposed that in pursuing such a woman you could only have motives of the very noblest kind, and so it is. You can gain nothing from her but the riches of the heart, and that is just as I would wish for you.

"She is magnificent, Darcy- a queen among women, if I may be so bold. She will defrost that tender heart of yours and still make you toe the line. My advice, Darcy, is to do whatever it takes to win her affections, regardless of how you must humble yourself to do it." Richard stretched sleepily and winked at his cousin. "Had she any dowry of her own, I might not advise you so, for I think she is quite a captivating woman myself! You always did have exquisite taste."

Darcy ignored his cousin's jab. "How am I to do so? If you and Miss Elizabeth are correct, I have managed to give offence at every turn. How am I to undo the mistakes of the past weeks, or the habits of half a lifetime?"

"Practice makes perfect, old man. Try starting with that mama of Miss Bennet's. No doubt she will seat you by herself at dinner tomor- I mean tonight. If you can stomach her effusions without making any of your haughty speeches, I would say you are well on your way to learning how to please a woman worthy of being pleased."

Darcy gulped, his eyes widened. "Do you really think that necessary?" For Elizabeth he would dare anything, risk any chance, but an entire evening trading inanities with Mrs Bennet? Torture!

"Can you think of a better one to practice on?"

Darcy groaned, knowing Richard was right, but dreading the discomfort a long conversation with Mrs Bennet would cost him. "Could we not dig up Wickham? Perhaps I could publicly exonerate him, hand him the keys to Pemberley, and find him a rich bride…."

Richard laughed. "Speaking of our old friend, he may be out of our hair."

"What? How would that be?"

"Well, I wouldn't put too much confidence in it. I saw him last evening and made note of the advantages of America. Much opportunity there for a man with ambition, they say."

"He would never go there willingly. Besides, the fare costs more than he has ever been able to hold on to for more than a week."

"Oh, I saw to it that was not a concern. He has ample funds for such a voyage."

Darcy narrowed his eyes. "And I suppose I am twelve guineas the poorer for it? I wondered why my purse seemed so light."

Richard shrugged, spreading his hands supplicatingly. "Call it an investment. Not that I would expect him to actually use the money as it was intended, but if he sells up here he will now have enough to purchase a Lieutenant's commission in the Regulars, or any number of more honourable options. He can have no excuse for sticking around to make trouble for you now; and if he does, well, he is being watched very closely. Colonel Forster and I go back a long way."

Darcy frowned thoughtfully. "It is an interesting plan, at least. I doubt he will make good use of the funds. More likely he will use it as seed money to fleece another unsuspecting 'friend', but it was worth a try to shield Georgiana- and Elizabeth's family from him. The younger girls are exactly the kind of empty-headed quarry he tended to favour when we were at school."

"From what you said, it sounds as though his tastes have lately coincided more with yours."

Darcy's face darkened. "He certainly found Miss Elizabeth appealing, for which I could blame no one, I suppose. He did not spare her his charm, either. However," Darcy rubbed his still-tender jaw, "I believe she will be safe from him now. She knows him for what he truly is, and I have proof that she has enough spunk to send him packing."

Richard's eyebrows rose in surprise. "You told her everything, didn't you? Darcy, I never thought to see you so wholly let your guard down. There may be hope for you yet, Cousin!" Richard gave him a playful shove on the shoulder.

Darcy smiled, a warm satisfaction growing. "I am glad you approve."

Richard grunted. "Now, if you please, my bed? I stayed out half the night drinking with the colonel for your sake, and I deserve my beauty sleep."

~

The gray dawn disappointed more than one person in the general vicinity of Meryton with its heavy downpour. At Longbourn, Elizabeth chafed at being denied the spirited long walk she had desired for herself. Some rebellious part of her had even fantasized that she might encounter Mr Darcy out on one of his early morning rides. A sly little smile curved her lip when she thought what a lovely backdrop Oakham Mount would make for a private conversation. She discovered that she truly wished to speak to him more, to study his character again in light of her new knowledge. *Will he still desire to speak to me?*

If Jane was correct, he would, and the idea was unreasonably flattering. Elizabeth was not insensible to the compliment of such a distinguished man's affections. What could have occasioned them? She had never sought his favour, but he seemed to have bestowed it despite her attacks on his honour. She pursed her lips thoughtfully. Only a man of true integrity- or unreasonable obstinacy- would maintain his attachment to a woman who was admittedly beneath his station *and* extremely rude to him.

She flushed with mortification at the things she had said. Such wrong assumptions she had made! For the first time she felt that her barbed tongue had led her into great error, and she began to almost see the sense of some of her mother's complaints. Mrs Bennet had always bemoaned her daughter's wit, claiming that no sensible gentleman would want a wife who fancied herself more clever than he. Elizabeth could not help her cleverness, the words simply came to her in the moment. Her father had trained her to think, and her mind was quick and nimble. If only her tongue were less so!

She owed him an apology, she knew. She recalled his stiff response from the day before when she had challenged him with his failure to correct an error. It was *she* who had made the error, and *he* who should have been granted the benefit of the doubt as an honourable man. *Well,* she resolved, *I will do it, no matter the cost to my pride.* She was still uncertain about the idea of marriage, but she felt fully convicted of her shameful treatment of him. He deserved at least to hear her apologize. After that, he was free to do as he chose.

Elizabeth went through the motions of her morning, doing her level best to tolerate her mother's gleeful praise. Nothing she could do was wrong in her mother's eyes today. She had supplanted Lydia as the favourite daughter and Jane as the most promising. The fickleness of her mother's compliments annoyed her so greatly that in self-defence she forced her thoughts in a happier direction. She withdrew to her father's room and Mrs Cooper's company to read aloud.

Charlotte Lucas paid Elizabeth a visit in mid-morning, sitting with her for a while as she read to her father. Elizabeth was grateful for her company, but she felt terribly awkward discussing her friend's engagement. Elizabeth could not easily reconcile herself to the idea of her intelligent, sensible friend wed to the pompous fool that she found Mr Collins to be. Still, she would not wound Charlotte for anything, and had recently good cause to regret hasty words. By tacit understanding, little was spoken of any engagements after the first acknowledgement of the news.

Mercifully, Mr Collins intended to take his leave this morning so he could return to Hunsford to make preparations for his wedding. Even now, the housemaid was preparing the room he had occupied for Aunt Gardiner's arrival. Despite her misgivings about relating all the events of the past days, Elizabeth looked forward to her aunt's visit with every expectation of pleasure and relief.

~

"The post is arrived, my lady," the aging butler sniveled, extending a small silver tray within his mistress' obliging reach.

Anne de Bourgh's eyes fluttered open at the intrusion. The remedies the doctor had been employing of late tended to make her very drowsy, and she had an unsettling habit of dropping off in the middle of meals. Mrs Jenkinson covered smoothly for her, bending her own lace-capped head near to block her mother's view.

"You are late, Thompson!" the lady's imperious tones scolded.

"Yes, my lady," the butler bowed mildly, backing out of the room. It was pointless to protest his innocence where the tardiness of the mail carrier was concerned. Safest, he had learned it was, to excuse himself quickly.

"Mrs Jenkinson, you put yourself too much forward! Anne must be able to see me!" The great lady's eyes narrowed disapprovingly. Mrs. Jenkinson fawned over Anne to the proper degree to please Her Ladyship, but occasionally forgot her place. That was what came of taking on a reduced gentlewoman, she observed.

Anne's pale face emerged from behind the laced cap. "Anne, you have not finished your soup. You must strive to improve your health! Little wonder Darcy has not formalized your engagement. Do not forget your duty, child!"

Anne was insensible to the exigency of a modest blush on her part in response to her mother's exhortations. For better than the last ten of her seven and twenty years, she had heard the same diatribe against her health and her own apparent lack of willpower. Clearly, the great lady who unfortunately must be counted as her mother considered Anne's indifferent state as a personal insult.

Lady Catherine frowningly surveyed the assortment of personages paying their respects via this day's post. Lady Whitcombe, Lady Bramburg, Lady Trenton... all included the ladies' burgeoning hopes of wishing Lady Catherine joy on her daughter's upcoming nuptials. Also described by all were vague mentions of hosting a gala at some point, but never a declaration of specific dates or a forthright invitation. Spineless! Why, in her day, a lady acted with decision. The de Bourgh dowager would lend distinction to any such paltry gathering, should she deign to attend. She could not fathom why such fine ladies of the *ton* would not simply pluck up and host their confounded events.

She had left the most satisfying letter for last. It always gratified her to read her parson's eminently sensible observations. That, she congratulated herself, had been a providential appointment. William Collins possessed the proper degree of humility and deference, and was not backward in paying his compliments.

Anne stirred her soup listlessly, lifting the spoon occasionally to watch the unappetizing liquid strain back into the bowl. A special healing recipe, it was supposed to be. Anne thought it more akin to affliction than remedy. She drizzled the spoonful down over the saucer, wrinkling her nose in disgust. At least she was safe from her mother's pointed observations as she did so- it was always obvious by the single-minded attention paid whenever her mother became engrossed in any correspondence from Collins.

She had just resolved to venture a single bite when an animal shriek split the room. Looking about instinctively for some poor scalded cat, her startled eyes at last found her mother. Lady Catherine rose shakily to her feet, her heirloom dining chair flung backward on the floor. Her face purpled, eyes flown wide in rage.

"Anne! We are leaving *instantly* for Hertfordshire!"

~

Madeline Gardiner arrived at Longbourn at two in the afternoon. She braced herself as the carriage drew to a halt. She felt deep sympathy for her sister and nieces for their present distress, but it would take every drop of her reserves to cope with Mrs Bennet's despair. She was grateful her new governess was already proving steady and reliable, so she needn't bring her children. It was a comfort to know they were well situated at home in London, so she could focus all her energies on the Bennets' present difficulties. She truly hoped that Mr Bennet had miraculously recovered since she had last had word from Jane.

The footman helped her out of the carriage and held an umbrella for her. She smiled her thanks and looked to the house. Instead of the tear-streaked girls she expected, Mrs Bennet herself bounded jubilantly out the front door. "Fanny! Is Mr Ben...."

"Oh my dearest sister!" Mrs Bennet cut her off, waving her lace handkerchief. "We are saved! You will never guess, so I will tell you. Lizzy, my dearest, sweetest girl, is engaged to Mr Darcy! Is that not splendid! Oh, I shall go distracted, it has been such a thing for our girls! She will have so many fine carriages, and you know, she will be able to throw the other girls into the way of other rich men. Ten thousand a year, sister! Why, 'tis as good as a lord! And you know, he has a house in Town, and that great estate in Derbyshire- Pemden or something like that."

Mrs Gardiner's eyebrows rose. "Pemberley?"

"Yes! Yes, that is it. Will she not be a great lady! I hear it is the finest estate in the entire country! My dearest, sweetest girl, I *knew* she could not be so clever for nothing! But come, come inside before you catch your death, and I will tell you everything!"

Feeling as though she had already been told almost everything, Mrs Gardiner followed, her eyes searching for her nieces. She was itching for a more sensible account of recent days' events. She spotted Lizzy with a basin of some kind, surreptitiously sneaking by the opening in the top of the stairwell as she passed beneath. Elizabeth met her aunt's questioning gaze with an awkward little smile and a small wave. She made a perfunctory gesture with her head toward her father's room at the end of the hall, and slunk away.

Mrs Gardiner's curiosity was truly piqued. Elizabeth engaged, and too embarrassed to come tell her of it- too abashed, even, to come greet her properly? That was *not* like Lizzy, who was always frank with her. Moreover, the family's letters had not breathed a word of any engagement besides Mrs Bennet's designs on one Mr Bingley for Jane. This all must have come about since Mr Bennet's accident.

She remembered Lizzy's last letter, written only the week before. Elizabeth had mentioned meeting Mr Darcy, but had not sounded very pleased with the acquaintance. Rather, she had written of a preference for a new recruit in the militia. Indeed, a great deal must have happened!

She gratefully laid aside her wet things and joined her sister-in-law in the drawing room by the fire. Mrs Bennet giddily filled her in on the juiciest gossip, including her frustration that Mr Bingley had not yet spoken for Jane. "I am sure, Sister, that it can only be a matter of time. Oh! If only Mr Bennet would hurry up and get well, perhaps Bingley can come ask for Jane properly! I am sure that can be all he is waiting for! And then Mary can live with them at Netherfield, while Kitty and Lydia go to Pembrook with Lizzy. Depend on it, Sister, I will have all my girls married to rich men by next summer!"

Jane appeared in the drawing room almost immediately to hug her aunt. The deepest affection had always existed between the two eldest girls and the Gardiners. Mrs Gardiner had lovingly taken the two under her wing, acting as advisor, confidante, and friend. She had at times suffered a mild pang of guilt that she did not share such a close bond with the three younger girls, but she had discovered it nearly impossible to find common ground with them. The eldest, however, was an open book to her as she studied Jane's reserved greeting. Her niece's eloquent face spoke volumes, and she understood there was much to tell once Mrs Bennet had exhausted her narrative.

Half an hour later, she was settled in her room. Jane had followed to help make her comfortable, pausing to rap lightly on Mr Bennet's door as they walked by. A moment later, Lizzy tiptoed into the room, closing the door softly behind her. Her aunt astutely surmised that Lizzy would have much to say, and preferred to do it in privacy.

Mrs Gardiner turned a quizzical eye on her nieces and gently demanded an accounting of their strange behaviour. She saw Jane raise her eyebrows pointedly at Elizabeth, and shifted her gaze to the younger of the two. "Lizzy? Have you something of interest to tell me?"

Elizabeth blew out a huff of air, then affected a light manner. "Papa is much better. He has been fluttering his eyelids, and drinking more broth today. Mrs Cooper feels he will wake fully within a day or two."

"And Mrs Cooper is?"

"Uhm… she is the nurse who tends to Papa."

"Really? I am glad to hear it, but are not nurses very expensive? Of course, your uncle and I will help with those expenses."

Elizabeth's eyes rolled hesitantly to Jane, who tilted her head silently with a sly little smile. "There is no need, Aunt," Jane answered for her. "Mr Darcy has already attended the matter."

Mrs Gardiner's eyes widened. "Lizzy, that is not proper! A gentleman must not take on such an interest in a lady's family, he is liable to compromise you!" She peered carefully at Lizzy's reddened face. "He has not already done so, has he? Is that why your mother says you are engaged?"

"No, Aunt," she replied lamely. "Well… perhaps a little." With another encouraging glance from Jane, she related to her aunt all the events of that fateful morning, not leaving out her own shameful conduct and bad judgement. She forced herself to brave the humiliation which was her due, and shared everything she had learned to discredit her prior opinions. The only details she kept private were those directly concerning Miss Darcy.

Mrs Gardiner's shock was evident. "This is surprising, indeed. And do you believe Mr Darcy truly cares for you?" Elizabeth was silent, but Jane nodded energetically.

"Lizzy, you know I grew up in Lambton, only five miles from Pemberley, and still have some connections there. The present Mr Darcy, like his father, has always had a good reputation as a liberal and honourable man, even if he is somewhat above his company as you have said. I remember Old Mr Wickham, he did a deal of business in Lambton on the estate's behalf, but I have no knowledge of the son. I can only tell you what people generally say of the current Mr Darcy, and there is nothing to reflect poorly on him."

Elizabeth shifted uncomfortably. "I know, Aunt. I have misjudged him."

Mrs Gardiner moved to sit next to Elizabeth and wrap a comforting arm around her. She gave her other to Jane, and pulled her two favourite nieces close. "Are you quite certain that Mr Wickham is the villain you say he is? I do not doubt Mr Darcy's honour in the matter, as his reputation is that of a fair and just man, but anyone can be mistaken. Your implications as to Mr Wickham's character are rather serious."

Elizabeth nodded. "Yes, Aunt, I am sure. I cannot say more, but he is not a man to be trusted. I have no fear for our own family, as we have no dowries to tempt him, but Lydia and Kitty, you know, they are not terribly circumspect. They *will* flirt with any man wearing a red coat, and I do not think Mr Wickham in possession of the kind of honour which would prevent him from leading them astray, should the opportunity avail itself. I think it would be wise if we were to find some quiet way to shield them from him."

"Can he be as bad as all that?" Surprise at such a categorical renunciation of a former favourite of Elizabeth's strained Mrs Gardiner's voice. She studied her nieces closely. "He must indeed be silver of tongue if even you were fooled, Lizzy! I have never known you to be easily deceived."

Elizabeth rested her head on her beloved aunt's shoulder. "No," she agreed softly. "But my usual perceptiveness, Aunt, has proven to be a folly of its own. Until yesterday, I never knew myself. I had allowed my vanity to lead me and to let me think ill of a decent man simply because he had offended me. I then believed I was right and justified because I usually *am* right about people. I suppose it amused me to take such a sensational dislike to so consequential a man as Mr Darcy. I had never known myself to be so vulnerable to my own feelings. How am I ever to be sure of not erring so dangerously again?"

"Well, we never can be sure, my dear. I trust you have put a great deal of thought into the matter. I know you, Lizzy, and I should be very surprised if another were ever able to deceive you again so easily. In addition, it seems you have gained for yourself a very wise and valuable ally." Mrs Gardiner allowed a small mischievous smile to play upon her lips.

Elizabeth reddened again. She looked down at the floor, mortified. Mrs Gardiner turned a questioning gaze on Jane.

"Do not worry, Aunt," Jane consoled her, an unusually impish expression on her face. "Lizzy is only embarrassed to admit that she thinks Mr Darcy the handsomest man of her acquaintance!"

Elizabeth turned scandalized eyes on her sister. "Jane!"

Jane was enjoying the opportunity to torment her sister for a change. "They do dance very well together, Aunt. It caused a stir indeed when Mr Darcy singled her out over everyone, but as Charlotte Lucas says, he has always looked her direction a good deal when they are in public."

Elizabeth scowled, but would not allow Jane to defeat her at her own game. "And how would you know this, Miss Jane? Your eyes have only been on Mr Bingley since the day he arrived in town!"

"Girls!" Mrs Gardiner quelled them, looking shocked. Jane and Elizabeth both began to laugh, Elizabeth's embarrassment temporarily banished. "Jane," Mrs Gardiner turned to her left, with a bluntness only she could get away with. "How do matters stand with Mr Bingley? Your mother is making quite a fuss about him. I should like to know the truth of the matter."

It was Jane's turn to blush, but she managed to share with her aunt the details of her understanding with Mr Bingley. Elizabeth arched her eyebrows and pursed her lips playfully, forcing Jane also to confess that she fully returned Mr Bingley's regard, and was in fact very pleased.

Aunt Gardiner seemed satisfied. "I have not yet received word back from your Uncle, though I should have expected that if a letter were to come, we might have word here as soon as tomorrow. I know he will want to come to us as soon as possible, Jane. Then your Mr Bingley can speak to him to obtain his conditional blessing. You said, I think Lizzy, that you are expecting your father to recover soon? Perhaps we will not need your Uncle's blessing after all."

She smiled sweetly at her girls. "Now, my dears, I should like to take a short rest before tea, but Lizzy," she leveled a gaze at her niece, "I wish to find time to speak with you privately at some point before your dinner guests begin to arrive."

Fifteen

Colonel Fitzwilliam lounged comfortably in Bingley's parlor, as far from Miss Bingley and as near Georgiana as he could situate himself. Georgiana's tiny pink tongue peeked over her lower lip as she tried to master a tricky new embroidery stitch she had learned just before leaving London. Miss Bingley assiduously praised her labors, while attempting nothing of the kind herself. Mrs Hurst was reading her correspondence while her husband snored placidly beside her.

Fitzwilliam had tried to content himself with watching Georgiana, but a minute whiff of air behind him kept tickling his neck. "Darcy, *do* sit down!" he finally snapped. He craned his head to stare down his restless cousin, who had been pacing the floor for the last ten minutes.

Bingley looked up from the fire he had been stoking with a bemused expression. "It is just as I have said before. There is no more awful object than Darcy on a lazy afternoon when he has nothing to do."

"Indeed, but normally he just sits as a great black cloud in the corner of a room with a book in his hand."

Darcy's gaze switched to his cousin and sister. Wordlessly, he stooped to resume his seat. Before he could regain it, Miss Bingley's voice chimed in. "I do *so* sympathize, Mr Darcy! Truly, one feels restless when the weather is so unpromising. You know how I ad*ore* a lovely stroll out of doors! It is not as though we can plan a great deal of entertainment either, what with such a *te*dious evening to look forward to."

She frowned, then rounded on her sister. "Louisa, would you favour us all with some music? We could all do with a diversion, and does not dancing sound lovely?" She rose, extending her arm expectantly to an

156

unwilling Darcy. He could not refuse her gracefully. "Brother, Miss Georgiana, will you join us?"

Georgiana shrank a little. Bingley crossed his arms, hovering resolutely by the fireplace with a defiant look toward his sister. Smilingly, the Colonel offered Georgiana his hand. Mrs Hurst opened the instrument and began a lively tune, to which the two present couples commenced to dance.

Darcy could not keep his eyes on his partner, hard as that lady was obviously trying to attract his notice. As they passed during the dance, her hands grasped his a little too warmly, lingering a little too long; his thoughts, however, were miles away... three miles, to be precise. With his mind so occupied, the dance passed in blissful oblivion.

As soon as Mrs Hurst plucked the last bar, and before Miss Bingley could request another song, he firmly disengaged himself. "Excuse me, there is a matter I promised to attend to, and I ought to do it before I retire to dress." He left the room briskly, leaving the knowing smiles of Georgiana and Colonel Fitzwilliam in his wake.

Frustrated, Caroline flopped back into her seat with a petulant frown. Mrs Hurst began to rise, but the Colonel petitioned her to remain at the instrument. "Come, Georgie, I will teach you to dance the reel. William would certainly mock my taste, but here is not here to disapprove for a few moments." He winked at his young cousin and drew her into a lively spin, evoking a girlish squeal of delight.

Bingley chuckled to himself. He had a sneaking suspicion that Darcy would not disapprove of the reel so heartily as the colonel suggested, if only a certain dark-haired lass were present to partner with.

~

Wickham had spent his day quietly observing the town of Meryton. Gathering information without attracting undue attention to himself was the object of his current occupation. One thing he had ascertained was that Colonel Forster had someone perpetually at his heels.

The current tail was young Marshall, nonchalantly standing about twenty paces away, but glancing his direction a little too often. Forster had indeed listened to Fitzwilliam, but he might have used more experienced spies. Wickham would have little trouble disappearing if need be.

Currently he amused himself by listening to a few of the young shoppers outside the millinery. He recognized one of them as the niece of Mrs Long, a particular friend of Mrs Bennet, so he attended the girl's conversations with interest. As he might have suspected, there was a good deal of chatter about the Bennet family, particularly that saucy Miss Elizabeth.

Wickham smirked a little. Despite how her modesty had led her to demur during their conversation, the lady's discomfiture over the town's presumption of her engagement to Darcy had been clearly evident. In short, she was furious, and she despised the man. The more he thought about it, the more firmly he concluded that Darcy may have finally bitten off more than he could chew. If there was one thing Wickham understood, it was how to read a woman. He grinned a little to himself. This particular woman possessed the unique ability to make his old companion miserable.

Little Elizabeth Bennet was more clever and more spirited than most, but ultimately she was naive and sheltered, just as society demanded of a maiden. She had swallowed his charmingly woven tale hook, line, and sinker, and he had no doubt the lady was firmly on his side of matters. *How clever of me to have early engaged her sympathies!*

Though he had never formed designs on Miss Elizabeth's person- could not have afforded to have- he had been delighted to make an ally where Darcy had made an enemy. In addition, she was well respected in the little community. Securing her good opinion of him had bought him introductions to many of the better houses in Meryton. Of course, as an officer of the regiment, he was automatically welcome in most drawing rooms, but his gambling habits often lost him their favour quickly. Miss Elizabeth's staunch friendship had resulted in protracted sympathies toward him from the general populace.

He had not been surprised to note, on more than one occasion, his old companion's gaze lingering on the Hertfordshire beauty. Any man could see her appeal, but, though for different reasons, Darcy could not afford her any more than he himself could. It had never truly occurred to him that Darcy might become entangled with the little spitfire.

In digging a little more deeply than most, he had uncovered the rumours that Darcy had acted to interrupt that parson's proposal. He knew his old friend too well, however, to attribute purely selfless motives to Fitzwilliam George Richard Darcy. The man had lost his head over a pert smile and a pair of sparkling eyes.

What luck for me! Somehow he sensed that there was an advantage to be exploited here. Colonel Fitzwilliam, ever Darcy's pet, had been willing to pay handsomely for him to stay away. If so much was offered so easily, more was most certainly available if he made them desperate. Darcy evidently wanted to purchase his silence.

Aha… a pleasing idea came to him. *Georgiana.* A slow smile spread over his face. Darcy would never have dared breathe a word of Georgiana's little indiscretions to anyone but Fitzwilliam, and he certainly would shield that precious little brat from the wild Bennet family. That information was a bombshell, one he believed he could set off right in the middle of Darcy's plans for domestic felicity. *The old sod, he's gone romantic.*

Miss Elizabeth was the key. He sensed in her a tendency to flaunt convention, but she was still a lady. She could not afford to associate with a fallen woman such as Georgiana Darcy, and she already had a low opinion of the family to start with. All he truly needed to do was succeed in turning her suspicions against the little heiress, a job which was already half done. If he could discredit Georgiana openly in Miss Bennet's face, but not so irreparably that a few well-placed words and perhaps an offer of marriage would not restore her respectability.... Darcy would pay a small fortune to both protect his sister and win the affections of his fair lady.

If that failed... well, there were still other options.

~

"Now, Lizzy," Mrs Gardiner instructed her niece, "In the quarter hour before your company arrive, I want you to tell me everything you have not yet told me about Mr Darcy, Mr Collins, Jane, Mr Bingley, and your father."

Elizabeth's downcast visage became overspread with a sly look. "That is a tall order, Aunt. Would you like me to take breaths between my sentences, or merely to wave my hands as punctuation?"

Mrs Gardiner laughed lightly. "First, perhaps we should discuss your papa. You mentioned his nurse. Has he had a doctor?"

"No, Mrs Cooper's husband is normally the nearest doctor, and her son as well, but they have been away in London. She expects them back by tomorrow. Our apothecary has been tending to him, but both assure me that at present, there is little a doctor could do for Papa. He does appear to be mending a little every day."

"That is good news. While I am sure your uncle will arrive as soon as possible to lend whatever aid necessary, of course we would all prefer to see your papa up and well again. Are there any immediate concerns for the estate?"

Elizabeth sighed. "One of the tenant families, the Browns, may have to remove. I have been taking baskets to them for a while- in fact I should have gone this morning. Their need has become rather great, for Mr Brown had a terrible accident behind his plow last spring. Both his legs were broken and a few ribs. Mr Jones has seen him and believes in some time he may recover, but never with his full strength, as the bones in one leg did not set at all properly. He has a wife and three young children to support, so naturally he wishes to keep his lease and farm again next year. At present, I do not think he can possibly continue."

"You would not bring such a concern up to me without already having thought of a solution. What do you propose, Lizzy?"

Elizabeth gave a little chuckle. "You mistake me Aunt, for in this situation I have not an answer. You know Papa has long done without a steward, as he knows as much about managing an estate as anyone. I know he wished to spare the rather large expense, but under such circumstances, I wish he had retained someone."

"It is a pity you are the only other person in your family with any experience at all in these matters," Mrs Gardiner mused. "You did mention your papa seems to be recovering. Is this not an issue that can wait some weeks until he has regained his faculties?"

Elizabeth shook her head sorrowfully. "Papa was just talking to me about it a few days ago, saying that if something is not changed soon, the family will rapidly become destitute beyond recovery. They are already in dire straits, as he was unable to farm at all this year. Many of his neighbours took pity and lent what aid they could, but his rent is very far behind and they have become almost entirely dependent upon charity.

"By rights, Papa should have evicted them long ago, but you know Papa. He would not do such a thing in the middle of winter, and to Mr Brown! He has always been such a good tenant. I wish Papa had not put off managing the situation though, for now I do not know what to do."

Mrs Gardiner pursed her lips thoughtfully. "If I were you, Lizzy, I would seek more experienced advice. You have, if I am not mistaken, not one but two estate owners coming to dine this evening. Why not put the question to them?"

Elizabeth stiffened. "Surely, Aunt, that is not necessary!"

"Why not?" Mrs Gardiner asked reasonably. "Mr Darcy is, as I have said, well respected in Lambton. Those are not London society folk there, you know, but simple farmers and tradesmen, just like here in Meryton. They would be quick enough to cast aspersions on his character if he were known to mistreat his tenants. Surely he has had experience in circumstances such as these. If the situation must be remedied soon, it seems you have a ready counselor at hand."

Elizabeth pouted a little. "Your answer is far too practical for my taste, Aunt. Of course, you are right, but I am not comfortable turning to him for advice under our present circumstances."

"And just what, may I ask, are those circumstances?" Mrs Gardiner flashed her niece a cunning expression. "You have told me all of the events which occurred, but you have not spoken of your revised opinion of the gentleman."

"I am not sure I have one yet. For nearly all of the little time I have spent in his company, I was operating under a false impression of him. I now know him to be a good and decent man. I still believe him to be arrogant, although Jane defends him by saying he is mostly shy. I find that a difficult assessment to agree with, as he is a man who has lived and moved a great deal in the world. I think it more likely that he feels he is above his company."

Mrs Gardiner nodded. "I would not be surprised at that. You know your uncle does business with many from the best circles, and they are a privileged set. I would expect anyone born to such a situation should have a touch of pride."

"I do not accept that excuse, Aunt. His friend Mr Bingley, as you will see, is quite affable. I think, by the way, that Jane has done very well and they will be very happy together. Back to the point, however; I do not believe the advantages of birth give one the right to be proud and disdainful of others."

"I do not defend it, Lizzy, I only say that the attitude is very likely what he was taught from his infancy and you should not immediately condemn the man for it. From what I hear, Jane's Mr Bingley had quite a more modest background. And you know, you do not make allowances for differences of temperament. Not all would enjoy the attention which naturally comes as a part of Mr Darcy's wealth and situation."

Elizabeth laughed. "Now it is you who begin to sound like Jane!" She shook her head gently. "It seems all of my dearest confidantes are in a conspiracy to convince me to like Mr Darcy!"

"Well, then, you do know what they say about that! Perhaps we are all of the same mind, in that we wish to see you happy and in a good situation. It seems that at present your respectability depends upon your going through with the engagement, however unconventional its beginnings."

"With a man I hardly know? I do not see how that can bring me happiness. I concede fully that he is a good and honourable man, but I still do not believe his temperament and mine could be compatible. I do not wish..." she looked to her aunt with some embarrassment, "...I do not wish to have the sort of marriage my parents have, where neither party is able to love or respect the other. That cannot be agreeable to either partner."

Mrs Gardiner gave her niece a sympathetic smile. "All is not yet lost, Lizzy. Let us see him tonight and give him a chance. Perhaps after the two of you know each other a little better, his manners may be softened. Who knows? Perhaps he may decide you are too opinionated for his taste, pay you a handsome settlement, and set you free," she finished with a wink.

Elizabeth chuckled lightly at her aunt's joke. "I think I can safely say that Mr Darcy is already well aware of my stubborn opinions, Aunt! In this, I am quite certain that he is likely the only man of my acquaintance who is at least as obstinate as I."

"Well, then, I will look forward to this evening with great interest! And now I think we must repair downstairs, as I believe I hear a carriage turning

161

in the drive. Shall we, my dear?"

Caroline Bingley sat impassively gazing out the window as the carriage approached Longbourn. They had been obliged by their numbers to take two carriages for comfort, and Caroline had made absolutely certain that she was in the same carriage as the Darcy siblings. Colonel Fitzwilliam, who had been following behind Georgiana, had abruptly changed course to take the other conveyance.

Despite the rapidly cooling weather, Mr Darcy had insisted that the coach travel with the shades open, and Caroline had quickly seconded his opinion. She shivered a little now, wondering what the man was about. *He has taken leave of his senses! Perhaps he ought to be examined by a doctor after all.*

She glanced at him, taking in the clenched jaw and the restless fingers drumming on his knee. *I have never seen him do that before. Such a crude mannerism, and from Mr Darcy!* His eyes were resolutely fixed on the house they approached, and he either did not or would not notice her doting look.

If only we could get back to London! Caroline knew that her brother still had business needing his personal attention, but he had so far shown no desire to resume his plans to return. Always in the past she had scorned the business which Charles had inherited from their father. It was a tangible reminder of their embarrassing connections to the manufacturing trade, and his affairs had more than once interrupted her social plans.

This time, however, she was most eager for the disruption. All of her attempts to make Charles remember his place had been brushed aside. By slipping quickly into his study earlier in the afternoon, she had even found a letter from his attorney indicating the man's willingness to come to Netherfield, so Bingley's business might be concluded without travel. Her last hope for immediate removal from this barbaric place was blasted.

Perhaps… a thought began to brew in her mind. She was in charge of organizing this ridiculous tenant's reception, after all. She could well invite whom she saw fit, could she not? Certainly a group of farmers would provide rather tedious company for the occupants of Netherfield. All that was really required for *them* was a decent meal and the gift basket Charles had insisted upon, which the cook could organize. If Caroline Bingley had to entertain, she would have quality guests and would do so in style. Then Darcy would be forced to acknowledge her qualities!

Caroline grimaced a little, seeing Darcy turn to his sister to help her get ready to disembark from the coach. Poor, dear Georgiana looked so cold!

To think of how he was treating his young sister with this sham of an engagement! The girl would be the darling of the *ton* once she was out, and Caroline had always had every intention of being the one to guide her amidst the swirling circles of society's finest and richest families. What harm would she suffer in her first season in the *ton* if her brother, one of the most sought-after bachelors in England, married an unsophisticated country nobody?

Elizabeth Bennet knew nothing of society, could certainly not advise a highly celebrated debutante as Miss Georgiana Darcy surely would be. Not only would the connection bring no material advantages to the girl, but her respectability among the best circles would be tainted. A sister-in-law whose family owned a warehouse in Cheapside! The best young men would not even call upon even Miss Darcy with such a stain upon her account.

Fortunately, there was still time to stop this charade. Who were the people of Meryton, after all? Miss Elizabeth Bennet's acquaintances, nothing more. No one of any real import was aware of all of this gossip yet; it was not likely that the rumours would follow Darcy to London or that anyone would credit them as true if they did. Surely all could still be silenced quickly with the right measures taken.

Sixteen

Bingley stepped into the Bennet's parlour and immediately his gaze sought his sweet Jane's. Her eyes were already on him as he entered, and she favoured him with the most stunning smile he had ever seen. *And this, the pleasure which will be mine every day!* Nowhere did there exist a more beautiful woman, he assured himself. Jane's beauty was not confined only to her lovely features, but was magnified and enhanced by her gentle spirit and cheerful nature.

Bingley knew he did not possess a deep and intricate character, such as his friend Darcy, but he felt none the poorer for it. He never presumed to be a difficult man to understand or please, and in all truth could have contented himself with any one of several women he had encountered. However, after meeting Jane Bennet, whose character was so very like his own, he began to understand the difference between blasé contentment and true belonging.

With her, he had discovered such an affinity of mind as he had never known possible. Within a very few moments after meeting her, he had found her to be kind and serene, not given to the manufacture of anxiety or strife. How refreshing her company was to him! He was hopelessly drawn to her beauty immediately, but the last weeks had afforded him an even better knowledge of her.

It was true that she was shy, and little given to demonstrative expression of her feelings, but she had gradually unfurled her full radiance to his approving eyes. She owned the most generous, loving nature he had ever known. He never heard her speak ill of anyone, and within a short time he discovered that was not disguise on her part, but a true depiction of her shining character. She could express disapproval; she was not deficient in discernment, but never did slanderous speech cross her lips.

Bingley had grown up with a critical family, and had seen the needless strife it caused. His father had been much like he himself was; open and carefree, a cheerful and engaging man who avoided conflict and unpleasantness whenever possible. He was not naïve, could not have been a successful businessman had he been, but like his son, Steven Bingley had been an incurable optimist. A marriage of convenience brought him a sizeable dowry with which to expand his business, but it had not brought love.

Lucinda Bingley had desired wealth and connection, and had never been able to forgive her older brother for marrying beneath himself and ruining her own chances for a better marriage. She endlessly picked at her husband, whose untroubled nature carelessly shrugged off his wife's malcontentedness. Charles, as the youngest, had come along at a time when his father had all but withdrawn to his work and the out of doors in self-defence. The son had spent most of his time following his father's example.

Until he met Jane Bennet, he had only aspired to a marriage with a woman of beauty and some accomplishment. In addition to these qualities, which she possessed in abundance, Jane brought a genuine kindness he had never dared hope to find. His heart swelled with joyful appreciation as she performed her curtsey and gave him a secret smile. He returned it and had to stop himself from taking his rightful place by her side. Their engagement was not yet official, and he did not wish to cause her any distress.

He continued his greetings to the rest of the family, noting vaguely that an answering spark of intelligence flickered in Miss Elizabeth's eyes. A little extra measure of warmth lit her expression and firmed her hand clasp. Perhaps her happiness over her sister's engagement would make things easier on Darcy this evening! He smiled winsomely at his future sister and was introduced to their aunt with pleasure.

~

Elizabeth greeted Georgiana with genuine affection, taking great delight in introducing her to her Aunt Gardiner. The latter's gentle ways quickly set the girl at her ease, and Elizabeth was at liberty to shift her eyes to the older brother.

Darcy's expressive gaze lingered on her a little longer than strictly proper, but he met her aunt with perfect equanimity. His measured and controlled demeanour was firmly back in place, but she was surprised at the lack of officiousness in his attitude. Her eyebrows rose as she watched him taking pains to get to know her aunt, facilitating discourse between Mrs Gardiner and Georgiana.

As all settled into comfortable conversation, Elizabeth turned to find Caroline Bingley at her side. "My dear Eliza, I hear congratulations are in order," she was sweetly intoning, with a larger-than-life smile plastered across her face.

Elizabeth fought an unaccustomed tremour of nervousness as she inclined her head politely. Of all the responses she had rehearsed for herself on this trying evening, she had not yet hit upon an honest way to answer Caroline Bingley. The best she could think of was a wordless acknowledgement of the statement. It was true the rumour was afoot, but she would not confess to more at this point.

That Miss Bingley was insanely jealous went without saying. Elizabeth could not help a miniscule flutter of victory at having unwittingly gained what Miss Bingley had been long angling for. *That,* she scolded herself, *is uncharitable. I have done nothing to earn the distinction of a proposal by Mr Darcy. Surely he only acted on a chivalrous impulse and likely regrets his actions by now!* Caroline might yet gain the point in seeing her not wed to Mr Darcy, although it was doubtful she would ever find herself so honoured instead. Elizabeth forced her feelings into a cheerful façade and tactfully turned the subject.

"I understand from Mr Bingley that you are presently organizing a reception for the tenants of Netherfield. Your party will be very well received indeed, as they have been largely without any sort of recognition from the Hall these three or four years."

Miss Bingley's expression cooled. "Yes, indeed. Charles feels it necessary to reward the farmers for… well, whatever it is they do. I am sure they will be most pleased by his condescension, as he has arranged a very generous gift for each family."

Elizabeth's eyes began to sparkle as she identified a weakness. "Oh, I am certain they will very much enjoy his gift! Mr Bingley is all that is generous and good. Do you know, I find that regardless of whatever gifts we give our tenants, what they tend to look forward to the most is the fall festival here on our lawn. It is most definitely the highlight of the harvest season!"

Miss Bingley's eyes sharpened upon her companion. "Well, of course, Netherfield can afford to be more generous with the tenant gifts than a smaller estate such as yours." She sniffed. "I am most certain that, though Charles chooses to host an event anyway, our tenants will need no further consolation than his rather generous basket."

"Indeed? When your Mrs Nicholls called on our own Mrs Hill today she went away intending to include almost the very same items we always give. I declare, you must have had some wonderful ideas of your own to add. I do hope you will share your thoughts?"

Caroline wavered between haughty disdain and mortification at discovery. "You cannot mean that you take a personal interest? A competent cook and housekeeper ought to be more than capable of assembling such a simple thing!"

Elizabeth smiled pertly. "Of course, I trust that I am in Mrs Hill's way more often than not, but it is my good fortune that she tolerates my interference. I have come to care a great deal for our tenants, which permits me personal knowledge of each family's needs."

Caroline lifted her nose fractionally. "Indeed you must spend a great deal of time on such pursuits. I commend you, Miss Eliza. It must be difficult to find time to tend your own affairs. It is fortunate that in a retiring, quiet community such as this, it is not so critical for ladies to always appear in the latest fashions. The gentlemen here cannot possibly have such discriminating taste as those in Town."

Much to Caroline's surprise, Elizabeth actually laughed. "It is true, Miss Bingley, that we mere country lasses do not dress so finely as the ladies of London! However, in my experience, it seems that the gentlemen of the countryside place a greater emphasis on a woman's pleasing manners and robust health, a natural consequence of spending a great deal of time out of doors. Do you not agree Colonel?" Elizabeth turned a devilish smirk to Fitzwilliam, who had been standing nearby with a fresh drink in his hand.

"I dare not contradict you, Miss Elizabeth," he winked and raised his glass to her. "In fact, present company considered, I would say you have ample evidence to the proof of your theory."

Elizabeth inclined her head graciously, enjoying the sight of Caroline Bingley fuming beside her. Darcy chose that moment to extricate himself from Mrs Gardiner and Georgiana, who were conversing pleasantly. He had overheard a good bit of their conversation and could not resist drawing near. He stepped to her side with a quirked brow, and for a shared heartbeat two pairs of eyes laughingly met one another. Elizabeth took a quick breath and returned her countenance to a carefully neutral expression.

"Miss Bingley," Fitzwilliam bowed in that lady's direction, "may I assist you to a drink before dinner? Mrs Bennet keeps an excellent sideboard." He crooked his arm to an unwilling Caroline, and she found one of her own favourite ploys turned against her. Fitzwilliam led her reluctantly away, casting a brief glance of martyrdom over his shoulder.

Darcy could not help a light chuckle under his breath. Fitzwilliam might well play the martyr, for he was not only shepherding Caroline Bingley away from him, but he also was moving to engage Mrs Bennet, leaving Charles and his Jane free. Shaking his head, he determined that he would never, ever complain about Richard helping himself to his purse whenever he saw fit. Still smiling, he turned his gaze to his own lady, finding her bright eyes resting on him and full of sceptical curiosity. Darcy cleared his throat uncomfortably. "May I ask, Miss Elizabeth, how does your father today?"

"He is a little better, sir. Mrs Cooper's opinion is that he is recovering rather well. I truly must thank you again," she added with sincerity, "for thinking of sending for her. Her presence has been most welcome to us at this time."

"I am very glad to hear it. I most earnestly wish to be of service to you and your family in any way I can." He paused, admiring the modest blush and the lowered lashes as they shaded her cheeks.

Daringly, he proceeded again, his voice lowered for her ears alone. "Miss Elizabeth, I will be frank. I am not well schooled in the arts of conversation, and you will likely find me too forward and blunt. However, I was hoping to secure an opportunity to speak with you in private for at least a few minutes, at your earliest convenience. We left things rather... unsettled yesterday, and it is my fervent wish to come to a better understanding between us."

Her eyes lifted again, an expression of wonder shining from them. *Indeed, he is blunt!* If anyone had told her to expect the staid and reserved Mr Darcy of her first acquaintance to consistently speak in such a forthright fashion, she would have laughed the notion off as ridiculous. Surely he knew that private conversations between unmarried people must be delicately managed and discretely chaperoned, yet he boldly asked again for that privilege.

Tilting her head, she considered his request for only an instant before responding. They had already shared more than one private conference, and in the eyes of others her honour was already committed. In truth, she found his naked hope refreshing. Giving a slow nod of assent, she reflected on how much more efficiently their situation might be resolved without the pretense of bland, socially correct conversation.

A small breath of relief escaped him. "Thank you," he managed. He was about to ask her when she would agree to meet with him when the dinner bell sounded in the parlour. Turning, he automatically proffered his arm. Elizabeth hesitated only a second, taking it with a shy smile and unconsciously fluttering lashes. *My word, she is lovely!* A broad smile lit his features and his chest swelled proudly at the honour of escorting her.

Glancing over his shoulder, he suddenly remembered his manners. "Mrs Gardiner? May I escort you as well?" He glanced to Georgiana with the smallest look of apology, one he knew she would understand. She grinned encouragingly at him as she accepted Mr Hurst's other arm and fell in behind them.

Mrs Gardiner graciously accepted his escort and the threesome followed Fitzwilliam with Mrs Bennet and Miss Bingley into the dining room. Mrs Gardiner carried herself with humble dignity, and Darcy was greatly impressed with her unassuming, amiable manner. *What a genteel lady she is! I can easily see where Elizabeth learned much of her grace and comportment… sadly it was not from her mother!* Darcy reflected on his pleased acquaintanceship with this elegant lady and what a fine influence she might be for Georgiana. *And this is the relation I once disdained for her situation in trade!*

Not for the first time since meeting Elizabeth Bennet, he found all his former notions of civility turned upside down. Not only was he perfectly delighted with this woman's conversation and manners, he wished to know more of her and her family. She had mentioned to him when they were first introduced that she had grown up in Lambton, and had even had the pleasure of meeting his mother once, many years ago. He appreciated that her information was given politely, with discretion, not as a blaring demand for recognition as many others might have done. He began to think that, perhaps, not *all* of Elizabeth's relatives were embarrassing.

Once into the dining room, his confidence began to flag. Where should he sit? Would it be too audacious to assume a seat near Elizabeth? If he were to take Richard's advice, he should seat himself near Mrs Bennet. A sudden nervousness caused him to tense until his eyes fell upon the table. Mrs Bennet had used place cards for the night! Stepping round the table, he was delighted to discover that his name appeared between Elizabeth's and Mrs Gardiner's. His happy gaze flew to Elizabeth's face, noting her shrewd smile.

He helped Mrs Gardiner into her chair first, then Elizabeth. As he bent low over her neck, admiring her curls once again, he murmured into her ear, "The cards are most helpful. Your handiwork, I presume?"

She tilted her head slightly, responding under her breath. "Jane's, actually. You know Jane always wishes for peace and harmony. I, on the other hand, tend to enjoy a good row on occasion, and might have seated you betwixt Miss Bingley and my mother!"

A look of horror crossed his face before he could quite squelch it, but the effect on Elizabeth was enchanting. She laughed merrily, with a small wink which he was quite certain she had never bestowed upon him before, and may have even been unconsciously done.

He broke into a relaxed grin. "Then Miss Bennet has my eternal gratitude. Not that I object to knowing your mother better, but I fear my meager dialogue skills are woefully inadequate for her liking."

Elizabeth laughed again, her dark eyes flashing, fully ensnaring him under her spell. "Mr Darcy, I believe you give yourself too little credit! I have had the pleasure of debating you on subjects of interest, and have not found you deficient. Indeed, you ought very much to enjoy getting to know my father better, once he is recovered, for he loves a spirited debate as dearly as I do."

A flush of pleasure tingled through him. By her own admission, she had not only assured him that he had the capacity to please her, but that she expected him to be around to spend time with her father! He wondered if her words had been intentionally chosen to grant him such confidence. By the sudden shift in demeanour he witnessed, he guessed it was not so, but her words thrilled him nonetheless.

Elizabeth quickly hid her fading smile behind a glass of claret. Casting about for some way of retrieving her good humour, he returned to the subject of her father. "I have, in fact, had the opportunity to speak with your father at great length. I met him out riding the other morning before his unfortunate accident. I found him to be a wealth of knowledge, as a matter of fact. We talked for some time and with great pleasure before parting company."

Elizabeth could not hide her surprise. "Truly? I had no idea. We knew very little of that morning's events, and Papa is not normally inclined to morning rides. Was it very early?"

He gave a short, silent laugh. The sentiments of the desperate man who took that wild ride and the hopeful one who sat at dinner this evening were so radically different that it seemed an age ago. "Yes, we rode some time before we watched the sun rise over Oakham Mount together. It is a lovely place. Your father mentioned that you have a special attachment to it."

She fixed him with a pensive little smile. "Yes," she replied slowly. "I have. It *is* a lovely place, affording an excellent view of the brash young horsemen from Town galloping across Purvis Lodge's fields."

He started. She had seen him, even before they had ever met at the Assembly? Of course, the interest their arrival generated would have fixed his and Bingley's identity in her memory as the future denizens of the vacant Hall nearby. He smiled at her confession of an early notice of him, enjoying her laughing eyes sparkling back at him.

With a tight yet emboldened smile, he turned his attention to the rest of the table. It would not do to ignore everyone else entirely! He noted that prudent Jane had seated herself and Charles on either side of Mrs Bennet, trusting in Charles' affability to defuse any improper behaviour from the matron of the house. Mrs Gardiner sat between himself and Bingley, near enough to assist in diverting Mrs Bennet.

To the other side of Elizabeth was Georgiana, and beyond her Kitty, then Lydia Bennet. Next to Jane, opposite Mrs Gardiner and Darcy were the Hursts. Richard found himself squarely between Mrs Hurst and Caroline, with silent Mary Bennet next to the latter. Richard appeared less than enthusiastic about the situation until he realized that Georgiana was near. Lydia Bennet also was not far away at the end of the table, and more than welcomed his frivolous attentions. Darcy relaxed, fully appreciating Jane Bennet's wisdom and looking forward to a pleasant evening.

~

Dinner did indeed pass pleasantly. Elizabeth had approached the event with much trepidation, but all her worry was for naught. Darcy had proven a surprisingly conversant dinner companion, both with herself and her aunt. Still labouring under her earlier impressions of him, she had truly been expecting him to shun her wonderful aunt's company. Instead, he had purposely engaged Mrs Gardiner, leaving Elizabeth free to get to know Georgiana better.

The girl appeared much recovered after her shock from the day before. Her spirits had returned, and she chattered delightfully with both Elizabeth and Kitty, and even Lydia when the latter was ignored by the handsome colonel. The younger girls enthusiastically mined her for information on the latest London fashions. Georgiana, for her part, verily sparkled with glee at the rare opportunity to speak with such unpretentious girls of her own age.

Elizabeth remarked to herself that Kitty was more reserved than normal, and that her hazel eyes flicked uncertainly between Georgiana and her own sister Lydia. Hope began to bud in Elizabeth's breast. Perhaps all was not lost for Kitty, if she was beginning to uncomfortably take note of the contrast between raucous Lydia and graceful Georgiana. She pursed her lips and decided to encourage that friendship.

Elizabeth's gaze swept the table. Jane was taking pains to become better acquainted with Louisa Hurst, and her efforts were beginning to bear fruit. Mr Hurst even found himself capable of responding to Jane's sweet cheer and thoughtful conversation. Elizabeth smothered a proud smile. Leave it to Jane to discover even in Mr Hurst a pleasant dinner companion!

Mary and Caroline Bingley had less than nothing to say to one another, ensuring quiet from that region of the table, although Mary gazed rather steadily at Georgiana. Caroline's attempts to control the conversations of others nearby were diligently thwarted by Colonel Fitzwilliam at every turn. Elizabeth felt a true regard for Darcy's cousin as she observed his cool dismissal of Miss Bingley and his careful manipulation of Lydia from across the table. The man was masterful! *Had he been the one to speak for me, I doubt I should have even objected!*

Her thoughts seized. Perhaps… Colonel Fitzwilliam was not shy about his lack of wealth. As he had hinted once the day before, he would need to marry a woman of fortune to maintain the lifestyle to which he had been brought up. She did not fit that criteria; nor seemed the colonel capable of a violent enough attachment, as far as she could tell, to overcome such a difficulty. As she had once reflected to herself regarding Wickham, a marriage of only tolerable felicity could turn sour quickly if a couple had not the proper resources to live as they were accustomed. Darcy certainly had that, and then some.

A conviction began to turn in her bosom. It was not Darcy's resources which began to improve her opinion of him. Though he was more recalcitrant than his cheerful cousin, there was a depth to Darcy that she felt she had only begun to plumb. As a student of characters, she had discovered early on that he was an interesting puzzle. How she could have misconstrued some of the most basic elements of his character, she still could not fathom, but the more she learned of him, the more fascinating he became.

He engaged her quite frequently over dinner in discussions of her favourite books and plays. She found they both favoured Milton, as well as Scott and Donne. She brought up the works of Byron, and Darcy made a face. Surprised, she asked, "Do you not like his works? I should have thought you might."

"His work is, I grant you, superior enough. His character I cannot abide. The man is a blackguard and a wastrel. A more unprincipled, hedonistic degenerate I never wish to encounter."

Elizabeth arched her brows, surprised almost beyond words that Darcy would excoriate the celebrated poet with even stronger language than he used for Wickham. "You know him?"

"Of course. We were at Cambridge together briefly, though we did not frequent the same circles. He came to me once to ask sponsorship for the publication of *English Bards*, though I expect he knew I would turn him down."

"May I ask, what is it about him you find so offensive?"

Darcy reddened, then lowered his voice. "I regret that I cannot relate more of my opinions in public, nor with an unmarried lady. It would be most unfitting, as there are some things I doubt your father would approve of me sharing with you."

Elizabeth cracked a sly smile in sudden comprehension. "And what, may I ask, do you think of Henry Fielding? I found *Tom Jones* to be excessively diverting!"

Darcy's face went ashen until he recognized her lilting drawl, a sure symptom of one of Elizabeth Bennet's infamous teases. Darting a quick glance around to make sure they had not been overheard, he leaned a little nearer. "I sincerely hope, Miss Elizabeth, that... *that* particular novel has not been a part of your repertoire!"

She chuckled, enjoying his discomfiture. "No, but I believe Papa has a copy somewhere. Would you like to borrow it, or do you already have your own? You seem familiar enough with it."

His eyes bulged, digesting this new side of the playful, yet heretofore entirely modest Elizabeth Bennet. She lifted her glass and sparkling eyes gazed at him contemplatively over the rim. *Daring. Oh, sweet Elizabeth, how I would enjoy lifting your veil of innocence! I feel beyond it lies a very passionate woman indeed.* A slow smile spread over his face. He could not disappoint her teasing provocation.

Not releasing her gaze for a second, he lowered his head, speaking nearly into her ear. "Indeed, I am familiar with the book. I have two copies; one in London and one at Pemberley- both gifts. I began to read it once but shelved it again, thinking it would be best to wait until I have an enchanting *wife* to read it with. It *is* rather comical, after all." He drew back, grinning roguishly. He fully enjoyed the effect on her flushed countenance, the scandalized but laughing eyes.

Elizabeth quickly brought her napkin to her lips to hide her guilty amusement. Mr Darcy had a sense of humour! Quite a wicked one as well, if she could believe her ears. She watched him nonchalantly take a sip of wine, smirking playfully back at her as he caught her gaze. He lowered his glass, smiling a little more placidly, then turned to answer a question from Mrs Gardiner.

Elizabeth felt her heart fluttering queerly. What a pleasant time she was having this night! Darcy had surpassed all her expectations as an agreeable companion. Why, the man *could* speak, and pleasantly, too! She had already known him to be well read, but that their tastes should match so exactly was a welcome surprise. She had anticipated that her little joke would entirely discompose him, but he had risen admirably to the challenge, parrying her playful jabs with a teasing thrust of his own. He had made it clear that he counted honour and integrity as paramount even in his choices of entertainment, but he was no stuffy prude.

Wonder at her new discovery held her silent for a few moments. Glancing to her left, she saw to her great satisfaction that Georgiana and Kitty were still busily engaged in chatter, with occasional input from Lydia. She nervously tossed the remaining ragout about her dish with her fork, her eyes rising across the table as she did so. Her little interchange with Darcy had not gone unnoticed. Caroline Bingley glowered icily, but Colonel Fitzwilliam tossed her a jaunty grin of encouragement.

Elizabeth smiled back to her plate. If she were to take her own former advice to herself regarding the opinions of people she trusted, she would side with the colonel. He seemed an honourable man, and he was clearly in favour of improving relations between herself and his cousin. Elizabeth's own rebellious nature reveled in the probability of perturbing Caroline Bingley with her efforts to warm to Darcy.

She glanced back to the tall gentleman by her side, who happened at that moment to be peeking at her. He flashed her yet another hopeful smile, revealing a tiny dimple she had somehow never noticed. In that moment,

Elizabeth made up her mind. She would give Fitzwilliam Darcy a chance to win her heart.

Seventeen

After dinner, the entire party adjourned to the sitting room together. It had seemed awkward for the ladies to separate from the gentlemen when the master of the house was unable to be in attendance. Mrs Bennet, who had been unable to shower her future son with her affections during dinner, shadowed Darcy as diligently as ever Caroline Bingley had. Caroline, at least, had discreetly distanced herself from Mrs Bennet, so he only had one challenging woman to cope with.

Elizabeth, who had been requested by her mother to serve the coffee, eyed him with some concern. She could not easily come to his rescue, nor was she quite certain she wished to. Though her sentiments had begun to sway in his favour, she honestly wanted to see how he conducted himself with her very trying mother.

Darcy was not insensitive to her attention as he attempted pleasantries with Mrs Bennet. The lady was enough in awe of him that she did not entirely monopolize the conversation, allowing him to distract her from her rather pointed questions about Bingley and her eldest daughter. His gaze returned occasionally to Elizabeth, finding her inscrutable eyes on him each time. After a decent interval, he bowed to Mrs Bennet, excusing himself.

He made his way to Elizabeth, extending his cup for her ministrations. She looked up to him with sly appraisal. Leaning fractionally closer, he murmured to her quietly, "How am I doing?"

Surprised conviction flashed across her face. "What can you mean, sir?"

"Come now, Miss Elizabeth, I know you are waiting for my horns to sprout! In truth, you have every reason to do so. I regret to admit that I

175

have been less than amiable since we first met. I hope I can remedy your first impressions of me."

She arched a brow, amused at his frankness. "I appreciate your candour, sir. However, if that be the case, and your sudden transformation is the result of a desire to improve my opinion of you, I wonder if the shift in your manner can be genuine?"

"And well you ought. I understand that you have little real knowledge of my character, and I respect your desire to remain circumspect for now. However," he gazed deeply into her chocolate brown eyes, his expression intently sincere, "disguise of every sort is my abhorrence. I am as you see me. Unfortunately, the pride you noted before is also a part of my character- one that I thought was under good regulation. You have taught me otherwise. I look forward, Miss Elizabeth, to whatever new revelations I may discover about myself under your tutelage."

Elizabeth stared back at him, her mouth slightly agape in astonishment. *My goodness, I have never heard a man speak as he does!* Her lips began to curl into a hesitant smile. The smile grew until it encompassed her whole expression, and a gentle laugh bubbled forth. She dropped her gaze, blushing furiously, and gave him a little nod of sweet surrender. Not sure of what to say in reply, she turned her attention to his cup- not allowing herself to flinch, however, when he let his fingers brush hers incidentally as she handed it back.

Darcy released a deep breath of satisfaction. His gamble had worked. He had spent the day pondering how best to approach her. He was not good with elaborate or subtle discourse. What he did possess was a blunt plainness, and he had hoped desperately that Elizabeth would be a woman who could appreciate fearless honesty. The surprised delight still glowing from her face assured him that his words had pleased her.

He dared not say more in the same vein while in company, but he no longer feared speaking to her. The thorns she had so carefully erected against him before seemed no longer in evidence. He was grateful he had said his peace quickly, for his attentions to Elizabeth could not go unremarked.

Caroline Bingley moved in their direction, making a great show of her empty coffee cup. She was followed doggedly by a very determined Georgiana. Intimidating Miss Bingley might be, but she was not about to allow her adored new friend and cherished brother's pleasant interlude to be completely disrupted!

Conversation waned, consisting mostly of the neighbourhood gossip and the weather. Darcy remarked that, though he had heard from a reliable source to expect a light winter in Hertfordshire this year, snow seemed likely within the next day or two. He and Elizabeth had exchanged an amused little smirk, and Georgiana giggled behind her hand. Caroline appeared mystified for a moment, but shifted the topics back to those in which she could take part. Her companions responded civilly to her comments, then gradually drifted away to other conversations as was suitable.

Darcy was keenly interested in learning more about Mrs Gardiner. Tactfully leaving Georgiana with Kitty and Mary Bennet, he moved in her direction. She was speaking animatedly to Bingley and the Hursts, and he stood where he could attend her words. A few moments later, Jane had a question for Louisa Hurst, and Darcy was left alone with Bingley and Mrs Gardiner.

For her part, Mrs Gardiner was pleased to have the two men who favoured her nieces to herself for a moment. She had begun to develop high opinions of both of them, and was in the way of thinking that her cherished girls had done well- very well, indeed.

Darcy in particular impressed her. His open earnestness appealed to her, though he did not speak as freely or as eloquently as his friend. She did not detect the haughtiness in his manner which had at first repelled Lizzy, but she did sense that the man might default to that posture when confronted with absurdity or banality. Her eyes flicked uncomfortably to her sister, who was energetically regaling Colonel Fitzwilliam with the local gossip. Yes, it was indeed understandable if the neighbourhood had at first taken the wrong impression of Mr Darcy.

Mrs Gardiner had no particular prejudice against the very rich, but she was not intimidated into obsequiousness either. She took Darcy as she found him, and decided that she agreed with what his reputation in Derbyshire had bespoken of him. He seemed a reasonable, sincere fellow, not given to flights of fancy or exaggeration.

He was clearly possessed of a keen mind and a thoughtful nature. She had the distinct impression that more went on in his head than he ever let on. *I can see why he might like Lizzy, she is not as easily seen through as most other young ladies. As for her, she might do very well with such a man*, she thought to herself. It was true he lacked Elizabeth's inimitable zest, but he was far from boring, and his acumen was very sharp. He would be a man her quick-witted niece could respect.

A swift intuition inspired her to maneuver the conversation back to Elizabeth. Her opportunity was perfect. Her reflections on her youth in Lambton and her mutual acquaintances with Darcy among the shopkeepers led to talk of a difficulty with one of his tenant farmers. Bingley interjected with an expression of woe, as he was still learning all the intricacies of being a landlord. Darcy nodded in commiseration, observing that a landlord's abilities at stewardship could make or break an entire community.

"That does remind me… I beg you would forgive my meddling, but Lizzy was mentioning to me some concerns they had. Unfortunately, Mr

Bennet is unable to tend his affairs at present, and Lizzy is worried for one of the families in the neighbourhood. Would you gentlemen find it possible to advise her?"

Both men perked up, Darcy in particular. "Lead on, good lady!" Bingley encouraged. "Let us hear what troubles her. Then Darcy will save the day, and I will learn how it is done!" He winked jovially at his friend. Darcy coloured a little, but he was in truth deeply interested in the matter. Elizabeth's potential as a mistress for Pemberley had of late become a subject of great curiosity for him. He was intrigued by her present situation, forcing her to manage affairs on her own, and he hoped fervently that he could be of help.

Mrs Gardiner conducted her little entourage across the room. Placing her hand gently on Lizzy's, she explained their purpose and how the subject had arisen. Elizabeth flashed a quick look of betrayal, but her aunt parried it with a stern expression. Sighing, she turned to the gentlemen and explained the situation with Mr Brown.

Darcy stroked his chin thoughtfully, his eyes unfocused as he listened to the story. Bingley watched Darcy, taking his cues from his more experienced friend. "Hmm, Miss Elizabeth, I do have one or two ideas I should like to discuss with you. I would like to hear more particulars of the case, and your opinions at length. Perhaps we could make a few suggestions to help you come to a decision. Would tomorrow morning, around ten, be convenient?"

Elizabeth blinked a little. A part of her had still anticipated the officious Master of Pemberley whom she had built up in her mind to expound on his condescending opinions, taking the matter effectively out of her hands. Instead she was pleasantly surprised to hear him carefully emphasizing his interest in her opinions and information. She nodded mutely, looking hesitantly to her aunt for her concurrence.

"Capital!" Bingley enthused. His own joy stemmed primarily from the very sound excuse for him and for Darcy to escape Netherfield without his sisters to visit his angel.

had just been manipulated by her innocent-looking aunt, and he did not wish Darcy watched Elizabeth's expression carefully. He sensed that clever Elizabeth to be party to anything which might distress or offend her. A little later, he was able to find out.

Bingley and Mrs Gardiner were drawn back into Mrs Bennet's web, affording him a precious few seconds to lean close to her ear. "I hope I have not overstepped my bounds, Miss Elizabeth. If you do not wish for my interference, please tell me so at once. I am, however, happy to be of service if I may."

She gazed up to him, fixing him with that meditative stare which she had worn much of the evening. She tilted her head, lips parted beguilingly. At length, after he had begun to shift his feet awkwardly, she made him an answer. "I thank you for your consideration, Mr Darcy. You have perplexed me greatly this night, I must say. I think it will do very well to have your thoughts on the matter. I yield to my aunt's wisdom; it is of course right and proper to seek the advice of someone more experienced than myself when a family's welfare is at stake, as is the case here. I look forward to your input."

He bowed graciously, glad to have once again seemingly judged her rightly. "I shall see you tomorrow morning, then. Perhaps, if it is amenable to you, we might walk out to meet the family in question, but I leave that to your discretion." She agreed, rewarding him with a sweet, if hesitant, smile and her thanks.

They had little opportunity for further discussion, and cards were out of the question, as Caroline, in a high dudgeon, had ordered the carriages unfortunately early. That lady blithely ignored the narrowed eyes and glowering expressions from many in her party.

She perfunctorily paid her compliments to her hostesses and propelled the Hursts to the first waiting carriage. She had been greatly snubbed by Eliza Bennet and largely ignored by the rest of the room, most especially Mr Darcy. In a silent huff, she vowed she would not remain a moment longer than strictly necessary. Not even attempting to finagle a way to ride with Mr Darcy, she ordered the driver to be off at once.

The remaining party from Netherfield shared frustrated expressions, but though they would have liked to have remained behind, it would have seemed awkward. Additionally, neither Darcy nor Bingley were in the habit of forcing their drivers to wait for them in the cold.

They made their polite farewells, with Bingley and Darcy lingering just a little behind the others in the foyer. Both wanted one last moment with their Bennet sister. Once her mother had retreated from sight, Jane shyly gave her hand to Bingley for a tender kiss. Elizabeth stiffened at witnessing the private moment. Despite her own discomfort, she was beyond pleased for her sister, and in truth was glad to see Jane make such a daring move before others. Certainly Mr Bingley was no longer in danger of persuasion from his sisters that Jane was indifferent to him!

Her eyes shifted uncomfortably to Darcy, fearing under the circumstances there might be some expectation for her to offer him some trifling farewell intimacy. She shrank back a fraction. Darcy solved the problem for her. He smiled, clicking his heels smartly, twirling his hat with a flourish, and offered her an exaggerated bow. "Until tomorrow, Fairest Miss Elizabeth!" he intoned gallantly.

He startled an endearing laugh out of her and she returned the gesture in kind, curtsying deeply as if she were before the Prince Regent. "Yes, Fair Sir, until tomorrow!" Still dipping low, she touched her fingertips together and gave a mock courtly nod, her lips twitching all the while with mirth.

Darcy spluttered involuntarily, then bit his lip to keep from roaring with laughter. He itched to offer her his hand to help her rise, but she was quicker than he. *It is enough,* he cautioned himself. He smiled again, his eyes speaking volumes of his admiration. She held his gaze for a moment, then the gentlemen stepped out into the night.

Jane turned to her sister in utter amazement. "Lizzy, what was *that* about?"

Elizabeth laughed out loud and shrugged. "I hardly know! But I think Mr Darcy improves upon closer acquaintance, do not you? Perhaps he is capable of pleasant manners after all!"

Jane, her eyes still wide, shook her head in wonder. "Do be careful, Lizzy. You will have the man so altered that even his close friends will fail to recognize him! It would be hardly convenient to have his own staff turn him out of Pemberley as an impostor. I did have my heart set on visiting you there at Christmas, you know."

Elizabeth made a jeering face, then the giggling sisters returned, arm in arm, to the drawing room.

~

Bingley stared pointedly at his friend all the way to the carriage. Darcy, glancing to the side with a sly little grin, attempted to ignore him. They mounted the steps and sat down inside, where Darcy was now subject to three impertinent stares.

"Was there something I could do for you all?" he queried, an unmistakable twinkle in his eye. He was completely satisfied with the evening. The temperature of Elizabeth's address had warmed most pleasantly, and, with her blessing, he had an appointment to spend time with her again on the morrow. He could not have hoped for more. Indeed, he would have been optimistic about much less!

"Well, Cousin," Richard drawled, "I was hoping to corner your enchanting lady once more this evening to, shall I say, add a little leaven to the lump. I never got the chance, however, as she seemed to spend much of the evening in close conversation with another gentleman of my party."

Georgiana giggled girlishly, snuggling close to his arm. "Tell us all, Brother! I heard her laugh many times tonight when you two were speaking. She was smiling when we left, too. I told you she would come to love you!"

"Wait, Georgie!" he pleaded, holding his hands up. "We are yet a long way from talk of love. We had a pleasant evening. Let us leave it at that."

"I say, what do you call that little scene at the door?" Bingley taunted from across the carriage. "Shameless flirtation, Colonel, that is what our Darcy has fallen to. Why, he was a regular Don Juan saying his farewells this evening."

"Call the doctor, Bingley," Fitzwilliam winked.

"I prefer rather Roland, or Arthur of the Round," Darcy remarked wryly, triggering a sly chortle out of his sister. "It is not my intention to seduce anyone."

"Well, be that as it may," Bingley grinned, "I believe the lady is looking forward to your visit tomorrow morning."

"You are going again tomorrow?" Georgiana squealed. "I will have a sister soon! Is it not wonderful, Richard? It is your turn next, you know! Brother," she returned to Darcy suddenly as her cousin began to sputter, "may I come with you tomorrow?"

"Our visit tomorrow is actually a business one, Georgie. Until Mr Bennet is well recovered, or their uncle Gardiner is able to arrive, Miss Elizabeth has been left in charge of the estate. She had some concerns in which she thought Bingley and I might be able to advise her."

"Say no more, Cousin," Richard waved his hand. "I have no interest in such matters. My yearly visit to Rosings is enough taste for me. It is just as well," he stretched his shoulders inside his tight-fitting red coat. "I only have leave through tomorrow, though I could have requested an extension. I know my mother would like me to stop for dinner at the townhouse, and as you seem to have your love life well in hand, I think I shall return in the morning."

"And leave me to my own devices? You are no friend."

"Just whom am I to entertain whilst the two of you are off rescuing damsels and wooing fair maidens?" Richard's eyes widened suggestively- he may not have been willing to slight Caroline aloud in her brother's presence, but no one could miss his implication.

"Richard, I will still be here," Georgiana pouted innocently. "Remember, you were going to teach me that scandalous new dance from the continent next... the waltz, did you call it?"

Darcy arched a critical brow at his cousin. "Indeed, Richard! Perhaps, Georgie, we may find a friend for you amongst the Bennet sisters who would behave with more decorum than your guardian."

Richard chuckled, shrugging helplessly. "Young people these days! They say the most confounded things! Now remember, Georgie, you promised not to tell him *everything*." Richard leaned forward conspiratorially, wagging his eyebrows to exaggerate whatever secret they had concocted.

Georgiana laughed gleefully. Despite his suspicions that his co-guardian was perhaps exerting a less-than-stellar influence, Darcy enjoyed her good spirits. The old Georgie was coming back to him. It was as though she had finally given herself permission to live again. Though he and Richard both had steadily poured love and support into her since her near-disaster, she had remained hesitant and insecure. He felt he could point to her new inspiration by Elizabeth Bennet as the turning point to a better tomorrow for his beloved sibling.

Bracing his arm around his little sister, he snuggled her close to keep her warm. Relief and satisfaction filled him. Had Georgie not begun to come round, Wickham would have still had his revenge, even unawares. He reflected with pleasure on his evening. Wickham had tried to taint and sully everything and everyone he cared about most, but now both the women who held his heart were immune to that scoundrel's poison. By thunder, things were going to turn right! Ignoring the knowing smirks from his companions, he smiled vacantly, the image of a vivacious beauty dangling before him the rest of the way to Netherfield.

Eighteen

"Colonel, I hope you are not leaving us so soon!" Caroline Bingley floated down the elegant staircase, her fingers trailing the polished walnut balustrade. She had lingered above stairs a great part of the morning, hoping to catch Mr Darcy, but she had finally concluded that he must have arisen far earlier and she was losing time with him.

Fitzwilliam, having just received his outercoat from a footman, turned to face her. He straightened upon seeing her, then, as an afterthought, gave her a strictly correct bow. "I am, Miss Bingley. I am to return to my regiment by this evening."

"I am indeed sorry to hear it. Poor Georgiana will miss you greatly." She smiled smoothly, coming to stand uncomfortably close to him.

"My cousin prefers her brother's company to mine, I assure you, Miss Bingley. She is most pleased to be staying behind." He finished buttoning his coat and began to turn when she put out a hand to stop him.

"Pray… stay a moment, Colonel."

He turned back, arching a quizzical brow. "Something I can do for you, Miss Bingley?"

"I wondered, sir… have you any concerns for the course our Mr Darcy has embarked upon?"

"Such as…?"

"Well, sir, of course by now you must be aware that the Bennet family are hardly presentable in the better circles. They are certainly not of the same caliber as *your* illustrious family, Colonel Fitzwilliam. Do you foresee any troubles for him among your extended relations? I should think that to begin with, obtaining the approval of the Earl for the marriage of his distinguished nephew to the daughter of a mere country squire might prove... trying. I only wish," she put on a convincingly mournful face, "to spare our mutual friend any grief and regret in the future."

Fitzwilliam began to smile slowly. "Darcy will indeed be glad to hear of your concern. I shall be sure to let him know that you wished to pave the way between himself and my father." He felt a swell of satisfaction as alarm grew on her face.

"In fact... now that you mention it, I believe I shall see what can be done to prepare Miss Elizabeth for her first meeting with my father. He is an old tyrant, you know, Miss Bingley. You have met him yourself, have you not? That was an unpleasant meeting for *one* of you, as I recall. Sure to rake the novice Miss Elizabeth over the coals, he is- until, of course, he falls victim to that rapier wit of hers for the first time. I have no doubt she will leave him vanquished on the field! The countess, now that *is* another matter, and I am very glad you bring it up."

He stroked his chin thoughtfully, then, his face brightening, snapped his fingers. "Aha! Mater has always been a soft mark for a young lass in the most fashionable attire- thinks it a mark of respectability or something of the kind. I shall mention to Georgiana that she should take her future sister to her own modiste in London before she meets my mother."

"Better yet... yes, that will do nicely. She and Miss Elizabeth are of much the same build, and William had just ordered Georgie a very generous winter wardrobe- more than she can ever wear, you understand- and she brought a good bit of it with her. You will make that recommendation to Georgiana for me, will you not, Miss Bingley? Your concern for your future sisters is truly touching." He performed a chivalrous half bow, favouring her with a suave smile.

Caroline did her best to swallow her dismay and consternation, swiftly replacing them with her mask of fond distress. Her façade cracked just at the end when the colonel referred to Eliza Bennet as her future sister. Impossible! Charles had gone and proposed to that ninny Jane Bennet over all her protestations! *Pull it together Caroline! You are worthy of Pemberley itself! Surely you can handle the insinuations of this clown!* She forced her rumpled sentiments back into order.

"Fine feathers, Colonel, that is all. There are any number of young ladies in the latest fashions," she squared her shoulders ever so slightly to make certain he noticed her rather generous bustline, accented so perfectly by her gold taffeta. "I highly doubt if Eliza Bennet should feel comfortable in a borrowed wardrobe... and in such attire as Miss Darcy owns! It is so far above that to which she has been used, do you see. Surely you must have noticed that she goes about rather... simply," she let the word linger with a faint sneer.

"Hmm, indeed, Miss Elizabeth needs very little enhancement," he stroked his chin in agreement. "Perhaps you are right, the woman is a natural beauty. Of course, as Darcy's wife she will come into the finest wardrobe money can buy, but I quite agree with you. There *are* any number of primped and powdered belles in London. Miss Elizabeth's native radiance should be allowed to shine when she is first introduced to her new relatives."

"*Natural beauty!*" Caroline's nostrils distended indignantly. "Why, the girl is half wild, the way she traipses about! I should not be surprised if she is at this very moment climbing trees, or slopping the pigs! The countess would be rightly affronted to be introduced to such a- a slatternly *farm girl!*"

Richard Fitzwilliam, well practiced at keeping his cool on the battlefield, began to laugh heartily. "I shall repeat your comments to Mater, she will be so highly amused!" He continued to laugh a little longer, enjoying the lady's fuming visage. "I can speak with some authority on this though; the Earl and the Countess had all but given up on my cousin. Pater was threatening to import some Indian princess if Georgiana married before William!"

He wiped an imaginary tear of laughter from his eye. "Quite seriously, I think they will agree that a farm girl is exactly what my antisocial cousin needs. He can retire peacefully to Pemberley and never be seen in Town again. She is of hardy stock too, my father will quite approve. 'Pemberley needs an heir!' he will say in that imperious way of his. Not that it will matter what their opinion is. Darcy is rather accustomed to having his way, regardless of the opinions of others."

Caroline's face was now beet red, fury seething from her dilated eyes. "I trust, Colonel, that you are correct and he will be happy with that... that *chit!* I would *hate* to see our dear friend at odds with his family!" she hissed in desperate reprisal. Balling her elegant hands into tight fists, she screwed her mouth shut and fled the foyer, taking the stairs so quickly she nearly stumbled.

Fitzwilliam was left chuckling to himself. "It is safe to come out now, William!" he called.

A very amused Darcy stepped from behind the study door, his face still suffused with mirth. "I hope you enjoyed yourself, Richard!"

"I did, rather." Smilingly, he pulled his gloves from his pockets and slowly began to pull them on.

"That bit about the Indian princess was a stroke of genius."

Richard guffawed loudly. "Yes, it was, if I do say so myself. Imagine you with a mail-order bride like some Colonist! You would have to build her her own house, you'd be too terrified to talk to her! Then again, if she spoke Hindi, maybe you would fare better."

Darcy chuckled. "No, thank you! I have enough women in my life to keep my hands full." He frowned and sighed heavily. "I am exceedingly troubled by Miss Bingley's actions. I shall have to speak to Charles."

"I heard enough of it," Bingley hopped off the bottom stair and approached. "I was just coming down the stairs when I heard her speaking to you, and I shamelessly eavesdropped on the entire conversation. I should have stopped it, I know, but I wanted to find out if she was sensible to correction. I am sorry to learn the opposite. I just stopped her on the landing and requested that she pack her bags this instant. I am sending her back to my townhouse this very afternoon."

Extending his hand to Fitzwilliam, he said, "I am very sorry, Colonel, for my sister's behaviour. And to you, Darcy," he turned to his old friend. "I must apologize. Caroline will not trouble you again."

Darcy heaved a long breath. "It is of no consequence, Bingley. She can change nothing, but I admit, it will be a relief to have her out of our hair for a time." Bingley nodded his full assent.

"Well, gents," Fitzwilliam donned his hat with a flourish. "The carriage awaits, and duty and honour call me away. You will send me a wedding invitation, will you not William? And you, Bingley," he reached to shake the other's hand, "I thank you for your hospitality. My very best wishes for your felicity. You both have found rare gems, I daresay!"

"I know not how to thank you, Richard," Darcy took his hand next, gazing sincerely into his cousin's eyes.

"Oh, I wager there will be many a broken heart after news of your engagement gets out. I've been waiting for that, you know, and you have tried my patience to the maximum, I tell you! I intend to scour the balls this spring and find myself a rich young debutante to comfort. An earl's son still fetches a respectable price on the open market." He winked jauntily and turned to the door, leaving his companions chortling in his wake.

"Colonel, I have a brilliant idea!" Bingley called as Fitzwilliam reached the door. "My sister has a dowry of twenty thousand. I would be most obliged if you would take her off my hands. I would even set you up with your own residence in Town! It is not a bad offer, and you and she get along so well, you know." Bingley sounded as if he were only half joking.

Fitzwilliam paused long enough to fire a scandalized glare over his shoulder. "Bingley, I hope to *retire* from combat, not plunge forever into the fray. Good day, gentlemen." He jerked the door open himself and scurried to the waiting carriage, as if he were afraid Bingley might think to ask him to take Caroline as a passenger.

"Well, Darcy?" Bingley turned to his companion. "We ought to be off as well. You promised Miss Elizabeth we would arrive by ten." He paused, making a face. "Perhaps you ought to go on your own, as I will have to make some arrangements for Caroline."

Darcy nodded in resignation. He would have preferred Bingley's company, but if doing without it for the morning meant that Caroline

Bingley would not be waiting like a spider in her lair when he returned, it was worth it. "Perhaps you will give me a few moments of your time before I leave."

"Certainly. In my study?"

"Yes, I already had some documents out."

"I say, you have been getting a little ahead of things, have you not? I presume you are still on the subject of Miss Elizabeth's present concerns?"

"Yes, and no." They gained the study door, and Darcy rang for the butler. "Would you please have Nancy and Sarah come to the study? Then if you please, I would like you to wait just outside with the door open."

"I beg your pardon, sirs, but Nancy is no longer employed here."

Darcy straightened. "Excuse me? Did you know of this, Bingley?"

Bingley shook his head, mystified. "I have no idea what you are talking about. I have dismissed no one. Is Nancy not the maid assigned to Georgiana?"

"If you please, sir, Nancy was dismissed by Miss Bingley yesterday."

Bingley stiffened, setting his mouth into a grim line. "Dawson, please send for Nancy, wherever she may be. My sister has no authority here any longer. Nancy is to be reinstated as of this moment, and I will add an extra week's pay for her trouble."

The butler bowed stiffly and went out. Bingley shook his head in awe and turned to his friend. "What is this all about, Darcy?"

Darcy picked up his pen, pointing with it to a few papers on the desk. "I had a rather revealing conversation with one your maids- Sarah, it was- yesterday morning. I inadvertently frightened the wits out of her, I'm afraid." He related the details of the pre-dawn conversation with the young maid to Bingley's amazed ears.

"The scoundrel!" Bingley spat. "I did not know Benson was so low. What do you propose?"

"Nothing, as yet. I have made inquiries, that is all so far. I am considering a way to provide a suitable dowry for Nancy to allow her to settle respectably. As for the other family- you have no vacant farms at present. Neither have I. I wish to know more of the circumstances to see if a good fit can be found."

He dropped his pen, draping his arm over the back of a chair. "This concern of Miss Elizabeth's may in fact turn out for the best. I hope to gather information from all parties concerned today, and will apprise you of my findings."

Bingley stroked his chin thoughtfully. "You will not score any marks with Miss Elizabeth by kicking out her tenant in favour of an inexperienced lad with few prospects."

"I do not intend to 'kick' anyone out. I am only seeking information."

"Well, you have my support in your endeavour, whatever you discover.

You ought to go. I can interview the maids when they arrive, and I will be certain to post someone at the door for propriety's sake. You must not keep your lovely lady waiting."

Darcy nodded. "Right, then. Will you come later to call on Miss Bennet?"

"Yes, I shall. Caroline will not ruin my entire day." Bingley scowled. "Stay a moment, would you carry her a note?" He leafed through the papers on top of his desk until he found a blank one.

Darcy left to grant him some privacy. He stepped outside to see if his horse was ready, and once again nearly bumped into Sarah as she hurried to the door of the study.

"I'm sorry Sir!" she squeaked timidly.

He gave her a quick greeting. "Do not be afraid, Sarah. Mr Bingley will see you in a moment. Thank you, Mr Dawson," he acknowledged the butler. "Please wait with her."

Bingley emerged almost immediately to hand Darcy his illegible note for his beloved- and fortunately very patient- angel. "Oh! Dawson, you are quick, man. Come in, come in. Good luck, Darcy!" he called to his friend as the latter turned to go.

~

Elizabeth was, once again, spending the morning in her father's room. Mr Jones had come and gone already this morning, and Mrs Cooper had finished Mr Bennet's morning breakfast. "Miss Elizabeth, would you help me to change the linens?" she asked.

Elizabeth frowned. "How are we to do it? We cannot move him, can we?"

"Oh," the lady chuckled, "there are ways. Come, I will lift the lower sheet under his body, and you can slide the fresh one beneath." Thanks to Mrs Cooper's deft, practiced fingers, they had the bed linens changed in good order. Elizabeth settled in her chair to read aloud again.

She was so engaged when there came a light knock upon the door. Mrs Gardiner opened it to Elizabeth's summons. "Lizzy, Mr Darcy is here to see you." She opened the door fully to reveal the tall man behind her, causing Elizabeth to start. "He expressed a wish to inquire after your father directly. I see no harm, do you?"

Elizabeth rose awkwardly. She had expected him to wait for her in the drawing room. She could not hide her surprise that he had come upstairs to see her- she had not expected such meek informality on his part. Darcy bowed his thanks to Mrs Gardiner, who cast a firm look to her niece. She stood back, allowing him room to pass by her. Darcy stood still a little hesitantly in the doorway, his fingers twitching at his sides. Elizabeth sighed, resolving to make herself amenable. "Would you care to come in, Mr Darcy?"

Mrs Gardiner abandoned him there, retreating back down the hall. He bowed and entered the modest room, his inquisitive gaze finding Mr Bennet's pale face. It was a reminder of the very real uncertainty which still lingered over his new friend, and the instability wrought upon his beloved's family.

"Mr Darcy, may I introduce you to Mrs Cooper?"

His attention rose back to the ladies facing him. Elizabeth's expression was warmly welcoming. His eyes lingered on her for the space of an extra breath before he turned to greet Mrs Cooper. He found her very agreeable, with a competent air and a comfortable demeanour.

"I am right pleased to meet you, Mr Darcy, sir," she curtseyed and met his gaze boldly. Though she had spent a great deal of her time shut away in this small room, the talk of Mr Darcy drifted through the door and permeated the servant's kitchen where she took her meals. This, she knew, was her silent employer *de facto*, and it was clear to her at first glance that he had taken quite a fancy to her favourite of the Bennet girls. *A very sensible man indeed*, she decided.

Darcy smiled at the woman's forthright manner. A servant from a great house- such as Pemberley, for instance- would not dare take such freedom in addressing him. Mrs Cooper, however, was a rustic sort of professional, and thus an independent of sorts. He had a feeling that she greeted him exactly as she would the family or friend of any of her patients, and he found that thought somehow liberating.

Elizabeth was turning to the woman now. "Mrs Cooper, would you care to refresh yourself? Mr Darcy can help me keep watch over Father for a while."

Mrs Cooper hid a knowing smile, murmured her thanks, and slipped past him, discreetly leaving the door ajar.

Darcy turned back to Elizabeth in complete surprise. "You do not wish for her company, as a chaperone?"

Elizabeth's eyes sparkled impishly. "Mr Darcy, is not my father's presence enough chaperonage? You would not accost a woman in her own father's sickroom, surely!"

His mouth dropped open, drawing a peal of delighted laughter from Elizabeth. Did she know how alluring she was, when she laughed and teased him so? "I am beginning to understand something about you, Miss Elizabeth."

She arched a brow, her smile unflagging. "Oh? Pray tell, what is that?"

He moved more deeply into the room, poising himself near a chair but not taking it until invited to do so. "Why, that you seem to find the greatest delight in provoking me. If that is true, I beg you would not stop. I would by no means suspend any pleasure of yours!"

Her smile broadened, and she took a seat with a gesture toward the chair he had intended to claim. He sat near her, leaning close so as not to miss a drop of whatever saucy remark she might make.

"Ah, but Mr Darcy, I thought it was impossible to laugh at you. We have established before that you have no faults but pride, and at that I cannot laugh. How ever am I to amuse myself if I do not have any foibles or weaknesses in your character to exploit?"

He felt his face warming and stretching into an uncharacteristically droll expression. "I beg you would not take another's opinion of me, but form your own. I trust *your* judgement of my character as infinitely more accurate."

She pursed her lips thoughtfully, her eyes still twinkling as she appraised him. "Perhaps I will begin my assessment by listing what I know of you. I might thereby identify some folly by which I may entertain myself."

"By all means," he sat back with a patient smile, preparing for her examination. Never before had he been nervous that he might be found wanting in another's eyes. Surprisingly, he actually wanted her to identify his flaws. He was well aware that he had them, and if she were to agree to be his wife, she would live with them daily. More vital to the moment, however, was the swaying of her opinion. Elizabeth was intelligent enough to be suspicious of the appearance of perfection, because she would know it to be artificial. He wanted to be real and authentic with her, of all people. He could only hope his flaws, when discovered, were not ones of such gravity as to make her turn from him.

"Very well," Elizabeth began after a nail-biting moment of reflection. "You are a kind brother, you have a loyal cousin and friend, you are a man of duty, very concerned with your estate. You are well traveled, exceedingly well read, and you care little for foolishness." She lifted one eyebrow, waiting for his answering smile in confirmation before she went on.

"You take your coffee with cream and two lumps of sugar, your tea you take without cream. You have a very fine carriage which I think seldom sees mud on its polished spokes, and you must pay a great deal for your valet, as that is the most exquisitely knotted cravat it has been my pleasure to admire in some while." She paused, enjoying his entertained expression. He dipped his head in acknowledgement and invitation for her to continue.

"You enjoy riding tremendously, which I find inconvenient, but the other day I noticed a small quantity of hair on your breeches, by which I assumed you must have tended your own animal. By all accounts you are a splendid hunter, and an avid outdoorsman. You do not enjoy balls, but I cannot fathom why, as you are always impeccably dressed- thanks, I think, to that wonderful valet- not to mention, you are a *superior* dancer." She placed an unmistakable inflection on her last phrase, reminiscent of Sir William Lucas.

Darcy could not help laughing out loud. Even at that awkward moment, she could look back and find a source of amusement. She tilted her head challengingly, daring him to answer her unspoken question.

"I cannot refute any of your findings. I am very blessed in my family, small as it is, and you are quite precise as to my tastes and experiences. I did, in fact, tend my own horse day before yesterday, much to my valet's chagrin. He has not yet forgiven me, but as you so astutely surmised, I make it well worth his trouble to tolerate my whims.

"I do not enjoy balls, I am sorry to say. I have not the talent for speaking easily to people I do not know. You, Miss Elizabeth, are rather skilled at catching the conversations of others and adding clever witticisms of your own. I have never yet learnt the knack."

"It is a matter of practice, Mr Darcy. I imagine that had I practiced my riding and my piano with as much enthusiasm as I honed my tongue, I might be accomplished at both and not nearly so liable to saying aloud the things which I will later come to regret."

His mouth twitched merrily. "So you are saying that to make myself invulnerable to your teasing, I ought to practice my conversation skills? I bow to your sage advice. I should enjoy such practice, however I am not altogether certain I wish to be rendered impervious to such a charming wit as yours." He paused, admiring the light filtering through the small window bouncing off her luscious curls.

She smiled archly at him, waiting for him to continue. "I recall at the Meryton Assembly you stated your belief that dancing provides an agreeable situation for people to become acquainted. Perhaps if the opportunity presents itself, you would agree to help me to practice those skills I seem to lack? As I recall, my performance of a few evenings ago was not one of which to boast."

Elizabeth affected an air of resigned disappointment. "Oh dear, Mr Darcy, I should be happy to oblige, but alas, I fear it may be impossible to find a woman in these parts handsome enough to tempt you to the floor. Perhaps in London you will have better luck!" She grinned challengingly, delighting in her ability to pull the rug from under his feet.

Darcy's mouth fell open again. He was silent for a moment as Elizabeth began to laugh. "You heard that?"

"I *was* seated rather nearby, and as I had no dance partner at the moment, I had no other amusement but to divert myself by observing those around me." She tilted her head and pursed her lips, pointedly smirking at his discomfiture.

"Oh." His eyes wandered to the window, seeking some excuse, then returned to her face. Observing her playful expression still in place, he bit his lip thoughtfully. "You have been waiting some while to say that to me, have you not?"

Her eyes sparkled more brightly and she laughed again. "I confess I have! What will you think then, sir, when I admit to sporting with your remarks in public and amusing myself at your expense?"

"Surely I must have given offence! You are too generous. I was wrong to speak so, and have no doubt wounded your sensibilities. It is little wonder you began our acquaintance prejudiced against me!"

Elizabeth sighed, her smile fading somewhat. "Mr Darcy, since we are confessing all, it must be apparent to you that I have more than my share of vanity. Rather than loudly taking offence, I gave vent to my feelings by jesting with my neighbours. I am afraid, sir, that you have me to blame in part for the generally poor opinion many here have of your character."

"No," he interjected firmly. "That blame is mine alone. I was brought up with proper manners, though I understand now I have not always employed them in company. I should have judged better to ask an introduction, I know. I doubt you will believe me when I say my comments truly had nothing to do with your person. I primarily wished to avoid dancing with a stranger, and to discourage Bingley from urging me to. You cannot know how I have regretted that decision!"

He reached cautiously for her hand, heat creeping into his voice. "I had scarcely even looked at you, locked as I was in my own selfish pride. It was within mere moments, I believe, that I began to wish for the opportunity again! I distinctly remember you passing by me with that bewitching twinkle in your lovely eyes, as though you were thoroughly amused with something. Now I know that to be my own folly, and I justly deserved your scorn! I believe I spent the rest of the evening, and nearly every meeting since, helplessly staring at you."

Elizabeth released a tight little laugh and dropped her eyes to hide her swell of feelings. Darcy's fingertips were tracing the top of her hand in a most distracting way. Her body filled with tension. He sensed it and stilled his fingers, contenting himself with simply clasping her small hand.

Elizabeth smiled faintly down at his fingers curling round hers. He was not backward in expressing his wishes, but his concern for her comfort was touching. She found her opinions of this man improving remarkably every time they spoke. There was a simple sincerity to his manner, and hiding very deeply beneath it that spark of playfulness she had detected the evening before.

There was more though... her eyes searched his carefully before dropping again, finally confessing to herself that what she saw was a consuming tenderness, the like of which she had never experienced. The imperturbable, consequential, perfectly poised Mr Darcy, ruled by a blindingly deep emotion... for her! *Could Jane have been right all along?* She had always enjoyed debating his keen mind, but always for her own momentary amusement, delighting in besting such a man. Never before had she considered there to be any true affinity.

His confession of such early feelings for her was quite surprising. Not even Elizabeth, spirited and independent as she was, could be immune to such a powerful, persistent admiration expressed by a handsome and honourable man. She swallowed.

Honourable he was, she could see that now. There was something delightfully pleasing in his openness with her. It was as if he dealt with her on an entirely different level than other men, as if he respected her well enough to hand her the keys to his private thoughts.

Warmth spreading upon her cheeks, she raised her gaze shyly to his. Those intense dark eyes arrested and bound her speechless. Boldly she held his regard, studying his face freely. That tiny dimple, only in evidence when he smiled deeply, caught her eyes. From there she traced a line to his mouth, shivering when she recalled his gentle kiss. She could not really be *falling* for him… could she?

Well, what matter if I am? she asked herself impatiently. It seemed impossible now to avoid a marriage. Caution would do her little good in this case. She may as well let her fancy run freely! She found herself fully enjoying her new understanding of this man, and regretting even more profoundly her previous errors. How could she have been so mistaken? Could he really be one and the same man with whom she had thought herself more than sufficiently acquainted? He had appeared so aloof before!

He seemed so warm and compassionate now, so unlike his previous chilly address. *Jane* was *right*, she affirmed. Georgiana was clearly suffering from painful shyness, and Jane was the first to recognize that the brother, too, was terribly uncomfortable. A man in his position would be forced to appear in public often; always at the head over his peers and a prime target for the offers of countless women, whether he liked it or not. Lacking the ease of his less affluent friend Mr Bingley, Darcy would naturally appear haughty and proud.

Darcy let his eyes rove over her lovely face as she contemplated him. Once before he would have grown uncomfortable under such serious scrutiny, but the opportunity to openly drink in her graceful presence was too delicious. If she wished to study him, and if such familiarity would grant her ease, he was more than willing to bask in her company. He lightly stroked the back of her hand with his thumb again, daring to press her for greater allowances. Her blush deepened, but she did not shift away from him.

A step creaked outside the door, and both quickly drew back their hands. Mrs Cooper's happy face appeared in the doorway, and she stopped. She was carrying a little tray for herself, but she had rather expected by now that this interview would have been brought to a close, or removed downstairs. Her practiced eye was quick to discern embarrassment on both faces, but she was too cagey to make her observation known. Rather, she settled for distraction. "Excuse me, Miss Elizabeth, Mr Darcy, sir. Mrs Hill asks if you would like some tea?"

Both quickly rose to their feet. "No- no thank you," stammered Elizabeth. "That will not be necessary, Mrs Cooper. We have business in Father's study…." Her eyes shifted nervously to her companion, whose tender expression of a moment ago had been wiped clean by his usual composed manner.

Darcy moved to allow Mrs Cooper to enter the room. He bowed politely, eliciting a thrilled little grin from the middle-aged nurse by his gentlemanly attention and that handsome dimple. Elizabeth smiled privately. She catalogued it as yet another insight into Mr Darcy that she had not expected- he was unfailingly polite to everyone in her household, treating all with respectful dignity and even friendliness. She began to imagine that his own staff might regard him very highly. It would be a telling caricature of the man, she decided. Who would know his qualities and flaws better than they?

In some wonder, she watched as he helped Mrs Cooper settle into one of the chairs, solicitously taking her tray and placing it near her for her convenience. Mrs Cooper beamed, catching Elizabeth's eye. It was clear that Mr Darcy had won her good opinion by his simple gestures. Elizabeth sighed and shook her head in cheerful resignation. Tally one more of her confidantes swayed to Darcy's favour.

Nineteen

Elizabeth and Mr Darcy excused themselves downstairs and made for the library, which doubled as a study for Mr Bennet. Elizabeth led the way, leaving Darcy free to admire her floating, graceful form as she descended before him.

At the bottom of the stairs, they were greeted by an inarticulate plinking on the pianoforte. The racket was dreadfully spine-shivering. Darcy did his best to conceal a shudder when a particularly sour note rang out. Elizabeth turned to him in embarrassment. "Lydia is taking lessons with Aunt this morning," she explained uncomfortably.

He schooled his expression and gave a curt nod, happy to have gained the solitude of library. Even there they could not fully escape the distracting clamour, as they could not in all propriety shut the door. At least the great plentitude of Mr Bennet's bookshelves insulated the room somewhat and dulled the noise from outside. Elizabeth began to show him to the desk and some papers she had drawn out for their conference.

"Oh! My dearest Lydia, you are doing splendidly!" Mrs Bennet screeched from the drawing room across the hall. Elizabeth cringed, peeking at Darcy. "Oh, my sweetest sister, is she not talented? I always said, Dearest Lydia, you could do just marvelously at anything you tried!" Mrs Gardiner's demure reply was barely audible. Elizabeth's lips thinned, and she reached for the sheaf of ledger paper on her father's desk.

They had no success here at conversation. Elizabeth peeped at him in humiliated torment. Darcy twisted his mouth into a firm line as he studied the documents she showed him, doing his best to appear unconcerned with the din from the drawing room. Elizabeth could not help a sympathetic smile. His efforts at nonchalance were valiant, but the tension in his shoulders was too obvious- at least, it was to her.

Elizabeth had called for a refreshment tray to be brought in, so that they might have the excuse of avoiding the midday meal when it was served. Some generous spirit within her wished to avoid subjecting Darcy to her entire family for a formal luncheon. Her gesture was not unappreciated. The relief in his face was palpable, though he strove mightily to conceal it. Both affected an air of indifference as they worked right through the late morning.

Darcy scanned the pages quickly, digesting another man's private financial matters as though they were his own concerns. Once or twice he glanced up to Elizabeth's face. He read her embarrassment at laying her family's affairs open before him, and met her eyes with complete gentleness. He needed her to trust him! Surely if he could gain her confidence here, where the evidence of their differences was so pronounced, he might have success in other areas as well.

At length, he cleared his throat and spoke. "It would appear that Mr Brown has been a steady and reliable tenant for many years up until this last one." A sour note clanged again on the piano, causing both to flinch and Darcy to lose his train of thought. How gratefully he had left behind him those early days of Georgiana's tutelage!

Elizabeth nodded emphatically, drawing his attention back to the subject at hand. "He is a good man, Mr Darcy," she replied with iron in her voice, as if daring him to contradict her. "He is honourable, and very wise. Papa thinks highly of him."

"Yes, I understand," he assured her. "However, you are unfortunately correct that his rent is seriously in arrears. It is doubtful he should ever in his lifetime be able to repay what is owed." He paused, watching her carefully. "It is, of course, your father's prerogative to attempt to collect on the debt or to make other arrangements. So far, I gather that Mr Bennet has chosen to allow time for Mr Brown's injuries to heal in hopes that he will be able to retain the farm next year. Is that correct?"

Elizabeth nodded quietly. She fingered another ledger, biting her lip. "I fear your assessment is more generous to my father's planning than is warranted. In truth, I believe he was merely trying to delay the inevitable. None of us wish to see any harm befall the family," she finished lowly.

"Hmm..." he stroked his lip as he surveyed another ledger sheet. His eyes narrowed and traced down the page again and again. Elizabeth did not fail to notice his sudden interest and raised a curious brow.

He returned his gaze to hers. "You do realize, Miss Bennet, that the matter cannot simply be allowed to slide. The lack of repayment may be overlooked by your father, but in the long run it is a substantial blow to the prosperity of Longbourn... one which, as heir, Mr Collins would be within his rights to prosecute... even years from now," he added quickly.

Elizabeth stared in shock. "I had not considered that!"

"May I?" he queried, gesturing toward another reef of papers. Mutely she passed them over and watched in fascination as he flipped back and forth through the pages. He seemed to be looking for something in particular, but as yet he was not telling her what it was.

As he was reading, there sounded a small tapping on the opened door of the study. The eyes of both turned to the sound. Kitty and Jane stood sheepishly in the doorway, sewing baskets in hand. "Lizzy, I am so sorry to interrupt, but might we join you in the study?" Jane was pleading. The pianoforte hammered once more for emphasis.

Sliding her gaze to Darcy, who looked quickly back to the ledgers, Elizabeth nodded. "At least now we can close the door!" she muttered under her breath. The gentleman beside her bit back a chortle, his eyes flashing to hers for only a second. As Kitty and Jane settled into a window seat, Elizabeth remained awkwardly near the desk. Darcy withdrew into silence once more, seemingly uncomfortable with their audience.

Elizabeth had begun to regret granting her sisters entry when he spoke abruptly. "Miss Elizabeth, would it be possible to meet this Mr Brown? I have a particular question which I should like to have answered."

She blinked in surprise. "I suppose it is. I expect he is at home." Privately she wondered what he could have in mind, but she sensed he would not say more until he had the information he sought.

With a bow to her sisters, Darcy moved to the door and held it for her, his warm gaze lingering on her face as she followed him through. She could sense without even looking the giddy nudges and giggles shared by her sisters as they quit the room.

~

"Miss Darcy is not at home? Nonsense! I shall set that girl right. She cannot refuse to see me! I am almost the nearest relation she has, and I am entitled to call upon her whenever I see fit!" Lady Catherine swept by the stoic butler, who managed to position himself artfully enough that he appeared forbidding without actually requiring the lady to push him out of the way.

"Yes, my lady," Drake commented neutrally. What she believed her rights and entitlements to be was not his business. He had already received particular instructions regarding this relative of his Master's, and it suited his purposes that she should enter the house of her own accord.

Lady Catherine descended upon a nearby footman, bloodshot eyes blazing and a fleck of spittle forming at the corners of her wrinkled mouth. "Miss de Bourgh requires assistance! What worthless staff you have here! I shall speak to my nephew directly." The young man could not have been flung out the front door more violently if she had dealt him a physical blow. The sheer force of her ire was more than sufficient. He scrambled to the carriage outside to do the noble woman's bidding.

Lady Catherine strode confidently to the music room. No matter that the house was virtually silent; Georgiana ought rightly to have been practicing at this time of the day, and was surely only waiting to receive her guest so she could begin a new piece after performing the requisite protocols. The room, however, was quite empty save for a very surprised housemaid with a dusting rag.

The august personage stood in mute astonishment for a moment. With some sense of imperious denial, her gaze swept the shadows behind the bookcases and even peered round the corners of the sofas before she had satisfied herself that her niece was truly not present. She whirled to face the butler when he appeared discretely behind her. "This is not to be borne! Send up for my niece immediately!"

Drake inclined his head. "As your ladyship must remember, Miss Darcy is away at present."

"Lies! She cannot be away. My nephew wrote me specifically not a fortnight ago and said my niece was to remain here through the holidays! Wait until my nephew hears of your *disgraceful* conduct!"

"As your ladyship pleases. Your ladyship will naturally desire to wait in comfort while Miss Georgiana is sent for. The rose drawing room at present enjoys the benefit of a robust blaze and Miss de Bourgh, I believe, is fond of that room. Would your ladyship care for some refreshment?"

Lady Catherine settled somewhat. At last they were getting somewhere! "That will suffice, and mind I am to be brought a cold water first. My doctor believes it good for the constitution, you know, and you must prevail upon your master to adopt my ways once he returns. Do not forget, Drake! My water is to be served with a slice of lemon- a *fresh* one this time- and my tea with a sprig of mint off to the side. Peach, rather than strawberry preserves, if you please; my doctor says it is better for the digestion. And no scones! Your cook nearly broke my tooth last time!"

Within a few moments, the ladies had settled into the designated sitting room. Anne, appearing weakened by her journey, swayed very slightly against her companion. Lady Catherine puckered her worn lips in disdain. If Anne would only exhibit a little willpower and pluck up, she would be Mistress of this house any day! It could not come soon enough, either.

What disreputable ways the staff had got into! It was not this way in the days of her brother-in-law!

An agreeable warmth stole across her features. Oh, no, it was not like this at all in the days of dear old George! Back in those days, the staff groveled properly at her feet. She had been sure he was on the brink of a proposal when he betrayed her for her younger sister. He had tried to make it up to her later, but it had been too little, too late for her forgiveness. Her lips coiled in resolve. She would see her daughter a Darcy, if not herself!

A freckled young maid appeared presently, wheeling a tea cart. "At last!" the great lady cried. "How long does it take to boil a pot of water? Your cook ought to be stoking her fires constantly. At Rosings, I never suffer the kitchen fire to be diminished in the slightest, even in the heat of the season," she huffed scornfully.

"As your ladyship pleases," the girl bobbed a cheeky curtsey.

"Where is my niece? She ought to be down by now! Go at once and summon her to take refreshment with us. Such a shameful lack of propriety and respect!"

"As your ladyship pleases," the girl repeated, with a spunk entirely too plucky for decorum. She curtseyed again, and the noble guest quite positively detected a mutinous gleam in the maid's eye.

"Go at once! I shall speak to the housekeeper if my niece is not brought to me instantly!"

"As your ladyship pleases," the girl parroted as she backed out of the room.

"Such insolence!" she declared. "I never in all my days...." her eyes fell to the tea tray. She lifted her glass of water suspiciously. It was quite warm, and a sprig of mint floated listlessly near the surface. She clenched her teeth. What utter incompetence! Inspecting further, she discovered a small dish of wilted lemon wedges placed between the cream and sugar. Next to them, a towering stack of scones dolloped generously with strawberry preserves adorned the centre of the cart.

~

Elizabeth had accepted Darcy's arm in escort, a carefully composed expression lingering on her face as she did so. She was not yet ready to display any flicker of her improving regard for him, although she expected it was obvious by her lack of verbal attack this past hour and a half. She peeked at him discreetly beneath the hood of her warm cloak, watching with interest how the tension left his features as they gained distance between themselves and the house.

For his part, Darcy was busy scolding himself into gentlemanly conduct. It did not matter that countless layers of fabric and leather lay between them; Elizabeth's taper fingers rested gently in the crook of his elbow, her beautiful curly head bobbing so fittingly by his side. Her smaller frame synchronized with his as they moved, and they stepped down the path in harmony.

He fought a little twinge of satisfaction from displaying itself in his manner. Elizabeth Bennet did not mince her steps, tiptoeing daintily like a lady of fashion. Rather, she strode purposefully, with decision, yet still carried herself with a modest feminine grace which he found irresistible.

Though he kept his face resolutely up and forward, his eyes continually drifted to the apparition at his side. He strove valiantly to introduce some interesting topic of conversation to ease their short journey, but continually drew a blank. It was Elizabeth, quite characteristically, who spoke first.

"Will you tell me now, sir, what it was which so suddenly caught your interest in my father's documents?" She fixed him with that temptingly arch expression of hers, her beautiful face a warm radiance backdropped by the chill grey of their surroundings.

He cleared his throat gently, straightening his shoulders uncomfortably. "I did say that it would be your father's prerogative to collect on the debt…."

"You did," she answered carefully. "Or, in his indisposition, the duty falls to me. Yet, as I have asked your advice, it might be said that you have a place in the matter as well."

"That is not quite what I meant," he returned, warmed and surprised that she would be defending his involvement in her family's affairs. "The debt can be collected… or *other* arrangements can be made to satisfy it." He let that statement linger, curiously watching the emotions playing across her lovely features.

Her able mind did not disappoint. Inspiration sparkled in those dark eyes and she rose them to meet his gaze. "What do you have in mind?" she asked hopefully.

"That is why I wished to meet with him. As yet, I do not have a suitable suggestion, but I hope to be able to make a sound recommendation to you after our conversation. I wish to assess the man's abilities. You speak so highly of him; it stands to reason that he must have other areas of expertise by which he might be able to both recompense the estate and provide for his family in the future."

Elizabeth's chocolate eyes crinkled in approval, an eloquent smile kindling. He returned it with good will. She was pleased with his ideas! He allowed himself just for a moment the very agreeable fantasy of taking Elizabeth Bennet as his confidante and partner, the one to whom he himself turned for advice and encouragement. Her lively intellect and warm loyalty could carry him through any difficulty. What a pleasure to closet himself for hours in his study with Elizabeth as his company, rather than his silent old hound!

Naturally of course, after working through whatever quandaries they might face together, he would thank her- most *ardently*- for her devoted succour. What freedoms could then be his, as her husband? Elizabeth would be no mousy prig, waiting silently and diffidently for him to exert his marital rights and leave her be. Not she! No, if there were any difficulties with Elizabeth Bennet, it might be said that she was rather a woman of too much feeling! Though at present her fiery and independent nature gave him great cause for anxiety, he had good reason to hope it would not always be so.

Elizabeth slyly peeped from beneath her hood after a few moments of awkward silence from Darcy. "May I ask, sir, what it is which amuses you so?"

Darcy's face flushed guiltily, his mouth opening to form some apology which would not come. "Amuses me, Miss Bennet?" he tried to sound innocent, but his traitorous voice cracked as his throat constricted. "I cannot know what you mean."

Elizabeth grinned challengingly, small pearly teeth peeking between those rosy lips. His heart, already agitated by his incongruous musings, performed a somersault and left him breathless. "Come, sir, I have not known you to bear such an agreeable expression without good cause! If it is your intention to improve my understanding of you, I would ask to be enlightened, if I may be so bold."

"I do not think that would be wise, Miss Bennet," he murmured huskily, a little twitter about the corner of his mouth.

"Very well, then, sir!" She lifted her chin airily and pretended to dismiss him. "I might add, however, that it is not at *all* gentlemanly to keep a secret from a lady."

"It would be far less 'gentlemanly' to reveal my thoughts to that same lady, Miss Bennet." He bent his head low, leveling an expressive and intimate smile.

Her eyes widened in convicted surprise as his meaning dawned. "Oh," she whispered involuntarily. She looked hastily away and lapsed into silence, her breath quickening.

They walked on with no words for some moments, remorse beginning to etch itself into Darcy's features. "Miss Bennet, I apologize if I have made you uncomfortable," he spoke lowly. "It was not my wish."

Her eyes flashed quickly to his. "I…."

"Well, well, Mr Darcy! And Miss Elizabeth, how do you do today!" a cheery voice interjected.

The attention of both turned to Sir William Lucas, who approached round a bend in the path. He was mounted on his old road horse, a very fine, if aged, greatcoat splayed from his shoulders down over his saddle. Elizabeth tensed. Of all the people to see her out walking alone with Mr Darcy! It could only be worse if it had been this man's wife they encountered!

Darcy bowed his head very properly to the titled gentleman. "Good Day, Sir William, how do you do?" he replied civilly.

"Oh, I am splendid, my dear sir, splendid! I see you and the lovely Miss Elizabeth are taking the air. Capital, capital! May I congratulate you sir, on carrying off the fairest gem of the county? What felicitations must be pouring in, eh my good man?"

Darcy opened his mouth to reply but the good Sir William had not yet exhausted his superfluity.

"I was just saying to my dear wife what a fine thing your arrival has been for the neighbourhood, Mr Darcy. Why, only consider all of these happy young couples; for where there is one engagement there are always more soon to follow, eh Mr Darcy? What a handsome pair your friend Bingley and the lovely Miss Jane Bennet make, Mr Darcy. Such a fine thing, and we are all expecting to hear word at any time of such a *desirable* event in the offing!" The gentleman's bushy eyebrows waggled significantly.

"You are well acquainted, I must expect Mr Darcy, with our dear Charlotte's happy news. Such a sensible and bright young man, my future son-in-law! He paints a lovely picture of the fair Rosings Park. Perhaps you can tell me, my dear sir, is the seat of the esteemed Lady Catherine de Bourgh," he uttered the name with reverent care, "as magnificent as he claims?"

Darcy's lips thinned. "Indeed, sir, it is very fine."

"Capital!" the jubilant father enthused. "What a fortuitous connection. A lucky girl, my Charlotte!"

Darcy's eyes flitted over Elizabeth's face, taking in her tight expression. "If you will forgive me, Sir William, I would have declared all the luck to be on Mr Collins' side. He is a fortunate man to have secured the hand of Miss Lucas." He felt rather than observed Elizabeth's swift and gratified glance in his direction. Her fingers tightened ever so imperceptibly on his arm. Rewarded again! His inner parts tingled with exhilaration.

"Oh, my dear sir, you flatter me! Such kind words, such condescension! Capital, I say. Oh, but Miss Elizabeth, do forgive my lack of breeding. How does our dear Mr Bennet this morning? I trust there is some improvement?"

"Indeed, sir," the young lady answered, a mortified flush staining her cheeks still from Sir William's callous remarks about Jane and Charlotte. Darcy, however, was soon privy to a willful shift in her expression. She blinked twice and that provocative sparkle returned to her eyes. Her lips curved deliciously. He held his breath, anxious to partake of the wit of his Elizabeth while her sword was pointed somewhere other than at himself.

"I believe, sir, that our dear Mr Collins will be most fittingly pleased to have many years yet to enjoy the beauty of Rosings and the very great patronage of the Lady Catherine de Bourgh. What a fortuitous thing it is!" She met Sir Lucas' eye with a sweet challenge, the corner of her mouth lifting ever so slightly.

"Well… yes, capital, I say." Sir Lucas' face clouded slightly. He possessed not the ability to mock himself, which often precluded the skill to rightly interpret some of his neighbour's pleasantries. The lady inclined her head and offered him a gracious smile, and the gentleman at her side bowed in proper respect, so quite surely there was nothing amiss. He touched his hat. "Well, then. A very good day to you, Miss Elizabeth, and to you, Mr Darcy." Still blinking and mystified, he gave his mount an uncoordinated nudge and moved off.

Darcy's gaze shifted to the impertinent young lady at his side. "You speak of my unprepossessing ways! I might say, Miss Elizabeth, that it is not terribly gracious to make sport of those who cannot defend themselves from your witticisms." He arched a brow, a hint of a smile teasing his mouth.

"Ah, but Mr Darcy, Sir William still believes me to be eminently genteel and modest, whereas you, who know better, I think are the more greatly entertained by my lack of proper deference! So, you see, no harm has been done."

"Perhaps I am at least glad to know I am not the *only* one obliged to surrender my sword in a match of wits."

Elizabeth laughed, those speaking eyes flashing beguilingly. "Very good, Mr Darcy! I shall return it to you, as is only sporting. You are a quick study, I daresay."

He grinned, his heart swelling in his chest. "Miss Bennet, do you know how we train our hunting dogs?"

Her brow furrowed, eyes still twinkling as she tilted her head curiously. "I beg your pardon? I have no knowledge of dog training."

"More is the pity, for you would prove a prodigiously talented handler. You see, Miss Bennet, a dog is ever eager to please. An unschooled pup blunders about, mayhem and destruction following in its wake. As it is offered instruction, it guesses what might be the desired response of its handler. Most of its guesses are far from the mark in the beginning, but the instant it makes a right move, the handler rewards it lavishly. Each correct response is praised, and gradually a new skill is learned. What was once an awkward and ignorant creature, capable only of causing confusion, becomes a loyal and clever partner, ever learning and desiring to be near its master."

Elizabeth narrowed her eyes slyly, an impish curve to her mouth. "The great Fitzwilliam Darcy of Pemberley, comparing himself to a gangling hound puppy? How very amusing!"

"It is a fortunate animal indeed which finds itself in the care of a highly skilled and, dare I say, *amiable* trainer," he winked daringly at her, enjoying the rosy warmth flooding her cheeks.

"And this trainer; does he come to care for his animals, or does he merely take satisfaction in the creation of a useful partner?"

"Both, it is to be hoped, for the most effective partnerships are ruled by a mutual attachment. Dogs can be very loyal and affectionate, you know." He hesitantly reached for her gloved hand and she surprised him by meeting him halfway, a sudden shyness fluttering her lashes low.

He clasped her hand breathlessly for a moment, quite at a loss for words when she submitted so gently to his desire to touch her. "Shall I interpret that," he rasped hoarsely, "as your way of rewarding your pupil?"

She slowly tipped her gaze up to his, a genuine rather than a provoking smile gradually lighting her features. "It would be unwise," she answered softly, "to neglect to praise such a promising protégé."

Twenty

"*Where is my niece?*" thundered Lady Catherine de Bourgh. She had given up waiting in the drawing room and now roved each of the downstairs rooms like a pirate searching out booty. The library! No. The sun room, the breakfast room, the gallery, the green parlour… no, no, no, no! "What do you mean, her maid is not available? Unconscionable! Let me to *someone* who knows where your mistress is to be found!"

A goodly number of Darcy's staff trailed along behind her, each offering cheerful suggestions as to Miss Darcy's favourite haunts about the large London house. None proved fruitful. Outraged, she charged the stairwell to begin pillaging the family's private quarters.

"Miss Darcy allus slept down theh, m'lady," a rather cockney young cook's assistant gestured to the third room in the western wing. "She'uhd hev me bring her cuppa in tha moarnin's."

Lady Catherine glared at the audacious little snippet. "How *dare* you presume to direct *me!* Go back to your kitchen, you insolent wench! I think I know my way around my own nephew's house!"

"Jest as yer laydeyship pleases," the girl's face glimmered with insubordinate merriment as she bobbed her curtsey and withdrew.

"Of all the cheek!" the fine lady shouted at the retreating figure. "You will never work in service again! Heaven and earth, that you should even *dare* to come above stairs, and in the presence of nobility! I shall have personal words with my nephew!" It did little good to shout further, as the young scullery maid had vanished without further sass.

205

The three other maids, their heads tipped reverently, immediately touched their fingers to their mouths. Lady Catherine eyed them cynically, assuming they, at least, were offering her wordless assertion that *they* would not presume to talk back to nobility. Glowering, she flung open the door to the room indicated. Not only was it devoid of the presence of any young lady, but the furniture was shrouded and looked as though it had not been in use for some time.

Irate, she spun around to face the staff assembled behind her. The eldest of them, standing somewhat at the front of her peers, perked in a little inspiration.

"I just remembered, your ladyship, Ma'am," she dipped a curtsey. "Miss Darcy was moved to another room last summer, when she returned from Ramsgate. It was near the Master's. If you would follow me, Ma'...."

"*I know where the Master's chambers are!*" the great lady fumed and stalked toward the other wing. She proceeded to examine every room, asserting her rights as family to search out her disobedient young niece. How dare that girl presume to hide from her! Boiling in anger, the great lady at last approached the Master's chambers. She reached for the door to cast it aside, but Darcy's butler materialized out of thin air.

"I have my orders, my lady," Drake bowed respectfully. "No one is ever granted access to the Master's private quarters, nor to his private study. I regret I cannot allow you to enter."

"I override your orders! Stand aside, you cannot dare deny access to a peeress!"

"I regret that I must, if I wish to keep my place, my lady. It is Mr Darcy to whom I answer, and none other. I apologize to your ladyship, but my Master's orders are quite inflexible on this point." He clasped his hands behind his back so that it might never be said he had laid a hand on a noblewoman, but his towering figure froze as an immovable statue.

"*You* said you would find my niece!" she roared. "*Where is Georgiana Darcy?*"

The man's face clouded. "Miss Darcy is not here, my lady. I believe I promised your ladyship that we would *send* for her, at your ladyship's command. It will be at least a full day before I receive any word back."

"*Send* for her? Why then did your staff send me on this wild goose chase if she is not here?"

"I beg your ladyship's pardon," the butler dipped his head apologetically. "I believed they understood your ladyship wished to know of Miss Darcy's most frequented rooms, so that your ladyship could ascertain all was properly in order for a young lady of her station."

"*In order!*" she snarled indelicately. "I want to see my niece! Where is she?"

"In point of fact, my lady, I cannot say precisely where Miss Darcy is. She is with her guardian, Colonel Fitzwilliam."

Lady Catherine screwed her mouth tightly in outrage. "Well, then! I shall know how to act. I am most *seriously* displeased with the performance of this household. Shameful, scandalous that the halls of George Darcy should fall into such disgrace!"

She spun about on her heel, and the elegant noblewoman swooped down the stairs where her pale daughter rested. "Anne! We are leaving at once, and without Miss Darcy! I shall speak to my nephew most severely regarding the *abominable* lack of decorum displayed by his staff! Anne! Attend me at once!"

Anne, who had been reclining with a cool cloth over her eyes and Mrs. Jenkinson carefully dabbing her forehead, groaned lowly. She moved to sit up, faltered dramatically, and was caught by Mrs. Jenkinson.

"Anne! Exert your willpower, girl!" Lady Catherine swept to the front door. With a glare at the footman, she floated gracefully through to her waiting….

"*Where is my carriage?*" Her driver was loitering in some embarrassment upon the curb, his hands clasped behind his back, but the horses and carriage were nowhere to be seen. Vitriol and savagery radiating from her, she pounced upon the poor reddening man. "Masterson! *What have you done with my carriage?*"

"Begging your ladyship's pardon," he faltered, his eyes returning to Drake who had followed her. "Mr Darcy's coachman, he noticed a cracked leaf spring. We cannot possibly go on, it would mean certain disaster…."

"*A cracked leaf spring!* My carriage is perfect! It is of the most expensive make available, and my man assures me there is no finer in all of Kent!"

The man panted a little, still darting his gaze nervously to the butler, hoping for his support. "Y-yes, my lady, only… well, we did hit that rut on the road…"

"*That was your fault!*"

"…and it has been a good six or seven year since your ladyship authorized a full restoration…."

"Unnecessary! Bring the carriage at once! Cracked leaf spring, indeed! I'll have no more of this nonsense, Masterson! I am leaving for Hertfordshire this minute!"

"I- I am afraid that is quite impossible, My Lady." His tones faltered to nearly a whisper. "Mr Carson, the coachman here, he sent it straight away to Mr Darcy's wainwright here in London. He said as how you wouldn't want for any delay, and it would be best to fix it immediately. We have only just returned from there, my lady. The wainwright, he told me he was setting to it instantly. It will be half torn apart by now, my lady."

"Then bring me Darcy's carriage at once, and let us have no more of this lunacy! I want those horses harnessed and in front of this door in under a quarter of an hour, *do you understand?*"

"Y-yes, my lady." Masterson gave a nervous little salute and moved off briskly. Five minutes later, he had returned for her and stood tremblingly at the door of the house.

"Begging your ladyship's pardon… Mr Carson says none of the Darcy carriages remain. Mr Darcy took the chaise, Colonel Fitzwilliam has the coach, and the curricle is also at the wainwright's for a new coat of paint- being the off-season and all. The other carriages are all back at Pemberley." The man looked as if he wished to melt into a puddle on the spot. Cringing, it was all he could do to force himself to meet his lady's gaze as she descended upon him.

"*Drake!*" the great lady bellowed. "What is the meaning of this rubbish?"

"I am afraid it is quite true, my lady. There are, of course, two drayage carts for the kitchen staff. I do believe there is an older gig still in the stable, kept for the use of Mr Carson or myself when Mr Darcy sends for an errand. Your ladyship would be most welcome to…."

"Unacceptable! In this weather? Three ladies cannot possibly travel in decency and comfort in such a vehicle!"

"Of course, my lady. I shall ring for a cab at once for your ladyship."

"You shall do no such thing! The heiress of Rosings cannot be seen in such a conveyance! Send word to my brother the earl this minute! I would see him here and have words with him!"

"As your ladyship pleases," Drake bowed. The Lady's face purpled at the repetition of that odious phrase. It seemed none in the house were capable of any other response. "If I may, my lady," Drake paused as he went off, "is there any refreshment I can have brought while your ladyship waits?"

"From *that* kitchen?" she sputtered incredulously. "Absolutely not, I would prefer not to be poisoned!"

"As your ladyship pleases." The door slammed behind him.

Bingley finally let go the breath he had been holding for most of the morning. He stood at the steps to his house, waving out of duty as the carriage pulled out of the drive, but of course there was no answering wave. It had taken hours to pack what necessities she deemed indispensable, but at last Caroline was safely bundled within, and on her way to London where she could do no further harm. *About damn time!* he thought savagely, then chided himself. It was not in his nature to harbour such ungenerous thoughts, even for his most trying sister. It was likely only his anxiety to see his precious angel, which had been wearing on him ever since Darcy had ridden off without him earlier.

He clapped his hands together eagerly, rubbing them in brisk anticipation as he stepped back into the house to find his butler. A quick change of clothes and a call for his favourite hunter would be just the thing! As he passed by the drawing room, however, a most forlorn sight diverted him.

The room was empty save for a lone figure in light blue near the window. Georgiana appeared to have wandered from the pianoforte and stood silently with her forehead against the window, her arms crossed over her breast. She jumped a little at his approach, having not noticed him until he was very near.

"Miss Georgiana? May I ask if you are well?" he inquired gently.

"Mr Bingley! Oh, yes, I am…" she faltered, her eyes darting about to hide her prevarication. Finally her shoulders drooped in a long sigh, and blinking, she met his gaze. "I suppose I wish I were not left behind again," she bit her lip, dropping her eyes once more.

She never could have confessed the depression of her feelings so freely a few days ago, but with Elizabeth's encouragement she had resolved to speak her mind more clearly in the future. There were few gentlemen safer than Bingley upon whom to venture her new forthrightness. She watched him hopefully for any sign of understanding.

"Is it that which troubles you! I am so sorry, I had no notion. It is really too bad your cousin could not remain another day or two to keep you company while Darcy is away."

"Yes," she answered softly, suddenly fascinated with her shoe ribbons. "It is a pity Richard could not stay."

"Well, Miss Darcy, I have the perfect solution. You must come with me to call upon the Bennets. I shall be leaving directly."

"Oh," she pled, "that… cannot be necessary, surely. Is it even proper? Miss Elizabeth and my brother will be occupied with business, and I should hate to interrupt. Miss Kitty and Miss Lydia called on me just a while ago. They did not stay long, but is it right that I should return the call on the same day?"

"The Bennets do not stand on ceremony, my dear Georgiana!" he laughed. He had not spoken her first name so simply in two or three years-since she had begun to resemble a grown woman, in fact. His light return to their old familiarity brought a smile to her face.

"I… I suppose I could. Miss Lydia and Miss Kitty were going to town from here, they said, but they oughtn't to be away long, so Miss Kitty said, with the snow threatening. Perhaps I could come…." Her brow furrowed. "Miss Kitty *did* say it would be a fine thing if I could play the pianoforte with her sister some day; perhaps we could learn from each other."

"Which sister?" Bingley asked mildly.

"Well, I should have hoped Miss Elizabeth, as I know her the best, but I do believe she indicated Miss Lydia today when she brought up the idea. She must be greatly accomplished! She said she practices very constantly."

Bingley let go with a most ungentlemanly guffaw before he could catch himself. "Truly! I imagine, Georgiana, that there *is* a great deal you could learn from each other, but I doubt your brother would quite approve of such a curriculum for you. Come, you must accompany me to pay the call! I will ring for the carriage while you make yourself ready."

Georgiana's bewildered expression blossomed into something more hopeful. She nodded agreeably and thanked him with a gracious smile as she turned to go.

"Oh, and Georgiana!" he called just before she was out of sight. "Be sure to ask your maid to attend us. We have had enough ladies' reputations compromised for one week!"

~

George Wickham smiled at the young lady across from him. Miss Mary King, whose unfortunate complexion always caused her to appear to be blushing whether she was or not, set her cup shakily down upon the tea tray. "I am sorry, Mr Wickham," she was saying, "that my uncle is away at present. I believe he would be very much honoured to make your acquaintance."

"Think nothing of it, Miss King," he replied gallantly. "I shall of course be eager for an introduction to him when he returns. At present, however, it is indeed no hardship, for I am quite able to enjoy your amiable company here at the estimable Mrs Long's. It is indeed fortunate for we friendless militia officers, is it not, that she is such an obliging hostess?"

Miss King's shoulders hunched slightly in bashful appreciation of his bold compliments. She clasped her hands together in her lap, her pale lashes shading her grey eyes. Such a pleasing address he had! She had not thought to attract the notice of the town darling- his attentions had always tended in another direction until very lately.

"La, there you are Mary!" Lydia Bennet's unmistakable voice caught the pair's attention. "What a good joke, I had not thought to find you out all alone today!" The flamboyant Bennet girl plopped herself down next to her slightly annoyed companion.

"Oh, Mr Wickham, what a fun thing to find you today!" Lydia plucked up a bit of biscuit from the tea tray, causing Miss King to glance at her in thinly veiled consternation. "I could do with some jolly good times. We had to suffer the *dullest* dinner last night. I declare, Miss Darcy is every bit as stuck up and boring as Mr Darcy is!"

Wickham gave a start which he barely concealed. "Miss Darcy is in town, you say?"

"Oh, my, yes. I suppose her brother forced her to come and meet Lizzy, though I daresay they cannot hope to like each other. Such a mousy little thing! The colonel, though, now *he* is quite a worthy acquaintance! What a shame- me and Kitty called at Netherfield this morning- on Miss Darcy, you know," she winked scandalously, "but the colonel had already departed again for London. I suppose he will be back for the wedding, but how dreary that he should have gone away already!"

"How very intriguing, Miss Lydia. Tell me, do you know how long Miss Darcy intends to remain?"

"Oh! La, I could not say. Me and Kitty left directly, there was nothing interesting to be had. That horrid Miss Bingley was not taking callers, and since the colonel was gone we wanted to get away before she came back downstairs."

Wickham recovered his voice smoothly. "Fitzwilliam gone away already? Hmm, I shouldn't wonder," he mused, allowing his thought to remain significantly incomplete.

Lydia Bennet may have been obtuse and flippant, but one thing she most definitely was *not* was insensible to the expressions of handsome gentlemen. She tilted her curly head, with a penetrating expression that Wickham found eerily similar to her more sensible sister. "Why should you not wonder, Mr Wickham? Do you mean to imply he is not well received? I think him perfectly amiable! I am quite sure he liked me too, you know he talked to me a great deal last night."

"Oh! Forgive me, Miss Lydia, I had no intention to cast aspersions upon any favourite of yours. I quite imagine the good colonel *did* like you very much. His tastes are… well, I should not go on, I fear I may already have said too much."

Though never fond of each other in any sense of the word, the two young ladies cast titillated glances toward one another. This had the ring of good gossip, of the very juiciest kind. If they were only persuasive enough, they might be counted among the privileged first to know. As one, they leaned forward with bated breath.

"You needn't fear anything *I* might say," Lydia flicked her brown eyes toward the other girl.

"Nor I!" Mary declared with spirit. She glared back at Lydia in challenge. "Do tell us, Mr Wickham, you know you can trust *us* with any secrets."

"Of course, you are quite right," he conceded with an air of reluctance. "I suppose it would be only right that I should tell you at least *some* of his affairs, so that you may be put on your guard." The girls' eyebrows rose in unison. A regretful tug softened his mouth, lending him such an air of benevolent authority that the young ladies in attendance hung devotedly on his every word.

"You know I grew up with Darcy, I expect, Miss Lydia? Has…" he paused, hesitantly. "Has your sister shared with you any of my history with the Darcy family?"

Lydia's brow furrowed, her eyes narrowed. It would not do to confess that she had not, in fact, heard any sumptuous rumours from her sister's lips. "I… I think she said he did you some wrong?" she guessed, hoping by his tones that she had judged his meaning rightly.

"One might say that, yes. I have, however, quite forgiven him, and bear him no malice. It is not of that matter I have to speak."

"Such forbearance!" murmured the awestruck Mary King. "Only a true gentleman can forgive such…" she glanced to Lydia for her concurrence, "…such a grievous wrong! You are too good, Mr Wickham."

"Oh, no," he shook his head modestly. "I am no greater than many others in my same position." The girls both sighed. Truly this was the finest among men!

Wickham went on. "It is, naturally, my youthful association with Darcy which brought me often into the company of his cousin the colonel. He was a few years older than I, of course, and as such was frequently our "captain", we called him. There were a few others who would join us, but old Richard- you will forgive me, ladies, if I slip in addressing the son of an earl by his boyhood name, as I knew him- Richard was always the roughest and toughest of the lot. I believe I might say we were all frightened of him. Not one of us could stand up to him when he commenced any endeavour, whether we wished to or not.

"I remember noticing his less than sterling character more than once, but until we were well past our boyhood- but not fully into manhood, you understand- I never thought him a dangerous fellow. Then I started hearing rumours of… oh, I must really stop there. It is not a thing which a gentleman ought to repeat before young ladies."

The girls, both leaning forward with their lips slightly parted in the most profound interest, each gave a little gulp of dismay. "Well, I don't care for all of that nonsense, Wickham!" Lydia asserted. "You *did* say, did you not, that we ought to hear the full truth for our own protection, did you not? You are too much the gentleman to withhold such valuable information!"

He smiled a little, relenting. Clearly his marvelous scruples warred within him, and the interests of the innocent young ladies before him won out. "Very well, Miss Lydia, I bow to your wisdom and discretion in the matter. Well, then, yes, there were many rumours of young ladies of the neighbouring towns and farms mysteriously sent away, for one poor excuse or another. I began to notice that most often a rash of such incidents would occur near the end of our summers home from school."

The girls' eyes were rounded in wonder, their pretty puckered lips drawn into delicious little rosebuds. "Did they…." Lydia leaned close, cupped her hand about her mouth and whispered something to him, causing Miss King to cover her own mouth in abject horror.

"I am afraid so, Miss Lydia. One poor young girl even died of it, she and… well, this is a respectable house, and I shall say no more aloud. It was some years, however, before I learned to suspect Fitzwilliam. Then one day, I caught him in the home of my neighbour. They… well, they had a fair young daughter. More than one scullery maid later confessed his attentions as well. It was always the youngest and most innocent he would prey upon-those who would never suspect."

Fifteen-year-old Lydia and seventeen-year-old Mary straightened, both squaring their shoulders with grave dignity. It was, Wickham reflected, a very beguiling enterprise, as a young lady with erect posture tended to show off her most pleasing attributes rather well.

"Well, I should just like to see him try me!" Lydia announced. "I am nobody's fool, and I shall be certain to tell him so should he ever again come near me!"

"I have no doubts about you," Wickham dipped his head respectfully. "You do, however, have sisters to protect, and I fear not all are as astute or as well-informed as yourself." Lydia nodded in hasty agreement.

"It likely does not matter, however. My old friend has since moved on to larger quarry. He still appreciates a pretty face often enough, I daresay, but he is getting older and must set up an establishment some day or another. The ladies I fear for are those with a large purse to their name as well as innocence and beauty. It is they who are at the greatest risk from him these days."

Lydia turned eyes wide in alarm to Miss King, whose typically ruddy complexion had gone quite pale. "Mary, you had better watch yourself! You know you are not always careful, and you do not have a Mama like mine to advise you!"

Mary King's pretty little mouth fell open in some outrage. "I, not careful! How dare you say such a thing to me Lydia Bennet?"

"Well, it is only the truth, you know, and with an inheritance such as yours, that awful colonel will be after you! La, he is so old! I cannot imagine!"

Mary King fumed impotently. Wickham was smiling with something of a mystified expression. "What can she mean, Miss King? Have you some means which might tempt the colonel? Forgive me, I had no idea. I never think of such things myself. Love, you see, is beyond price. I do exhort you, however, to please be cautious, for my sake, should the colonel return to town. I know for a fact that he has already attempted to seduce one heiress, and it was a lucky thing for her that her brother found them out when he did."

Mary King, trembling a little that anyone could treat a young lady in such a dastardly fashion, touched the tips of her fingers to her lips. "Do... do you know who the poor girl was, Mr Wickham?"

"Why, certainly. It was Miss Georgiana Darcy."

Twenty-One

"Mr Darcy, may I present Mr Jeremiah Brown and his wife Susan." Elizabeth stood just ahead of him near the open doorway, a calculating little smile on her face.

Darcy drew a deep breath. If this was a test, he was determined to pass. "It is an honour to make your acquaintance, sir. Miss Bennet speaks very highly of you."

Mr Brown's expression lit in shy felicity. He looked hesitantly to Elizabeth. Clearly he was comfortable with her presence, but the eminent Mr Darcy's reputation went before him, and the modest farmer could never have expected the prestigious gentleman to appear on his own doorstep. He was not quite certain what civilities might be expected. Hobbling on a little crutch, he backed into his humble abode, gesturing invitingly to the gentleman. "Do, please suhr, come i' ou' o' the weather."

"Thank you." Darcy removed his hat and ducked his tall frame inside the door. "This seems a very comfortable house," he complimented his hostess, casting his eyes about the family's cozy arrangements. A gaggle of small children in the corner caught his interest. "Hullo! What have we here?" he smiled kindly down at the farmer's little brood. He directed his attention to the oldest of the lot, a boy of about ten. "My name is Darcy. What is yours?"

The lad's eyes darted hesitantly to his father, but he plucked up his courage. He stood to greet the gentleman properly as he had been taught. "Willy, suhr."

Darcy's eyes rose briefly to Elizabeth's, as she had come to stand near the children. "A very fine name, my boy," he smiled.

"'T'was after me grandpapa, suhr," the boy answered proudly. "Tha's me sister Millie and me brother Jack."

Darcy greeted the younger two, both looking to be about four or five. Millie immediately grasped his finger and giggled. Mrs Brown started in embarrassment, meaning to pull her daughter from the gentleman, but he assured her politely that he had no objections to the children. The youngest two gathered about his legs in friendly awe.

"Come, William," Elizabeth suggested gently, extending her hands to the younger children. "Will you show me how your little peahens are coming along?" She glanced up at Darcy by way of explanation. "One of the neighbours had an unseasonably late brood, and they thought young William here would make a fine gamekeeper," she winked. Whether it was that bold gesture or her easy employment of the child's name, Darcy's heart flipped again.

Her gaze returned to the children as she ushered them toward the door. "They must have grown so much since last week! Have they been keeping warm enough?" Elizabeth chatted amicably with the children as she led them out to a little soddy near the house, leaving Darcy gaping behind her. He stared at her back until after the door had closed, then shook himself. He turned again to the farmer and his wife.

"Taik a seat, please suhr," Mr Brown offered. The man's wife came to him and the small party all sat, occupying most of the furniture in the little house. "Mr Darcy, I know wha' this is abou'," the man's head hung, his bearing resigned to his fate. "Me rent. I canna' maik i', I know. How soon must w'all be out?"

Darcy shook his head. "You mistake me, sir. Miss Bennet has asked my advice in resolving the affair while her father is indisposed, but it is not for me to decide anything. I believe the family's intentions are to find a workable solution which will keep your family in good security while recompensing the estate. It is Miss Bennet's wish to settle the matter in Mr Bennet's lifetime, rather than leaving things to the heir of Longbourn to decide."

"Aye. I taik yer meanin', suhr." Mr Brown nodded, a faint hope flickering again on his face.

"To that end," Darcy went on, "it was my hope to learn something of your experience. How long have you been a tenant here at Longbourn?"

"A' me life, suhr. Me father was old Samuel Bennet's arb'rist, and he tau' me a' 'e knew."

"Arborist? How is it you became a farmer instead?"

Mr Brown shifted hesitantly. "Th'estate, y'see suhr... Mrs Bennet dinn' see any point to the fancy orch'rds whe' Mr Bennet brou' 'er 'ere. Waste o' money, she ca'ed it, keepin' an arb'rist on. Now i's jest the season'l 'help as is required." He shrugged, masking his disappointment with what surely had been a tremendous blow to his livelihood. Darcy's lips thinned. He wondered what the current Mrs Bennet had found to be a better use of the estate's funds. "Farmin' suited me a'most 's well," Mr Brown added with forced cheer.

"And so…" Darcy shifted his tall frame uncomfortably in the little seat, "I suppose you are indeed familiar with the curious little orchard in the hollow, near the edge of the Longbourn property. Your father must have had some hand in its management, though it has gone quite wild now. I have some interest in that persimmons tree. Tell me, if you can, is it possible to take a start of such a tree? I should like to know how it would fare in my conservatory."

"Oh, I wouldna' do tha', suhr," the man shook his head with authority. "Tha' tree, i' likes the cold i' does. It'd never thrive in an conservatory… beggin' your pardon, suhr."

"Indeed?" Darcy raised an eyebrow in interest. "Cold we have aplenty in Derbyshire. Is it possible to graft the tree?"

"Aye, suhr, tha'd be the best way. Tricky, those persimmons trees are, 'till a man gets 'em started." He went on to elaborate some of the difficulties his father had had in propagating young starts from the tree, and what they had learned. Darcy listened raptly as the man humbly expounded upon his knowledge.

At about this time, a crisp snowy breeze blew Elizabeth and the children back through the door, little flecks of white shimmering on their outer clothing. Elizabeth's smile was fresh and radiant, full of life, and it reflected in the rosy cheeks of the children. Darcy felt his breath leave him once again. Oh, to have this joy for his own! He stood, helplessly drawn near to her. Her vibrant face turned up to his, and he watched in mesmerized fascination as the last snowflake melted off the tip of her nose.

Mr Brown cleared his throat. "I thaink you for ca'ing on us, Mr Darcy and Miss 'Liz'beth. As it is though, I s'pect it'd be best if you get to back to th' 'ouse soon, bein' on foot and a'. I'd hait to see Miss 'Liz'beth taik cold."

"Nonsense, Mr Brown, you always fear such for me, and it has never yet occurred!" Elizabeth teased. "It is a very light snow, and not threatening more at the moment." She turned her sparkling eyes back to Darcy, arching her brow expectantly.

"Yes, well," Darcy straightened his coat, recalling the purpose of his visit. "Miss Bennet, would you despise me very much if I made your favourite tenant an offer of employment?"

The man and his wife turned shocked gazes to one another as Elizabeth's eyes rounded. "Excuse me, Mr Darcy?"

"Your Mr Brown is quite an expert in an area which intrigues me very much. I have an arborist for my orchards, of course, as well as three assistants for seasonal work, but the grounds at Pemberley are exceedingly large, and their hands are full. Mr Brown has knowledge which none of them possess, and I imagine when old Stevens seeks to retire in a few years, I shall be looking for a suitable replacement. I believe I have found him; by your leave, of course, Miss Bennet."

He turned to the man and his wife, still gaping in wonder. "And yours, naturally, Mr and Mrs Brown. It is only fair to warn you that the climate in Derbyshire is somewhat harsher than what you are accustomed to, and I will completely understand if you do not desire the change."

Mr and Mrs Brown shared the barest of wordless exchanges before their eyes turned back to the oddity before them. Never did it happen, that a wealthy gentleman strode into the middle of one's need and simply set all the past on its ear. "I…" Brown choked out a whisper. "I don' ge' 'round s'easy, suhr," he gestured to his bum leg.

"That is no bother," Darcy waved. "We have any number of two-wheeled carts for use about the estate, and I will see to it you always have one at your disposal, and a horse exclusively for your own use. As for your leg, of course, we will want to make sure it continues to heal as much as can be. We do have an apothecary resident in Lambton, as well as a doctor in the next town. It is not necessary for you to decide immediately…."

Brown and his wife glanced at each other once again. "Wi' respect, suhr, I think we've decided. I'd be right pleased. But," he turned his gaze to Elizabeth, "what of my debt to the Bennets? I can'n leave."

Elizabeth offered her old friend a shimmering smile. "Fear not, Mr Brown, if I know Mr Darcy, he already has a solution in mind for that as well." She turned a light expression on the gentleman, who appeared for a moment to have lost whatever ideas he might once have possessed.

"Ah…" he stuttered. Recollecting himself, he started again. "Well, it is quite simple, really. I know the sum required, and I can assure you that your new wages will allow you to repay the debt rather quickly. So that the Bennet family may not suffer by my gain, I shall purchase the debt, and you may settle it with me, on very easy terms. Will that be agreeable, Mr Brown?"

Mr Brown straightened to his fullest height for the first time that day, straining on his wounded leg. "Yes, suhr. I'd be right honoured, suhr!"

Darcy smiled. "I will make the necessary arrangements. Can your family be ready to remove by the end of the week?" The man answered tremblingly in the affirmative. Darcy nodded in acknowledgement. He then knelt before the children, his fine buckskin breeches directly on the sod floor. "Well, Master William, it seems you and I will be seeing more of each other. Will you bring your peahens with you to Derbyshire? We can always use some healthy fowl about, as well as clever hands to tend them."

Willy swallowed, stiffened, and nodded smartly, the mirror image of his father. "Yes, suhr!"

"Good," Darcy rose. "You will be a most welcomed addition to Pemberley, my good fellow." He smiled gently at the younger children, sparking return smiles from each of them. With a light heart, he took his leave of the little family and ushered the lady out of the door.

In some hesitation, he offered Elizabeth his elbow once more. Was she pleased? Had he overstepped? Her face was turned from him momentarily; he could not read her feelings. He caught his breath, waiting.

Wondrously, she took a firm, possessive hold of his forearm and drew herself near. Her bonnet tipped out of the way as she raised her face, and Darcy was treated to the most glorious smile he had ever seen. A broad grin split his face and he gestured gallantly to the road with his free hand. "Shall we, Miss Bennet?"

"By all means, Mr Darcy." She fell into step beside him as they set out for her home. A light snow salted her clothing, the heavy grey sky muffling all sound save their own breath and the light crunch of frosty ground beneath their feet. Darcy felt he had stepped out of time and space into this private little interval, a respite from the world.

"Miss Bennet," he began softly, waiting for her to look at him again with those glorious eyes. She did so easily, and he gazed quietly into them before continuing. "I hope you are not displeased by the arrangements we discussed. It was not my wish to subvert your- you father's- authority where your tenants are concerned."

She tilted her head, a fine line appearing where a smile tugged at the corner of her mouth. "And how have you done so, sir? Have you paid other visits I am not aware of? Shall we be growing beans instead of potatoes in the lower field next year?"

He could not help a low laugh. "I believe you know what I mean. The solution seemed very tidy, and I believe all concerned will be the better off for it, but I gave you very little chance to object."

"I do not see how it would have been my place to do so," she replied easily. "Have you not the right to offer employment to whomever you wish? If his debt to my father's estate is to be reconciled, he has no further obligation to my family, and may take any situation he chooses. I expect you already have some answer for the problem of our now vacant farm?"

Her suspicions were confirmed with a glance up at his face. A cautious smile wavered, his eyes twinkling significantly. "I believe Mr Bingley might. You are not displeased?"

"Terribly so!"

Darcy froze abruptly in his tracks. "I beg your pardon, Miss Elizabeth. I have not the pleasure of understanding you. What is it, specifically, that displeases you? I beg you would tell me so it can be rectified."

"Why," she shrugged dramatically, "I shall be losing my favourite playmates! The Brown children are great companions of mine, you must know, Mr Darcy."

He started breathing again. "I know," he answered at length, beginning to walk once more. At her questioning glance, he admitted, "I happened upon you once as you were playing with them. You ought to pay more attention to your surroundings, Miss Elizabeth, as I watched you- not very discreetly either, I daresay- for a very long time without ever attracting your notice."

"Mr Darcy! You are a sneak!"

"Sneaking, while riding a seventeen-and-a-half hand horse? Impossible!"

"A gentleman would have made his presence known!" she arched a playful look at him.

"And interrupt such a lovely scene? You quite mistake me, Miss Bennet, if you think me capable of that. I am a selfish creature, I am afraid, and I derived much enjoyment from watching you and the children at your sport."

"Well," she tossed her head blithely, "I shall have to think of some suitable punishment for you."

"Oh, back to that, are we? What, then, of my reward for rendering my assistance? Do I merit any sort of favour?"

A sly curve came to her lips. "Perhaps the one cancels out the other!"

"No better than that? Do I not earn some benefit by my honesty? I might well never have told you, you know, and never have been forced to pay that particular debt."

She laughed. "Quite true, Mr Darcy! Tell me what reward my 'pupil' would request, then, and I shall consider it."

Darcy stopped her, looking seriously down into her face. "A very near one to my heart, Miss Bennet," he whispered. He took her hand off his elbow and clasped it tenderly.

Elizabeth's breath caught. He had been so light-hearted and easy, she had not expected such a serious shift. Was he going to press her for her acceptance again so soon? Both knew it to be an inevitability by this point, but just for a time she had enjoyed the fantasy that she still had some choice in the matter, and that he was a devoted suitor actively trying to curry her favour.

Darcy reached hesitantly for her other hand, and blinking, unable to meet his eyes, she allowed him to take it. "Miss Bennet," he murmured, "I find myself a very jealous man."

Surprised, she glanced up. "J-jealous?" she stammered. "I do not understand, sir. Have you some cause to doubt me?"

"You, no. I am quite envious, however, of another young man bearing the moniker of William, with whose name you seem quite familiar."

"Wh-what?" she broke into a confused grin, starting to chuckle.

"And my own sister, who makes free with your Christian name! Not a good example to set, is it Miss Bennet, that a girl of less than a day's acquaintance should have enjoyed such a privilege while I, who have known you two months almost, am constrained to formalities?"

Elizabeth eyed him appraisingly, amusement sparkling. He gazed down tenderly, admiring the tiny drifting snowflakes beginning to gather on her lashes.

"What say you… *Elizabeth*?" he whispered. He tipped his head lower, closer to her face. "Will you allow me to call you by your given name, or is there some other which you would prefer?"

She forced herself to remain still, not flinching away at his closeness. It was not uncomfortable to be so near him, but it made her heart flutter queerly, uncontrollably. Her voice caught breathlessly. "My most *particular* friends call me 'Lizzy'. Is that the name to which you refer?"

His hands, cradling hers, raised them to his chest, in near reach of his lips. Gloves or no, her eyes became riveted on them, wondering at his intentions. "If that is what those dearest to you call you, then yes. I do ask for that freedom. What think you of my boldness? Am I incorrigible… Lizzy?"

"Very nearly," her words rasped in her throat. "What am I to do with you?"

His mouth softened. "Say you will return the favour. It would give me the very greatest pleasure… Lizzy."

Spirit returned to her eyes, and she lifted her chin. "Or perhaps, Mr Darcy, if I am clever, I should withhold that particular prize until you have done something rather singular to earn it!"

"Refusing to make it easy on me, are you not?" he grinned in some delight.

Elizabeth fluttered her lashes coquettishly. "A lady must have *some* tricks up her sleeve, would you not agree? Else how shall I endeavour to exert any influence at all?"

"I think you will find, Elizabeth, that a smile from you is all that is required to sway me." He dipped his head still lower, his voice dropping huskily. His hands tightened around hers and he held her eyes intently.

She gazed back, wordlessly studying the depth of feeling mirrored in his expression, trembling in his voice. Slowly she nodded. "Very well, William," she whispered evenly.

His held breath rushed to the fore, his entire body shuddering in release. His eyes blinked rapidly and without even consciously willing it, his right hand left hers. Thoughtlessly he reached the glove-tipped fingers up to brush a stray snowflake from her cheek, but stopped himself just short of touching her. He hesitated, fearing he had gone too far, but her gaze never wavered. Her breathing had quickened and those marvelous eyes dilated, but she remained still.

Boldly, daringly, he closed the distance to her soft skin. The kid leather of his glove molded to her cheek, dissolving the flakes as they touched down. He held his hand there, she permitting his caress with uncertainty speaking from her eyes.

"Elizabeth," he whispered, so lowly the word was almost inaudible. "Lizzy…." Her eyes fell closed in unconscious invitation.

His heart in his throat, he tipped his face lower. He could feel the puff of her breath warming his cheek, the heat of her skin radiating in the chilled space between them. It was a siren call, an irresistible beckoning, and he had not the strength to deny it. Delicately, fearfully, his curled fingers offered the barest nudge to her cheek, coaxing her to welcome him. He drew in one final breath, then those delicious lips found his.

He lingered there, barely touching his mouth to hers, for long intoxicating seconds. Slowly and carefully, he parted his lips to cup them around her lower one, drawing it between them. Elizabeth was nearly panting, so rapid and shallow was her breathing, but she held herself rigidly still. He released her lip, then took it again. He gave the gentlest of tugs, and her jaw relaxed.

At his third brush, she met him with softened lips. His heart soared. Pressing a little more insistently, he encouraged her to release her mouth to him. With modest reserve, she did. Her breath became his as their lips tangled sweetly, softly. He lost count of their kisses as they merged together into one seamless, rapturous caress. His other hand had joined the first, and together they cradled her lovely face while Elizabeth's hands, stranded somewhere near his chest, fisted and rested lightly on the lapels of his overcoat.

Euphoric, he tilted his head slightly to the side, approaching her more intimately. Her graceful neck flexed, curving to tip her delicate jaw to accommodate his attentions. His smallest fingers trailed down the grooves of her throat, etching her shape and feel into his hands. *What cruel fancy struck me this morning to make me remember my gloves?* He forgot them often enough when at home, why could he not have done so today?

His entire being quivered, a deep groan of ecstasy suppressed. Who was he kidding? The gloves could not matter. Even swathed and bundled beneath layers of outerwear, he had never felt so laid bare, so deeply entwined with anyone. Elizabeth, his extraordinary Elizabeth, so sweetly surrendering! Could it be possible?

Elizabeth was experiencing some crisis of feeling. She had been determined to challenge him a little more, to exact a little more studious conversation from him so that she might better examine his character. *Oh, why must I be so willful?* What more proof did she truly need that he was honourable and devoted?

Surely she had given him every opportunity and excuse to turn tail and run, yet he had remained to shield her. He could easily have sworn her off- or worse yet, he could have turned brutish, forcing her to follow through with an engagement whether she hated him or not. Instead he had humbled himself, made himself utterly vulnerable, and in the process begun to reveal his true nature to her wondering eyes. The more closely she looked, the more inevitable it seemed that her heart would abandon her.

Allowing herself to trust him was a tremendous gamble, a daunting plunge. Her body tensed, still unwilling to wholly submit. Patiently, gently, he persuaded her to lower her guard. At last, something inside of her let go. She *wanted* him, and finally she came to admit it to herself. She drew back fractionally, her lips still hovering near his- just enough to catch his notice and cause him to open his eyes. Deliberately, so that he would know beyond a doubt that it had been her own volition, she moved into him again.

Darcy did vocalize his pleasure then. An unconscious throaty moan rumbled low in his chest, and an answering quiver trembled in Elizabeth's core. He traced the crisp edges of her full lips with his own, drinking in her willing reception. Gently he pressed a withdrawing kiss to her upper lip, and still cupping her face, gazed down into her eyes. "Elizabeth," he whispered reverently, stroking her cheekbones with his thumbs. "My Lizzy... you asked me before what I had been thinking, do you remember?"

She nodded ever so slightly, not wishing to disturb the tenuous contact of his fingers. He tilted his head a little, smiling gently. "It was this. It was you, and my dreams of being with you like this. It was the hope that you would be so warm, so tender. I am afraid, my Lizzy, that you have quite made me your slave."

Her mouth quirked- that delicious mouth! Now he knew it to be such for himself! "That is well, sir, for it seems I shall require some means of keeping you biddable for the foreseeable future."

His expression turned to one of awe. "Elizabeth!" he whispered. "Does that mean....?"

Her face dropped a little, bashful for the first time. She peeked up at him through the shade of her frosted lashes. "I do not make a habit of allowing just *any* gentleman such liberties, as you may well remember sir."

"*William.*" His body pulsing, he touched her chin to lift her gaze.

"William," she murmured, his name spoken with gentle affection.

He stood breathless, staring, wishing to burn this moment into his lifelong memories. His thumb brushed over her chin, and unable to resist, he lowered his face again to hers. This time he did not confine his attentions to her glorious mouth, but explored her cheeks, her forehead, even brushing light kisses over her snowy lashes. Elizabeth leaned into him, willing and pliant, and he was helpless to deny the deep tremour of pure elation washing through him.

Conscience tickled his thoughts at last, and he drew back. "We are quite exposed here, Elizabeth," he murmured. "Anyone could happen along, and I fear that will do our reputations no good whatsoever!"

She smiled, a pert twist returning to her lips. "Do you forget we have already been seen unchaperoned together by Sir William Lucas? He will have us marching down the aisle by special license within the fortnight, if I know him at all. There really can be no more compromising witnesses abroad today!"

Darcy laughed, still stroking her cheeks. "If that be the case, I shall not fear! I must confess though; I will have to admit to a sudden admiration for Sir William's way of thinking." He drew her close once more, savouring her luscious sweetness.

Elizabeth flattened her hands upon his chest, no longer pressing them cautiously against him, but tenderly to him. She spread her fingers over his thick coat, sensing his chest rising and falling with his breath, the steady thrum of his heart. There was something delectable and exhilarating about such intimacy with him, something she had never thought to expect. It almost frightened her to consider how rapidly she had become at home in his embrace. Enthralled and thoroughly hypnotized, she leaned her body closer to his as he tenderly caressed her mouth once more.

Approaching hoofbeats from around a grove of trees caused her to blink and pull back. Darcy too, attempted to compose himself, but in both cases their flushed complexions gave them away. The rider was upon them quickly, moving in a brisk trot, and before they could step apart the man had pulled up. He halted his mount, and with an air of some disbelief, lowered his woolen scarf from his face.

"Well, Lizzy! I trust you have some explanation for what I think I am seeing!"

Darcy turned his shoulder slightly, an implicit warning, interposing himself between Elizabeth and the stranger.

Elizabeth herself had gone quite pale. She bit her lip and glued her eyes on the rider's saddle. "Good afternoon, Uncle."

Twenty-Two

Georgiana had found Mary Bennet the only sister available to visit with her. Kitty and Lydia had not yet returned. Mrs Bennet was also in town, and Mrs Gardiner seemed nowhere about. Mr Bingley had retired to the opposite side of the room with his Jane, and Georgiana had to make do with the least receptive member of the family for her companion.

She glanced in the betrothed couple's direction occasionally. She liked Jane, though she had had little enough opportunity to actually speak with her. She seemed genuinely kind and affable, like Bingley. She may have lacked the lively energy which characterized her sister, but there was a serenity about her that seemed so restful after days in a household with Caroline Bingley. She supposed that was why Charles liked her so much, and could not blame him.

Mary was quite a different story. Neither she nor Georgiana were in the slightest at ease, and it remained to be seen which would pluck up the courage to draw the other out of her shell. Mary sat silently across from her, eyes largely on the floor and her hands resolutely clasping her cooling teacup.

"I believe that Miss Kitty and Miss Lydia mentioned they expected their visit to town to be but a short one?" Georgiana put forward awkwardly.

"It seldom is," Mary mumbled, a faint bitter edge to her voice.

Georgiana caught herself in a little surprise. Mary seemed to have no notion that her discourteous response showed an odious lack of breeding; in fact, her manner was exactly the same as it had been before the question had ever been put to her. She stared vacantly at the rug, sullen and stony.

Georgiana swallowed. *Perhaps* she ventured *I am not the only one who is painfully shy!* It would be difficult for an introverted girl to survive at the very centre of such a boisterous household full of siblings, but one so completely the opposite of each of her other sisters, one who lacked many of the charms the others flaunted, could quite possibly be thoroughly miserable. Steeling her resolve, Georgiana tried harder.

"Do you play, Miss Mary? I have heard that Elizabeth does. Miss Kitty mentioned something this morning about Miss Lydia's expertise on the pianoforte."

Mary's hazel eyes leapt to meet hers at last. "*Lydia?*" she asked incredulously. "She said that?"

Georgiana's face fell. "Why, yes, she did- they both did!"

Mary's mouth crinkled and she began blinking rapidly. She looked quickly about, seeking to hide her shift in expression from her guest but failing miserably.

"Miss Mary? I do not understand! Have I said something wrong? I do beg your pardon!"

Mary's hand was covering her mouth and her shoulders had begun to shake uncontrollably. Georgiana gasped in horror at herself. She had made her hostess cry! Abominable! What a wretched girl Miss Mary must think her!

"M-miss Mary, please, I am so sorry! I do not know what I have said, but…."

Mary raised her face back to her then, lowering her hand slightly, and a squelched peal of laughter escaped her. Stunned, Georgiana studied her a minute. Mary was not crying, she was monstrously amused! Her brow furrowed in wonder, Georgiana watched as stoic Mary Bennet strove to contain her laughter.

"Can it really be that bad?" she whispered in awe.

"You have no idea!" giggled Mary. "Kitty must be pulling one over on you. Even Jane had to hide in Papa's study! My poor aunt has been lying down with a headache ever since!" Mary hid behind her hand again, struggling to regain proper deportment, but this time she was not alone in her labours. Georgiana bit back a most indecorous chortle, certain that her face was by now a brilliant crimson.

After an uncomfortable moment spent composing themselves, Mary pressed her mouth into a tight, thoughtful expression. She glanced toward the end of the room, noting that Jane and Mr Bingley seemed completely absorbed in their own conversation. Blinking hesitantly and drawing a shaky breath, she turned back to her guest. "*I* play, Miss Darcy, but no one ever wants to listen to me- unless they want to dance and I am the one at the instrument."

Georgiana's mind fixed on those words. They sounded uncannily like her own words to Elizabeth. How she had hung on that unwavering encouragement offered! She leaned slightly forward. "I will listen to you, Miss Mary. Perhaps we could try a duet!"

Georgiana learned quickly the reason no one wanted to listen to Mary. It was not her technical expertise, for that was superior and rivaled her own. Rather, it was her pedantic air and the dreary pieces she selected. She could do nothing about the other girl's personal taste, she supposed, but she was watching Mary carefully and began to realize something. "Mary," she asked softly, gently. "Do you *like* playing?"

Mary's hands dropped from the instrument. She stared with her mouth slightly agape. "No one has ever asked me that before. I never thought of it." She faced forward, gazing blankly at the sheet of music before her. Georgiana glanced away, granting Mary her privacy.

"It is the only thing I am good at," Mary shrugged at last. "I suppose I play because I do not know what else to do but read."

Georgiana held her peace another moment, considering. At last she ventured, "You are *very* good, Miss Mary."

Mary's eyes turned sharply toward Georgiana. The other girl's tone was sincere and kind, and absent was the silent "but" which always characterized that statement when uttered by her family. She waited for it, but it did not come.

"You think me dull, do you not?" she prodded, unable to take the compliment at face value.

"Not at all," Georgiana returned stoutly. "You have a natural talent, and if you had the masters I had, you could be shockingly good! I just wonder if you enjoy it- if you appreciate it." Georgiana did her best to temper her tone with humility. She feared that her reference to her superior masters would sound snobbish and vain.

Fortunately, it was the words of praise which Mary took to her heart. It was doubtful she had heard many. She lifted her fingers again to the keys, tracing C# thoughtfully with her thumb. She looked again to her companion and a hint of warmth lit her eyes. "I think I should enjoy playing with you, Miss Darcy. May we try something together?"

They were so employed when Lydia and Kitty Bennet returned. The very frames of the house shuddered with their unflagging obstreperousness. The two chilled girls gathered around the fire in the drawing room and their voices drowned out even the pianoforte.

Georgiana's gaze drifted to them occasionally, but socially fragile Mary had only just opened up to her. She dared not leave her to visit with the others. It was obvious they had not noticed her presence at the instrument as yet, so much did they take Mary's constant playing for granted.

"La, it is so cold!" Lydia stuck her hands before the fire. "Jane, did you see, it is starting to snow at last!" Jane offered some murmured reply, but Lydia paid little attention. The room was filled with the clatter of their hot cups and saucers as they tried to warm up.

"Mary!" Lydia turned their way at last. "We heard the most delicious... Oh! Miss Darcy!" Lydia elbowed her sister and both stared in some surprise.

Georgiana was turning pages and could not politely rise from the instrument, but she greeted them as cordially as was possible. "Good afternoon, Miss Kitty and Miss Lydia. I trust you had a pleasant time in town?"

"Oh, we had a *most revealing* visit," Lydia's head was bobbing. Kitty snickered beside her. Georgiana's brow puckered. These girls were merry enough, but their manners were nothing like those of their genteel older sisters.

"Me and Kitty and that dreadful Mary King, we heard something *very* interesting today." Kitty, not as bold or quick-witted as her younger sister, giggled in response, but offered no comments of her own.

"Oh?" Georgiana's eyes widened innocently. Clearly the girls were involved in some kind of gossip. While she felt surely her brother would not approve of her indulging in the same activity, she did not know of a gracious way to excuse herself. It seemed that she would be required to hear.

"Aye, indeed!" Lydia averred. She and her sister shared significant glances. Mary had ceased playing and folded her hands disinterestedly in her lap. "Would you believe," Lydia went on with a conspiratorial whisper, "that there is- or *was*- a gentleman in our very own town with a *most* dastardly history?"

Georgiana felt the blood run from her face. She dropped her eyes, struck speechless.

"A young lady of breeding and character does not espouse rumours, Lydia." Mary spoke with prim sharpness. Her face had dropped back into her customary scowl. She glanced sideways at Georgiana, and the remainder of the speech she had prepared for just such an occasion went unsaid. Somehow it seemed pompous and out of place in such gentle company.

"Oh, but this is no mere rumour! I have it as a fact, from a very *reliable* source- meant as a warning, I shall have you know! I shall be on my guard, make no mistake. You ought to hear all!"

"I am always on my guard," Mary mumbled. "Young ladies cannot be too careful where their virtue regarding members of the other sex is concerned."

"You are so strange, Mary!" Lydia giggled dismissively. "I know Miss Darcy understands the importance of warnings. Is that not so, Miss Darcy?"

Georgiana had begun to tremble. Was it possible? Her chest heaved slightly. Could her story have been relayed to strangers? She turned her eyes back to Lydia's sly grin. Her only hope lay in silence, and in the slight chance that she had mistaken the girl's meaning.

"You see, it is as I told you, Kitty! Well, I think you were abominably ill-used, Miss Darcy, and so I told Maria Lucas when she heard…"

"H-heard… what?" Georgiana began to shake.

"…and my aunt Philips, she said she was glad the man never came to *her* door, I can tell you!"

"What have you heard?" Georgiana's voice dropped to a trembling, desperate whisper.

"Why, 'tis nothing! Only that there was a 'gentleman' in town who barely wanted the name, but he is gone now. It was someone you knew, Miss Darcy, that is all." Lydia tried her hand at coy subtlety, but there was nothing artful in Lydia Bennet. She was all brass and vulgarity, and poor Georgiana was turning redder by the second.

"G-gone, you say?" Georgiana stammered. Her last shreds of dignity were fading away, as every comment of Lydia's hit nearer the mark.

"Oh, yes! For surely your brother would not suffer him to remain, after his monstrous behaviour to you!"

Hot tears began pooling in Georgiana's eyes. Ruined! All of this time it had seemed her secret was safe. Just when she had dared to live again, all was dashed at a whim! A sob broke in her chest and she put the heel of her hand to her forehead.

"Miss Darcy?" a low voice inquired. Mary, still sitting near her on the piano bench, slid her hand over Georgiana's other in awkward sympathy. Georgiana pinched the other girl's fingers rather desperately, aching for some sort of steady comfort.

"La, see, Kitty, I told you that man was dangerous! Only look how frightened poor Miss Darcy is!"

In a rush of vehement despair, Georgiana bolted to her feet. "Let me tell you something, Miss Lydia! That man *is* dangerous! Do you want to know how I know? I saw it for myself! I saw him change from someone I trusted into a devious villain! I cared for him and all he wanted to do was use me!" She covered her face with her hands and began to sob uncontrollably.

Bingley, who had paid absolutely no attention to Lydia's careless banter, was on his feet in an instant and crossing the room to stand near Georgiana. Gently, protectively, he put his hand at her elbow. "Georgiana!" he hissed into her ear. "Use caution! Your words are rather compromising!"

"It is too late for that!" Georgiana wailed. She pushed his hand away and ran from the room. She scrambled to the front door, mindless of the cold and her thin muslin. Jerking it open, she nearly fell into her brother's arms.

"Georgie! Whatever is the matter?" he exclaimed. He reached to steady her and peered fearfully into her tear-streaked face. Elizabeth, white and shaken, stood next to him. Just behind them both towered a grim-faced gentleman she had not seen before. She stared back and forth at them, still choking on her tears.

"Georgiana!" William bent to cradle his long arm around her. "What is it, Sweetling?"

Elizabeth, too, reached for her, taking Georgiana's free hand. "Dear Georgie," she whispered. "How can we help?"

Georgiana's face hardened. Glaring at Elizabeth, she jerked her hand away. "Do not come near me ever again, Elizabeth Bennet! How could you? I trusted you! *How could you do it?*"

Elizabeth and Darcy's shock was equal. "Georgiana! How dare you speak in that tone!"

"Wait, please, William," Elizabeth held a quelling hand to him, which proved instantly effective. "Georgie, have I hurt you somehow? Please tell me what it is that troubles you."

Georgiana screwed her mouth tightly, drew back her hand, and slapped Elizabeth soundly across the cheek. "You lied to me!" she sobbed. Her voice shook and the tears took over. She broke down completely. She pushed her way past her brother- successfully so only because he stood thoroughly flabbergasted and helpless. She set out in a run, tripped in her skirts, and tumbled to the frozen earth only a few paces away.

Her brother was instantly upon her, seizing her shoulders and dragging her to her feet. "*Georgiana! What is the meaning of this?*" She flinched through her tears. She did not remember ever hearing William so angry. She closed her eyes tightly, biting her lip. "Answer me! Why did you strike Elizabeth?" he demanded.

She squinted her eyes open and Bingley was there, forcing her brother's hands down. "Darcy, let me. I believe Miss Darcy had a hard time of it in there."

Darcy turned away, flinging his arms and sputtering in furious vexation. He froze with his back to her, anchoring his fists at his hips. "*This* is a wretched beginning!" he thundered, to no one in particular.

Georgiana was terrified. She had reacted in rage and passion, a thing she had always been taught not to do. William could never understand! Thankfully, Bingley at least was treating her gently- for now. He led her to a small stone bench near the garden and pressed a handkerchief into her fingers. She nodded gratefully and looked up in time to see Elizabeth pacing briskly toward her brother.

Darcy's shoulders drooped and he held out his hand for Elizabeth. She took it, drawing near with her face full of questions.

"*Lizzy!*" a loud voice snapped. Georgiana's gaze followed the sound. The unknown gentleman she had seen before was marching toward Elizabeth, fire in his eyes. Mrs. Gardiner was out now, and hurrying up behind him. "Get back in the house, Elizabeth!" he ordered. "I have seen enough!"

Elizabeth turned in some defiance. "Uncle, there is much you do not know! Please, let me expl-"

"*Now*, Elizabeth!" the man roared. He turned his glare on Darcy. "I will have words with my niece *alone*, sir!"

Georgiana could not see her brother's face, but she could well imagine it. Fitzwilliam Darcy was not in the habit of backing down to any man. She watched Elizabeth turn quietly to him and give him a look of such warm reassurance that it would have made her heart soar- if only she were not convinced that Elizabeth had betrayed her.

William deflated. She could see all of the starch go out of his manner even from behind. Deliberately, he gave Elizabeth back her hand and forlornly gazed after her retreating figure. Elizabeth glanced over her shoulder more than once, but she obeyed her uncle. The entire Bennet family, save for Jane, filed into the house and the door banged closed, rattling on its hinges.

Georgiana clenched her eyes shut and buried her face in Bingley's handkerchief. The sobs began anew. Everything was wrong! Her life as she knew it was over, and William's chances with Elizabeth were blasted. Not that she ought to regret that, if Elizabeth had violated her confidence, but he had been so hopeful! Her dear brother had found love at last, and it was all a sham!

A gentle hand rested on her shoulder and she looked up, stunned that William could be approaching her so kindly after what she had just done. It was not he. Jane's sweet face, warmed by an understanding softness, smiled into her own. "Come, Miss Darcy. Shall we find some place out of the cold where we can talk?"

~

"Elizabeth Bennet, are you out of your senses?" Edward Gardiner paced the floor in his brother-in-law's cramped study. His niece hunched in a seat, her hands pressed anxiously together between her knees and her eyes studying the carpet. "Lizzy! Look at me!" he snapped impatiently.

Elizabeth raised her face. He could still see the bright mark against her cheek from that horrible Darcy girl. "How did you become mixed up with this dreadful family? Indecent, both of them! I will not see this go any further!"

Elizabeth closed her eyes and a fat tear escaped. What she would have given two days ago to be able to depend upon just such a determination from her uncle! Now, searching her feelings, she found it was the last thing she wished. "Uncle, please, there is so much you do not know! Please let me try to explain!"

He blew air through his teeth, running his fingers over his thinning pate. Exasperated, he at last took a seat. His vibrant and spirited niece sat wilted and lost before him, dejected and defeated. No, he could not allow this to continue! Whoever this Darcy fellow was, if he held this kind of power over the indomitable Elizabeth Bennet, his society must not be tolerated.

Elizabeth took a deep breath to begin, but the door to the study creaked open. Holding up his hand to stay her explanation, he looked to find his wife entering the room. She closed the door softly behind herself and took a seat next to Elizabeth, patting her niece's hand. Mr Gardiner studied his wife shrewdly. Madeline had a fair bit of the romantic in her, but she was not known to him to take leave of her senses where the decent comportment of young ladies was concerned.

"Well, then. Which of you is going to tell me what is going on?" His gaze shifted from one to the other. The women exchanged a look, Elizabeth surrendering easily to her aunt's firmness.

"My dear, it is not as bad as it appears," Mrs Gardiner suggested sweetly. "Perhaps if I start at the beginning?" She repeated to her husband what Elizabeth had told her of the hours immediately following Mr Bennet's accident and Darcy's unexpected announcement, keeping her eyes on her niece's for confirmation that she had got it right.

Mr Gardiner pinched the bridge of his nose. "My dear, what you are telling me does not improve my opinion of the gentleman. And you, Lizzy, I have never known you to tolerate officiousness! How is it you can accept this situation with equanimity?"

"I did not, Uncle. Not at first." Elizabeth spoke around the tightening in her throat, willing her heart to steady and her breathing to slow. Carefully, she spent some minutes elaborating on her improved understanding of the man in question. With deepest humility she laid bare all her misconceptions and regrettable conduct. "I have come to see that I was wrong about him, Uncle!" she concluded. "You must believe me, he is a good and honourable man."

"Indeed. Is that why I caught the two of you in a compromising position in the middle of the road?" Mr Gardiner spoke with a brittle edge in his voice. "Well, tell me Lizzy! Are those the actions of an 'honourable' man?"

Mrs Gardiner turned widened eyes on her niece. Elizabeth flushed guiltily, confirming her uncle's accusation. "Lizzy!" she whispered in scandalized awe.

"And that sister of his!" Mr Gardiner continued. "An unprincipled hoyden! She attacked you, Lizzy! Scandal or no, I will not permit you to ally yourself with such a family!"

"Miss Darcy was not herself!" Elizabeth cried defensively. "She is a sweet and vulnerable girl, Uncle! I do not know what has set her off, but she clearly believes I have wronged her somehow." Suddenly she straightened. "Where is she, Aunt? Did she go? Poor Georgiana!"

Her uncle snorted derisively and rose, stalking to the window.

"I expect she has returned to Netherfield, Lizzy," Mrs Gardiner supplied. "Her maid left the kitchen a while ago. I believe Jane and Mr Bingley saw her home."

Relief washed over Elizabeth's face. "Dearest Jane! She will know what to do. Is Mr Darcy…?"

"Do you mean that rather pathetic figure in the garden?" Her uncle turned a wry expression on her. Elizabeth leapt to her feet, joining her uncle at the window. Darcy did indeed look morose. He sat alone on a little stone bench, his head in his hands and light snow crusting his greatcoat.

Elizabeth's breath fogged the glass, and she lightly traced a small hole in the mist so she could still make out his shape. Mr Gardiner watched her carefully. He had never seen Elizabeth offer the slightest concern for any gentleman, but she seemed markedly anxious over this fellow's disturbance of mind. It showed some propriety of feeling, he supposed, that the gentleman had remained at Longbourn after the others had departed, and by all appearances suffered greatly over the afternoon's events.

Mr Gardiner sighed. "Send him in, Lizzy. I will speak with the man—*alone*."

~

Caroline Bingley had spent three out of the four hours it took to travel to London weeping in desolation. All of her plans were lost to her! There would be no glorious Pemberley to impress her friends, no handsome and prestigious Mr Darcy to usher her about London society. He was so perfect for her! Why could he not see it?

Everything was going along so smoothly until those wretched Bennet sisters had spoilt it all! Jane had begun it, with her porcelain face and milk toast ways. Ninny that she was, Caroline could have predicted Charles would fall for her. Why could he not have pursued Georgiana Darcy instead, as she had desired? Jane possessed no virtues that the Darcy heiress did not, and was penniless besides!

Still, all might not have been lost if it had not been for that horrid Eliza Bennet. What on earth was Darcy *thinking*? If he wanted a woman with a little spirit to warm his bed, she would have been more than willing to fit that bill! Had she not always been enthusiastic and clever when he was around? Impossible man!

Eventually she dried her tears. It would take a good hour's rest for the effects of her lamentations to fade decently enough to make herself presentable at her London home. She closed her eyes in thoughtful repose. Surely it was not yet too late! What could she do, so far from the centre of it all?

She had to concoct some excuse, some means of returning to their prior intimacy. There remained no avenues before her! Desperation turned in her breast. She needed Darcy! Hours- years!- spent gazing longingly at his chiseled profile had cultivated a powerful feeling within her. Dared she call it love? It was near enough. What was love but a strong desire and affinity of disposition? He would make her the perfect husband!

His ample material consequence and his established societal capital were his primary attractions, but Caroline was no ice queen. Darcy's person was by far the most pleasing she had encountered in her circles of influence. She had come to believe that his physical assets matched to perfection what she had always sought in her ideal mate.

His deep voice, with its rich timbre, made her inner parts tremble. That dark hair, the way it curled just a little over those expressive eyes! She imagined running her fingers through it as he exerted his rights over her. A shudder ran through her. No unpleasant duty would it be to tolerate his attentions! She could almost feel his heat, his strength. That firm mouth, those sensual hands and powerful shoulders....

The carriage jolted as it left the rougher roads and entered the cobbled pavers of the city. Caroline swallowed, ashamed at her scandalous musings. London was closing in upon her, but she was no nearer relinquishing her designs on Mr Darcy. There had to be some last option available to her!

It is a well-known fact that despair does not often make one wise, and so it was with Caroline Bingley. Her anguished mind dredged up a succession of ideas, most of which she dismissed as impossibly gauche. At last a thought took seed and blossomed in her mind.

She rapped on the outer door of her carriage, summoning her driver's attention. "Daniels, I should like to pay a call before I return to the Townhouse. Take me to Grosvenor Square."

Twenty-Three

"Miss Georgiana, is there something I can bring for your present relief? A glass of wine? Can I get you anything?" Bingley stood helplessly outside her bedroom, arms twitching randomly as though they itched to be of some service but had no direction.

Georgiana shook her head miserably. Bingley cast a plaintive glance to Jane, who wrapped an arm comfortingly over her shoulders. "Come, Miss Darcy," she gently suggested. "Let us help you get comfortable." Bingley stood back in agonized resignation and Jane closed the door.

Jane and her maid helped to ease her into her bed, still fully dressed. Jane brought her a damp cloth to freshen her face and with a quiet look, dismissed Georgiana's maid. Jane herself remained in staunch support, neither pressing her for words nor abandoning her to face her feelings alone.

Georgiana swallowed painfully. "You must think me dreadfully wicked!" she whispered.

Jane laughed gently. "Miss Darcy, I have four younger sisters, at least three of whom are regularly capable of far more shocking behaviour than yours!"

Georgiana tried to smile, even to make reply, but all she could manage was a sob. Jane soothed her kindly, sweeping the wisps of hair out of her face and cradling her head- just as Elizabeth had done two days ago. Georgiana's dry heaves turned to anguished tears. How she had hoped such sisterly affection was not all a fantasy!

"Miss Darcy," Jane's voice was sweet, but brooked no arguments. "I fear there must be some dreadful mistake. I understand you are quite undone by something, but I believe if you will speak to me of it, we can begin to set things right and clear up any misunderstandings. I would not wish you to cause yourself more pain than necessary."

Georgiana sniffled and endeavoured to bring herself under regulation. It was some minutes before she had composed herself enough to form an articulate sentence. Jane waited patiently, offering a handkerchief when it was needed. At last she drew a shuddering breath.

"Did… did Miss Elizabeth tell you anything about… about me?" She raised timid eyes to Jane's face.

Jane blinked, hesitating before making reply. Her reluctance was plain.

Georgiana began to sob once more. "I th-thought I could t-trust her!" she mumbled tearfully.

Jane placed a hand on the girl's shoulder. "There were some things that Lizzy told me in the strictest confidence, and only because she was in some deep perplexity regarding her previous understanding of Mr Wickham, as well as Mr Darcy. I know she told no one else- not even our aunt, in whose discretion I would have the utmost confidence. Lizzy would never hurt you, Miss Darcy, and nor would I."

"Wh-why w-would L-lydia say s-such things? How did she hear th-them?" Georgiana's features contorted and her voice rose in pitch as she strove mightily against her tears and the gasping hiccoughs interrupting her speech.

Jane narrowed her eyes. "What did she say?"

With much agony, she listened as Georgiana struggled through the details of what Lydia had related. She pressed her lips together in angry silence. She had absolutely no doubts of Elizabeth's secrecy, but things did look rather damaging to Georgiana's trust in her. And this poor girl! Her reputation would be in shreds!

"Miss Darcy, who else could have known of these things?"

Georgiana gulped. "Not even my maid knew! It could only be my brother and Richard… Colonel Fitzwilliam. And Mr W- you know, *him*."

"I see." Jane gazed thoughtfully at the closed door of the bedroom. She turned her eyes back to the sniffling girl and stroked her hair behind her ears. "Can you rest alone for a little while? I should like to see what I can learn."

Georgiana assented numbly. Sleep sounded heavenly.

~

"At last! *Where* have you been, James? I summoned you *hours* ago!" Lady Catherine remained seated, gesturing regally to the chair opposite herself. She had no intentions of hurrying to make herself amenable to her brother.

"Summoned, eh?" James Fitzwilliam, the Earl of Matlock snorted as he entered the room. "I am not your toady, Catherine."

"You owe it to decency, to honour, to come at once! I am your last living sister and I required your presence hours ago!"

"I see. Well, then, as it is quite too late for that, I shall be going. Come along, Richard." The earl did an about-face just before taking the indicated seat, drawing his son into step with him.

"You shall do no such thing!" Lady Catherine's eyes sharpened upon her nephew. "Fitzwilliam! Have you brought me my niece?"

Colonel Fitzwilliam tilted his head curiously. "My sister remains at the townhouse with my mother, Madam, but I will be sure to convey your well wishes."

"You know very well what I mean! I know she was with you! Bring me Georgiana *at once!*"

"Georgiana? Why, no, she is with Darcy. With me! What a preposterous notion! I am bound for my regiment, Aunt, and I do not believe my cousin would be allowed to remain with me in the barracks."

Lady Catherine rose shakily on her cane, seething red. "*How dare!* I will have none of your insolence, Richard Fitzwilliam! I came here to settle a matter of the very gravest importance, and I require the entire family's support!"

"Anne has decided to sell Rosings?" the earl guessed, placing a little extra emphasis on his niece's name. Catherine still pretended Anne was a child. "About bleeding time. She will never get what it is worth, though- too many repairs needed in the village."

A thin line of froth began to form at the corners of the lady's mouth. "*I am speaking* of the purported engagement of *your* nephew- *Fitzwilliam Darcy*, in case you decide to willfully misunderstand me- to a country nobody of no status whatsoever! He has betrayed my Anne and gone against the express wishes of the entire family!"

Fitzwilliam, standing behind his father's shoulder, raised his hand. "Not mine," he put in helpfully.

"*Obstinate boy!* Be silent, I am ashamed of you!" she thundered. Turning back to her brother, she continued her diatribe. "That chit has lured him on with her arts! No doubt she has compromised his honour and devised some scheme for his entrapment! She has made him forget his place, what he owes to his family!"

"And just what is that, dear Sister?" The earl crossed his arms, leveling a flat stare at her. "Respect? Filial devotion? What a pity he has not at present any source of inspiration for such noble sentiments."

"*He is promised to my Anne!* There, now what have you say to that?"

The earl narrowed his eyes and his hands fell menacingly to his sides once more. He stepped nearer, his words coming in a dangerous hiss. "I think you and I both know why that would be a bad idea, Catherine." He held her gaze in a steely lock, unflinching and unblinking.

Her nostrils flared and her eyes widened even further, if that were possible. Richard could see the thin red veins lining the white orbs. Mad energy seized her and she shot a thin hand out to her brother's collar. "*You know nothing of the kind!*" she screeched. "Anne deserves to be a Darcy and it *will* be so!"

Grimacing, the earl wrenched her wiry grip from his clothing and took a long step away from her. "I will not support you in this, Catherine. Go back to Rosings!"

He turned on his heel and began to march out, but she followed him. "He will never be received anywhere! He will be the laughingstock of all London! You cannot seriously deny the claims of duty, honour and interest! Fitzwilliam Darcy of Pemberley *must* marry within his own sphere and he *must keep his word to Anne!*"

The earl continued walking, his voice carrying over his shoulder. "He has made no promise to Anne. As far as station, from what I hear the young woman is a gentleman's daughter, so she must be suitable."

"Suitable, my eye!" she stormed after him. "I *will* have satisfaction! I insist you provide me a carriage at once! I am leaving for Hertfordshire at first light to put a stop to this charade!"

The earl stopped and turned at last, a tiny curl to the corner of his mouth. "Take your own carriage- or did you fly down here on your broom?"

"Buffoon!" she snarled. "This incompetent staff sent my carriage away! They can do nothing right! It will be an entire day, perhaps two before mine is assembled again. I require your coach!"

· "No, Catherine! Not a single wheel nor bit of harness will I lend you to wreak your mischief. Let Darcy alone or you shall have me to deal with!" At those last words, the Fitzwilliam men departed the house, leaving the refined lady in a towering wrath.

Chuckling, Richard held the carriage door for his father while the older gentleman mounted the box. "You poked the bear tonight!" he laughed as they were seated.

The elder Fitzwilliam grunted. "I would be lying if I said I hadn't enjoyed that at least a little. I wonder, though, at that carriage of hers. Odd that Darcy's staff would have sent it away." He fixed his son with a penetrating stare, a little sparkle in his eye.

"Indeed!" Richard stroked his chin thoughtfully, gazing out the open window of the carriage to avoid revealing his self-satisfied grin.

"What of this girl, Richard? Tell me, is she respectable? I'll not see Darcy wed to Anne, but tell me at least he has not attached himself to some odious bumpkin."

"You know Darcy better than that. 'Insupportable!'" he mimicked his cousin's best stodgy tone, drawing a snort from his father.

"Is she quite fetching?"

"Devastatingly so- at least to Darcy's mind, I should think. She is just the sort to fix him. Perhaps she is not a conventional beauty, but she is quite striking and terribly clever. I imagine he likes her wit quite as well as her face."

"But not impertinent? Dear heavens, anything but a brazen, uneducated snippet. Or a fortune hunter! There would be nothing like that to prove Catherine right!"

"Not at all. Well… perhaps she is a little impertinent, but quite delightfully so. She is utterly ladylike, Father. Very respectable, I should say."

"You said Darcy acted rather on the spur of the moment. Do you think his attachment to her is an enduring one? I should hate to see him make such a move, only to regret it."

"I never saw a more promising inclination. He is eaten up by it, Father. Poor Darcy! You know he has so little patience with feminine wiles and foibles, and at last he has found a woman who is completely artless and forthright- so much so that she has made him work for every ounce of her regard, without respect for his pocketbook. Whether she causes a sensation in London remains to be seen, though it is possible I suppose. He cares nothing for that, Father. She fascinates him and he will have no other at this point."

The earl leaned back against the carriage seat, straightening his jacket front with a jerk. "I had expected he would do better- *far* better, it was to be hoped. There was Lord Ellsworth's daughter, not to mention Miss Chesterton, with her fifty thousand, but I could not get the boy to even call a second time." He sighed in resignation. "I collect he has no political ambitions, and Pemberley is quite solvent. Monk that he is, I suppose I ought to be grateful he has taken marriage into his head at all," the earl grumbled.

Richard laughed. "You will not sway him, Father, best not to even attempt it!"

Matlock gazed thoughtfully at his son for a moment, then spoke up with decision. "My boy, see about extending your leave. I think we ought to pay a visit to Hertfordshire tomorrow."

~

"Well, Mr Darcy, it seems at present I must withdraw my objections to your 'understanding' with my niece." Gardiner stood, lifting a sceptical eyebrow. "Know this, however- I will expect your behaviour to be above reproach, and you will wait to make any formal announcement until we know more of Mr Bennet's condition. If I have any cause for concern whatsoever, I will hold you responsible. Do I make myself clear?"

"Perfectly, sir." Darcy offered the man a respectful bow.

The uncle was far less indolent than the father. Darcy found himself wishing fleetingly that their positions had been reversed- that it had been Mr Gardiner in charge of the upbringing of the youngest Bennet girls and Mr Bennet to whom he now had to make explanation. Gardiner, for all his intimidating posturing, seemed a highly respectable and gentlemanly sort of fellow. A watchful guardian he would have made. Darcy had a suspicion that the changeful father, on the other hand, might have found the entire situation highly amusing and may have even poured him a drink after they had done.

Mr Gardiner dismissed him, and with great relief, Darcy took his escape. His thoughts had dwelt for the entire conversation on Elizabeth and Georgiana. What could have occasioned such an outburst? He felt reasonably assured that Elizabeth bore no grudge for the attack on her person, but what of Georgiana? She had never lashed out in such a way! His duty as her guardian and his affection as her brother warred within him.

He relaxed greatly when he found Elizabeth anxiously waiting for him just outside the library. The worry in her eyes pained him, but also relieved his own uncertainties. If she had turned against him, she surely would not be here now, looking for all the world like she wished to comfort him.

"Your uncle has granted his conditional blessing," he sighed.

Elizabeth nodded. She'd had no doubt of that. Her uncle could bluster and storm, but she knew him to be truly generous and soft-hearted. "He only wished to know that I was well," she assured him.

"Yes, so I understand. I cannot fault him for that." It would have eased his heart to pull her close, but he dared not even touch her under the circumstances. Marriage could not come soon enough, he decided. What he would have given to draw her aside and speak openly of his fears and doubts!

Interpreting his feelings remarkably well for such a short acquaintance, Elizabeth took a small step nearer and gazed up into his face. "William," she spoke softly. "We have a much bigger problem than my uncle."

His expression dropped seriously. "Do you know what is happening with Georgiana?"

Elizabeth glanced hesitantly over her shoulder to the drawing room beyond. "In part. It seems there were some rumours in town. My sisters overheard them, and I am ashamed to admit that they no doubt had a hand in their propagation."

Darcy narrowed his eyes, clenching his fists. "What rumours?"

Elizabeth swallowed a lump in her throat. "Insinuations regarding a certain gentleman of your family's acquaintance and Georgiana." She dared to look at him. Darcy had gone thoroughly red, his jaw set. He glared at the room beyond as though he would have liked to permanently silence Lydia Bennet.

"*I'll kill him!*" Darcy snarled. He locked his jaw, desperate to avoid losing his temper in front of Elizabeth- particularly with her uncle just through the closed door behind him. He shook with impotent rage, closing his eyes. "Excuse me, Elizabeth. I will call again when I can." He reached to yank the front door open himself.

"William, there is more!" Elizabeth put a hand on his arm to stay him. She drew close, her voice low. "Lydia confessed that the rumour did indeed come from Mr Wickham, but *he* is not the man implicated."

Darcy felt his stomach knot. "Who is?"

Elizabeth bit her lip, hating what she had to tell him. "Colonel Fitzwilliam."

"Good evening, Miss Bingley."

Caroline poised herself gracefully upon the steps of Darcy house, peering fashionably down her nose at the stuffy old butler, a relic from the days of Darcy's father. Mentally she grasped for a name. What was it? "Good evening, Mr Dale," she greeted him airily. "Will you tell Mrs Nielson, the housekeeper, that I have arrived?" She moved toward him, blithely assuming his compliance.

Drake rooted firmly to his spot. "I was not informed you were expected, Miss Bingley."

"Not... well, I never! You did not receive word from your master this morning that I would be calling this evening? Such an inconvenience! Ah, well, it cannot be helped. Mr Darcy had a particular wish for me to speak with Mrs Nielson, and so I have come- all the way from Hertfordshire! Will you have her meet me in the rose drawing room, please?"

She brushed past him in elegant nonchalance, ushering herself into the fine entryway of the home. She cast her eyes about the surroundings in pleasure. Ah, yes, this home would suit her very nicely! Some of the furnishings declared their dated selection by Darcy's mother, but they could be replaced easily enough.

Drake trailed behind her in some bewilderment, but he could not in good form toss the lady out on her ear. Better, he had apparently decided, to allow her her head. "I shall speak with Mrs *Nelson* at once," he informed her stiffly. She bit her lip at her error, but recovered quickly.

Caroline breezed into the drawing room, wholly unaware that it was not unoccupied. She caught herself in an graceless stumble upon beholding the glowering presence before her. An elderly woman wreathed in layers upon layers of black silk and lace prowled before the fire. She turned sharply at the intrusion.

"Who are you?" the woman demanded. Caroline glanced over her shoulder in dismay at the vanishing butler. Was that a spark of mischief she had detected in his eye?

Caroline preened a little. She had no notion of cowering before this woman; neither would she allow her the upper hand. Who was this audacious person who assumed residence at the Darcy house when neither the Master nor Miss Darcy were at home? "I am a very *close* associate of Mr and Miss Darcy's. Whom might I have the pleasure of addressing?" She tempered her speech with just the precise mixture of polished ease and unwelcoming coolness as to establish her credibility.

"How can you not know who *I* am? Insolent chit!" Caroline's eyes widened in shock at the insult. "*I* am Lady Catherine de Bourgh, aunt of Mr Darcy and mother Anne de Bourgh- Heiress of Rosings Park and Mr Darcy's betrothed! Now, I demand you declare your business here or be off!"

An indignant huff escaped her. The nerve of the woman! To speak to *her* in such a way, as if she were some insignificant servant! Of course she had heard for years of Lady Catherine and her ridiculous intentions for that sickly daughter of hers, but had never been required to tolerate the woman in person.

"*I* have come on a matter of some urgency directly from Hertfordshire! It is imperative that I speak with Mr Darcy's housekeeper at once. Kindly excuse me!" Caroline turned to go.

"Hertfordshire?" the woman stalked nearer with imperious haste. "What is your name? You cannot possibly be that wretched Elizabeth Bennet!"

"*Hardly!*" Caroline glared sulkily. "How dare you insult me so?" she scowled. "I am Caroline Bingley, and my family has enjoyed intimate ties to the Darcy family for years!"

The noblewoman straightened, and Caroline recognized the calculating gleam in her eye for what it was. "Forgive me, I can see that *you* are no crass strumpet. Tell me, Miss Barnley, has my nephew made an offer to that odious Bennet person?"

Why, she can't even remember my name! The woman is senile! Caroline realized. Still, she had a purpose in coming here and would not see it suffer by an old woman's insulting memory. "Impossible, your ladyship! Indeed, I believe he has quite been taken the fool, and it is my intention to spare his reputation such an unlucky smear if at all I can."

"It is as I thought! This charade must be stopped instantly before more harm is done! Tell me, Miss Bramley, how is it you arrived here all alone? I do not approve of young ladies traveling post-chase."

"I am not alone! My brother has supplied me with a carriage and a man-servant at my disposal. Once I have seen to my private affairs, I shall be retiring to my townhome in Piccadilly." She placed a little extra emphasis on the name of her neighbourhood.

Lady Catherine snorted with great delicacy. "Only upstarts and nouveau riche claim that as their residence" she sneered, enjoying the flush on the haughty vixen's face. With swift decision, she turned a commanding air on this little pretender. "We are departing at the stroke of dawn for Hertfordshire to set this matter straight. You look to be a woman of some sense and decorum, and perhaps your influence may prove valuable. You may attend us if you wish."

Caroline gave herself pause. Better still than her plan of involving Darcy's staff in her undertaking was the prospect of allying herself with his family. Lady Catherine certainly had her own objectives in mind, but Caroline had no fear for any competition from Anne de Bourgh. Darcy would never consider marrying his sickly cousin- the man needed an heir, after all! The aunt, however, might just prove a powerful enough opponent to the match with Elizabeth Bennet that he would be forced to give her up.

She drew herself to her full regal height. "What an excellent idea, my lady," she inclined her head graciously. "I would be most pleased to accept your offer. I shall have my coachman provide my address. What time shall I expect your call?"

"I, call for you? Nonsense," the peeress huffed. "The country roads are dirty at this time of year, I cannot spare my carriage for such abuse. We shall travel in yours."

~

Charles Bingley had issued swift instructions immediately after his private conference with Jane. None of the staff were to go into Meryton, and no callers whatsoever- even the tenants- were to be received. Netherfield was locked down. Louisa would whine plaintively when she discovered her hothouse flowers could not be got, but he would not be shaken.

He called for the carriage to take Jane home, while he himself rode next to it. Winter darkness was already settling over the frosted landscape, but it was not difficult, after about a mile, to recognize the rider galloping pell-mell in their direction. Bingley ordered the carriage to halt. "Darcy!" he beckoned.

Darcy, who was at that moment approaching the turn which would take him into Meryton, reined in his mount. "Take Miss Bennet home," he instructed his driver. Jane offered a parting gesture of her fingers through the shutters as the carriage rattled off.

Bingley caught up to his friend. "I thought we would call at Colonel Forster's first."

Darcy stared, he and his mount still breathing heavily. He considered in silence for a moment. "Thank you, Charles," he yielded at last. "I should be most grateful for your company."

They set out together in a brisk trot, giving Darcy's horse a breather after his two mile gallop. "What do you intend to do?" Bingley asked.

"What I should have done long ago," Darcy growled between clenched teeth. "I am going to call that blackguard out!"

"Darcy, you cannot! Think of the risk!"

"It is high time he is stopped. I can defeat him at any weapon of his choice!"

"Yes, and spend the rest of your days in prison, if you are lucky!" Bingley retorted. "There can be no victory in that. Georgiana deserves better, to say nothing of Miss Elizabeth!"

The bluish silhouette in the darkness suffered a moment in silence. "I am sorry I never told you, old friend."

Bingley glanced to his left in some surprise. "I would not have expected you to. No, Darcy, do not be sorry. You must know, though, that Georgiana is like a sister to me. I would have protected her just as you and Fitzwilliam have."

"How much have you heard?"

"Only what Jane knew- that Wickham tried to use Georgiana to revenge himself on you."

Darcy set his teeth. "It seems this time he may have succeeded!" He screwed his mouth shut in sudden rage, then without warning lashed out an epithet to the darkness.

Bingley regarded him mildly. He had witnessed more emotion from Fitzwilliam Darcy in the past four days than in as many years before. If it was true that still waters ran deep, Bingley began to worry for the devastation which might be unleashed when the fathoms were at last stirred. "Do you know the substance of the rumours?" he asked cautiously.

"Yes," was the simple reply, and apparently all the answer he was getting. After another moment, "I need Richard."

"What does Fitzwilliam have to do with it?"

"I thought once that Wickham's jealousy was confined to me. I was a fool. He is trying to destroy everyone connected with me."

Bingley stared at the rising moon over his horse's ears, considering. "What of Miss Elizabeth- and Jane? Is their family safe from scandal at present?"

"Do you mean have the younger sisters been brought into order? We can only hope. Mr Gardiner seems less inclined to tolerate foolishness."

"And… Miss Elizabeth? How is she handling this unpleasantness with Georgiana?"

Bingley could hear his friend sigh at last, and he caught a glimpse of white teeth flashing in the moonlight. "Beautifully, Charles. She is perfection."

Twenty-Four

"Gentlemen, I am sorry to report that my man has lost track of George Wickham." Colonel Forster re-entered the room where his guests waited. He clasped his hands dejectedly behind his back.

Darcy shot to his feet. "Lost track of him? How is that possible, Colonel?"

"It seems the Lieutenant was calling at the home of one of the better respected residents in the town. My man was obliged to await him without, but the Lieutenant never reappeared. I suspect, Mr Darcy, that he ingratiated himself to some of the servants of that household and was able to leave through the back entrance. By the time it was realized that something was amiss, he was nowhere to be found."

"So," Darcy's tone dropped dangerously, "in addition to slandering a respectable young woman *and* a decorated war hero with noble connections, he is also guilty of desertion in a time of war. Have I got it all, Colonel, or have I missed something?" Darcy stared icily- of course there was more. This was Wickham!

Forster's face reddened, and he cast the gentlemen a pained expression. "I have been making inquiries. He owes money to several shops in Meryton. He has also been implicated in the disgrace of two of the local tradesmen's daughters. He has debts of honour as well."

Darcy paced, his jaw and mind working ostensibly in conjunction. Bingley watched the play of muscles in Darcy's cheek with some amusement. His old friend was boiling in rage, but few would ever have known it. *I bet*

Elizabeth would notice. The thought came seemingly from nowhere. Yet, he was quite sure of its accuracy. Her sharp wits and keen discernment were surely marks in her favour in the eyes of the highly private man before him. Yes, regardless of her station, she was exactly what his old friend needed.

"Colonel, have you any notion where he might have gone?" Darcy ventured at last, recalling Bingley's mind to the trouble at hand.

"Not as yet," Forster sighed. "Desertion is a very serious charge, not one we take lightly even in the local militia. I have my eyes and ears out for him, but my resources are tapped. What of Fitzwilliam? The man is part bloodhound, Darcy. He has means which I do not."

"I intend to get him here again, to clear his and my sister's reputations if nothing else. I have no idea how I shall go about that bit, however."

The colonel shook his head unhelpfully. "I wish I knew, Mr Darcy. I will send you word immediately should anything be found out regarding Wickham."

Darcy and Bingley took their leave and emerged into the crackling winter air. They set out for Netherfield again at an easy jog, not wishing to overheat their horses. Bingley gazed idly up at the stars and waited for his friend to speak. He was waiting for a long time.

"I wish to pay a call to Longbourn first thing in the morning," Darcy spoke at last.

"Why so early? I imagine Mr Gardiner will not smile upon such audaciousness from a suitor who so recently caused such a stir."

"I am betrothed to a daughter of the house- at least conditionally," he reasoned. "It is only natural that my welcome should not be confined to the traditional visiting hours. Much as I desire to speak with Elizabeth, though, that is not my primary motivation."

"Shall I ask, or would I do better to wait and watch?"

"Georgiana. We have to set things right." Darcy grunted a little as his horse fumbled in an unseen rut along the road.

"Yes, she ought to apologize. Do not go too hard on her, Darcy- she was quite overwrought. Of course she was in the wrong, but I suppose it was understandable for her to be so. Just... I beg you would not frighten her more than she already is, Darce."

"You ought to know me better than that, Charles. I shall traumatize her no further, but she must apologize to Elizabeth. Such an attack on my wife I will not tolerate, even from her!"

"Getting a little ahead of things, are you not?"

Darcy shook his head wearily. "Forgive me, it seems I am a little overwrought myself." He sighed and continued. "I hope to amend Mr Gardiner's first impression. I fear it was not one of which to boast- and that was *before* Georgiana's little scene."

Bingley fixed his friend's shadow with a presumptuous stare. "You don't say," he drawled.

Darcy glared back. "*And* there is the matter of Georgiana's reputation. It occurs to me that it should be dealt with at the source."

"We cannot find him. How do you hope to do that?"

"Not Wickham." Darcy smiled to himself. How had he not thought of this earlier? "Lydia Bennet. Two can play at this game."

~

"My dear, what do you make of all this?" Mr Gardiner drew his wife down to sit upon the still-made bed in the guest room after the family's somewhat melancholy dinner. Madeline draped her head over his shoulder in weary relief. What a trying day it had been!

Lydia and Kitty had been ordered to their room with strict instructions to speak to no one. Mary and Elizabeth had trained their gazes steadfastly upon their largely empty plates, eating little and speaking less. Jane had returned only very lately from Netherfield, providing Elizabeth, at least, with an excuse to see her sister upstairs.

Mrs Bennet had appeared the only family member whose spirits remained unflagging. She, of course, had heard the shocking reports of "that poor Darcy girl and that dreadful colonel!". "I *knew* him to be a dangerous sort, and so I told the girls!" she stated emphatically. Her endless chatter she had couched in her anxious concerns for that "sweet Darcy girl, poor little fool", but "such a shocking lack of guardianship from her brother" she declared she should never understand. A rational mind, upon believing such vagaries, would naturally leap to wonder how a poor guardian of a sister could hope to prove a worthy husband, but it seemed Mrs Bennet was not capable of such a conclusion.

Mary had left the room in disgust soon after Elizabeth's silent retreat, abandoning the Gardiners to face the matron's ramblings alone. When her talk had turned to wedding lace and the various calls she was expected to make, the visiting in-laws had quite bluntly recommended they all withdraw to retire early for the evening.

Edward Gardiner heaved a long sigh of fatigue. His journey had been a hasty and uncomfortable one, undertaken with expedience as his primary motivation. Rather than the distressed and mournful family he had expected to find, he had stumbled upon a hopeless tangle of scandal and romantic conundra. "My dear?" he queried again. "You have not yet made any answer."

"I was trying to decide which to answer first. You, no doubt, are most concerned for Lizzy, but I do not feel equal to addressing that scenario before laying out what I know of other matters."

"By all means." He rubbed his tired eyes, waiting.

"Thomas is showing steady improvement. This evening while Lizzy was sitting with him he squeezed her hand in answer to her voice. Mrs Cooper says that is a very good sign, indeed."

"Forgive me, my love, but how is it again that the nurse came?"

"Mr Darcy sent for her- immediately upon hearing of the accident, it seems."

"Why would he do such a thing? I wonder if the man can be quite sensible."

Mrs Gardiner laughed lightly. "Tell me a man violently in love who is?"

"You really think his feelings are so strong? He seemed rather distracted when I spoke with him."

"So you would be as well, I imagine. Miss Darcy's behaviour rather puzzled him."

"He is not the only one!" he interjected. "But go on."

"I was only going to add that perhaps he was also somewhat preoccupied by his private walk with Lizzy." A knowing little smile curved her lips as she tilted her face up to her husband's.

Gardiner narrowed his eyes at his wife's playfulness. "Is that what you call it? Pray tell, how did an unchaperoned walk come about? Where was everyone else?"

"Oh, dear!" Madeline described the morning's events and the couple's endeavours with estate business. "I really did not think it would come to the point so quickly," she flushed guiltily. "My concerns were more for the younger girls' impropriety. Perhaps a chaperone should have been found, but here on the estate, practically within sight of the house, none could have thought...."

Gardiner gave a short wry huff. "You were not privy to the little scene I witnessed! It seems, my dear, that our Lizzy either blows hot or cold. The young lady I observed seemed to have no reservations whatsoever about the gentleman."

Madeline sighed. "I suppose that is just as well- she has little enough choice in the matter, and I am glad to see she has turned her sentiments in his favour. I do think him a fine young man, Edward. There is something very pleasing about his manner. He may appear proud at first, but that impression wears off quickly. I believe him quite taken with Lizzy."

"What is to be done about that sister of his? Gossip and tittle-tattle I care nothing about, but if she is as ill-tempered as my first impression...."

"Oh, no my dear! I do not believe she is. It seems that Elizabeth held some details of Miss Darcy's past in trust, and when these tidings were aired, she feared herself betrayed. The poor girl! I do hope Mr Darcy can patch things up for her!"

"Well," he declared with decision, "our family will do nothing to further such slander. I will not have the girls abroad at all, save perhaps Jane. I trust *her* discretion at least, unless she should desire to walk alone with her own young man," he shot his wife a wink. "Fanny we shall have to detain as well. I cannot as easily order my sister to remain within her own doors, but we must preoccupy her somehow. I am afraid, my dear, that we are set for a few trying days ahead."

Mrs Gardiner let go a long sigh of resignation. "Such a fate!" she moaned dramatically.

"I have every confidence in your fortitude and ingenuity, my dear," he answered her dryly.

~

"Georgiana?" Darcy tapped his fingers hesitantly upon his sister's bedroom door. He could not decide whether it would be safer to let her rest, or to present himself with the contrition he felt was her due. He stood in silent attendance, straining for any creak of the furniture within which would declare his sister's wakefulness.

After a few moments he moved to step away, only to have the door opened to him. Georgiana had never changed for bed, but her rumpled clothing attested to the restless few hours she had spent. She crossed her arms sullenly and looked up to him with swollen eyes.

Compassion tugged at his heart. "Oh, Georgie," he sighed, opening his arms to her. With a trembling shudder, she came willingly to him and buried her face in his chest. Somewhat awkwardly, he waltzed her back into her bedroom so he could close the door, then held her for long minutes.

Her tears had begun anew. "William," she blubbered at length, "what is to become of me now?"

He grit his teeth, wishing he could supply her with a confident answer that all would be well. "I do not know," he admitted finally. "The rumours have no doubt taken on a life of their own by now. Still," he drew back enough to force her to look at him, "this is a small town, and one fantastic story will quickly be supplanted by another."

"That is not how you felt about the matter when the rumours were about Miss Elizabeth," she retorted bitterly.

He sighed and put his hands on her shoulders. "This is Miss Elizabeth's home town. She had no means of escape, no recourse to counter such slander, and no hope of forming any other respectable establishment. *You* are not quite so unprotected." He struggled against the irritation in his voice. He did not like her petulant attitude, but he could sympathize. His sister was immature and very badly hurt, and he resolved to handle her as gently as possible.

Georgiana continued silent and morose for another moment. Then, timidly, "Are you going to send me away?"

"That would only confirm the rumours, would it not? No, Georgie, we are going on the offensive."

Her head lifted, curiosity sparking through her tears. "How do you mean?"

He braced her shoulders carefully, gazing into her streaked face. "Georgie, how much of the rumour did you actually hear? Did you know they do not have the right of it?"

Her eyes reflecting confusion, she shook her head.

"It is not Wickham your name is linked with. It is Richard."

Horror crossed the girl's features. "No! Richard would *never*...!"

William raised his hand, interrupting her. "I know, Sweetling, but apparently your outburst at Longbourn confirmed some part of it, at any rate, as true."

Georgiana began to sob again. "Poor Richard! If I had only known! Why, I should have simply laughed, like Miss Elizabeth does! Now I have ruined him, as well as myself!"

"If it is any comfort, I do not believe your reaction can have spread to other ears yet, and I suspect the persons who witnessed it to have a short memory."

Georgiana wiped her face. "What is to be done?" She began to wring her hands in worry.

"Sweetling, it seems to me that the best way to combat an enticing tale is to put forward an even more interesting one. I do not mean we ought to lie," he added quickly, noting the concern on her face, "but we can clear up matters somewhat."

"But how?" The frustrated tears wavered in her voice again. "We cannot simply declare Mr W- *him* a liar. He will only tell the real truth, and that is worse!"

"I do not think he would do so. He likes having the general public's good esteem. I think it pleases him to be better thought of in company than I. Regardless, that is not my intention. Please do not ask me more as yet, though. I am still trying to decide what is best to be done."

She firmed her mouth. She would trust her brother; he always knew what was right. Dearest William! He was so good to her, even after her unsurpassable foolishness. A long breath of remorse left her. "Have I..." she hesitated, fearful, then resolved to start again. "Have I ruined things with Miss Elizabeth? Does she hate me now?"

He gave a wry chuckle. "Not in the slightest. She was very worried for you, Georgie."

"She cannot have forgiven me so easily! I was so vicious and unreasonable! The things I accused her of!"

"Yet she has, and I do not believe it was through any superhuman effort. She has a very generous nature, Georgie, and her sympathies are quite engaged for you. Not," he held up an admonishing finger, "that you will not be expected to apologize, for I shall insist upon it, but you need not fear any harsh feelings from her."

Georgiana stared in wonder, a little comforted. "And… what of you, William? Do her sympathies include you now?" She peeked timidly at his face and was treated to a sly little grin. She brightened instantly, her woes temporarily banished. "Oh, William, tell me, please!" she begged.

"I certainly shall not!" he drew to his full height, a faint return to the masterful demeanour he affected before others.

"Very well, I shall just have to ask Lizzy when I see her next," she tilted her head teasingly.

"Perhaps I shall have to rethink my previous good opinion of her influence upon you," he quirked an eyebrow.

"It is too late for that now, Brother," she informed him archly. "If I am to understand you correctly, I will have much opportunity in the future to be influenced by her!"

A satisfied smile slowly blossomed on his face and he acknowledged the truth. "She has obliged me with her acceptance." His pleasure clouded slightly. "Her uncle is more sceptical of my intentions, but I am not without hope there. He seems a worthy man, and after today I would not blame him for any reservations he might hold."

Guilt washed over Georgiana's features once more. "I did not help, did I?" she whispered.

"Hardly," he observed dryly. "Though I would not have you think that all of the blame can be assigned to you. I regret that Mr Gardiner first happened upon us just after Elizabeth's acceptance, at a moment when I was not yet master of my feelings." He paused, a distant little smile warming his eyes again. "Elizabeth is a woman of strong affections," he murmured, almost to himself.

Georgiana covered her mouth with her fingertips, both embarrassed and thrilled at her brother's confession. "William!" she scolded laughingly.

"Oh, yes, I deserve your censure. I should not have mentioned a word of my transgressions to my impressionable sister, should I? I do so because I would not have you believe I am without fault. I am perfectly capable of folly of my own."

"Yes, but at least Elizabeth is respectable and trustworthy, unlike… well, unlike some others. You may be faulted for some things, perhaps, but it cannot be said your faith is ill-placed. Nor can anyone accuse you of shirking your responsibilities to her."

"No!" he declared vehemently. "I intend to marry her as soon as it can be arranged!"

Georgiana fell laughing into his arms. "Oh, William, I am so happy for you! Richard told me this morning, he said… Oh! I nearly forgot!"

She spun away from him and went to rummage in her jewelry case. He waited for her, perplexed. "What did Richard say? I did not know you had even seen him before he left."

"Hmm? Oh, it was nothing, he only knocked to say goodbye. I was taking an early breakfast in here." She left her reason unsaid, but it seemed plausible that avoiding Miss Bingley might have been a motive for taking a tray in her room. She kept her eyes resolutely on her jewelry case as she searched for something among its many contents. At last she found what she sought and came forward, hiding it in her hand.

He arched a brow. "What did Richard say?" he demanded again.

Her lashes fluttered hesitantly. "That… that it was well you had found love, and that he hoped others in our family might one day do the same. Here," she thrust the object in her hand into his, changing the subject. "It was Richard's idea that I should bring it."

He turned over a small velvet sack, closed by a drawstring. "So this is that secret you had concocted? I wondered what you two were up to." Opening the drawstring, he dumped out the prize hidden within. "Aha. I might have known," he smiled. He opened his hand to reveal a lovely antique ring; a ½ carat emerald stone crusted all about with a tight and dazzling array of diamonds.

She smiled shyly. "I didn't know Miss Elizabeth's tastes, so Drake suggested I choose the one Papa gave to Mama. I hope I have done right…."

"It was very thoughtful of you, Sweetling. I think she will like it very much; green is a favourite colour of hers, though I daresay this ring will be too ornate to befit her simpler tastes for every day. Now that I consider it, there is not a ring in all the Darcy coffers which truly suits her- she is cut from quite a different cloth! Still, this is a fine heirloom to gift my bride until a more suitable one can be made. Thank you, Georgie." He tucked the ring back into its velvet case, then secreted it into his pocket. Georgiana drew a satisfied but trembling little sigh.

He smiled commiseratingly at his sweetest little sister. "I am glad you can put aside your fears for a time. I wish you to rest at peace tonight. It will not do for you to appear worn and guilt-ridden on the morrow!" He drew her into his arms for a tight hug, planting a brotherly kiss on her forehead. "Sleep now, and we will face tomorrow together."

She drew another long breath, squeezing her eyes shut and relaxing in his embrace. "Thank you, William."

Twenty-Five

Darcy's thoughts were still stewing early the next morning. Though he had admonished Georgiana to take care to rest well, he had not done the same himself. He had managed to conquer his overwhelming desire to ride off in singlehanded search of Wickham, but he had lain awake much of the night.

Much depended upon how quickly he could secure Richard's return. An express message sent late the evening before had urged haste, but Richard had a higher authority to whom he must answer. Darcy would have to take a back seat to the colonel's commanding officer. He hoped the man would be reasonable and generous with his cousin's leave. Georgiana's respectability perhaps depended upon the cousins presenting a united front.

He had fretted some while longer over what he must do, but in good time his thoughts had turned to the brightest moment of his day- that shining instant forever seared into his memory when Elizabeth had returned his affections. Hs valet discovered him early the next morning, soundly asleep with a light smile upon his face.

"Excuse me, sir, but you wished to be awakened early," Wilson whispered.

Darcy awoke with a start. "So I did. Thank you." He sat up, rubbing his bristling face. "No, no shave just yet. I desire a ride and I shall return shortly." Darcy dressed quickly and made his way to the stables.

A half hour later saw him in a headlong sprint over the fields, thrilling in Pluto's powerful strides and the stinging wind whipping his face. It was dark yet, the hazy outlines of the landscape rolling beneath his horse's hooves. Darcy guided him single-mindedly to that spot where he had last spoken with Mr Bennet.

As he had dared to fantasize, Elizabeth was there, even so early. She stood quietly, bundled in her warm cloak and watching his approach. All his hopes centred upon that one hooded figure, the one in all the world he could truly open his whole heart to. He dismounted smoothly, scarcely noticing the distance between his horse and her until he had crossed it and the rein looped over his arm tugged the horse closer.

He reached his free hand boldly for hers, and she took it. At her touch, his entire body relaxed and he knew peace. "I was hoping to see you this morning," he spoke softly, wrapping his other hand possessively over hers.

She turned a welcoming smile up to him. "I thought you might be out early today, and I wanted to see you, too."

"You did?" Gratitude lit his eyes. He peered carefully into her upturned face. "Truly, you wished to see me?" He could still scarcely believe she had so suddenly and wholly committed herself to the match she had vehemently attempted to cry off only a few days before.

"I thought you might need a friend," she replied simply.

His face fell. "It was not merely a 'friend' I hoped to find, Elizabeth."

She laughed, that teasing lilt in her voice. "I suppose it would be uncharitable of me to disappoint, would it not?" She stood on her toes and surprised him with a quick, daring kiss to his chin.

"Elizabeth!" Pleasure mixed with fear in his tones. "We should not- your uncle already disapproves of me!"

"Nothing of the kind. It is *this* he disapproves of." She took his face in her other hand and pressed another firm kiss to his cheek.

"Elizabeth Bennet!" he gasped- not very harshly. "This is most immodest! I cannot condone...."

He was silenced by another kiss, this one much softer and placed in a far more distracting location. She slowly dropped down again and shrugged helplessly, her tones both teasing and sultry. "It is the dreadful company I have been keeping recently! This is one particular fellow in the neighbourhood who, I fear, has been a shockingly bad influence upon me."

"And here I was quite certain it was the other way around." *If only he could swallow!* None but Elizabeth could tease him so provocatively, conjuring images both of a spirited chess match and a duel of quite another kind in the very same moment.

She eyed him appraisingly, alerted to the deeper timbre in his voice and aware that they must not tempt one another too far. "Entirely possible," she decided, her manner lightening. "I say, have you seen that gentleman of late? Tall, silent, rather disapproving? Goes about avoiding people? I cannot imagine where I might have mislaid him!"

"Gone forever," he asserted. "I gave him the shove-off myself."

"Ah, that is well. I should hate for him to be jealous if he were to catch me doing this." She stood on her tiptoes again and waited with closed eyes. Caution was overrated, after all.

Darcy, grinning despite himself, tipped his head low to oblige her. She was so soft and welcoming! He pulled her close, wrapping his arms around her for the first time and reveling in her tender ministrations. How he cherished the reassuring comfort she offered! She slid her arms up around his neck and allowed him to hold her long, sharing the warmth of her heavy cloak against the cold morning. He kissed her as fervently as he dared—thrilling in the rapturous intimacy but knowing clearly that he must at length pull back.

"Thank you," he whispered at last, pressing one more kiss near her ear. "You cannot know how badly I needed a little reassurance today."

The teasing light in her eyes vanished, replaced by sincere feeling. "What are you going to do?"

He shook his head doubtfully and began to elaborate his immediate plans to her. Elizabeth listened thoughtfully, her brow furrowed. "I was hoping," he finished, "to enlist your family's assistance in some part. Do you think your uncle would agree?"

"He will," she declared stoutly. "It is high time Lydia was made to feel the import of her words. She ought to face the consequences for once, rather than having them foisted upon others! I will make Uncle listen to you. He has already made it plain that Lydia and Kitty shall not be allowed further opportunities for gossip."

"Actually, it is your sisters' proclivity toward idle talk that I am hoping to exploit. I… I beg you would forgive me for such a nefarious undertaking…." He looked at her questioningly.

A spark of mischief again came to her face. Those intelligent eyes twinkled back at him and she cocked him a calculating grin. "Are you certain it is your cousin who is the military strategist?"

"Quite! Richard is the master, I am merely the student." He glanced at the skyline. Somewhere during those glorious moments in Elizabeth's arms, the sun had crested the horizon and the new day was underway.

She caught the direction of his gaze. "I should be getting back," she thought aloud. "Uncle has forbidden trips to Meryton, but he did not expressly prohibit any early morning walks. I suspect that was merely an omission, and he shall repent of it once he learns where I have been."

"Yet another insight into your character, Miss Bennet," his mouth twitched. She arched a brow at his return to the more formal address. "I shall have to take care to express my wishes specifically and clearly in the future. You have a very devious turn of mind!"

"You have no idea," she agreed. Her eyes shifted to the stallion just behind him as the horse gave a sudden tug on the rein. The great steed was in determined search of a mouthful of grass, yanking Darcy's arm away from her.

Darcy turned. He had nearly forgotten about the hulking giant at his side. He stepped aside a little. "This is Pluto," he introduced.

Elizabeth's eyes returned hesitantly to his face. She put out a cautious hand to the horse's nose.

"Not there," Darcy took her hand in his own and placed it on his horse's neck. She left it there, stroking the thick hair gently.

"How is it you have not much experience with horses?" he wondered. "I should have thought you, of all ladies, would enjoy riding."

"Riding takes practice," she answered pragmatically. "I do not dislike horses, but I am afraid you will find that once I gain a modest competence at something, I often do not return to improve myself. It is a terrible habit to have got into," she arched a mock serious gaze at him. "Perhaps I was never required to tender any great effort toward such enterprises. I expect," she looked back at the horse, "you will tell me I should give myself the trouble to improve my skills."

"The Mistress of Pemberley ought to be an accomplished horsewoman," he grinned in agreement. "What would the neighbours say if they saw my wife attempting to scale the rocky cliffs in a phaeton?"

"I can walk very well, sir!"

"Not even you can walk that much. Come, let me sit you on Pluto."

"Oh, no indeed! I shall require a much shorter mount, thank you very much! A lady's saddle would not be amiss either- or is that a part of your wicked scheme, Mr Darcy? You would place me on a monstrous beast where I must sit indecently if I am to be at all secure, not to mention utterly dependent upon your help to both mount and dismount?"

"My dearest Elizabeth, you do me so little credit! I had also thought to swing up behind you and take you for a truly terrifying ride over the fields, where you would be obliged to allow my arms snugly round your waist to keep you aboard."

"And to think I had considered you steady and trustworthy!"

"Not a bit of it. Did you hear that, Pluto? She thinks I am a sedate gentleman. You know better the wild, reckless rides we take, do you not?" The horse blew a gentle sneeze, and Darcy rubbed his shoulder affectionately.

Elizabeth laughed heartily. That insufferably taciturn and prideful man she had known last week was standing before her in barely civilized attire, jesting lightly with his horse! "Do you have a Persephone at home?" she chuckled. "Pluto is a curious name."

"My father always named his stallions after the Greek heroes. I suppose I have continued the tradition, but with the Roman names. I have a grey most fittingly named Neptune at home, and of course Pluto earned his name by his colour as well."

She crossed her arms, a sly smile cracking. "And how convenient for you that we already have a pomegranate tree."

He laughed suddenly, reminding her that she quite liked the sound, and inspiring her to tempt him to it often. "I had not thought of that! Shall you be avoiding the fruit in the future, my Lizzy?"

"I should say it is quite too late for that."

"I am glad to hear it." He stepped close again, cupping his gloved hand over her cheek. "I would not wish to entrap you, my queen."

Elizabeth blushed vividly at such a bold endearment. Her gaze faltered, but her smile grew. He tipped her chin back up to meet his eyes.

"I have something for you before we part, my love," he murmured. "It may be a bit premature for your uncle's liking, but I wish to give it to you all the same, if you will allow it." He slipped off his gloves, then brazenly tugged the gloves off her hands. Elizabeth watched him with widened eyes as he reached to the inner pockets of his clothing to withdraw a small item. He pulled away the case to reveal the stunning ring.

"An engagement gift," he bashfully explained, sliding the jewel up one of her fingers. "I had not thought this to be your wedding band, although it can be if you like." He clasped her fingers, sensitive to her overwhelmed expression. "It was my mother's, and my grandmother's before her," he continued softly. "Georgiana thought you would like it."

Elizabeth swallowed hard and nodded wordlessly. Darcy's wealth she had suddenly come to take for granted. It was some ephemeral trait he had possessed upon their first acquaintance, now thoroughly forgotten in the light of the tender heart he wore for her alone. The weighty bauble on her finger was a tangible reminder that he came from a world vastly different from her own- a world where one was judged by the size of the ring his wife brandished, or the modishness of each dazzling new gown. It was a world where appearances mattered more than substance, connections could make or break a fortune, and honour could be bought for a trifle.

Women- scores of them- far more pretentious and ambitious than Caroline Bingley, would be forever vying for her husband's attention, and she was not naive enough to think that would cease with his marriage. Every move she ever made would be constantly scrutinized and whispered over by those who might desire her fall from grace. This would be her future.

A fist curled in her stomach. What chance had a simple country girl against all the finery of London? She began to blink rapidly. She could not- would not!- be merely a wife of fashion, a healthy young woman required only to produce an heir while her husband slaked his desires elsewhere. A small sound choked from her.

"Is it too much?" he asked hesitantly. He feared that she might feel he was flaunting his riches, though that had not been his intention. *Brash idiot*, he castigated himself. He had only just overcome her dislike of his pride, yet he could not stop himself from pressing her with what now surely appeared an ostentatious display. His shoulders drooped in defeat and annoyance with himself.

But Elizabeth was shaking her head, her gaze still lowered. "No... thank you, William, it is beautiful. It is just... are you certain you want me?" Her eyes rose to his in earnest appeal. "I will surely seem unsophisticated and shabby in your world. I do not think I could bear it if... if I lost your regard. I feel quite unworthy." Secure, self-assured Elizabeth Bennet trembled slightly with doubt.

He let out a breath of relief. "You, my Lizzy?" He took her in his arms again. "Did you never wonder why I am yet a bachelor? Why I have never even dared to give any woman a second glance before you stole my entire attention? It was not for want of 'elegant and sophisticated' females, I assure you. It was because until you, I had never encountered a woman of true worth, one I could wish to share my life with. I cannot fix the hour or the spot, but I was well in the middle of my devotion to you before I even knew it had begun. You have grown so steadily in my heart that I do not believe I could ever be content without you, my dearest, loveliest Elizabeth. There could never be any other for me."

He touched her face with his bare fingers, gently tracing each little crevice and groove and delighting in the tickle of her warm breath on his hands. Beneath his tender fingertips the corners of her mouth lifted once more. Smiling, he tipped his own face near to lightly caress her lips with his own. He nearly came undone when he felt her velvet fingers reach for his own cheeks, teasing his chin.

Elizabeth released a long breath. She began at last to appreciate the struggles Darcy had faced in the *ton*, and yet another mysterious layer to his character peeled away. He was a man without peer, to have been relentlessly pursued as he had and to still emerge unscathed by the temptations and expectations of high society. She pulled a little closer, trusting in his embrace.

"Elizabeth," he whispered lovingly.

"Hmm?" was the muffled reply.

"I should wish to remain all day as we are, but there is something I must tell you."

"What is that?" she lifted her mouth from his to nuzzle his cheek.

"Your hands are cold. And so is your nose."

She drew back with a start, removing her hands from his face and stammering an apology. He laughed easily. "I was not concerned for my own comfort! You, however, must get back home before you take a chill."

"And before I offend my uncle!"

"Yes, that too." He returned her gloves, helping her to tug the one over the large ring and enjoying her smile as he did so. "Will there be any objections to us calling around ten?"

"None whatever. I shall tell my uncle you will be desiring a private conference."

"Thank you." He pressed one last kiss to her cheek, then swung up on Pluto. "I shall see you shortly, my Lizzy." With a broad smile and a click to his mount, he galloped away.

~

It had been some long while since Caroline Bingley had been obliged to ride rear facing in a carriage. Her *own* carriage, no less! Lady Catherine had not left that avenue available to her when the four ladies had set out from Darcy House that morning. Anne de Bourgh was bundled and swathed with hot bricks and a bevy of quilts, consuming most of the forward facing seat, but her spindly mother had managed to find herself a niche nonetheless.

Caroline cast a dispassionate eye on the great lady. She wondered at the woman's obtuse lack of discernment. Even in the short while it had taken Darcy's staff to help the ladies to the carriage, it was obvious to her where their sympathies lay. All treated Anne, and even her companion with gentle deference. The highest honour and care was paid to the sickly young woman and her quiet attendant, but Lady Catherine's machinations were deliberately frustrated at every turn.

Caroline had scarcely refrained from laughing out loud when Lady Catherine required not one but four separate footmen to procure her traveling cloak. "Misplaced, with sincerest apologies, my lady," had been the dry butler's excuse. Great had been the tongue lashing she imparted as he had helped her into the carriage, but the butler had merely bowed in simple deference with a quiet, "As your ladyship pleases." Lady Catherine had exchanged her flushed scarlet countenance for one of flaming violet at the butler's words. It had been a scene which Caroline was likely to relive with amusement for years to come.

"I say, Miss Bington," Lady Catherine began.

"Bingley," Caroline corrected her, indiscreetly omitting the proper address.

Lady Catherine's eyes narrowed. "Miss *Bingley*," she intoned heavily. "You say your brother has an estate where we shall be welcomed to pass the night. Is it near this… Bennet place?"

Caroline swallowed. She had not counted on this difficulty. Charles would no doubt be unwilling to welcome her back. *Well!* She would demand entry anyway. After all, it was only by some cruel trick of fate that he, the younger brother, was master over their father's holdings, while she, but a woman, could claim only a handsome dowry. What business ought he truly to have in denying her the benefits of their inheritance?

"Absolutely, my lady," she answered smoothly. "As to location, I believe it is approximately three miles to Longbourn, the little farm the Bennets call their estate."

"And you say Georgiana Darcy is staying at Netherfield?"

"Yes, my lady," she smiled, trying to cover how much she despised having to answer so.

"With your brother?"

"Well… yes, I suppose so, my lady. Mr Darcy stays there as well, of course."

"Of course." Lady Catherine sat back, a smug expression on her lined face. Caroline began to wonder just what she had let herself in for.

"I still do not see why we had to leave so bleeding early in the morning," grumbled the Earl of Matlock. He watched his breath fog in the carriage and tugged his long gloves for emphasis.

"I told you, Father, I received a message from Darcy in the middle of the night."

"We were coming anyway, what can the rush all be about?" he groused in irritation.

"He did not say, Father, but Darcy does not send such messages on a whim. I suspect something truly awful must be afoot. I hope it is not bad news to do with Mr Bennet."

"So what if it is? I daresay your cousin is overreacting. What can he expect you to do?"

Richard shook his head. "I've no idea. The thought has occurred to me… well, let us hope that is not the case."

"What? You speak in riddles, my boy."

"Do you remember George Wickham, the son of old Darcy's steward?"

The earl snorted. "A worthless rascal if there ever was one. Has he been imprisoned or shot yet?"

"No, but it was a very near thing once or twice. He has joined the militia stationed in Meryton and still has no generous feelings for Darcy."

"Still chasing skirts as well, I imagine? Ah, I see. Here I thought to anticipate a rather dull stay in Hertfordshire. This could prove a very entertaining visit."

~

"Lizzy, where have you been? Oh, we are all in an uproar!" Mrs Bennet, waving a laced kerchief, chased her daughter into the entryway of the house.

Elizabeth sighed. She had expected she might be missed, and braced herself for the explanation which would surely be required. "I went for a walk Mama, as I often do," she replied patiently. She flipped the scarf off her neck and began to put away her outerwear.

"Oh, hang your walks! Your father is awake!"

"What! Oh, Mama, is it true?" Elizabeth eagerly clasped her mother's hand. "Papa!" she began calling before he could be reasonably expected to answer, and raced up the stairs. "Papa!" She burst into the room. Jane and her aunt sat with Mrs Cooper, but her father's eyes were quite firmly closed.

She looked to each of the faces in dismay. "I thought… Mama said…." she trailed off miserably.

"He opened his eyes for a moment, Lizzy," Jane answered her. "It was only a moment. He seemed to look at us, but he did not speak."

Elizabeth sank down on the corner of her father's bed, deflated. "Oh," she responded sadly.

"Do not fret, Dearie," came Mrs Cooper's kind voice. "'Tis as promising as anything, I declare! I'd a letter from the doctor yesterday and he intended to journey from London this morning. He will be stopping to check on your dear Papa, Miss Elizabeth."

Elizabeth forced a cheerful reply. "That is good news," she returned softly. "Excuse me, please, I… I should go change."

Jane began to rise to follow her, but Mrs Gardiner put out a staying hand. Jane glanced from her aunt to Elizabeth's drooping shoulders, and acquiesced.

Twenty-Six

The messenger arrived at Netherfield just before nine in the morning. Darcy had been prowling the drawing room, chafing at the societal sensibilities which prevented him calling on the Bennet family any earlier. He would drop a comforting hand on Georgiana's shoulder occasionally as he passed by, not failing to note her pale visage.

At the ring of the bell, both Bingley and Darcy sprang to the entryway. "Excuse me, sirs, I have a message for Mr Darcy from Colonel Forster," the young officer explained. "I am to await a reply," he continued.

Darcy, stroking his jaw with his hand as he had begun to read, acknowledged the statement with a bare nod of his head. He scanned the note quickly and his expression fell into a scowl. Wordlessly he passed the note to Bingley.

"No!" Bingley cried as he read. A warning glance from Darcy silenced further outbursts. Chagrined, he dropped his eyes back to the page and finished reading. When he looked up, he caught his friend's stony gaze.

"Wait a moment and I shall have your answer for the colonel," Darcy told the messenger. Bingley followed him into the study and they closed the door.

"Miss King! She seemed such a quiet, proper girl!" Bingley exclaimed.

"And possessed of a fine fortune and an absent guardian," Darcy lifted his brow.

"Do you think she is with Wickham? Forster did not sound so certain. Can he have compromised her?"

"Of course. I sincerely doubt, however, if that is the end of his devilry. He intends to marry her, I should think, to obtain control over her inheritance. The colonel had traced her coach toward London, but it is rather soon to discover if they have arrived or if they have journeyed beyond."

"Yes, so I saw," Bingley mused. He watched as Darcy paced, his hands on his hips and his mouth pressed tightly. "Well, I suppose we have seen the last of him, have we not? It is a pity, though, for poor Miss King."

"You think we have? I think he has not abandoned his other quest, but has only found a tool. Mark my words, Wickham will not be satisfied until he has wrought some further damage to myself and had the satisfaction of witnessing it."

"I thought he had done an estimable job at that already."

"Not by half." Darcy sighed, dropping his fists. "I shall compose a reply. Would you be so good as to keep Georgiana company for a few moments? I do not like leaving her much alone today."

"You will be certain the colonel tracks down Miss King's uncle?"

"I imagine he has already endeavoured to do so, but I shall offer what assistance we can."

~

"Stop the coach! Wait, please!"

Caroline cocked her head at the distant shout from outside. "Did you hear that?" She glanced questioningly to the other occupants of the coach. Anne de Bourgh appeared to be asleep, seeming truly ill. Mrs Jenkinson looked as though she would have liked to agree with Caroline's ears, but dared not lift her voice.

"I heard nothing," Lady Catherine declared.

Caroline furrowed her brow, listening carefully. "I hear it again. Someone is hailing us from without."

"Nonsense. I do believe your head is addled, Miss Bingson. You must commence my doctor's healing soup regimen."

Caroline made a face. It was scarcely half way into their journey, and she already wanted to commit the most dreadfully uncivilized deeds. If she heard one more bit of advice from Lady Catherine's doctor…. "I am quite certain," she repeated herself firmly. *It is my carriage, after all!*

"Daniels!" she put her head out the window. "Is there someone trying to catch us up?"

"Yes, Miss Bingley," his voice filtered through the box. "A fellow what looks like a parson, on an old post nag. Not much of a rider, I'd say. Do you want I should wait? I worried he might be up to no good, Miss."

Caroline strained her neck but could not see the figure apparently trailing behind them. A little more loudly now she could hear another plaintive appeal for the carriage to stop.

"William Collins!" Lady Catherine announced. "Why did you not tell me he was trying to gain our attention! By all means, we must stop."

Caroline rolled her eyes at the shutters and made the request of her driver. In very little time the sweating, broad-faced man she remembered from the Netherfield ball had presented himself at the window of their carriage.

"Your ladyship!" He swept off his rented horse and stooped a low bow. "I flatter myself, nothing but Providence could have brought me into your ladyship's company for the present journey!"

"Collins! Where have you been? I required you two days ago!"

"But… your ladyship, I had only just departed Hertfordshire…. I must acquaint you with my most joyous news! I have secured the hand of the fairest creature who ever walked! I have the very greatest confidence, my lady, that when introduced to the vision who is my dearest Miss Charlotte Lucas, daughter of Sir William-"

"Never mind that, Collins! What are you doing following us *back* to Hertfordshire?"

He reddened a little, a sheen of perspiration on his brow despite the cool weather. "Why, I thought to attend your ladyship! When I returned to Hunsford and was notified your ladyship had set out, of course, I took it upon myself to… and when I called at Darcy House I was told…."

"And I suppose you have no idea what that chit of a cousin of yours is up to all this while? I am surprised at you, Collins! You ought to have known your duty to the de Bourgh family!"

"Y-yes, my lady," he bobbed his head, clutching his hat. "Of course, by all means, it is incumbent upon me to… forgive me, I have not the pleasure of understanding your ladyship," he faltered at last.

"Insolent fool! Why, you must have seen your way to stop this charade, this stain upon my nephew's account! That silly little minx is your kinswoman, is she not? You must have exerted your influence to impress upon her father what a foolish, insulting notion she had got into her head! To think my nephew could be imposed upon in such a fashion!"

"Naturally, your ladyship is quite correct," he bowed his head, chastised. "Your ladyship must comprehend, however, that Miss Bennet's father…."

"Is not worth my regard! If he cannot keep his daughters in check and their expectations confined within their own sphere, I have no sentiments to spare the man. We have stopped here long enough! Daniels! Drive on, and Collins, do you keep up. I shall require you to make the introductions at Longbourn."

Caroline ground her teeth in irritation. Lady Catherine certainly made free enough with a carriage and a driver which were not her own! A start pricked her awareness. The noblewoman remembered everyone else's name and every detail of every conversation with electrifying precision, but Caroline's own name came out bungled every time. *Is that how it is going to be?* Her white hands clenched inside her muff. Caroline Bingley was nobody's doormat.

~

"Mr Gardiner, I thank you for agreeing to speak with me." Darcy took the offered seat in Mr Bennet's study, carefully evaluating the other man's manner.

"My niece informs me," Gardiner eased himself into another chair, "that she will make my existence miserable should I fail to hear you out."

Darcy's eyes widened in mute surprise, triggering a sly chuckle from the older man. "Fear not, my dear sir, she did not put it quite so plainly! I know my niece, however, and have had cause in the past to regret when I did not put faith in her judgement. She told me you had something of rather great import to discuss."

Darcy bit back a long sigh, straightening in his chair. "Indeed. Firstly, sir, I must again beg your forgiveness for the events of yesterday. I assure you, I do not make a habit of compromising young ladies."

"Nor does Lizzy have a history of permitting such liberties. If it were one of the younger girls you had settled upon, we would be having a much more serious discussion, as I would be entertaining doubts about your good sense."

"I understand, sir." Darcy tried to contain a small twitch to the corner of his mouth. Perhaps Mr Gardiner would prove even more amiable than he had hoped. "My sister, as well, is apologizing to Miss Bennet as we speak. I hope you comprehend, sir, with what profound consternation I observed her behaviour to El… to Miss Bennet. She is exceedingly remorseful, I assure you."

"That is as it should be, but I think it hardly necessary." He paused, looking penetratingly at the humbled man before him. "I had a long talk with my niece, Mr Darcy, and she conveyed to me what she knew of Miss Darcy's history. You may be assured that I shall keep this knowledge in strictest confidence, but Lizzy felt it necessary to the preservation of my sympathies toward your family."

Darcy felt a wry expression growing. He found it ironic that to secure the good opinion of Elizabeth's family, his own mistakes and secrets must be laid bare. In any other family, the opposite would have been the case. "I have confidence in your discretion, sir, as I have the utmost faith in Miss Bennet's. The reason she spoke of such things to you is that I had hoped to secure the assistance of your family in repairing the damage to my sister's reputation."

Gardiner pinched between his eyes, a pained expression in evidence. "Lydia...." he muttered under his breath. "She is currently confined to her room. I shall be keeping a tight rein on my niece for the time being, I assure you."

"In truth, sir, I had rather hoped you would not." Gardiner's forehead puckered in interest as he listened to Darcy's plan.

~

Georgiana had looked forward to the call with fear and trembling, but instead of the affronted and indignant family she had every right to expect, she found herself welcomed with open arms. Elizabeth had been the first to greet her, with a warm embrace and a sincere smile. Jane and Mrs Gardiner had rapidly followed suit.

Mary Bennet, curiously, remained somewhat aloof, but would not suffer herself to be very far parted from Georgiana. Though largely silent, she remained constantly nearby- a dispassionate bodyguard, as it were. Bingley immediately retired to a corner with Jane, and Georgiana quickly found herself once again at ease with the remaining family. Perhaps not all was lost, after all.

In some wonder, she glanced about the room after several minutes. "Forgive me, Miss Elizabeth, but is your mother unwell this morning?"

"You need not address me so formally, Georgiana," Elizabeth winked. "However, Mama is quite well. She is very busy, I believe, with some personal matters."

"Oh, I see." Her brow furrowed. She did not see, in fact, but felt it rude to inquire further. It was, however, not long before she would receive her explanation.

The housekeeper appeared at the door of the sitting room, beckoning Mrs Gardiner. "Mrs Stewart requests your attendance, Ma'am."

Georgiana shot Elizabeth a questioning glance as Mrs Gardiner excused herself.

"Aunt Gardiner thought it best to begin soliciting Mama's advice on colours and lace," Elizabeth supplied. "With Papa ill and so much to contrive, Aunt Gardiner suggested it might be in better taste that the dressmaker might come to Longbourn for the morning. It is indeed a distinction, for the last time Mrs Stewart made a house call was for the wedding of Miss Keston of Mayweather, when she wed that wealthy gentleman worth eight thousand a year.

"Mama intends to spend a few hours at least looking over samples. Unhappily for me, she has no faith in my taste in fashion, so I expect I shall be consulted at some later date. I believe Mrs Hill's kitchen has been entirely commandeered." Another small wink accompanied these remarks, and Georgiana began to understand. Elizabeth and her aunt were geniuses of the first order.

Shortly thereafter, her brother appeared again in the sitting room, accompanied by Elizabeth's uncle. Georgiana tensed involuntarily. The gentleman, however, came to her directly and offered a bow. "My sister, Georgiana," William drew her forward. "Georgiana, may I present Mr Edward Gardiner."

"Delighted, Miss Darcy," Gardiner smiled with genuine affability.

She glanced quickly toward her brother. His intentionally light manner helped her to understand how to receive the man. "I am delighted as well, Mr Gardiner," she answered humbly. "I thank you for your hospitality."

"The pleasure is ours, Miss Darcy." Gardiner cast a surreptitious eye toward Bingley, who had drawn close and was hovering with some anxiety, rather like a hopeful puppy. With a tightly hidden smile which was only perceived by Elizabeth, Darcy performed the introductions.

"Mr Gardiner," Bingley began, a little anticipatory tension in his voice, "may I trouble you for a few moments of your time?"

Gardiner cocked a mirthful glance at Jane. "By all means, my good sir," he replied, and the two departed.

Darcy caught Elizabeth's gaze with a significant look. She nodded and left the room. Georgiana watched their exchange with growing wonder. "William?" she whispered questioningly.

He took her hand and gave it a cheerful squeeze. "All will be well, Sweetling. Take courage," he murmured softly.

A scarce moment later, a thunderous clamour arose from the stairs. Lydia and Kitty Bennet had been sprung from their prison. Georgiana's tension began to return, but William placed a comforting hand on her shoulder.

"La, it is about time!" Lydia was declaring. She addressed herself immediately to her bonnet and gloves in the hall, overlooking their guests entirely, but a ring of the bell distracted her. "Why, it's Maria!"

Elizabeth had rejoined the party in the sitting room by now, wearing a conspiratorial smirk reserved for Darcy.

"Thank you for your note, Lydia!" Miss Lucas' voice came through from the hall. "I could not wait to see your new bonnet!"

"New bonnet?" Lydia's muffled voice replied. "But I have no new bonnet!"

"Oh, but you have! You told me it was the latest fashion in velvets!"

"La, you are so strange, Maria! You must mean that one we admired in the window yesterday, but it was so dear! I declare, Papa does not give me enough allowance."

"But I was quite certain…."

Elizabeth interrupted the girls here. "Lydia, Kitty, dears, do come in here!" she called from the doorway.

Three girls, half decked out in outerwear, followed Elizabeth's voice into the sitting room. They all stopped upon beholding Georgiana. "Oh!" Kitty ejaculated, the first articulate utterance heard from her since she had emerged from her confinement.

Darcy smiled graciously at his future sisters. "Miss Catherine, and Miss Lydia," he bowed. "And Miss Lucas! I am most delighted to see you again so soon!"

His magnanimous greeting caught the girls off their guard. They paused hesitantly, various warm articles dangling uselessly from their hands. "What a happy thing it is you could join us," Darcy continued. "I feared we might have missed you."

Lydia perked up primly. "Why, not at all, Mr Darcy" she returned, attempting a hint of her older sister's disdain, but not succeeding quite so gracefully. "Me and Kitty were just about to go to town. We are sure of meeting with good company *there*." She lifted her nose fractionally.

Kitty attempted no such raillery. She merely shrank closer to Maria, glancing with significant amusement in Georgiana's direction.

"Pray, do not go just yet," Darcy invited. "I beg you would indulge me for just a moment- Miss Jane, and Miss Mary, as well. I had hoped to present an early Christmas gift to my future sisters. I saw no point in waiting halfway through the cold months before you were able to enjoy the use of… well, I perhaps oughtn't spoil the surprise. If you will excuse me only a moment." Darcy stepped outside, and with a word to a manservant waiting at the coach, returned.

He was followed by five of Bingley's footmen, each toting two large parcels. A few audible gasps accompanied them. "Ladies," Darcy gestured invitingly, "I shall be required to return to London very shortly, for how long I do not know. As my plans are yet uncertain, I have asked your uncle's blessing to present these today. He did not think it improper, in light of my understanding with Miss Elizabeth. Please accept these with my warmest felicitations. Let me see… ah, this one is for you, Miss Lydia."

He presented each little stack of boxes in turn. With the exception of Elizabeth, the Bennet girls each received, to their complete amazement, a beautiful new woolen cloak and one of the most delicious new offerings from the millinery shop. An additional pair of boxes was set to the side for Mrs Bennet, but none wished to disturb her labours at the moment.

Kitty and Jane both thanked Darcy graciously. Mary's stony face softened as her fingers reverently stroked the thick cloak. It was far finer than the second-hand one her mother had passed her from Jane. She rose grateful eyes to the gentleman and offered him a shy smile.

Lydia, for once, was struck speechless. She stared at Darcy as though he had grown a second head, while Maria Lucas did full justice to the lovely bonnet in her hands. Such peace did not last long, but the reprieve was long enough for Mr Bingley and Mr Gardiner to emerge, each appearing well satisfied with the other. Many in the room fixed the pair with blatant stares, but by them nothing was mentioned other than their mutual felicity in the acquaintance.

While they were yet speaking so, the crunch of gravel outside roused everyone's attention. Lydia, possessing less tact than many others, was the first to rush to the window and peer out. "Jane, Lizzy, look!" she beckoned them all to the window. "The most enormous carriage has arrived!"

~

"One can see, my lady, the very agreeable countryside of Hertfordshire is most suitably furnished with serviceable roads, and, I flatter myself, all have been skillfully maintained even in the wet seasons. Your ladyship will surely appreciate the many abundantly productive orchards to be found in this country. Your ladyship will no doubt be quite expertly acquainted with the ideal type of land suited for growing...."

Caroline wanted to cram her fingers in her ears. That sycophant had not ceased his prattle since the moment he had fallen into league with them. Lady Catherine kept the window on their side of the carriage open so she could listen to his droning. Caroline shrank further down into her furs, shrugging her layers up over her ears and cheeks.

A glance across the carriage at just the right time revealed Anne de Bourgh peeping at her through half-lidded eyes. Caught, Anne immediately closed her eyes again and assumed once more the aura of the sleeper. Caroline arched a brow thoughtfully. Perhaps Anne de Bourgh had contrived a way to avoid conversing with that insipid mother of hers!

Caroline briefly toyed with the notion herself, but another glance out the window revealed a landscape all too familiar. They were very close to their destination. Caroline felt a quivering thrill in anticipation of the triumph she was about to witness. No, she could not sleep now, nor even pretend to!

Lady Catherine sat up suddenly in interest. "Collins! Is that the estate up ahead?"

Caroline was, of course, handicapped by the awkward angle of the window, thanks to her unfortunate placement on the rear-facing seat, but she had been through the area often enough. She could see Collins, however. The parson must have had weak eyes, for he squinted carefully before answering.

"Your ladyship is as discerning as ever! Why yes, it is. your ladyship must quite agree that, while nothing to the glory of Rosings Park…."

Caroline finally succeeded in blocking him out. She began to smile, the first time she had done so all day. Arrogant and poorly bred as Lady Catherine was, she was firmly on Caroline's side of matters. This was going to be an encounter to remember.

"Mama, Aunt, we have guests arriving." Elizabeth bit her lip painfully. How she wished she did not have to call her mother away from her amusements! Darcy, however, had clearly recognized the coach, and desired that the lady of the house should be present to welcome it. She had silently pled against such a course, but recognized that he was correct. Anything less would be bad form. Her mother would have to be alerted to the presence of their visitors.

"Guests, my love?" Mrs Bennet was all tender affection for the bride-elect. "They must have come to wish you well, is that not so? Come my dear, we shall be happy to receive them!"

By the time Elizabeth had emerged from the kitchen with her mother and aunt in tow, their guests had already entered the drawing room. Elizabeth braced herself. Such a large carriage could only mean….

"Darcy! There you are!" a strident voice carried to her. Taking a deep breath, she pushed the door aside. Elizabeth, her aunt and her mother filed silently into the sitting room behind the new arrivals.

The figure before her turned sharply at her entrance. "Colonel Fitzwilliam!" she greeted him joyfully.

"Miss Elizabeth!" he swept her a bow. "Darcy, you must allow me to perform the introductions. Father, this is Miss Elizabeth Bennet, Darcy's betrothed. My father, Miss Elizabeth, the Earl of Matlock."

Elizabeth dipped a curtsey. "I am honoured to make your lordship's acquaintance."

"The honour is mine, I assure you, Miss Bennet," the earl offered a reserved smile.

"May I present my mother, my lord?" Mrs Bennet was truly aghast. Pale and speechless, she fumbled a curtsey to the earl. Somehow it had escaped her notice that the handsome colonel she had so roundly abused on the previous evening was the son of nobility. That, to her mind, was enough exoneration to secure her good opinion of him. Elizabeth had momentary reason to hope that her mother's excitable spirits might suffer enough of a shock to diminish them through the duration of the earl's visit.

Elizabeth discreetly found her way to Darcy's side as he took it upon himself to make the remainder of the introductions to his uncle. She recognized a calculating gleam in his eye, and began to relax some. Perhaps he had planned this, too!

The earl quickly fell into easy conversation with her uncle Gardiner, a fact which readily surprised Elizabeth. She still felt the gentleman's eye upon her rather frequently. She found herself wishing that her younger sisters had made an opportunity to excuse themselves to town before the earl's visit, but even Lydia was sensible to the import of such a call. The girls settled on the sofa, but mercifully remained somewhat mannerly- if one overlooked the occasional inexplicable giggle and bold stares originating from that region of the room. Even Mrs Bennet was in sufficient awe that Mrs Gardiner was usually able to tactfully direct her.

"Richard," Darcy drew near his cousin, "how did you find her ladyship your mother?"

"Why, she is… she is well enough, Darcy." The colonel's eyes narrowed curiously. Darcy never referred to his aunt by her title when he could help it. Why would he make a point of doing so now?

"I thought you had told me she was doing rather poorly? I am glad to hear you found her improved." Darcy leveled an arched brow at his cousin.

"Oh…" the colonel inhaled sharply. "Yes, she suffers somewhat, the poor dear, but she rallies as best she can."

"Are you to take over the management of your grandfather's estate, then? Her ladyship had some concerns about the steward, the last I heard."

"Why… not as yet, Darcy." Fitzwilliam tilted his head, confused at his highly private cousin's mention of family affairs before a public audience. Darcy flicked his eyes silently toward the youngest Bennet sisters, who had ceased their quiet chatter and leaned forward in earnest attendance. "I recall," he added cautiously, watching his cousin's face for signs of approval, "that she did make mention of securing a pension against old Bayard's coming retirement."

"Yes, of course, that is proper. When you are ready to interview potential new stewards, I shall be glad to offer you any recommendations."

"Darcy, you know I have not inherited the estate in my own right-

Grandfather left it to Mother, you know, as there was no entail. She desires it to come to me eventually, but for now any changes are surely up to M… her ladyship," he corrected himself at a look from Darcy. "She would take *your* advice over mine, I am not involved at all." Richard glanced about the room. By now more than the youngest Bennet sisters overheard their conversation. Mrs Bennet eavesdropped shamelessly, and he could see even his father and Elizabeth's uncle were sparing some attention for Darcy's remarks.

"That is not how she was speaking of the matter at her last visit to Pemberley," Darcy continued, drawing a nearly horrified expression from Fitzwilliam. What had come over his cousin? "Do you not recall?" Darcy gave another meaningful cock of his eye. "She was rather insistent that a certain nameless gentleman in our family should continue to pay court to Lord Ellsworth's daughter to secure a future heir for the estate."

"Darcy! That was y-" he coloured and broke off, darting his eyes to the earthy beauty standing at Darcy's side. *Closely* at his side. Evidently a deal had happened in a day. Her dark eyes sparkled roguishly and she cast him a barely perceptible wink. He looked back to Darcy, who pinned him with a compelling gaze. *What the devil is the old man up to?*

"Georgiana!" Darcy beckoned abruptly. "Why have you not yet greeted your cousin?"

Richard turned, thoroughly befuddled. Georgiana drew near, her light blue eyes cast to the floor and her hands clasped before her. "Dearest Georgie!" he welcomed his cousin. At least *her* he would be able to comprehend.

"Good morning, Cousin," she acknowledged him softly, offering her hand for him. Her eyes remained cast down, her cheeks stained brightly, but she smiled a little at the carpet as he took her hand. Georgiana too bashful to look up to him? What was going on?

"Richard," Darcy brought his attention back, "I am glad you are here. I find it necessary to return to London for a few days. Georgiana wishes to remain to further her acquaintance with Miss Bennet, but of course she cannot do so without one of us near. Might I presume to hope that you would be able to look after her for a few days while I am away?"

"Why… of course, Darcy, by all means. I expect Pater will return just after you; he only intended a short visit, but I have several days' leave."

"Excellent, I thank you." Darcy directed his gaze toward Elizabeth, pointedly leaving Fitzwilliam alone with Georgiana. Fitzwilliam shot him a brief curious glare, then turned his attention to the less mysterious of his two cousins.

Twenty-Seven

As the carriage neared the small turnabout which served Longbourn as a courtyard, Caroline glanced out the window at the pompous black figure on his rented horse. His lips were curling in smug satisfaction, and she could scarcely feel less pleased herself. At last, a cohort of influential personages were come together to impress upon Darcy what he owed to himself and to Georgiana. It was for his own good! That strumpet Eliza Bennet would simply have to be put aside!

Peering out the window nearest the house, Lady Catherine gave an unexpected start. Caroline looked to see what had discomposed the great lady and discovered another carriage, twice as fine as her own, already gracing the driveway behind Darcy's.

She squinted her eyes somewhat and was able to make out the Earl of Matlock's crest on the door. Perfect! The earl would give no quarter to an upstart country nobody! Caroline preened a little. She would look forward to renewing her acquaintance with the earl. She feared he had been left with a deceptively poor impression of her true qualities.

Lady Catherine, however, was rapping on the carriage. "Drive on immediately! Take us to Netherfield at once!"

Collins had reined in, preparing to dismount, but stopped himself in dismay. "Your ladyship, I assure you, this is the right place! I regret that the situation may not be-"

"I said drive on! It is not up for conjecture, Collins!" Lady Catherine, frowning her great displeasure, reared back on the seat of the carriage and glowered.

Caroline bit back her frustration. Perhaps Lady Catherine already knew the earl's intentions, and had decided to cause Darcy no further public disgrace. She could hardly lament such a motive. After all, the man must still have some credibility left when his family had done with him, if she were to agree to be the next Mrs Darcy!

~

Elizabeth smiled as Darcy drew her aside and spoke lowly, "Handsomely done, sir. You have given the good people of Meryton fodder for several days!"

"Awkwardly done, you mean. I should rather have been more subtle, but clumsy as I was, I expect it will suffice." He released a long, slow breath and glanced across the room where three young girls tittered behind gloved hands. "Richard's arrival could not have been timed more perfectly."

"Yes, quite the coincidence, I daresay," she chuckled, then sobered. "Must you really leave so soon?" she asked softly.

She did not wish him to go any more than he himself desired it! Could it be true? Oh, how he could crush her to him! "I am afraid so, my Lizzy," he answered in a low murmur, for her ears alone. "I intended to leave directly from here; my horse is already outside tied to the rear of the coach. The fellow who began all this trouble has yet to satisfy himself. I cannot allow him to continue to harm others as he has done."

"You speak as though he is your responsibility," she smiled warmly.

"So he is, or he was my father's at any rate. I suppose I have inherited the reprobate. Had I put pin to his appetites months ago, these things could not have happened, but as I was eager to protect Georgiana, I did not pursue him as far as I ought. Now another has paid the price."

She tilted her head. "Another? What has happened?"

He thinned his lips. "I am not certain of anything. However, you might employ sensitivity where Miss King is concerned."

Elizabeth gasped. "No!" she blinked away a sudden terror.

Darcy put a hand out to reassure her, but his eyes quickly shifted to her left and his voice took on its usual commanding tone. "Uncle James, we are honoured by your visit." Elizabeth composed herself quickly and curtseyed again to the approaching earl.

"Your uncle is a man of sense, Miss Bennet," the elder Fitzwilliam began. "Darcy, I have just discovered that your Miss Bennet's uncle is something of a magnate, you might say. My broker has been investing in the

Gardiner's enterprises for some while and I have had no cause to regret it."

"I am glad to hear it, Uncle," Darcy smiled. "I find him to be quite amiable."

"Indeed. Well, Miss Bennet, my son tells me that you gave Darcy here a rather hard time. I do hope so, Miss Bennet, for my nephew has had entirely too smooth of an existence thus far."

"Does His Lordship value an intractable lady, then?" she raised a pert smile to Darcy's uncle. "If that be the case, I shall look forward to meeting Lady Matlock with much enthusiasm!"

Matlock startled into a great laugh, clapping Darcy on the back. "Just the thing! I say, Darcy, she has quite taken the likeness of your aunt, has she not?" He winked genially at his nephew. "Oh, do forgive me, Miss Bennet. She is a fine woman, Lady Matlock, but occasionally she sees fit to remind me who the real authority in the family is."

"Truly?" Elizabeth raised her eyebrows innocently. "Perhaps I ought to beg his lordship for any advice he might be able to offer. I should dearly like to make a good first impression upon her ladyship."

"Simple enough, really, Miss Bennet. You must take care to compliment her rather questionable taste in art, sample whatever new culinary concoction she has ordered from that blasted French chef, and by all means flatter her sons."

Elizabeth smiled, aware that her conversation still had its attendants. "While I shall endeavour to do what I can as regards the former- I have no taste in art and simple culinary preferences- the last will be no great burden, I assure your lordship. Colonel Fitzwilliam is one of the finest gentlemen I have encountered- in my limited experience," she dipped a cheerful half-curtsey.

The earl laughed. "But not so fine as my nephew, eh, Miss Bennet?"

"Certainly less taciturn and forbidding!" Elizabeth slanted an impish smile toward Darcy. "In fact, now that I think of it, my lord, I may have chosen the wrong cousin entirely!"

Darcy's eyes widened in some alarm, drawing a pleased chortle from his uncle and a swift reassuring smile from Elizabeth. He bent his head lowly, speaking only loudly enough for their small party to hear. "You forget, Miss Bennet, that you had quite little choice in the matter! It is most unfortunate for you, I am afraid, but it is too late to change your course now."

The earl clapped a hand over his midsection and bellowed in laughter, drawing curious gazes from about the room. "I say, Miss Bennet, you have quite ruined our boy! Where is my sour old nephew?"

"Sour? Oh, no, my lord. Mr Darcy can be quite charming, but I beg you would keep that information close." She tipped nearer with hushed conspiratorial tones. "We should not wish to reveal *all* of his secrets." She cast sparkling eyes to her betrothed, who seemed not at all discomposed by her plundering of his deepest confidences.

Elizabeth watched Darcy carefully. He had only begun to learn to be teased, and she feared taking too many liberties before his relatives. His uncle seemed a man of hearty good humour, putting Elizabeth perhaps a little too much at her ease. She had no doubts that he was, in truth, more sly and cunning even than she herself. It was high time to divert the man's attention away from tormenting his nephew!

"My lord," she brightened, "I am quite looking forward to making my acquaintance with Derbyshire. I understand my lord hails from the region as well. Can your lordship tell something of the landscape?"

"Indeed, Miss Bennet. It is harsh and unforgiving, the rocks break the plowshares and the blistering cold nips the buds from the trees. The only blasted things that grow are brambles and burs. The game is scarce, save for some half-starved coneys and rats. Rats the size of felines, Miss Bennet! Every home in Derbyshire is ramshackle and replete with the pests. The only saving grace is the mongrel dogs that roam everywhere at liberty, eating them almost as fast as they can breed. It was a shame last year when the rats ran out, but we only lost one or two farm hands to the feral pack."

Elizabeth's face shone with ebullient laughter as the earl continued with his sardonic description, not sparing even the great Pemberley with his glib insults. Darcy was gazing back in wry confusion, marveling at his uncle's easy satire.

"I now no longer wonder at the immense height of your horse, Mr Darcy!" Elizabeth chuckled, then tipped a sweet smile up at him. "He must keep you well off the ground and out of harm's way! Are there snakes as well, my lord?"

"Vipers, Miss Bennet, hundreds of them," Matlock confirmed with a droll wink. Darcy nearly bit off his own tongue when he witnessed it. He watched some minutes longer in speechless awe as his little country miss parlayed disarmingly with one of the greatest men in England. It was apparent that Elizabeth had utterly cast her spell over James Fitzwilliam, the Earl of Matlock. *Leave it to my Lizzy to take the measure of the man so quickly!*

"Uncle," Darcy interjected at last, "pray, do not give Miss Bennet false ideas of Derbyshire! I had nearly convinced her that it was a habitable and welcoming place. I beg you would not let slip anything," he leaned close, lifting his eyebrows significantly, "*shocking*. It is only Pemberley's western wing which leaks, and it has been some while since we 'misplaced' any of our guests. You know we dealt with that she-dragon in the back wood last season, and I do not think her brood in the cave can have gained their full maturity as yet."

Elizabeth by now was daintily covering her mouth with the tips of her fingers and striving to contain the great belly laugh which threatened to undermine her reputation as a lady. "Oh! Dragons!" she cried with enthusiasm. "How exciting, Mr Darcy! Oh, now you have quite captured my interest!" She turned a bright grin and admiring eyes up to him. *Ah, there is my reward!* he thought with a warm tingling thrill. It would be no hardship to endure his lessons from his Mistress!

Matlock eyed the couple appraisingly as Darcy tried to rectify his uncle's cynical description of Derbyshire. He had been concerned for Darcy for years. Either the motherless young man would be taken in by a gold-digger like that Bingley woman, or he would waste the prime of his strength away, never allowing anything at all to touch his heart. So far, it had appeared that the latter would be the case. He had taken life and his responsibilities altogether too seriously, and no lady was ever found who could meet his exacting standards.

Now, that other thing he had feared had come to pass. His highly sought-after nephew had fallen prey to a penniless young nobody. Yet, the earl could not in this circumstance find it within himself to feel disapproval. The girl did not seem in the slightest impressed by Darcy's wealth or stature, a thing utterly unheard of. She appeared to hold the man himself highly in her regard, treating him with the respect due to one's affianced, but with a light, familiar attitude which seemed utterly to have bewitched the young man. Matlock watched in some fascination as proud and serious Darcy stood before him jesting fancifully with a witty young girl of no consequence whatsoever.

There could be no doubt about it; the lady had clearly wrapped his nephew around her little finger. By Richard's assertion, it had been quite unconsciously done on her part! Never had he expected Darcy to fall so easily to a woman's charms, but this particular woman was something unique. Matlock listened a little longer to his nephew's easy repartee with the bright young lady and sighed inwardly. His nephew was lost, and if he wished to uphold cordial family relations, there was nothing to do but endorse the match.

~

Bingley's butler braced himself at the door of the Hall, wide-eyed and quaking. "The gentlemen left no indication that your arrival was expected, Madam," Dawson answered nervously.

"How *dare* you address me so! Do you not recognize nobility when you see it? Such an ignorant, backward country!"

Dawson gulped. "Forgive me, my lady, I did not know!" His gaze slid surreptitiously to Miss Bingley. "May our coach house offer your ladyship's horses fresh bait along the journey?"

"The horses! Fool, I shall see my nephew! We shall wait for him in the drawing room. I expect he shall be returning immediately he has paid his call."

"I-I regret, my lady, that I cannot do that." The butler cringed, waiting for the blustering assault on his character and respectability which he knew was to come.

The explosion was immediate and violent. *"Cannot do that? How dare! Stand aside, you cannot deny access to me! Do you know who I am?"*

Dawson, lacking the cool pluck of Darcy's carefully schooled staff in London, cowered slightly. His own sweet-tempered employer had rather spoiled him, and great had been that wondrous day- yesterday, in fact- when the Master had evicted the only resident source of strife from the household. "I... I have no idea, my lady," he ventured lamely.

Lady Catherine glared silently for a moment, fuming. "Collins! Tell this worthless fool who I am!"

Caroline rolled her eyes as the subservient little twit came forward, bowing repeatedly before his wrathful patroness. He opened his mouth to speak, but the butler, having been exposed to Collins' rambling on a previous occasion, moved to intervene.

"I regret, my lady, that it matters not. My master has ordered that Miss Bingley must not be granted entry- nor any of her guests... regardless of their identity." The last part came out with admirably little tremble in his voice. Dawson straightened and squared his jaw, affecting more courage and adamance than he truly possessed.

Lady Catherine whirled on Caroline, rage and betrayal sparking from her faded eyes. *"What is this?"* she hissed in fury.

Caroline blanched, but recovered smoothly. "My brother, your ladyship," she intoned sweetly. "He is quite blinded as well, and fancies himself attached to Miss Bennet's older sister. He did not favour my disapproval of the Bennet family, either for himself or Mr Darcy. So, it is, My Lady," she adopted a slightly martyred expression, "one cannot act upon good intentions without occasionally being made to suffer for it."

Lady Catherine's seemed to shrink somewhat, her towering ire against Caroline, at least, abated for the moment. She cast a vengeful expression back to the butler. "I have not yet done! This house is not worthy of our regard! I am most *seriously* displeased. My nephew shall hear of this!" She continued her litany against the household, the persons who dwelt within, and the entire Hertfordshire countryside until she had ascended once more into her- or rather, Caroline's- carriage.

Once settled within, Lady Catherine put her head graciously out the window so that her parson might have the honour of hearing her private directives to him. "Collins! Do you take us to the home of your betrothed. I believe you said her father bears some manner of title. *He* shall know how I am to be received!"

~

The half hour the earl spent visiting with Miss Bennet's family passed agreeably enough. He glanced once more about the room, mentally ticking off his final thoughts on his future relations.

That Mama of Miss Bennet's seemed a mousy thing, easily cowed by her relatives. He had been surprised to discover that; he had thought Richard had made some derogatory mention of the woman's brazen manners. He decided the woman was a powder keg- innocuous for the moment, but poised at any public moment to shower embarrassment upon those too closely affiliated with her.

The two younger sisters had caused him to raise his eyebrows more than once. It was plain that they, along with their companion, appeared over-eager to quit the house as soon as he had removed his arduous presence from their home. The blatant and hungry stares directed toward Richard did nothing to improve his impression of them.

That middle sister he could not quite put his finger on. She had posted herself loyally near his niece, saying little, but never far removed. He wondered briefly if the young woman had tried to attach herself to shy Georgiana, hoping to gain by circumstance. He would be sure to make mention of his concerns to Richard.

Despite all, he had been surprisingly impressed by Miss Bennet's aunt and uncle. They had paid him the respectful civilities due one of his status, but their manner was gracious and humble without descending into obsequiousness. They struck quite the perfect balance, and the earl went away with the impression that Mr Gardiner was in all probability the most genteel and respectable tradesman he had yet encountered.

The eldest sister- the one favoured by Darcy's friend- was one of the most stunning creatures he had ever beheld. She was perfectly enchanting, and unconnected as she was, she still struck him as more than suitable for a man of Bingley's status. She was everything maidenly and innocent, and the earl thought fleetingly of a few London girls who could stand to gain by her example. Even so, her classic beauty paled next to her sister's lively sparkle.

By far the most fascinating diversion in the room, and likely in all of Hertfordshire, was Darcy's affianced. The girl's effervescence had revealed a new nephew to him. It was as though she alone had been privy to the man beneath the mask of stoicism, and had taken it upon herself to unveil her loyalty to that man to the world, while still somehow respecting his deep privacy. He had never seen Darcy so at his ease since he was a child.

The earl still suffered somewhat in confusion at their circumstances. Richard had not neglected to inform him of the details of Darcy's relationship to the young lady, and had led him to believe that she still remained noncommittal about their proposed union. No such reluctance was apparent now!

It was refreshing, he supposed, that the lady had required a little convincing from his nephew. Curiously absent in Elizabeth Bennet were the ambitions which marked many women who approached Darcy, but it seemed clear enough to the earl that he had at last won her honest regard.

As the proper length of their visit drew to a close, the earl moved to bid his farewells. "Miss Bennet," he bowed to Elizabeth, "it has been my pleasure to make your acquaintance. I do hope your father continues in his recovery."

Elizabeth curtseyed very properly. "Thank you, my lord. We have every hope that he shall."

"Just so. Darcy," he turned to his nephew, "you must bring Miss Bennet to London as soon as may be. Your aunt is most eager to make her acquaintance."

Elizabeth's face clouded slightly. "I was most sorry to hear of her ladyship's indisposition. I do hope she may recover soon!"

"Indisposition?" The earl shot a questioning gaze across the room at his son, who was still trying to avoid Darcy's confusing presence. "Why, no, her ladyship is quite well. She only fancies herself greatly beset in the cold months, and refuses to stir abroad! My son is rather too prone to indulge his mother's complaints, I fear."

Elizabeth nodded her acknowledgement and slanted a curious look at her betrothed. Darcy's hid his satisfied smirk rather poorly. While a careful examination of his statements yielded no untruths regarding his cousin's situation, he had certainly allowed idle minds to believe what they would. No one could now find Colonel Fitzwilliam a man motivated to seduce innocent young heiresses, nor could his cousin's confidence in him be questioned.

Upon their departure, the gentlemen decided among themselves that Fitzwilliam would return to Netherfield with Bingley and Georgiana. The earl, determining to return to London himself, desired his nephew to keep him company. Darcy agreed to ride the first part of the journey back to London in his uncle's coach, but for the sake of speed he would take his leave and depart on horseback at the first coaching station.

The earl settled back on the plush squabs, fixing his nephew with a firm stare. No harm in testing the besotted young man a little. "I am quite disappointed in you, my boy," he began.

Darcy merely smiled. "I had expected you might be."

"A man of your station has no business meddling with the impoverished daughter of a modest country squire."

"You are quite correct, Uncle," he agreed.

"The estate cannot be worth more than two thousand a year, at best, and likely entailed besides."

"Two thousand, one hundred, to be exact, and the heir is a toad," Darcy supplied.

His uncle cocked a questioning eyebrow. "With her connections to trade, she will suffer in the *ton*."

"Miss Bennet will have the *ton* at her feet by the end of the first Season, if I know her at all. Those holdouts who are not swayed to her favour are not worth my trouble."

"You do not fear that Georgiana's chances may be harmed by the association?"

"Georgiana is quite taken with Miss Bennet, and has no desire to be the darling of the *ton*. I rather think she would fancy not having a Season altogether."

His uncle paused in surprise. He squinted penetratingly. "The youngest sisters are barely respectable. One of them for certain is set to bring disgrace upon the family if not properly checked."

Darcy lifted his brow in silent accord.

"And that mother- quiet enough today, I grant you, but Richard assures me her company can be most tedious, even bordering on alarming."

"All true," Darcy draped his arm across the back of his seat and crossed his calves comfortably.

"And yet you are determined to have her? There are other arrangements possible, you know."

Darcy dropped his arm and both feet thudded to the floor of the coach, his features hardening and his voice turning brittle. "Out of the question! I would never stoop to such disgrace, and even less would I ask it of Miss Bennet! Uncle, if you disapprove of Miss Bennet, make your opinion known. You shall not cause me to alter my course, but your answer determines whether you shall be welcome to our homes in the future!"

Matlock roared in delight. "Calm yourself, my boy! I mean no disrespect to your future bride! I am only surprised at you."

Darcy relaxed somewhat. "As was I myself, I assure you. However, I am quite satisfied that she is exactly the wife I should desire. It is just as I would wish."

The earl frowned, but it was not an unfriendly expression. "She is clever, Darcy, and accustomed to much liberty. I doubt not that she will challenge your authority."

Darcy grinned unrepentantly. "I would expect nothing less from her! Bingley tells me I have been too long without some iron edge against which I myself might be sharpened."

"Then, my boy, you have quite met your match. Do you know, I have the unsettling impression that after this first meeting, she still knows a deal more about me than I know about her."

"I often feel the same, Uncle!" Darcy laughed.

"I say," Matlock changed the subject abruptly, "what calls you so urgently to London? I should have thought you most reluctant to leave your enchanting lady. You are not rushing into a special license, are you? Is her father's condition truly so precarious?"

"No!" Darcy jumped in alarm. "That is, my trip had nothing to do with.... Although it is an interesting idea you have just given me."

"Not the first time you have thought it, no doubt," the earl commented dryly.

"Certainly not," his nephew agreed. "However…" he sighed, thinning his lips in uncertainty. "How well do you remember George Wickham?"

"Not *him* again."

"The same. He has been spreading rumours about Georgiana to harm her, linking her name with Richard's when… well, let me simply say that I do not believe Wickham traveled to London alone. "

The earl's face turned to granite. "He said *what* about my niece? And Richard! I will break him! Darcy, you may count on my assistance. I'll not have the Fitzwilliam name slandered!"

"I thank you, Uncle, but I believe I can handle Wickham," Darcy replied, trying to keep an edge of nervousness out of his voice. There was much he still preferred to keep private from his uncle.

"You will have your hands full when you get to London," the earl grunted. He squinted in surprise at his nephew's questioning glance. "Why, did Drake not send you word? Oh, I suppose it may have missed you. Your aunt came to Town, and she does not look upon your marriage with a favourable eye."

Darcy sagged, pressing his fingers into his eyes. "She came to your house?"

"No! To yours!" the earl laughed. "Had a devilish time of it too! Stranded, she is, or was yesterday."

Darcy's lips twitched a little. *Richard!* He sighed. "I suppose the conversation had to happen. I never intended to marry Anne, but she has not believed me."

The earl narrowed his eyes. "Yes, whatever you do, you must not marry Anne." He was then silent for a long time.

Twenty-Eight

It was with the very greatest satisfaction, for a change, that Elizabeth observed the departure of her mother and sisters from the house just after their hasty luncheon. Primped and powdered, and each of them decked in their Christmas gifts from Mr Darcy, the Bennet entourage set upon the unsuspecting town of Meryton with the very juiciest gossip. The presence in town of a handsome colonel, son of an earl, who stood someday to inherit- the imminence of such event and the size of the estate mattered not- was not a thing lightly to be dismissed!

Elizabeth and Jane had elected to remain behind, but Mary, curiously, had followed the others to town. Elizabeth suspected that sweet Georgiana had somehow won Mary's loyalty, and that the quiet middle sister wished to see her friend's reputation exonerated.

Elizabeth was pleased, on the heels of everyone else's departure, to welcome Charlotte Lucas. Together they and Jane drew chairs around Mr Bennet's bedside. Mrs Cooper cheerfully made way in the cramped room for them, listening with much enjoyment to the plans of three young maidens on the cusp of matrimony.

Jane confessed, in strictest confidence, that Mr Bingley had obtained their uncle's conditional blessing upon their marriage, but in light of their father's improvement, it had been decided to keep their engagement private until Mr Bennet could have his say. Nevertheless, Bingley would now, in their uncle's eyes at least, be accorded the privileges of one affianced to a daughter of the house, and Jane might consider herself an engaged woman.

Several things became readily apparent to Mrs Cooper's wise discerning. She observed with satisfaction that her favourite Bennet sister at last looked forward to her inevitable marriage with pleasure. A fine thing, it was. Too often bright young women with no dowry were shackled to insufferable husbands, but it seemed Miss Elizabeth had escaped that fate. That sweet Jane also bubbled with shy enthusiasm and hopeful pleasure.

Miss Lucas, however, seemed much more pragmatic about her approaching nuptials. There was certainly nothing wrong with a level head, but Mrs Cooper thought she detected a little wistful longing in the eldest of the prospective brides. Ah, well, not all could marry for love. It sounded as though the girl would be well provided for, and that was surely a mercy.

At two o'clock in the afternoon the bell was rung, and Mrs Hill arrived shortly at the door of Mr Bennet's sickroom. With her were two men instantly recognized by Mrs Cooper. The comfortable little woman wasted no time in introducing the young ladies to her husband the Doctor, and to her son who also wore a doctor's smock. The elder Dr Cooper stood about Mr Bennet's height, with kindly greying eyes and soft weathered hands. Somehow he was exactly what Elizabeth had expected him to be.

The younger, however, stood a head taller than his father with a broader form. He appeared to be about thirty years of age, with an average face, sandy hair, and bright green eyes. Though merely a country doctor of modest means, he obviously took gentlemanly care about his person and address. His manner to the ladies was pleasantly direct and unassuming. He smiled a little timidly at the pretty faces introduced to him by his mother.

Somewhat awkwardly, due to the tight spaces, the young ladies attempted to file out of the room so that the doctors might examine Mr Bennet. Elizabeth and Jane escaped neatly, but Charlotte stumbled a little over the post of the bed. It would perhaps have been to her better interests to be watching her path, rather than trying to steal discreet glances at the young doctor. She suffered no major misfortune for it, as that young man was compelled to put out a hand for her support.

Blushing furiously and stammering her thanks, Charlotte reclaimed her elbow from the doctor and scurried out to the hallway. There, she encountered a knowing twinkle in her friend's eye. She scowled, a most unaccustomed expression for her. "Stop it, Lizzy!"

Elizabeth affected an innocent look. "Stop what? I am only pleased that my father appears to be in good hands- very *strong* hands."

Charlotte's face flushed a deeper shade of ruby, causing even Jane to dip her head to hide a smile. "I am going home," she mumbled uncomfortably.

Elizabeth did not let her friend escape without a warm embrace, but was not above a guilty chuckle at her expense once the door had closed.

"Well, Miss Bennet," the doctor straightened at last, "I believe your father shall make a good recovery in time."

Elizabeth and Jane, standing side by side and clutching each other's hands, shared a glance. "When do you think he will wake?" Elizabeth ventured first.

"Oh, quite soon, I should think. I do not think him comatose, but rather in a very deep sleep," he explained. "That may sound discouraging, but after such an injury it is well, as it will allow greater healing. My wife's testimony confirms for me that he is mending, to be sure. I have bled him, but I fear doing it much more. I understand Jones has been tending to him? Yes, well, I expect he has been at it with those leeches of his again."

The doctors spent well over an hour fussing over Mr Bennet, part of which time Jane and Elizabeth evacuated the room to respect their father's privacy. It was apparent to the girls that the married couple had missed one another during their separation, which would continue some while longer as Mrs Cooper determined to stay on with Mr Bennet. They parted with a reluctance all too obvious to the lovelorn girls observing them.

After the two doctors had taken their leave, Jane whispered confidentially to Elizabeth, "Don't you think it will be a pleasant change from what we have known for us to miss our husbands when they are away?"

Elizabeth smiled privately. "Do you mean rather like Uncle and Aunt Gardiner? Yes, that will indeed be a pleasure. I should much prefer to regret my husband's absence than to wish for it."

"Exactly." Jane suddenly glanced about herself. "Speaking of our aunt and uncle, where are they? I have not seen them since Mama left!"

Elizabeth hid a smirk. "I believe they are resting. Uncle must be very worn out from his journey, I should think."

Jane simply stared in mute confusion. At last a spark came to her face and she blushed. "Oh."

"So! *This* is your fiancée, Collins?"

Charlotte froze in bewilderment as an imperious woman with a hawk-like nose peered closely into her face. She'd had no inkling that her fiancé had returned, and even less that he could have brought with him the magnificent Lady Catherine de Bourgh of whom he was so enamoured. It seemed that during her brief sojourn, the pair had comfortably installed themselves at Lucas Lodge. The event was remarkable enough, but the presence of Caroline Bingley utterly befuddled her. What could have occasioned that alliance?

The grand lady drew back at last. "She seems a genteel sort of girl, Mr Collins. Not very pretty, but that is as it ought to be for the wife of a clergyman."

Charlotte's face burned. She knew very well that she was no great beauty, but no young lady enjoyed hearing her looks maligned in before others. It galled her somewhat that not a single person present- including her parents, brothers, and her betrothed- thought to contradict or even look chagrined at the lady's brash insult. Her eyes slid helplessly to Caroline Bingley, who looked quickly away, her half-lidded eyes admiring her immaculately buffed nails.

"Now, Miss Lucas, you will tell me what you know of this Elizabeth Bennet. She is your friend, I am to understand. Collins, I do have to doubt your young lady's taste on that point. I do hope she can redeem my opinion of her good sense."

Charlotte found herself seated and gazing back in mute wonder at the withered face. Lady Catherine, leaning forward upon a silver cane, seated herself opposite. Collins came to stand at the lady's shoulder, a condescending smirk firmly plastered over his face. Charlotte drew a deep breath, bracing herself for a most unpleasant interview.

~

"Welcome home, Mr Darcy." Drake dipped his head deferentially to his master while a footman took Darcy's soiled greatcoat.

"Good afternoon, Drake. I trust all is well?" Darcy arched a knowing brow at his butler.

"Indeed, sir. It would be of note to mention that Lady Catherine called during your absence."

"Yes, I heard as much. I trust she found the accommodations comfortable?" Darcy offered his trusted employee a sly upward turn of his lip.

"I am afraid her ladyship suffers somewhat from a depressed appetite, sir. You will be delighted to hear, of course, that her ladyship's carriage is expected to be completed by this evening."

Darcy pressed his lips into a thin almost-smile, but then stiffened somewhat, assuming his most regal air. "Is she in the drawing room, then?" He began to turn toward that room.

"No, sir. She departed early this morning with Miss Bingley."

Darcy spun. "What? Surely I must have heard you incorrectly!"

Drake shook his head. "Not at all, I am afraid, sir. Miss Bingley called late last evening, claiming to have been sent by you yourself. Lady Catherine desired the use of the coach, and Miss Bingley obliged."

Darcy stood in absolute shock for a moment, his mind reeling. His breath caught. Elizabeth was unprotected! He had only barely won her consent! If Lady Catherine bullied her into renouncing him… dire thoughts rolled through his imagination, predicting woeful consequences for his relative.

He needed to get back to Hertfordshire! He had only just set foot into his own home, and had anticipated a long delay before he would be able to wrap up the duties which had called him to London. Wickham had to be stopped and that young lady brought to safety, there was no doubt of it, but the longer he tarried, the more volatile the situation in Meryton was about to become.

He viciously clamped down his frustration. It would never do to betray his feelings before his staff. Drake, who had known him since he was in short pants, discreetly held his peace while the young master deliberated another moment.

His clattering pulse began to slow a little as reason took over. Elizabeth was too headstrong and loyal to give him up at Lady Catherine's pleasure. He could only hope her family would be equally so. He could not risk losing her! A daring move… yes, that was it. One that would risk her uncle's displeasure, but he hoped he could obtain the amiable Mr Gardiner's forgiveness.

Darcy met his butler's gaze at last, a small twinkle in his eye. "Drake, please arrange for an announcement in the Times. I am to be married."

Drake almost concealed his very unprofessional pleasure, but not quite. "Very good, sir."

~

"He said *what?*" Colonel Fitzwilliam, seated at last in solitude with Bingley in the Netherfield library, lurched to his feet in fury.

Bingley lounged patiently. He had expected such a reaction, which was why he had forced the colonel to wait for an explanation of Darcy's unaccounted behaviour. Georgiana must not be present for this discussion, and it had obviously distressed her earlier in the day to be parted from both her brother and her cousin at once. At last she had retired for a time, and he had pulled the colonel aside.

Fitzwilliam had begun to pace in agitation. Snatches of his voice carried to Bingley as the man moved briskly about the room, the growled tones biting out the colonel's opinions of Wickham's parentage and how decorative he might look with his head on a pike. With abrupt ferocity he stopped and spun toward Bingley. "What has been done to clear Georgiana's reputation?" he snapped.

"You did it yourself, by arriving at such a convenient moment. I expect that... uh... the conversation with Darcy was overheard." Bingley wrinkled his nose in faint displeasure. He adored his angel, though her family did trouble him somewhat. In this instance, however, Darcy had exploited the mother and younger sisters' weaknesses with precision.

Fitzwilliam was not satisfied. He resumed his pacing, shooting occasional sceptical glares at Bingley. Bingley sighed at last and spread his hands supplicatingly. "Darcy told me all about Wickham. I wish to protect Miss Darcy as well. He has gone to London to track the blackguard down; it seems one of the local minor heiresses may have fallen prey to his wiles. That is why he desired you to remain- not only to protect Miss Darcy, but to prove that he trusted you with her even while he was away."

Fitzwilliam stopped and stared vacantly out the window in silence, chewing his inner cheeks in frustration. He could have been of much use to Darcy in searching out Wickham, but that was not an option now. Georgiana's immediate safety, and by extension the safety of her reputation, had been assigned to him.

Another sigh from Bingley drew his attention back. Fitzwilliam sharpened his gaze on the other man. "Is there more?"

"Caroline tried to come back."

It took Fitzwilliam a moment to recover from that shock. Not her! "Come back, how do you mean?"

"It seems she rallied some person of influence from London to come with her, and they tried to gain entry to the house while we were away. Dawson managed to repel them, but I do not know who the other woman was, nor where they have gone to." Bingley creased his brow in some confusion. "He also said Collins was with her! I believe he must have made some mistake. Caroline would never travel with that man!"

Fitzwilliam fisted his hands on his hips, an expression of horror mingled with amusement dawning. "Collins, you say? Isn't that that parson cousin of the Bennets'? I know who the other lady was, and she will be more trouble than two of your sister!"

~

Darcy sent a hasty dispatch to his uncle. He considered sending an express to Bingley and Fitzwilliam, but it was likely, he thought in frustration, that the pair had already borne a visit from his aunt. Lady Catherine had some particular fascination for Georgiana, and would try to browbeat the girl into standing with her against his marriage to Elizabeth. Fitzwilliam would never hear of her even visiting Georgiana under the circumstances, but his aunt would certainly have made her presence known.

He sent a letter to his solicitor, called for a fresh horse to be saddled, and donned a clean set of traveling clothes. Wickham would have to wait. Elizabeth was more important!

He wondered in some amazement at the involvement of Caroline Bingley. He could well imagine what had led to that particular alliance, and it pleased him not in the slightest. He worried for what damage the pair could do to his plans for happiness at last. How would they work on Elizabeth without him there to shield her? Bold confrontation was his aunt's style, but certainly not the limit of her ingenuity. He knew well that Elizabeth would indignantly thwart any open attempt to overthrow her, but he hated that he had left her unguarded against his aunt's more pernicious wiles. He began composing an apology in his head for when he saw her next.

Mrs Nelson, upon learning that the Master had returned, had scrambled to oversee a fitting meal prepared for him. Great was her consternation when he informed her he had no intention of staying long enough to enjoy it. She shoved her hands into her motherly hips and fixed him with that stare she had once used on the wayward boy. "Master, sir, you will plumb wear yourself out! No food, no rest! But that's the way of you heedless young men these days!"

Darcy broke into a wide grin, shaking his head in acquiescence. Less than a handful of his father's old staff ventured the authority to speak so to the boy they had watched grow to manhood. His father had advised him on his deathbed to always give rein to his trusted old housekeepers and butlers. None of them ever dared abuse that privilege, so he always took it to heart when they spoke.

Mrs Nelson clucked over him while he took a few hurried bites from a tray, not even sitting down. "You will give yourself the stomach ache, you will!" she predicted dolefully.

His cheeks dimpled disarmingly as he swallowed a mouthful of bread and cheese. "You can cease worrying about me, Mrs Nelson. I shall soon have another to do it for me."

The woman's eyes lit up. "Heaven and saints bless us!" Shyly, a little uncertainly, she ventured, "Would it be fitting to know the young lady's name just yet?"

Darcy offered a bashful smile to his old housekeeper, and if she had been less than the perfect professional she was, he doubted not that she would have been patting his face in praise. "Miss Elizabeth Bennet. You will not have heard of her, she is not of the *ton*."

As it happened, Mrs Nelson *had* heard a few whispered references to that name, but she was content to allow the Master to think otherwise. Though her face glowed, she murmured the proper deferences expected when one's employer announced there was to be a new Mistress.

Feeling all the more awkward, Darcy promised Mrs Nelson that he would manage to finish the remainder of his meal without supervision. She bustled off with a new vigour enlivening her aging bones. He calculated that within a quarter of an hour, his entire staff would know of his betrothal and half the maids would be scouring the future Mistress' chambers, left untouched for so many years. In two more days, Mrs Reynolds would no doubt be subjecting Pemberley to the same treatment. Darcy felt his chest swell hugely as he choked down the last of his sustenance for the road.

Only minutes before he would have set out, Drake himself ushered in a red-faced messenger in a sopping wet uniform. "Pardon the interruption, sir, but I believed you would wish to speak to this young man yourself."

Darcy handed back the fresh greatcoat he had been about to don and turned to the young enlistee with curiosity. "What can I do for you?" he asked brusquely, but not unkindly.

"Message from Colonel Forster, sir." The lad handed him a pressed parchment, preserved from the rain in an oilskin.

Darcy took it and read briefly. The words caused him to pinch his lips thoughtfully. "What are you orders?" he asked the young man.

The red-coat came to attention. "I am to await a reply and then return directly, sir."

Darcy glanced to one of the footmen at the door. "Take some refreshment and get warmed before you go, and see that your horse is well baited. If you please, inform the colonel that I intend to call on him in the morning. I shall be just ahead of you on the road."

Darcy reclaimed his coat and passed by Drake on his way out his own door. "Send another message to the Earl of Matlock for me…."

~

Caroline Bingley had remained as aloof as she possibly could in the Lucas' drawing room, hoping to rebuff the patronizing monologue of the master of the house. Fortunately, he stood in such awe of his noble guests that his mouth had remained largely closed, while his eyes glazed wide with hopeful docility. Every civility was paid with nauseating distinction.

Lady Catherine seemed well pleased by the attentions, which, of course, surprised Caroline not at all. Occasionally she caught fleeting glimpses of boredom from Anne de Bourgh, but she could not be certain if the expression was born out of ill health or actual displeasure. Most of the time, Mrs Jenkinson acted to block the view of the heiress' face from the rest of the room.

Lady Catherine had grilled poor Charlotte Lucas mercilessly, extracting every detail the young woman could tell about the Bennet family, Mr Darcy, Mr Bingley, and Miss Darcy. Miss Lucas was no fool and had been clearly reluctant to divulge what she knew, but the authority of her father and the pleasure of her betrothed compelled her to hold nothing back. Once or twice, Caroline was treated to a baleful glance from the plain young woman, but she quickly averted her eyes each time.

Lady Catherine certainly had the right of it when she insisted that Darcy could not marry Eliza Bennet, but her methods and her casual dismissal of all before her galled Caroline. Prideful in her own right, she detested being made to feel less consequential in the eyes of her prior acquaintances. The only good to come of Lady Catherine's autocratic coup of Lucas Lodge was that its occupants were far too intimidated to ask why she, sister of a local resident, would be quartered at their home instead of her brother's. Soon, she comforted herself, all would be put to rights.

"Collins!" the lady summoned.

Caroline watched as the parson, that witless fop, demeaned himself before his patroness. "Yes, your ladyship! I am in constant attendance! I beg your ladyship to-"

"You will draft a letter for me. We shall retire to the study, Lucas, and I require privacy while we carry out our task. I shall also require pen and ink. Your means are clearly modest, but I trust you keep a good supply of such items?"

"Oh! Yes, your ladyship!" Sir William trailed behind his future son-in-law as the lady showed herself to the room she desired.

Charlotte Lucas had begun to edge closer to the exit when the lady turned back. "Miss Lucas! I shall desire you to remain. Lucas, do you require your daughter to return to her room and consider carefully in what manner the future mistress of Hunsford parsonage ought to comport herself."

Charlotte Lucas took a deep breath, lacing her hands and dropping her gaze demurely before the lady and her future husband. After the pair had passed on, her features hardened and she fired a glare at Caroline which could have scorched the frozen landscape outside.

Twenty-Nine

Elizabeth and Jane reclined comfortably by the fire in the drawing room, having been shooed out of their father's room by well-meaning Mrs Cooper. "Young ladies cannot spend all their energies in a sick-room! You both have other claims upon your attention," she had insisted with a twinkle in her eye.

Elizabeth gave every appearance of poring over a book, but her mind wandered. She slid the tip of her finger under the next page, but it hovered so for a long time. Her imagination tended to dwell instead on a tall gentleman with a sonorous voice and the most unforgettable dimple she had ever seen.

Her eyes drifted from the print to the gold band on her finger. It was a little too large for her, and the heavy jewel insisted upon spinning downward toward her palm. She had not objected, as it made the ring less noticeable for the time, and she did not care to hear more of her mother's triumphing over her new status. Now she flipped the ring over and admired the sparkling facets, her memory turning pleasantly back to the hopeful man who had offered it.

How secure and at home she had felt with him that morning! Rosy blushes came and went from her cheeks when she thought of his gentle touch and his tender kisses. His open vulnerability enchanted her. He so obviously aspired to her pleasure, and she was helpless to withhold it. How could such an arrogant man have altered so abruptly? Of course, she knew the truth now. He never was arrogant. Her lips curved in innocent pleasure, reflecting upon the noble, kind heart she had discovered beneath his carefully polished exterior. She was very much going to relish peering into his private character further, and most assuredly planned to encourage more of his recent lapses in protocol.

"And just what are you girls doing?" Mrs Gardiner, fresh from a short walk with her husband, smiled at her favourite nieces as she joined them. She took a seat opposite Jane.

"I am trying to finish this point lace, and Lizzy is daydreaming about Mr Darcy," Jane peeked slyly at her sister, waiting for the mortified glance which would admit her sister's guilt. She would be disappointed.

Elizabeth perked up to return the volley. "Yes, I was just reflecting upon how agreeable it is to find oneself engaged to a handsome man of pleasing manners. He is wealthy as well, which a young man ought to be if he can possibly help it, but most importantly I find his person and address quite amiable."

"And he appears to be possessed of good judgement," winked Mrs Gardiner. "Altogether a fine catch, I daresay!"

Elizabeth chuckled lightly, then glanced over her shoulder out the window when she heard some sound. "Ah, I see Mama and the others have returned." She gave up trying to read her book and set it aside.

"Oh, my dears!" Mrs Bennet gushed as she re-entered the house. "It is all the talk! I never saw anything like it. Everyone is quite set against that dreadful Mr Wickham! Why, they say he has run off with Miss King, and her uncle still away! Did I not tell you, my loves, to be careful of a man who seems too amiable? What a foolish girl! Why, I am sure she had no great beauty, he can only have been after her ten thousand pounds!"

Elizabeth wilted in horror. Poor Mary King! Darcy had been hopeful that she could be found before talk escalated, but he had apparently underestimated the vigour and imagination of a town full of frivolous housewives with nothing better to do. Still, she was proud of him for trying to help a girl who could claim no connection to himself. He was good... and he was hers!

"Oh, Mama!" Jane interjected. "Pray, do not continue so! We do not know what may have happened!"

"Oh, yes, yes we do!" Mrs Bennet cried with energy, darting a significant glance at the other married lady in the room. Mrs Gardiner hid her eyes in shame for the poor Miss King.

Kitty and Lydia had retired upstairs to carry on their own prattle uninterrupted. Mary plopped herself near Elizabeth, sharing a woeful glance with her next older sister. As Mrs Bennet continued her scandalized description of the town's chatter, Elizabeth leaned near to Mary. "Georgiana?" she whispered.

Mary answered with a firm, satisfied expression. "Not even mentioned.

Everyone is talking about how evil Mr Wickham is and how they all want to invite Colonel Fitzwilliam to dine. I daresay his evenings will be full while he remains in town."

Elizabeth closed her eyes and drew a long sigh. "At least there is that." Pity for Mary King stole the rest of her speech. Of course, the girl ought to have known better than to run off with that man! Now, however, Elizabeth understood how easily a sheltered, innocent young gentlewoman could be deceived. Naivety was absolutely required of a young lady, rendering her utterly vulnerable to such an artful deceiver as Wickham. Her heart broke for the girl's future. There would be little Darcy could do for her now, even if he could find her. Once a young lady's ruin had been pronounced, it was nearly set in stone.

Elizabeth's eyes were still down, but Mary stiffened beside her, drawing her attention back. She looked up and followed her sister's gaze to the window. Her brow furrowed.

"Why, it's Mr Bingley's carriage!" Jane exclaimed. "But he was already here this morning...." Her tones mixed with confusion and pleasure, Jane rose to greet her betrothed.

It was not, however, Mr Bingley who dismounted the coach. The ladies watched in stunned fascination as first Mr Collins, then Miss Bingley descended from the box. At last a stern-faced personage of great perceived importance stepped majestically down, making the humble yard of Longbourn shrink by her august presence.

"Who can that be?" wondered Mrs Bennet aloud. Propriety soon took hold, as it became apparent that their guests would naturally expect to be received. A flurry of activity ensued; books, bonnets, scraps of fabric and lace were snatched and stuffed out of sight in drawers, behind cupboards, and under cushions. In less than a minute, two decorous matrons and three proper maidens sat poised upon bulging cushions as they waited to receive their guests.

The elderly lady entered first and her sharp gaze flew about the room's occupants until it rested upon Elizabeth. "You!" She stalked closer, quite rudely ignoring everyone else. "Yes, it must be you. Just the sort to tempt him. Elizabeth Bennet, I presume?"

Elizabeth rose, composing a serene façade in the face of the lady's brazen lack of civility. "I am, Madam. May I have the honour of knowing your name, Mrs...?"

Collins chose that moment to dart from behind the woman. "Cousin Elizabeth! You address a member of the nobility! *This* is Lady Catherine de Bourgh, my most honoured and esteemed patroness, mistress of Rosings Park and aunt of Mr Darcy himself! You must pay your respects!"

Elizabeth spared the most withering of glances for her cousin and a swift, curiously arched brow for Caroline Bingley, who remained near the door.

Caroline met her eye with cool disregard, then looked away. She seemed to be both endorsing whatever the woman had come for, and at the same time distancing herself from the great lady's manners. In truth, Caroline would rather have been anywhere else, but the prospect of allowing Lady Catherine unrestrained freedom with her carriage, combined with the hope of witnessing the downfall of Eliza Bennet, had been enough to bind her to the lady's company.

"Forgive me, my lady," Elizabeth dipped her head politely as Lady Catherine seethed before her. She tipped her chin up again, meeting the peeress' icy gaze with artless maidenly freedom. "May I present my mother Mrs Bennet, my aunt Mrs Gardiner, and two of my sisters Jane and Mary… and my uncle Mr Gardiner," she added as that gentleman entered the room.

Lady Catherine waved her introductions away. "I will speak with you in private, Miss Bennet!" Her tone was brittle and demanding.

Elizabeth glanced out the window at a cold rain beginning to pelt Caroline Bingley's driver and horses, then traded brief eye contact with her uncle. She schooled her tones, forbidding herself to appear anything but genteel and refined for Darcy's sake. She had watched Jane's calm sweetness for years, after all. How hard could it be?

"Of course, my lady, we may retire to my father's library. It is just through here," she blithely walked past the black figure, extending her arm toward that room.

She paused as she moved by Caroline Bingley. "Miss Bingley, do please invite your driver to take advantage of our stables. I should hate for your team to take a chill, it would be most terribly inconvenient." Elizabeth thought she detected a flicker of triumph from Miss Bingley, but would not allow herself the pleasure of witnessing how it was received by Lady Catherine.

"We *shall not* be here long enough for that," Lady Catherine put in icily. She glowered back at both Elizabeth and Caroline.

Elizabeth pulled on a sweet smile and dipped her head. "As your ladyship pleases." She was quite certain that Miss Bingley choked a little, but spared her no attention to discern why as she led Lady Catherine out of the room. She opened the door to the library and allowed the lady to precede her.

"You can be at no loss, Miss Bennet, to understand the reason for my visit," Lady Catherine began, bracing herself grandly upon her silver cane.

"Truly, your ladyship, I find myself quite unable to account for the honour of your call. I do trust you have had comfortable travels? I fear it is not the most pleasant time of year for such a long journey."

Lady Catherine squinted in irritation. "I undertake what I must for my nephew's sake, as I always do! Do not distract me from the point, Miss Bennet. A most alarming report came to me that you were expected to be united to my nephew, my own nephew Mr Darcy! Is that true?"

Elizabeth tilted her head, lifting her eyebrows in gentle acquiescence. "Indeed, your ladyship, I had heard the same report."

"Do not play coy with me! I demand satisfaction! My nephew must marry within his own sphere of consequence. *Impossible* that he should ally himself with one such a yourself! Now, tell me the truth- has my nephew made you an offer of marriage?"

Elizabeth's cheek tugged slightly to the side. "Your ladyship has just declared it to be impossible," she retorted obtusely.

"Impossible! It ought to be!" Lady Catherine fairly growled at the impertinence of this country upstart. "He knows the claims of duty, honour, and interest, and would not dare risk the displeasure of his entire family!"

Elizabeth tilted her head slightly in agreement. "As Mr Darcy *is* such a man of duty and cares a great deal about his family's pleasure, I must wonder why your ladyship undertook such a journey. What can you hope to accomplish by coming to me?"

"Indecent girl! I will have this heinous report universally contradicted! You have obviously drawn him on with your arts and allurements. Oh, yes, I know all about your *unchaperoned* interludes! I even know how you attempted to draw on your cousin to an illicit liaison *after* you rejected him!"

"Your ladyship might refer to your parson's lack of breeding and integrity, as ought to befit a single man residing in a house full of young ladies." Elizabeth's lips twitched, amused by the shocking memory despite herself.

"Aye, and so *that* is how you conduct yourself! What spell have you cast over my nephew? You hoped to entrap him, but I will not allow it! I will see this nonsense categorically denied and rejected for the foolishness it is! I will not see his reputation debased further!"

"As your ladyship's arrival can only confirm the report, then an immediate denial of it would certainly *harm* rather than improve your nephew's reputation as a gentleman."

"A mere trifle to one of my nephew's consequence! Men of his station are known to have their…" she sneered down her nose, "*dalliances*," she finished distastefully. "He is born to the very best circles and cannot marry a woman who is not his equal!"

Elizabeth's heart lurched as Lady Catherine touched upon her very own fears. She stretched her frame, standing somewhat taller and taking a little step closer. She kept her voice firm and steady. "He is a gentleman, and I am a gentleman's daughter; therefore we *are* equal."

Lady Catherine's eyes widened at Elizabeth's subtle threatening manner. No one ever dared such presumption! "And those people I met just outside? Do not think I do not know who they are! They are in trade! Oh, yes, Miss Bennet, I know *all* about you! Your people are barely respectable;

their only honour in society comes from their connections to your father's meagre competence! Your little farm here is so small it can scarcely be called a gentleman's estate, and allied with merchants besides!"

Elizabeth's lip curved slightly at the corner. "It is a happy circumstance, is it not, your ladyship? Truly, the very prosperity of even Rosings Park must depend both upon farming and its connections to trade."

Elizabeth could not have uttered a more provoking phrase. Lady Catherine's face purpled and her mouth dropped in open horror. "*Shameful* girl! To make such insinuations! Do you *know* who I am?"

"Were you not Lady Catherine de Bourgh of Rosings Park?" Elizabeth replied innocently.

"Insolent girl!" she spat. "We *will* come back to the point! This match you aspire to can *never* take place! Mr Darcy is engaged to *my daughter!* Now, what can you have to say?" Not one to be outdone, Lady Catherine took a great stride closer to Elizabeth, her fisted hands cocked behind her wiry frame in challenge.

Elizabeth smiled sweetly. "If he is truly so, why would your ladyship fear that he would engage himself to me? We have already established that he *is* a man of honour."

Lady Catherine narrowed her eyes. "Their arrangement has existed since their infancy! Darcy has yet to formalize it, but the united voices of their families have long desired it. I will not see nearly three decades of planning thrown over for a greedy pretender!"

"It must be very tragic to all of your ladyship's sensibilities," Elizabeth shook her head in sympathy, then brightened deliberately. "However, it is quite impossible for one of my paltry status to alleviate my lady's hardship. Lowly as I am, I am determined to act in a manner to ensure my own happiness, as I must. If Mr Darcy had desired to marry Miss de Bourgh, surely he would already have done so long before I made his acquaintance."

"Unfeeling, selfish girl!" the lady roared, stalking another stride closer and waving her cane threateningly. "You would ruin him in the eyes of the world! You are a brazen trollop! How is it you imposed upon him? I insist that you must confess all immediately! I am almost the nearest relation he has, and entitled to know all of his concerns!"

Elizabeth dropped her voice to a hushed, flinty tone, as if she were speaking to a rebellious child. "Your ladyship is not, however, entitled to know mine, nor is such behaviour as this likely to procure my cooperation."

Lady Catherine screwed her mouth shut, flaring her nostrils. "*Harlot!* You *will* tell me once and for all, *are you engaged to him?*"

Elizabeth offered a glowing smile and dipped her ladyship a deep, respectful curtsey. "I am, your ladyship, and I am most pleased to make the acquaintance of my future family." As she gathered her skirts, she strategically flicked her fingers so the stunning emerald from Mr Darcy rotated to the fore, catching a ray of light.

Lady Catherine would have to have been blind not to notice it. As Elizabeth had expected, she was not so. The lady glared in abject loathing, curling her upper lip in abhorrence. "Very well! I shall know how to act!" She brushed past Elizabeth in a great huff, marching toward the door and pausing as if she expected someone to open it for her.

Abruptly she whirled back to face Elizabeth once more. Her tones sweetened with a sickening twist to her mouth. "I understand you have a particular fondness for my niece, Miss Georgiana Darcy."

This Elizabeth refused to deny. "I have," she responded levelly. "She is one of the most delightful people I have ever met." She arched a brow meaningfully, wordlessly emphasizing the contrast between the engaging niece and the rather less-than-genial aunt.

"Just so." Lady Catherine's tones dropped menacingly as she shot another icy glare at her, then opened the door herself.

"Collins! We are leaving this disgraceful house! I take no leave, I offer no compliments to the hostess. They deserve no such regard!" The black skirts swished as the lady marched to the front door and hovered expectantly for Collins to perform his toadly obeisance.

Elizabeth emerged from the library just as Caroline Bingley rounded the corner into the entryway. Their eyes met briefly, Elizabeth holding the other's gaze with cheerful archness. It was Caroline who backed down first, but not before Elizabeth caught the faintest glimmer of grudging respect in her eyes. Her gaze slid away, but she threw back her shoulders and flowed gracefully out the door after Lady Catherine.

Elizabeth released a pent-up breath and looked to her uncle, who had followed after Caroline. He furnished her with a commiserating half-smile. "I suppose you want to know why she called," she offered unwillingly.

"No," he answered, eyes twinkling. "Everyone heard it all. She has rather strident tones."

"She does that!" Elizabeth chuckled. What else was there to do but laugh? She was too spirited to cry, when she did truly have the assurances of the man she cared for. His aunt was a harassment, that was all. A most vexing one, to be sure! She dropped her gaze to her hands, but glanced back up to her uncle when he placed a hand upon her shoulder.

"You would have enjoyed watching Mr Collins and Miss Bingley's faces," he whispered conspiratorially. "Your father would be very proud of you, Lizzy. I do wonder, however, why Mr Collins turned such a brilliant shade of red when Lady Catherine mentioned the time he stayed in this house." He accompanied that comment with a sly wink.

A genuine smile at last broke through and she drew a long breath of fresh air. "I imagine he would prefer not to have that known! Thank you for your support, Uncle. We must send word of this to Colonel Fitzwilliam at

Netherfield."

He nodded. "I will take care of it, Lizzy. Go to your mother, I fear she is near hysterics."

~

Richard Fitzwilliam swung off his horse- or, rather, Bingley's horse- at Colonel Forster's residence, tossing the reins to a young officer. He dusted his hat as he removed it, then passed cold fingers through his hair. A maid showed him to the colonel's study, where he found his old comrade in the process of raising a glass to his lips.

"Fitzwilliam!" he rose to greet his guest. "I was not expecting you!"

"As I see. Drinking on duty, Forster?" Fitzwilliam's mouth curved in a wry grin.

"Commanding officer's prerogative. I have granted myself temporary leave," Forster winked, then poured another glass. "I expect you've come about Wickham."

"Either to pound him senseless if you have caught him, or to sniff out his trail if you have not," Richard confirmed.

"I am sorry to say I cannot help with the former, but I may have some little information on the latter. We thought at first he had gone to London, but the coach we were tracking did not yield his miserable carcass."

"Miss King's coach?"

"I see Darcy has filled you in. Yes, an interesting case, that. The young lady arrived in London, but then disappeared again almost immediately. We questioned the coaching inn, but Wickham was not seen, and we have no idea where the young lady has gone to. It seems she slipped away unnoticed, which I can hardly credit. Fancy that, a young lady of means traveling alone and not attracting enough attention for one to gather where she has gone off to!"

Richard sat back against the cushions, his bushy eyebrows working as he scrutinized his glass. "I wish to heaven Darcy had allowed me to accompany him. I know Wickham's usual haunts better than he."

"He may not have even gone to London," Forster maintained. "We cannot find any trace of the scoundrel."

"Hah! Wickham not attaching himself by the ribbons to an unprotected young heiress? Of course he did. He must know you would have the dogs after him and is using a little extra caution, but I would wager my best horse he'll be safely married to the poor thing and have her tucked securely somewhere out of the way."

"She is not entirely unprotected. Her uncle was in London on some business. We sent word to him, and from what I hear he is not a man to cross."

Richard screwed his mouth into a grimace, ignoring the colonel's comment. "And I, fool that I am, saw to it he had plenty of funds to fleece that poor girl!" He fisted his knuckles and plopped his chin on his hand, furious with himself.

Forster regarded him somewhat quizzically, but when Richard offered no more, he shrugged and his expression cleared. "Well, Fitzwilliam, I would keep a sharp eye out if I were you. I would not be surprised if he did not go far. Bloody foolish of him to stick around here, but if he has it in for you and Darcy…." He shook his head and rose, signaling the end of their interview.

Richard's shoulders drooped, defeated for the moment. He had counted on some reassurance from his old comrade, but none was forthcoming. He would just have to protect Georgiana the old fashioned way- by keeping her in sight at all times.

~

Darcy shifted uncomfortably in the saddle. He had chosen to ride again for the speed it offered, but even he, consummate horseman that he was, did not relish quite so many hours in one day on horseback, and in a pouring rain besides. He grimaced against his seizing muscles. Now he remembered why he had relegated the sorrel gelding to his London house. He was a fine-looking animal with flashy paces, but blasted uncomfortable to ride for more than half an hour. Darcy flexed his thighs against the awkward twist of his fancy park saddle- made, of course, to fit this wretched horse- cursing even that unfortunate item in his gnawing displeasure.

If he was correct in his guess, he had less than an hour to go on this uncomfortable journey. He could survive sopping, freezing cold and stiff saddles and rough horses if he could just find himself again in Elizabeth's loving arms at the end of it all. How freely she had welcomed him that very morning in the sunrise! It was worth a lifetime of devotion just to be blessed with her sweet smile, the warm fragrance of her as he pressed her close to him at last. No other woman could fit so perfectly into his heart! It was as though she had always belonged there, and he had only needed to slough his cursed pride to be worthy of her.

A smile began to grow, despite the water droplets running down his face.

No, he was still not worthy of her, but she had promised to have him regardless. His precious Elizabeth would be his forevermore! He pushed aside thoughts of his aunt's schemes for the moment. He would not allow himself to dwell on his darker thoughts and fears while he yet struggled with his momentary hardships. If he could only get back to her warm embrace and assure himself of her continued attachment, all would be well.

He closed his eyes to blot out the rain, assuming his clumsy mount would manage to keep on all fours for the space of a few breaths, at least. He pictured his sweet Lizzy at Pemberley, filling his home with her laughter. Rooms long left shrouded and untouched would flood once more with the warmth and light of their Mistress- and the Master's heart would fare even better!

Which would be her favourite walks and groves? With a twitching mouth, he determined that he would personally be there for each of them as she made up her mind- most particularly those which afforded some modicum of privacy! He burned with impatience to see his home through the eyes of the woman he so longed to please. He felt sure that the lively and authentic Elizabeth would appreciate Pemberley's natural landscape and sprawling vistas. It was highly likely, he mused, that she might even introduce him to facets of his home that even he had yet to discover.

After their long walks, of course, he would have to see to it that his pearl was not over tired. She must rest! Only *his* chambers would do, to be sure, where he could personally ascertain that she was comfortable and well coddled. Oh, yes, he had every intention of coddling her, and with his recent glimpses of her breathless response to his affections, he felt sure she would allow him to pamper her as he saw fit.

Her restrictive attire, made for public eyes, must in the end give way to her comfort. He would start with her shoes, inspecting and massaging her dainty feet to be sure that her exertions had not caused any discomfort. His fingers laced unconsciously through his horse's mane as he next envisioned freeing her rebellious curls. Her shining hair, that perfect combination of twining ringlets and soft silkiness, would coil over his fingers as he kissed the elegant and forbidden column of her neck.

His arm he would keep wound securely about her as he caressed her so that she might not suffer any danger from her weakening knees, as he had proudly begun to sense the day before. Oh, no, better yet, he would help her to recline comfortably on…. *Good heavens.* He gulped, his pulse skittering.

Indulging his fondest desires, he allowed his passionate fantasy to continue. Her confining stockings would obviously have to go, as well as the stiff garters holding them in place. What would her bared skin feel like beneath his fingertips? Would she permit him to wander freely, acquainting himself intimately with all her secrets, every hidden delight?

He smiled against the raindrops hovering on his lips. Oh, yes, his passionate Lizzy would put aside her modesty for him, and for him alone. He did not deserve her caress or her open reception of his advances, but his generous Elizabeth would lovingly bestow them nonetheless.

His hands curled as he imagined sliding his fingers up beyond her garters, drawing aside the final barriers between them. What unparalleled beauty would be his to behold? He forgot to breathe for a moment as his mind kissed and blessed her sweet form in his dreams. Her sighs of pleasure almost reached his ears as he imagined lowering himself over her at last, forming a protective cocoon around her body with his arms and sharing her breath in the most intimate embrace afforded a man and a woman.

A cold splash over his knees jarred him at last from his pleasant reverie. His blasted horse lurched to the side as he tried to avoid a pocket of muddy water sprawling across the road. Grunting, Darcy vowed to himself he would sell the intractable beast as soon as may be. Squeezing his calves mercilessly, he urged the spoiled town-dwelling brute across the puddle. The horse made an awkward lunge, fearful of falling into the great black chasm of nothingness stretched before him. *Chicken-heart!* thought his owner sourly, all the more cross because his dreamy musings had been so dashedly interrupted.

Darcy sent the horse off once again, looking about himself. He was only five minutes nearer Elizabeth than he had been before, and it had long been quite dark. He shrugged his shoulders, chilled, and a fresh rivulet of water cascaded down his collar under his oilskin. He heaved a weary sigh. Bedraggled mop that he would appear, he intended to see his love first and ascertain that she was well before he made himself presentable at Netherfield.

~

Charlotte Lucas crouched sulkily on her bed, her arms wrapped about her knees and her scowling visage propped upon her thighs. Maria had visited her briefly in her confinement, but so far her father felt it best that she heed Lady Catherine's advice to solitary reflection.

The opinion, of course, was seconded by her affianced. Charlotte ground her teeth. She had endeavoured to regard Collins as tolerable because of the independence he offered, but even that highly desirable prize had started to pale. She began, like Elizabeth, to question if the respectability of a married woman was worth the price of her entire future.

There was a soft knock at the door, so light that Charlotte almost missed it in her self-pity. "Yes?" she answered.

The door pushed open to admit a furtive shape, then closed quickly. Charlotte blinked in some amazement. "Miss de Bourgh?"

Anne de Bourgh held a finger to her lips, glancing back at the door. "My mother is in the next room," she whispered.

Charlotte stared curiously, slowly adjusting her slovenly seat upon the bed and inviting Miss de Bourgh to sit opposite her. Anne accepted, her face bright with her exertion. "Can I help you?" Charlotte ventured cautiously at last.

Anne nodded, smiling faintly and putting her hand to her breast as she caught her breath. "You can tell me about your friend."

Thirty

Elizabeth had gently demanded that Mrs Cooper take a rest. She had spent the last few days eating and sleeping in this little room for the most part. With her husband's assurances and her own belief that her patient was improving, she was finally persuaded to take a real bed for the night. Elizabeth took her post with a candle and a book for her company- but not her only company. She allowed herself a sly smile. The truth was that she had begun to cherish each moment she shared with Darcy, and even Jane's unobtrusive presence put a damper on her delicious reminiscing.

She worried ever so slightly about Lady Catherine's threats. She knew that Darcy was dependent upon none of his relations, and that there was no real power his aunt held over him, but she did not like that his family would be displeased by their marriage. She pitied poor Anne de Bourgh if she were truly disappointed, but took some comfort in the fact that his uncle and certainly his other cousin appeared to look upon their union favourably. She shook her head. Surely Lady Catherine was justifiably vexed in the dashing of her every expectation. It could not excuse the lady's atrocious conduct to herself, but even that Elizabeth could find in her heart to forgive. She had Darcy's assurances, and that was all she really cared for.

She luxuriated in a little sigh of pleasure as she sank into her chair and admired her ring once more. In character and talents, there could not be a man better suited to her. His understanding was excellent, and though he was little inclined to lighthearted small talk, he spoke freely and eloquently enough when they were alone. She smiled privately, wondering how long it would be before she was able to spend a *great deal* of time alone with him.

The door opened and she looked up, expecting Jane, or perhaps her aunt. It was Darcy, sopping wet and frigid. "William!" she gasped, and sprang to her feet immediately.

She moved into his arms without hesitation, impulsively wishing to share her warmth with him. His face softened, the weary lines giving way to a meek smile as he stepped back from her. "I am all wet, Elizabeth."

She frowned impatiently. "And freezing! Take that coat off! Let me." He allowed her to spin him bodily about, chuckling a little in obvious delight as she ordered him around and stripped his wet garments off his shoulders. She wrapped him in a spare blanket almost instantly, scrubbing her hands roughly over his arms to warm him as though he were one of her younger sisters. Slowly she stopped, surprised at her bold assertiveness. She raised bashful eyes to his face.

"Are you finished?" he asked, a hint of laughter in his tones. That dimple of his flashed most distractingly.

"Uhm. I'm sorry," she mumbled uncomfortably, dropping her hands.

"Do not be sorry! I have not had such a welcome from the cold since I was a child!" He bent to touch a chilly kiss to her forehead, admiring her softened appearance. She wore a simple gown, unembellished by anything but her rich tresses. Only a portion of her hair had been swept up from her face as the rest spilled gloriously over her shoulders. She had never looked more beautiful. "I already missed you, Elizabeth," he murmured gently.

She flung herself into his embrace then, contentedly burrowing under his blanketed arms. "I did not look for your return for days yet! What are you doing riding in the rain, and traveling so late at night? You will catch your death!" Her voice attempted to sound like a fierce admonishment, but her face pressed warmly to his chest gave lie to her scolding lecture.

He laughed, pillowing his cold cheeks in her soft, lavender-scented hair. "I came to save you from my aunt. I heard she was intending a visit."

"Ah, yes. We had the pleasure this afternoon."

He groaned. "I am sorry. Was she very horrible?"

"Oh, no, quite the contrary! I found it to be a very enjoyable visit."

"To be sure," he returned dryly.

"Oh, but I mean it! I found her company very... amusing. I cannot say the same for Lady Catherine. I do not think she enjoyed herself, nor went away satisfied."

Darcy laughed easily, relieved beyond expression that Elizabeth had not been intimidated by his aunt. She had not needed him to save her after all! "I can well imagine! What did she say to you?"

"First things first." She pushed him into her old chair, then, avoiding his astonished gaze, bent to tug his wet boots off as she had done so many times for her father. What large feet the man had! Sensing the outrageous lack of decorum she displayed, her cheeks fanned a brilliant crimson, but she was determined to prevent his taking a serious chill. Fixing her eyes to his masculine calves- such *long* legs he had!- she silently set about her self-appointed duty. It was her nature to care for those she loved, and quite of a sudden, Darcy topped that list.

Darcy watched her in mute amazement and wonder. All of his wildest fantasies were playing out before his eyes! Elizabeth fussed over him with tender concern, her small gentle hands bestowing comfort such as he had never known. Her loving ministrations, combined with the genuine respect she had recently extended, swirled intoxicatingly in his heart. He felt twice the man he had been!

Edified by the care and devotion of such a noble woman, he at long last felt worthy of all the accolades showered upon him since his birth. He would forever after hold his head high among men; not because of any merit of his own, but because *she* declared her estimation of his virtues in her every look and gesture. The dam holding back the tide of his feelings burst, and he was overswept by such a drowning flood of love for her that he could scarcely draw breath.

Elizabeth was wholly unaware of the battle waged and won in her lover's heart. She tugged valiantly against the wet, skin-tight leather, demonstrating not only her fierce resolve toward his benefit but also some passing familiarity with masculine footwear. He bit back a trembling chortle as he tried to imagine one of Miss Bingley's ilk stooping to such a task. At last she rose, placing his boots by the small hearth and fetching another blanket for his knees. She began to move away from him to locate another chair for herself when his long arms pulled her close again.

"If you wish to enhance my comfort, Elizabeth, do me the pleasure of staying here with me," he pleaded in a low voice. She narrowed her eyes sceptically at him. He leveled her a rakish little smile. "You need not fear I would take advantage of you in your father's sick room! I only wish to partake of your warmth a little longer."

She cautiously allowed him to draw her to his lap, draping her knees over the armrest of the chair and her arm over his shoulders. She moved willingly, but stiffly, to accommodate his needful plea. He tucked the blanket over his shoulders snugly about them both and pressed his forehead again into her luscious hair.

"William, you know my aunt must be aware of your presence," she whispered nervously, her back still ramrod straight. Most of the family were abed, but someone must have let him in. The door was wide open, and though the hall was conspicuously vacant, it might not remain so. "She, or even my uncle could come in at any moment!"

"And then I will be forced to do my duty as a gentleman and marry you on the morrow?" he conjectured, his face still hidden from her. "I can think of many worse fates." He lifted his face to look at her, brushing those unruly curls aside as he had imagined doing so many times before. "At present, however, there is no cause for concern. I promised your uncle I would behave as befits a gentleman. Being a very sympathetic man, and in light off my pitiful, road-weary appearance, he granted me leave to see you alone for a short while."

"I imagine this is not quite the 'gentlemanly behaviour' he had in mind," she retorted sharply, arching her neck away from him to look him in the eye.

"A man's life and well-being must take precedence over proper decorum at certain times, do you not agree? I was just informed by a source very dear to me that I am perilously close to freezing to death. Would you withhold life-saving measures in such an instance?"

"I am not so mean as that!"

"I had not thought you so." He tightened his arms around her and she slowly melted into his cradling embrace. He rested his head gratefully against hers, closing his eyes and breathing deeply of her scent. *Here* at last, he was to learn what it was to love and be loved. Here in her arms everything else he was slipped away. Pemberley, his status and responsibilities, and all of those lonely years without anyone to share his burden; all were forgotten. He was simply a man in love with the most breathtaking woman he had ever known. His precious Elizabeth melded to him, her soft form pressing into his until all that could be discerned from without was one shape drawing breath under their blanket.

Not for the first time in the past days, his thoughts lingered on that old passage referring to man and wife becoming one flesh. Nothing could sound more heavenly! He allowed himself a lopsided grin as he considered, only for a moment, that he would someday soon be granted an even deeper level of intimacy with this remarkable woman, his love and his very heart. He murmured soft words of endearment as she turned her face to nuzzle his cheek. Exhausted and sore as he was, her warm presence was having a profound effect on his person. He shifted a little, hoping to spare her maidenly sensibilities any embarrassing discomfort. He would not have her move from him just now for all the world!

It had been his intention, when it first became obvious that a rapid marriage without the benefit of a courtship would be necessary, that he would not press her for intimacy until she had had time to accustom herself to the idea- no matter how long that took. What a man desired of his wife was primal, urgent, and overpowering. No gently bred maiden should be subject to such raw yearnings unless her heart were fully engaged. Her love was like the finest of masterpieces. Rushing matters would shatter the treasure, like leeching all the spice and power out of the new wine or scorching the silver before it was refined. She was worth waiting for, even down to the last delicious, stubborn, glorious curl of her beautiful head.

Somehow, he had promised himself, he must learn restraint, and that most dastardly of all virtues- *patience*. It would be painful, but absolutely vital! He knew well that once he had tasted of her sweetness, he would be as helplessly bound by his desire for her as a broken warrior who cried out for an opiate, always longing for more and never satisfied.

He could not allow himself to… *oh*. He groaned headily as she moved from nuzzling to kissing that tender place next to his ear. Oh, what was the use? He was already a man hopelessly lost at sea, and only she could cast him a rope. Mercifully for him, she seemed to have every intention of doing so. In fact, she appeared more than willing to offer the succour he craved.

At last he broke his peace, aware that Mr Gardiner, though a magnanimous man, still took his guardianship rather seriously. He could not afford to linger much longer, though tearing himself from her would be like ripping the bandage from raw flesh. He slid his hand up her shoulder, regretfully signaling her to cease her delectable attentions.

"I am loath to ask, Elizabeth, but I fear I must. What did my aunt say to you?" Once he had spoken, he returned his face to its proper home- buried in her luxurious curls- while he waited for her response.

"Oh, dear," she sighed reluctantly. Haltingly, not wishing to sound slanderous against his nevertheless deserving relation, she described her encounter with the lady. She could feel the tightening of his jaw as his prickling cheeks tangled in her hair.

A strangled hiss escaped him as she related Lady Catherine's irate pronouncements. He had no doubt she was making light of his aunt's colourful insults- he was, after all, rather well acquainted with the lady himself. At last her narrative drew to an awkward close. "Is that all she said?" he probed.

"No…" her brow creased in some concern. "Just as she was leaving the study, she asked me whether I were fond of Georgiana. I answered that I was, of course. She seemed satisfied in that, and left."

He pricked up his expression and stared at her carefully. "Fond of Georgiana… oh blast and damn." The oath escaped softly, but then a sudden pallour overcame him when he recognized his outrageously unbecoming language. "Forgive me, Elizabeth!"

She shook her head, absolving him immediately. Her eyes were full only of concern. "William, what is it?"

He drew a shuddering sigh, touching his forehead lightly to hers. Would she always be so gentle with him? What had he done to deserve her patient tenderness? He was silent a moment, and she waited without pressing him further. Another long breath heralded a swelling in his chest as his love for this exhilarating woman crashed over his senses.

She was still waiting, her uneasiness growing in her eyes. He pulled back to meet them. Her right brow dipped slightly- a mannerism he had never seen employed by anyone, but from his expressive Elizabeth, he understood its meaning instantly. She was begging him to relieve her worry, and would not allow him to escape without some explanation.

"My aunt has some special resentment regarding Georgiana," he admitted at last. "I do not understand why, exactly. She has oft declared that she herself would have been a better guardian, rather than a pair of very young bachelors."

He shrugged self-deprecatingly. "I know well my own failings, but I thank heaven my father's will in that regard was iron-clad. My aunt Helen- Richard's mother- was designated to take on Georgiana's sponsorship in the *ton*, rather than Aunt Catherine. *That* codicil set her into a righteous fury." He heaved a bitter sigh, pressing his lips rigidly in frustration.

Elizabeth shook her head slightly in bafflement. "I do not understand, then. If your father's will is so sufficient, what can she do? You feel she is threatening Georgiana somehow?"

"Oh, she can still do plenty. We have received an education only this week in how rapidly talk of any lady's disgrace can ruin her future. Aunt Catherine still has her contacts- spiteful old cats, all of them, who will look on our engagement less than favourably." He drew back fractionally with a pained expression, speaking softly. "Aunt Catherine is far from the only matron who has coveted the Darcy name for her daughter."

Elizabeth paled, her stomach dropping. So, Darcy, and by extension Georgiana, would truly suffer for his connection to her. She had once furiously dismissed the conceited words, but now the full weight of his position settled uncomfortably over her small shoulders. She was not equal to it. She bowed her head, her heart swimming and eyes stinging.

"Elizabeth? I did not mean to give you pain! Lizzy, my Lizzy, please do not cry!" His words of panicked concern broke over her, and she looked up to him once more, blinking rapidly. In a rush of breath, he crushed her to him, kissing her temple as it was nearest his mouth. "I see it in your eyes, Elizabeth. Do not you dare consider abandoning me now! Do not fancy you would be doing it for my own good, for nothing could destroy me more than to lose you!"

"But if Georgiana is to be harmed…" she began to protest, tears choking her voice.

"Shhh," he interrupted her with a gentle press of his lips to hers. "Georgiana needs you almost as much as I do. Almost," he repeated with emphasis, lovingly caressing her cheeks. "I would have you put it out of your mind. I beg you, my Lizzy, think no more on it. I will manage my aunt."

"I cannot simply cease to worry, William! You are in distress, and your concerns are mine, are they not? It is because of me that Georgiana may be at risk. You cannot be master of every problem on your own, William."

A glorious smile suddenly overspread his face, and Elizabeth could not be certain, but she thought she may have identified a second dimple on his other cheek before his next words distracted her. "And this, dearest Elizabeth, is why there can be no other for me!" With rapturous joy, he claimed her mouth. She yielded easily, tipping back against his shoulder as her arms tightened around his neck. He followed her, leaning tenderly over her as he braced her gently against the arm of the chair.

Her awkward posture, quite unfortunately, required a little more support than merely the uncomfortable arm of the chair. Smiling as he kissed her, he slid his hand up her back, delighting in the feminine arches and curves he detected beneath her gown. It was perhaps best that his actual support was required, or his fingers would have taken on a life of their own, placed daringly low on her frame as they were.

Elizabeth's hand dropped from the back of his neck to the front, one finger hooking in the top of his cravat and the others tickling over his throat. His pulse clattered wildly. Oh, no, he would not have to wait long for her! She arched her neck and allowed him to explore her mouth more deeply. Their lips and tongues met and swirled in a provocative dance, coming together and separating in a timeless synchrony known only to lovers.

A whisper of conscience tickled him; that quiet voice of his inner being reminding him of his position and hers, and the respect he owed to her and to her family. Even as the thought caused him to pull back slightly, he caught the glimmer of moonlight shivering upon her moistened lips those delicious, honey-dewed lips which were even now whispering his name, softly demanding more of him. He could not deny her!

A low conflicted cry wrung from his own lips as his mind battled for all that was right. She was a lady, an innocent! It was wrong to tempt her so. It was wrong to awaken her ardour when he could not satisfy it. It was wrong to remain in her arms, pressing her tantalizingly female curves to his masculine form, when he had promised her uncle to behave as a gentleman! It was wrong- so very, very wrong- to compromise her honour while pretending her wounded father did not lay a scant yard away, unable to object. Oh, but yet, it was *so right* to hold her like this.

A wordless endearment- a sigh, really- and he dropped his face helplessly to her neck. She tipped her chin obligingly, gasping as his lips brushed her milky throat for the first time. She trusted him, and the agony of that burden seared through his conscience. He must release her! She was a maiden, spotless and pure, and... and her fingers were running through his hair. Heaven help him.

He unleashed the full tenderness of his mouth on her neck, sliding up to her ear lobes and down to the point of lace at her collarbone. The woman in his arms fairly ignited. Banished for now was the gentleman's daughter with her demure glances and modest blushes. A stormy tempest brewed in his embrace, promising the hopeful lover a lifetime of memorable nights. Darcy covered her insatiable mouth again with his own, shivering when an answering whimper of pleasure reached his ears.

He moaned softly, his lips searching over her lovely face for any hidden places they might have neglected. Her breath warmed his cheek as her lips parted slightly and another muffled sound came... except this sound had not come from either of them. He drew back, his brow furrowed as he gazed at her curiously. "Did you...?"

She shook her head slightly, eyes widening as she heard it again. It sounded suspiciously like raspy chuckles, and by now, neither of them were in the slightest mood for such mirth. Her heart pounding in combined hope and mortification, she deliberately turned to the bed... slowly, so Darcy could not miss the direction of her gaze.

Mr Bennet's eyes were open and a disreputable grin played at his mouth. "Mr Darcy, good of you to drop by." His voice was rusted and graveled from disuse, but his words were clear enough. "I wonder, sir, if you would be so good as to look out that window there, and tell me if my prize sow has just flown away."

Darcy bolted to his feet, then stammered an embarrassed apology to Elizabeth for nearly upending her on the floor. Mr Bennet chuckled once more, then his eyes drifted shut, not to open again until morning.

"What are you doing back so soon?"

Darcy looked up from his third cup of coffee as his cousin, pressed and polished to a spit shine, finally graced Netherfield's breakfast room with his presence. Richard pulled up short as he peered his cousin in the face.

"You look a fright. Did you leave your valet in London?"

"You ought to know. It looks as though you made use of his services."

Richard shrugged with a grin. "Guilty as charged."

Darcy poured himself some more coffee. "I thought you military men were early risers."

"We are also practical. Where there is no lad blowing away at his blasted trumpet, we take our rest when we can. That does not answer my question. Were you not on Wickham's tail?"

"Probably not, but it matters little at the moment. Aunt Catherine seems to have slipped that snare you set at Darcy House."

"Oh, yes, I heard something about that." Richard pulled back a chair and helped himself to the pot of coffee, glancing up at Darcy in annoyance when only a trickle came out.

Darcy could not help a little smirk. "Has she turned up here, then?"

"Yesterday morning while we were all at Longbourn, but we have not heard a peep since then. Mr Gardiner came to speak with me yesterday evening, but I was out. He told Bingley that it had something to do with our aunt, but he did not wish to leave any written message. I had intended to ride over this morning to see what it was. Did you know," Richard laughed, "she seems to have traveled with Caroline Bingley?" Richard shook his head, a little hiss escaping as he tamped down another wave of wondering laughter. "That is one carriage I would be happy to escort- from *horseback*."

"Yes, I heard. They paid a visit to Elizabeth yesterday afternoon."

"What! She would not!" Richard brandished his practically empty coffee cup expressively. "They have never been introduced! Furious she is, I expect, but stooping to visit a farm of no account and have words with a girl of no name with no proper introduction? She would never demean herself!"

Darcy slammed his fist on the table. "*That* is my future wife you are insulting!" he snarled.

Richard shrank, holding up a hand in a gesture of defeat. "I did not mean it quite that way. Did you sleep at all last night?"

Darcy sighed, dropping his face to his hand as his elbow propped on the table. "Not exactly." He volunteered nothing else.

Richard, still cringing, waited a moment, then another. Had Darcy fallen asleep at the table? "So…" he probed at last, "this visit our aunt paid to your Miss Bennet… she did not frighten the young lady off, did she?"

A sly smile cracked below the hand, but the eyes remained hidden for just another moment. "No."

Richard drew a long breath in relief. Darcy was a changed man when Elizabeth Bennet was about, and it did his cousin's heart good to see it. Darcy was more a brother to him than his own brother, the viscount, ever had been. The surly bear who had replaced the amiable fellow at his father's death had finally begun to crawl back into its cage, at the command of a pert young woman. An exceedingly pert one, perhaps.

"Are you going to tell me what happened between Miss Bennet and our aunt, or are you leaving me in suspense?"

Darcy dropped his hand, a broad grin livening his tired features. "Elizabeth has found the perfect way to deal with our aunt, and she did it in a matter of seconds. Cheerful obstinacy. I understand Drake was the first to hit upon that, but it took him years, and she was not even married to Sir Lewis at the time. I never had the courage, myself. I was always afraid to appear ungentlemanly, but I doubt anyone witnessing the exchange yesterday at Longbourn could have wondered which was the real lady of the two."

"Would that I had seen it!" Richard chuckled longingly. "So, vanquished as she apparently was, has she flown back to Kent?"

"Hardly. She has not given up quite yet."

"Perhaps not, but where would she go? You said yourself that this is the finest house in the neighbourhood, and with Caroline in her company she was not welcomed here. You know our aunt would never room in the lodgings in Meryton. She has probably returned to London and imposed herself on my mother."

"Did you not hear of the other member of their party?"

Fitzwilliam's brow furrowed, then cleared. "Oh, yes, that parson fellow. Of what significance is that?"

"He happens to be engaged to one of Elizabeth's friends, a Miss Charlotte Lucas. Her father is a knight, though an impoverished one."

Richard's face whitened in a mixture of lively amusement and horror. "She wouldn't!"

"She is very determined. She has some special obsession with Anne becoming a Darcy." He shrugged. "Even sickly as she is, Anne is heiress to a title and an estate in her own right. She could have done much better than me, but she follows her mother's lead. It must be difficult to do otherwise.

"As for Miss Bingley, she knows I would never marry Anne, but I expect she hoped our aunt could do enough to turn me away from Elizabeth. Neither of them is quite rational about the matter. No, I imagine they have not gone to London, but have installed themselves at Lucas Lodge, which means we should be expecting a call... right about now."

Even as he spoke, Richard's head came up at the grinding sound of carriage wheels on the drive. He looked back to Darcy, eyes narrowed. "You should have gone into the military." Darcy's eyes crinkled over his cup as he drained the last dregs of coffee.

Thirty-One

"Aunt Catherine! How wonderful to see you this morning! I do hope you have not given yourself too much trouble in coming to us here in Hertfordshire." Richard bowed grandly before his aunt. "And Cousin Anne, delightful to see you again! I had no notion you had traveled as well." Richard gently took his cousin's hand and led her to a comfortable chaise within convenient distance of the hearth.

Bingley had joined Fitzwilliam in solidarity as the guests entered his parlour, but with one look at Caroline, he commanded his sister to withdraw. She followed him with an astounding meekness, possibly boding well for future relations between brother and sister. The pair retreated from the ensuing family spectacle, Bingley casting a brief commiserating glance toward Fitzwilliam.

"Fitzwilliam!" Lady Catherine spat. "Where is Georgiana?"

"Oh, likely still dressing, Aunt. Darcy spoils her, you know. She never rises above ten in the morning."

Lady Catherine pointed her cane at him. "She is a Darcy! I know better, Fitzwilliam. Bring her to me at once!"

"Still in her night dress! Why, of course, Aunt, I shall try, but her maid is a rather stout young thing. She will not take kindly to…."

"Have her sent down immediately, with all of her luggage!" Lady Catherine bellowed. "I am taking my niece and leaving this barbaric country!"

"Oh, I wouldn't do that, Aunt," Richard shook his head, his manner

318

hardening somewhat. "Darcy wishes for her to remain where she is, and do you know… I saw the guardianship papers myself." His voice was soft, but a practiced ear could discern the threatening edge to his tone.

"How dare you, Richard Fitzwilliam!" Lady Catherine raised her cane again as if to strike. "I can bury you! One letter to your commanding officer…."

"And what, Catherine?" boomed a deep voice.

Lady Catherine whirled, her face blanching in denial. Her nephew and brother had entered the room, both looking something the worse for their hasty travels. Darcy had hurriedly donned a fresh coat and combed his hair, but his blouse ruffles remained limp, his cravat pitiful, and his breeches dotted still with flecks of mud.

Matlock crossed his arms, a manner he affected only with wayward children and his recalcitrant sister. "You were saying something to my son, Catherine?" he demanded again.

She found her voice. "You went back to London! What are you doing here, James? Of all the deceitful, manipulative, unworthy conduct!"

"Yes, that is how I would characterize it," he leveled an icy stare at his sister. "It so happens that I enjoy traveling in freezing weather in the dead of the night. Let me be understood, Catherine. My son is *not* your concern!"

Lady Catherine's ire switched to Darcy. "My *nephew* is! Fitzwilliam George Richard Darcy, you will go down on your knee *this instant* and do your duty to your cousin! You have shirked your responsibilities for far too long, and your lack of honour has had serious consequences on Anne's health! You have distressed her long enough, and this time, *you will* capitulate!"

"No, Aunt Catherine, I will not." Darcy's voice was steady and even, as though he were discussing crop rotation with his steward. "I regret to cause my cousin any pain, but I have never desired the connection you say exists. Even should I wish it, my hand is no longer my own to bestow. Another has a claim on my honour."

"That *vile temptress*! You cannot ally yourself with that *chit*, Darcy! She would taint us all! That the shades of Pemberley should be polluted by such a - a scheming, low-born…" Her words were cut off when Darcy took three long strides and towered over her, his face inches from hers and his eyes blazing.

"You would do well to check your words, *Madam*!" The lady reeled and her mouth dropped in scandalized fury at Darcy's blatant omission of her title. "Miss Bennet is to be Mistress of Pemberley and of Darcy House, and guests shall be welcomed or repulsed at *her* pleasure. Her nature is more generous than mine, but I promise you, *Madam*, I will not tolerate any insults to my wife!"

Lady Catherine trembled, her gnarled fingers reaching blindly for a piece of furniture by which she might support herself. "Did you hear that,

Brother? Your nephew has lost his mind and become violent besides! I shall see your reputation *ruined* in the *ton*, Darcy!"

The earl laughed menacingly. "How might you expect to do that, Catherine? You will exhaust your daughter's resources and ruin yourself in the process!"

She shot out her hand, extending one long withered finger. "I am not without my means, James!" She rounded on Darcy, pointing that same finger at him. "I know all about Georgiana!"

Darcy staggered back and paled. "What?"

Fitzwilliam was at his side in a moment. "Impossible!" he cried. "What can you possibly...." Darcy stopped him with a subtle shake of his head.

Their fearful exchange was not lost on any of the room's occupants. Anne's eyes widened and Matlock glared quizzically at the pair.

Lady Catherine smelled blood in the water. A triumphant smirk blossomed on her face. "I know," she stalked closer, "that she was alone at Netherfield with that son of a tradesman! You abandoned your duty to her, Darcy, to call on that trollop, and left Georgiana to be compromised! I know he was alone in a carriage with her! She is ruined, Darcy, or will be when my solicitor receives the notice I posted to him yesterday."

Darcy and Fitzwilliam both stared in dumbfounded bewilderment. Then, as one, their frames began to quiver. Darcy, however, was beginning to laugh, while Fitzwilliam trembled with rage. "How dare you do such a thing!" the colonel snarled. Had his aunt not been a woman- the word *lady* was questionably and rather too generously applied- he would have had his hands about her throat.

Darcy halted him with a hand on his shoulder. "An interesting attempt, Aunt Catherine, but Bingley is an engaged man. Additionally, he is very strict with chaperones. There is never a room without a footman, and Georgiana's maid accompanies her at all times."

"That matters not," she waved a hand blithely. "A hint of scandal is all that is required. Do you seriously think anyone would take the word of a maid over mine? She will never make her presentation at court, Darcy! No one would risk an association with a tainted woman. That friend of yours will be forced to marry her if she is to save face at all, and what will happen to your pretty little Miss Bennet then? I fancy she will not defend the Darcy family quite so well once her sister has been abandoned for their sake, will she?

"You see..." she raised her cane, stepping forward, "I know all about her, too! You only barely won her consent, Darcy, and you certainly have not her father's yet. Her greed may have caused her to accept you after a fashion, but she does not like you. The insolent little chit may have some sense, after all- you never had any prepossessing traits Darcy! Too much like your father, but that matters not to me. I have only to threaten

Georgiana and offend that Bennet girl, and you have no recourse but to do as I wish!"

"Enough!" Matlock pushed between his son and nephew, both of whom by now were taking turns between anguished pallour and righteous fury. "Catherine, you go too far!"

"Do I, James? Why have you never checked him? He has been allowed to disappoint Anne for far too long! Unconscionable that a Darcy should shirk his duty!"

Matlock clenched his fists, then his glare shifted from his sister to, surprisingly, his niece. "Anne?" He lifted his bushy brows in an unspoken question.

Darcy was struggling and gasping for breath with the torrent of feeling washing over him. His selfish obsession with Elizabeth Bennet may have involved those dearest to him in a scandal of magnificent proportions. Regret for Bingley, fear for Georgiana, and abject terror at the threat of losing Elizabeth now mingled with remorse for his treatment of his cousin. Anne had done nothing to deserve his vehement rejection, yet he had stood in this very room and declared a stranger more important to him than the cousin he had known since infancy. What disgust she must feel!

His eyes leaden with sorrow, he watched as Anne rose from the chaise with quiet strength. With each step toward them, she seemed to grow in confidence. By the time she had drawn close, Darcy's eyebrows were arched in wonder. Anne de Bourgh, his sickly cousin, poised herself next to her mother with every inch the dignity and grace of her rank. His shock at her sudden shift in manner was only exceeded by the soft words which she now spoke.

"Mother, I have no wish to marry my brother."

The two young men were absolutely speechless with horror, but their reaction paled beside the wrathful being of their aunt. "*Anne!*" She made a grasp for her daughter's person, which Anne swiftly dodged with surprising adeptness. "*You are not well!*" her mother snarled, her lips curled and her bloodshot eyes flashing. Another vicious swipe of her hand landed on Anne's shoulder, pushing the young woman back so that, without a quick save by Fitzwilliam, she might truly have fallen.

She recovered swiftly and spun with new energy to face her mother. "No, Mother, I am quite well, and I have been so for years." She turned her light eyes to Darcy's, and for the first time, he noticed how very much like Georgiana she did look. Her burst of vigour lent new spirit to her features, and he stared back into the face of… whom? His sister?

Anne darted quick glance to her uncle, desiring his reassurance, and then drew a deep fortifying breath. "Yes, William. Uncle told me years ago. He thought I had a right to know. I was fifteen, and Mother was starting to make demands on you already."

"I have heard enough of this!" Lady Catherine sliced her finger toward Matlock's chest, as though she would have skewered him had it been a mite longer. "Anne, we are leaving!"

"*You* are going nowhere, Catherine!" the earl roared, his face more violent than either his son or nephew had ever seen. "It is time this was known! I will not see you continue to try to force Darcy into such a shameful, sinful union! Had he shown any inclination for it, I would have told him as well, years ago! Now he deserves to know what you have been trying to foist upon him!"

"*You know nothing!*" she shrieked. "*I will see you ruined as well, James Fitzwilliam!*"

"You would not dare risk it," he scoffed. Turning back to Darcy, his tones mellowed in consideration for his nephew, who looked nearly faint. "My father, the earl, was good friends with your grandfather, Darcy. They determined when we were young that their eldest children- your father and Catherine- should marry. However, your father had his sights set on Anne, the youngest of all of us. He was almost as stubborn as you, are, I'm afraid, and eventually his suit was accepted. Catherine," he shot his sister a moody glare, "was obsessed with your father, and I believe Pemberley as well, and never forgave him for passing her over."

He stopped his narrative to calmly deflect a savage blow from that lady's cane. With a hand tightened around her upper arm, the earl shoved the great and noble lady toward the door. She writhed, her feet dragging behind as she slashed and howled, spewing all manner of vitriol at her relatives. With a firm yank, the earl opened the door of the sitting room and commanded two footmen at the door, "See her to her carriage. Miss de Bourgh shall be staying behind."

Lady Catherine flailed wildly, thrashing her arms. "*Unhand me! How dare you lay a hand on a peeress!*"

"They dare at *my* command, Catherine!" the earl hissed menacingly. "You would do well to remember that! Go back to Rosings, and take that vermin of a parson with you!" He slammed the door of the study, only slightly muting the outraged cries of his sister as the strong young footmen dragged her bodily to her carriage.

Matlock returned to the three young people, his manner nonchalant. Anne was smothering a little smile, but Darcy and Richard were by no means master of themselves. Both were white as ghosts. It was Darcy's place to speak, but it was another moment before he could find any words. At last he managed a shaky beginning.

"Uncle," his voice was nearly a whisper, "you level a very serious accusation at my father's door."

The earl heaved the weary sigh of the aged. "It was not quite like that, my boy." He glanced at Anne, then continued. "I doubt he would have even realized… your mother was very ill after your birth, Darcy. It took her years to conceive, and when she did, she had a dreadful time of it. We all thought we had lost her. Your father took it very hard, blamed himself. He spent most evenings closeted in his study with a large bottle. I think the Darcy cellars have never suffered as much plundering as they did in those days. I thank heaven, my boy, that you are not one given to drink! A wealthy man in his cups can be very vulnerable under such an influence." He shook his head regretfully. "George was not at all master of himself when he drank."

Darcy and Fitzwilliam exchanged a quick, bemused glance, which the earl promised himself he would get to the bottom of later. Shrugging his shoulders, however, he forged on. "I was at Pemberley, as were most of the family when your mother was so ill. I remember going to check on your father in his study and Catherine had just emerged. No one else was about. She passed it off as of no consequence, but Anne's birth later that year was rather coincidentally timed." He spared his niece a sympathetic smile. "Catherine looked a deal like your mother still in those days. Old Sir Lewis never had any children with his first wife, and there were never any others after Anne."

Darcy was trembling, and he put a shaking hand to his forehead. "I need to sit down, Uncle." Fitzwilliam, beginning to recover more quickly, clapped him comfortingly on the shoulder and steered him to the sofa.

Darcy was blinking rapidly, his eyes blurring with the scandalized fear and outrage of what his aunt had wrought. His own father imposed upon, taken advantage of, his cousin the unwitting result of an illicit union, and his own prospects only narrowly escaping such a blight. It was beyond the pale! Nothing could have previously induced him to believe his own family might have concealed such a black secret.

"I know what you're thinking, my boy," the earl sighed again, finding his own seat. "Why did I not tell you sooner?"

"I- I suspect that might have come to mind next, had my thoughts been able to organize so well."

"Well, I never could bear to let your father know. He never would have forgiven himself. I told Anne, and of course my lady Matlock. We three decided that Anne should feign poor health until we could decide what else could be done about Catherine's expectations. You needed a healthy bride, of course; your father was rather insistent on that point after losing your mother. Catherine never would have accepted another suitor for Anne unless you were off the market, my boy. Bloody long time you took going about it."

Darcy looked again at Anne, the mystery still holding him in awe. "But I have seen you! You are so pale, Anne, and you do not eat…."

Anne's mouth pulled to the side in a shy smile. "Mother would not be satisfied until I had seen her doctor. He bleeds me frequently and keeps me on the strictest of regimens. I do not get much exercise. Those concoctions he has been using recently make me even more fatigued. Mrs Jenkinson helps me keep up the act as well."

Darcy dropped his face to his hands, his mind registering the selfish role he had played in the living nightmare his cousin had been subjected to. "I am sorry, Anne," he murmured. "Had I only acted sooner…."

"It is not your fault William," she answered softly. "Uncle has been offering me sanctuary and help claiming my inheritance for years, but I never had the courage to accept. I am going to now." She held her hand out to him, and with a new appreciation for his cousin- or whatever she was- he took it.

"Do not worry about that letter mother sent the solicitor. Miss Bingley quietly arranged through her coachman for me to send another directly on the heels of it. Rosings is mine, after all, and mother's solicitor truly answers to me. I made it clear that if he released any harmful information as she had directed, he would never have an income again."

Darcy's face grew into a slow smile. "You are remarkable, Anne. I am sorry I had never seen it. All of these years- how can I make it up to you?"

She shook her head modestly, dropping her gaze with a soft blush. "I should like very much to be introduced to your Miss Elizabeth. She sounds wonderful, William. I hope I will be welcomed at Pemberley to come to know her, and… and my sister."

Darcy placed his second hand firmly over the first. "Of course, you will always be welcome. Georgiana has often lamented that she never got to know you. I never felt safe having her long in your mother's company. I suppose now I know why. Anne, will you have the goodness to never reveal to her what we have spoken of here? I do not think she would understand about Father. She does not need to be so confused just now."

Her eyes widened emphatically. "You must know, I have an interest in keeping these things quiet as well!"

"Well, that's settled!" The earl slapped his knee in satisfaction. "Let the matter rest forevermore. Anne, Lady Matlock accompanied me. I am certain she would wish to visit with you. She also is desirous of meeting Darcy's betrothed, but that cold journey took some of the starch out of her. I expect she is just emerging from her bath. Shall we impose on your friend, Darcy, to see if a room can be found for Anne?"

Darcy grinned. "By all means."

~

Blissfully unaware of the stewing hurricane raging in his drawing room, Bingley had retired to the library with Caroline. Not a word had they spoken. Bingley's newfound confidence seemed to grow him in her eyes, and instead of a younger brother, Caroline was put very much in mind of her father.

Stiffly, but not unkindly, he directed his sister to take a chair while he seated himself behind his desk. Never before had he deliberately placed himself in such a position of authority with her, but he had seen Darcy employ the intimidating manoeuver countless times. If it worked for Fitzwilliam Darcy, it was not too good for Charles Bingley. The second act of the play was to subject his relative to stony silence, which he engaged in with a flourish. His fingers drummed expectantly on the desk.

Caroline slumped in her chair, not even bothering to put on her airs. Her eyes rested on his fingers. Bingley watched as she drew a shuddering breath. "I was wrong," she confessed at last.

The fingers stopped abruptly. "Excuse me?"

Caroline squeezed her eyes shut, humiliated at what she had said and then shamed that she was required to repeat it. "I was wrong." Her tones were hushed.

"How so?" he demanded. He would not be content unless she rendered a full confession and of her own volition.

She set her jaw, her old willfulness flaming, fading, and at last guttering out. "I ought never to have interfered with Darcy," she mumbled reluctantly.

Bingley arched a brow.

"*Mr* Darcy," she corrected. She glanced up at him and could see he was not yet satisfied. She heaved a deep breath. Her debasement was nearly complete, and there was no further point in trying to save face. Though she would never know the full measure of Lady Catherine's depravity, she had witnessed firsthand the wholly unbecoming state to which the woman had sunk in her mindless pursuit of the Darcy name. There was *nothing*, not even the triumph of seeing him reject Eliza Bennet, which could induce her to follow in that lady's footsteps.

"I will never impose myself upon any of the Darcy family again."

Bingley stared.

Caroline blinked, her voice cracking with intimidation. "I will beg Mr Darcy and Miss Darcy's forgiveness for my vanity."

Bingley's lips twitched.

Caroline sighed, exasperated. "And I will apologize to Eliza Bennet! Are you happy, Charles?"

"To whom?"

She set her teeth. "Miss Elizabeth Bennet."

"And what of my staff?"

She hung her head. "They are under your authority," she muttered.

"Excellent. I believe just now Mrs Nicholls could use some help in organizing the tenant baskets for next week's festivities."

Caroline's eyes flashed to his uncertainly. "Do you mean…?"

"You cannot shirk your duty, Caroline." His tone was set in iron, but a slight lift of the ruddy brow over his bright eyes gave her hope.

"Yes, Charles." She rose directly and betook herself to the kitchens.

Bingley grinned hugely, lacing his fingers behind his head and leaning back in his chair. "Dawson!" he called loudly. The butler appeared promptly. "Please give the staff these directions when interacting with Miss Bingley…."

Elizabeth finally rolled out of bed at half past ten. She was not being slovenly, she rationalized. After all, she had sat up all night in her father's room, relieved only at six by Mrs Cooper. After the… well, the rather embarrassing interruption of her "conversation" with Darcy, she had remained in wakeful vigil the rest of the night.

Elizabeth's cheeks warmed pleasantly. It was a most agreeable memory-if, that is, one left out the part about being caught in a passionate embrace with her betrothed by her snickering father. She could only hope that his head injury would prevent him from remembering that event when he regained full consciousness. Darcy might never recover from his mortification!

Jane entered the room as Elizabeth was finishing her hair, all smiles and sunshine despite the wintery day. Elizabeth slanted a knowing glance over her shoulder. "Expecting Mr Bingley to call this morning?"

"Naturally," Jane sighed. "Lizzy, I am so relieved that Father is improving! Mrs Cooper said he roused long enough to drink on his own this morning. Did he really speak to you last night? Uncle said he awoke for a moment while Mr Darcy was calling. What did he say?"

Elizabeth coloured and made no answer. Jane's brow dropped suspiciously and she stepped closer, peering into the mirror over Elizabeth's shoulder. "Lizzy?"

"Hmm?" Elizabeth inquired around the hairpins she had just stuffed into her mouth.

"Was Mr Darcy in the room with you?"

"Hummm."

"Alone?"

"Hmmmmhmmm."

Jane tilted her head. "What were the two of you talking about?"

"Nfffnnggg." Elizabeth focused her gaze steadily on her reflection, her hands busily engaged with a stubborn coil.

"Apparently." Jane narrowed her eyes playfully. "And what was it that Father said?"

Elizabeth removed the last pin from her mouth and blew an errant curl off her forehead. She turned to her sister, her lips twitching. "I believe he made some reference to pigs flying."

Jane sputtered, her hand flying to her mouth to avoid a noisy shriek of laughter. Elizabeth waved her hands, trying to hush her sister's amusement. "You will have our aunt in here, and I cannot avoid explaining to her if *you* are laughing so!"

Jane's eyes clenched, squeezing out a stray tear as her body shook with laughter. She gasped for breath, at length wiping her face. Elizabeth rolled her eyes, trying not to show the smile that threatened to overturn her very proper embarrassment.

"What did Mr Darcy do?" Jane finally managed.

"Dumped me on the floor."

Jane choked and doubled over, now thoroughly breathless. She clamped both her hands tightly over her own mouth, but little yelping sounds squeaked through her fingers. Helpless to remain on her feet, she sought the bed and curled up on it, burying her face into the covers to smother her squeals. "Oh Lizzy!" she gasped finally. "I cannot condone this! It is too shocking!"

"Yes, you look very grave and disapproving," Elizabeth smirked.

"Oh, but I am! Lizzy, you must marry that man right away before you do something truly scandalous!"

"I will take that under advisement."

"What did our uncle do about it?"

"What, do you think I *told* him?" Elizabeth was incredulous. "Poor Mr Darcy almost melted through the floorboards as it was!"

"So, he left right away? I cannot imagine he would have remained longer!"

"Sort of."

"Lizzy...."

"You do not think me the kind of woman who would not offer some comfort to a man in distress, do you?"

Jane shook her head. "You had better be planning on a short engagement."

Thirty-Two

It was a merry party which set out for Longbourn later that morning. Two persons, however, were less than delighted with the event. One was Caroline Bingley, whose reception back into her home depended upon her carrying out Charles' wishes to the letter. At the moment, that entailed helping Mrs Nicholls in the kitchen. Mrs Nicholls' sentiments in the matter would be too long and unflattering an account to include in this work.

The other person whose spirits flagged was Mr Darcy himself. With the very heaviest reluctance, he had set out for Colonel Forster's residence to obtain more information about George Wickham. Duty must overcome his desires. Besides, thought he smugly, it had not been so very many hours since he had last seen Elizabeth.

Shortly after his ardour had received such a dousing the prior evening, he had unwillingly taken his leave. The rest of the family had been abed, except for Mr Gardiner, who had been waiting with an open door, sharp ears, and a book in the library. He had already apprised the older man of his findings in London and his concerns regarding both his aunt and his childhood friend. Neither would be tolerated to interfere with the Darcy or Bennet families ever again. His aunt they had dispatched quite satisfactorily, but George Wickham remained at large. A long circuitous ride through the night had verified that none of the local lodging houses could boast his presence.

Darcy regretted that he would not be the one to first introduce his stunning bride to his aunt or his cousin, but Elizabeth had already thoroughly proven her graceful aplomb. He smiled warmly. Yes, she would make a fine Mistress for his home, one he would never cease to be proud of. He had every confidence in her.

Besides, the drawing room would be exceedingly full with the entire Netherfield party, and he, Darcy, would likely be relegated to the corners of the room while his female relatives monopolized Elizabeth and his male relatives descended upon Mr Gardiner. That would leave him with… oh, no, not that. Touching his whip to his mount, Darcy picked up the pace. He would rather face Wickham with bare knuckles than Mrs Bennet with a tea cup.

"Darcy, hold up!"

He jerked the reins, so great was his surprise at hearing his name that he nearly unsettled his mount. With a silent apology to the poor beast- and gratitude that it was not that clumsy hack from London- he patted the horse's neck and turned.

"Richard, I thought you were going to Longbourn!"

"I didn't want to get stuck in a corner with Mrs Bennet." Richard cantered up to his side and slowed his mount.

Darcy grinned, then broke into a chuckle. Richard's face beamed. "What has happened to you, Cousin? You are almost cheerful these days!"

"I have quite lost my mind, Richard. That is what has happened."

"And your heart, I daresay." Richard shook his head. "Too bad you and Bingley snatched up the only sensible Bennet sisters."

"There may be some hope for the middle one. Georgiana finds her quite amiable."

"Not for me, Darcy. Your Elizabeth has spunk, Binley's 'angel' has sweetness. All I am able to look for is a dowry." He sounded almost sullen.

Darcy sobered. "There are plenty of women out there, Richard…."

"Ah, yes, the *ton*. Tell me again how many worthy heiresses you found."

"What about Anne? She surprised me, Richard. There may be more to her than we have ever known."

"Perhaps." His head was down as he stared sulkily at the ground.

Darcy was quiet, studying his suddenly gloomy cousin. "There is someone, isn't there? Someone out of your reach?"

Fitzwilliam's eyes leaped back up, conviction and mortification flashing over his face.

"Who is it?"

Fitzwilliam turned his face straight forward. "No one you know," was the curt reply.

Darcy rode on in silence. "Richard," he ventured at length, "I have an estate not fifty miles from Pemberley that Father purchased as an investment. It brings in a modest but respectable income, about three thousand a year."

"I never knew about that," Richard replied disinterestedly.

"Nor did most. I do not like to advertise it. I would, however, like to part with it. My hands are full."

Richard turned sceptical eyes to him, then looked away almost as quickly. "So include it in Georgiana's dowry."

"Georgiana is well enough set up. Another is very dear to me as well. Would you sell your commission if I made it worth your while?"

Fitzwilliam looked again to his cousin. He stared thoughtfully without answering until Darcy began to grow uncomfortable for offering. "You know, Cousin," he said finally, "I believe your Miss Bennet has swapped you out for a changeling. She has my eternal gratitude."

Darcy smiled. "Mine as well."

Elizabeth was greatly surprised with the two new arrivals in her drawing room that morning. The awe of hosting the countess now, as well as the earl, was only overshadowed by Anne de Bourgh's gracious well wishes for her happiness. She could have sworn the young woman had been described to her as sickly and pallid, having no strength or interest in much of life with the exception of one Derbyshire gentleman. The Anne she met, however, seemed very much like Georgiana in her shy hopefulness. Elizabeth wondered what sort of fracture had occurred between the young lady and her mother, because apparently their desires did not align as well as had been represented.

Lady Matlock was a tall, large-boned woman with a stately, gracious bearing. She at once cornered Elizabeth and her mother, along with Mrs Gardiner. There was nothing terribly haughty in her manner, but she was clearly well used to being the most prominent woman in the room. Elizabeth found she could not begrudge the lady that, as her conversation and manners proved most agreeable. Mrs Bennet had found the woman sufficiently intimidating that she ventured few words to begin with.

"So, Miss Bennet, I understand my nephew intends a short engagement. Have you determined a date yet?" Lady Matlock's silver hair somehow sparkled in the light of the window, a feat Elizabeth had never before seen accomplished by tresses of that shade.

"Not as yet, your ladyship. Mr Darcy intends to properly address my father before any formal arrangements are made. As he is improving rapidly, we have high hopes that might take place soon."

"That is most suitable," the lady nodded affirmatively. "You must come to London to shop for your trousseau. I shall be pleased to host a soirée for you and to introduce you about Town as my future niece."

Elizabeth drew a grateful smile. "I thank you, your ladyship. My aunt and my mother have been helping to make a beginning here, as we felt it in better taste at present."

Lady Matlock blinked in some surprise. "The future Mrs Darcy, obtaining her wedding clothes from Meryton? Well, now that is… original. I commend your practicality, Miss Bennet. You will, of course, need at least a few items to begin with from the top tier seamstresses in London." She sniffed, then her tones softened reasonably, so that even Mrs Gardiner could not feel slighted, though she was quite firm. "You will occupy a rather notable position in London Society from now on, my dear, and you must make an impression in the beginning to smooth your way. However, I applaud your taste and resourcefulness at the present moment; it is far more than most young ladies would consider."

Elizabeth dipped her head at the rather backhanded compliment. "I thank you, your ladyship."

"Mrs Gardiner," the lady turned toward Elizabeth's aunt, "my husband tells me you have some connection to Lambton. It is not far from the Matlock estate, you know. Are you familiar with the Boyce family?" The two chatted amiably, finding a few mutual acquaintances. Elizabeth was surprised at the breadth of Lady Matlock's knowledge of the local merchants. Evidently she and her sister-in-law were not of a kind.

After a pleasant interlude, Lady Matlock tactfully turned her attention at last to Mrs Bennet. Elizabeth could not decide if she had been coached, or if Darcy's aunt had intuitively discerned that Mrs Bennet would perform better if given some time for her nerves to settle. Either way, Elizabeth was grateful. She queried Mrs Bennet about the best local millinery, the militia, and even found gentle questions soliciting Mrs Bennet's advice on her economical housekeeping.

Elizabeth and Mrs Gardiner exchanged wide-eyed glances. Mrs Bennet had clearly never felt quite so honoured. While still not fully grasping the differences between her own station and Lady Matlock's, Mrs Bennet managed to conduct herself with minimal embarrassment for her daughter. She slowly monopolized the conversation with boisterous phrases and expressive hand gestures, though Elizabeth noted a twinkle in Lady Matlock's eye. It was not without her leave that Mrs Bennet was suffered to prattle on.

The peeress was subjected to a treatise on Jane's beauty, Mr Darcy's magnificence, Mr Bingley's amiability, Mary's cleverness, and Lydia and Kitty's lively cheer. A flick of Lady Matlock's gaze indicated that she, too, had observed the youngest girls' high spirits. Anne de Bourgh and Georgiana were doing their best to keep up with the younger girls' enthusiasm. Elizabeth hid a smile. She was going to enjoy her new relatives.

"My lady," Mrs Bennet ventured with growing boldness, "May I say, we are pleased to see you in such health. Why, I feared such a journey to come to us here in Hertfordshire might be too much!"

Lady Matlock looked curiously at Elizabeth. She had quickly discovered the young lady to be uncommonly clever, and caught a small wink. An audacious gesture, to be sure, but something of a kinship grew out of it. Her future niece would have something to explain later, she sensed.

"No, Mrs Bennet," she returned to that lady. "My health is quite sound." She did not elaborate further, but she was quick to discern a faint dampening of Mrs Bennet's spirits. Before she could wonder at it, Mrs Bennet spoke up again. "I understand, my lady, that there is another estate in your family? Might I... inquire as to... where it might be?"

"Oh, that place!" Lady Matlock trilled a hearty laugh. "A tumbled-down castle in Ireland! Oh, my dear Papa left me that ruin, and I have not the least idea what to do with it! It is more a liability than an asset, I assure you, Mrs Bennet." The lady smiled charmingly back at her inquisitor as more good cheer slid from Mrs Bennet's hopeful face.

Elizabeth felt her cheeks tugging mercilessly and decided she ought to save her mother. "My lady, may I say I have been greatly honoured to become acquainted with Colonel Fitzwilliam. He is a kind and noble man. Your ladyship must be very proud."

"Ah, Richard, yes. He is a good son." Lady Matlock's shrewd gaze lingered on Mrs Bennet another moment. Elizabeth's hint had confirmed for her the other matron's rather mercenary motives, but rather than offence, she could only find amusement. After all, when a woman had five daughters to marry off, it behooved her to take an active interest in the sport.

~

As the visiting nobility began to make their farewells, Bingley, who had no intention of leaving his fair one so soon, suggested a walk for the younger crowd. All accepted, even Anne de Bourgh, to Elizabeth's great surprise. The rain had ceased with the prior night's darkness, and the parties involved feared a dreary afternoon indoors more than a little mud. The earl and Lady Matlock determined that they would remain at Netherfield for a few days, at least, so they could become better acquainted with their future niece, and to that house they repaired.

The walking crowd quickly split into two factions. Kitty and Lydia parted company from the others rather quickly, as they had shopping in mind and the slower pace of the lovers bored them. Elizabeth, Mary, Georgiana, and Anne de Bourgh contented themselves with strolling behind Bingley and Jane. As Mary had once again attached herself to Georgiana, Elizabeth found herself beside Anne.

They had exchanged only a few words at the house, but now Anne gushed forth with her pleasure at Elizabeth's engagement to Darcy. "I am so looking forward to getting to know you! You would not know, perhaps you could not, that William has always been rather quiet and not one to assert his opinions where it came to personal matters. I never saw anyone so altered as he was today!"

Elizabeth laughed. "Do you mean he is often unsociable and taciturn?"

"Oh, no. He was always very amiable. I know he avoided me because of my mother; he did not want to give rise to any hopes, although his efforts did not seem to clarify anything for my mother." There was a hint of sadness in her tone, but she brightened again instantly. "I was always a little afraid of him. He seemed so imposing and aloof. I watched him, though, and he always seemed sociable enough with Richard, and of course perfectly solicitous with Georgiana, but I could not believe he was really so amicable. I saw a new side of him today, and I think that is thanks to you, Miss Bennet. I hope now I will be able to come to know all of them better- and of course, you too."

Elizabeth smiled, a genuine heartfelt expression. "I should like that, Miss de Bourgh."

By the time their party reached Meryton, Anne and Elizabeth were on first-name terms and they had firmly and unequivocally decided to become as sisters. Anne's quiet delight knew no bounds. For too many years she had lived in her mother's long shadow. That was at an end now.

"So you still have no idea where he is?" Fitzwilliam was flabbergasted. "How can he just disappear?"

Forster held up his hands. "I told you, Fitzwilliam, my resources are tapped. I have a brigade full of new recruits and only a handful of officers qualified to train them. I cannot spare all of my best men to hunt out one deserter. It sets a bad example, to be sure, but I was hoping you could help me a little more. You know the kind of haunts he frequents."

Richard scowled, crossing his arms. "We take these things a little more seriously in the Regulars," he sneered. Immediately he regretted it. "I'm sorry, Forster."

The colonel waved a tired hand. "Darcy, you asked me to get in touch with Miss King's uncle. I did send him an express, but the messenger returned saying he was not to be found. My hope is that he is already aware of the young lady's absence and had taken matters into his own hands before my man arrived, but I have no way of knowing. The butler apparently was less than forthcoming about his master's travel arrangements."

Darcy sighed. Spots danced before his eyes and he rubbed them with his fingertips. A warm bed was nearly all he could think of at the moment… that, and a little company to go with it. "I understand, Colonel. Do keep us apprised, will you? In the meantime, we will try to turn up whatever we can. My uncle, the earl of Matlock, has taken special offence to some of Wickham's lies. He has set his own investigator from Bow Street Runners about London, and I have done the same. If Wickham turns up there, we should know about it."

The colonel shook his head. "It's a puzzle. Still, Darcy, Fitzwilliam, I thank you for your help. It is not often a regimental commander can expect aid from the gentry in such a matter."

"Thank you, Colonel, for your information." Darcy rose, and with a compelling look toward his cousin, made for the door. Fitzwilliam grimaced and followed him with less felicity, but equal enthusiasm. He had not suffered lack of sleep for the night, and was bursting with energy to rid his corner of the world of this scourge, once and for all.

~

George Wickham tugged aside the drape of his boarding house, peering down at the street. The rain had stopped, and true to form, the Bennet family had emerged. He sat on the bed, positioned conveniently next to the window, and tilted his head to peer around the corner of the casement. Lydia and Kitty Bennet. Hmmm. Entertaining, to be sure, but not very valuable. Not worth tipping his hand for.

A little more patience rewarded him with the sight he was hoping for. Elizabeth Bennet and her entourage strolled into town, genially greeting everyone they encountered. Only one man was present. Charles Bingley was not such a challenge. Wickham had some passing acquaintance with the fellow from their school days, but by the time Darcy had become acquainted with Bingley, he and Wickham had largely parted company. Still, he was familiar enough with the man to suppose that Bingley ought to be easily distracted. It should not be difficult, for all the fellow had eyes for was that eldest Bennet girl.

Wickham peered more closely, just long enough to ascertain that Georgiana was, indeed, present and without any further male escort. He swung his feet off the bed, slapping the round rump under the covers as he did so. The girl gave a squeak, and then a fair curly head popped up from beneath the blanket.

"I'm going out," he announced. "Call up for tea, and make sure to tip well." He dumped a pile of coins on the bedside table. Darcy's money was ensuring that he could live in secrecy and in style, hidden right under the man's nose.

~

Once in town, the parties broke up even further. Bingley, with a sly smile, drew Jane into a local watch and jeweler's establishment. Jane blushed, but it was not as though their visit would give rise to any further rumours about the couple than already ran rampant.

Kitty and Lydia had already descended upon the milliner's shop, and they were joined later by Georgiana and Mary. Georgiana, lightly teasing Mary, promised herself that she would see the plainest of the Bennet girls decked out most becomingly by the end of her stay. She suspected that Mary's unwillingness was largely a show, and with gentle prodding, she coaxed the other girl to accompany her.

Elizabeth shrugged with a grin and offered to lead Anne to the book seller's, which was a favourite establishment of hers. Anne agreed with enthusiasm. The pair rapidly became lost among the shelves, admiring the new arrivals and affectionately touching old favourites. Anne's face shone. She had scarcely been permitted the liberty of making her own selections. The Rosings library was as well stocked as its dowager mistress deemed fitting, and it was always a struggle to obtain anything new. Darcy's birthday and Christmas gifts had always been her primary sources of interesting material, and Lady Catherine had been far from objecting to any gifts from that quarter.

Elizabeth picked up one new leather bound novel, turning it over with curious eyes. The title piqued her interest, but the place for the author's name simply read "By A Lady." She fingered the pages, skimming a couple of the paragraphs and chuckling at the author's dry wit. It reminded her very much of her father. She enjoyed novels on occasion, but wondered briefly if her serious-minded betrothed would object to her continued pursuit of that guilty pleasure.

Anne came up behind her. "Oh, I have that one! Darcy gave it to me for Christmas last year. Mother said it was shameful. I think you would like it, Elizabeth," she grinned bashfully.

Well, so much for worry over Darcy's disapproval! Anne took the book from Elizabeth's hands with a shy smile while the latter cocked a curious brow.

Drawing out her reticule, Anne walked that book, as well as a second by the same "Lady," up to the counter. "An engagement gift," she informed her future cousin. Laughing lightly, Elizabeth thanked her.

Arm in arm, the pair eventually moved on out of the bookseller's. A glance in the windows of both the milliner and the dressmaker confirmed that the remainder of their party may well have already made their way home. Anne's surprise was mild until Elizabeth informed her that Kitty and Lydia never, ever parted from either shop in under half an hour.

"Were we really so long?" Anne laughed. "I do believe I was enjoying myself too much!"

They sauntered casually through the small town, passing each little row of shops, then set out for Longbourn once more. Their quiet afternoon together had served to allow them a chance to become better acquainted than weeks in a formal drawing room might have. Elizabeth gestured to the building they approached, arching a watchful brow at the other young woman. "That is the residence of my aunt and uncle Philips. His legal offices are on the lower level."

Anne visibly gulped, blinked twice, and paled slightly. Darcy approved of Miss Bennet, and she would do the same, but a lifetime under her mother's rule had left its mark. It would take some while to overcome her ingrained disdain of Elizabeth's low connections, but she determined to give it her every effort. "That… that must be very agreeable to have family so near," she managed diplomatically.

Elizabeth flashed the beguiling smile which had no doubt so enthralled Darcy. "Indeed."

Elizabeth turned her face away for a moment to glance far down the street where Kitty and Lydia were just emerging from a second, smaller dress shop down the way. They had already attracted the notice of two officers. She shook her head in some embarrassment and began to turn back to Anne when the other's arm was jerked roughly away from her.

Thirty-Three

Elizabeth reeled back, staggered slightly by the shoulder of a man as he brushed between them and pushed Anne backward against the very building Elizabeth had just pointed out to her. Anne spun about to escape, but the man's arm detained her.

"Georgiana!" Elizabeth easily recognized George Wickham's silky tones. "I looked for you in London, but you were not where you said you-gnnggghhh!" His words strangled back into his throat when Elizabeth made a snatch at the back of his collar, dragging him away from Anne.

Wickham turned with a grimace and swiped Elizabeth off of him as though she had been no more than a fly, but it diverted his attention long enough for Anne to collect herself. Employing a move she had seen often threatened by her mother, she swung her reticule- loaded with coins- to box him in the ear. Wickham yelped in surprise, but was not greatly discouraged.

Ducking a second blow, he wrapped his hands around Anne's waist and pressed her up against the Philips' residence. Before Elizabeth could reach for him again, he had locked the other woman in a passionate kiss, right before the entire town. Anne's hands helplessly flew up in a warding gesture, her small fists falling like pattering rain on Wickham's shoulders. Elizabeth gathered her wits and her weapons. Her heavy new books swung at the back of his lungs from their convenient canvas satchel took the zeal out of him.

Wickham made a choking sound and spun to face her, one hand still roughly clenching Anne's arm and the other reaching to seize Elizabeth's striking hand. "Why, it is the future Mrs Darcy! Good day, Miss Bennet. What kind of way is this to greet your future brother?"

Anne twisted away sharply and spun to glare Wickham down with all the scalding iciness of the de Bourgh heritage. "Who *exactly* do you think I am?" she demanded, her head thrown back furiously.

Wickham glanced nonchalantly away from Elizabeth to make reply, but swirled in a double take and fixed his incredulous gaze on Anne. "Anne!" Wickham's face paled and Elizabeth took advantage of his distraction to yank her hand free.

Anne had not spent seven and twenty years under her mother's tutelage for nothing. She marched imperiously closer. "That is *Miss Anne de Bourgh* to you, Mr Wickham! What excuse have you for this attack on my person?"

"Forgive me, I thought you were…" he gulped and broke off. He could have sworn it was Georgiana! Anne de Bourgh, the near-dead pawn of the officious Lady Catherine, walking and laughing merrily in this insignificant town with none other than her avowed rival for Darcy's hand? He took a step back.

Elizabeth glanced about as her peripheral vision caught movement. Her stomach pitted. Everyone on the street had seen Wickham's assault on Anne, and naturally quite a few curious onlookers began to gather and whisper behind their gloves. She made a swift decision.

"You thought she was what, Mr Wickham? One of your loose women? One of your paid companions?" Elizabeth fisted her hand on her hip and leaned threateningly toward him. "How *dare* you insult a lady in this way?"

Wickham was stepping back from them now, slowly, with his hands lifting in an unconscious gesture of supplication. Elizabeth was not finished. She stalked after him, now waving her finger.

"I know how you treat ladies, Mr Wickham! I know you are in debt-probably to half of the good people of this town! I know how you ought to have been a successful attorney by now, but you are a reckless gamester with no principles and cannot even make a respectable militia officer! I know how you try to manipulate and harm others through deceit and extortion! You oil your way into others' good graces and slander good, decent people like the Darcys because of your insatiable jealousy! You could have had every opportunity, Mr Wickham, but you squandered your chances in ruin and dissipation!"

Wickham had continued backing away from the wrathful Elizabeth, his eyes wide. Heavens but she was magnificent when riled! Her colour was heightened, her eyes flashed, and her bearing reflected graceful sovereignty and righteous passion. Darcy had better be careful! His steps dragged reluctantly. She had astounded him in her willingness to loudly and publicly castigate him, rather than flee in modesty as he had expected of a lady. What glorious sort of woman would unabashedly stand up to a man on a public thoroughfare? A pity that this masterpiece, too, should in the end belong to Darcy.

His admiration took a sudden turn as a glance over his shoulder revealed flashes of red moving in his direction. He groaned. He had planned to slip away quickly, intending to remain only long enough to openly damage Georgiana's maidenly credibility and then steal away. How could he then drop threats to Darcy if he had not his liberty? He took a long step in preparation to turn and run from the approaching militiamen, but he backed instead into something firm and unyielding. He turned his head and swallowed. Colonel Fitzwilliam clamped an iron hand to his shoulder.

Elizabeth had not yet arrested her tirade, marching still toward the retreating weasel and scolding him heatedly. Just as she registered Colonel Fitzwilliam's presence, a gentle hand at her own shoulder stilled her. "Elizabeth," Darcy called softly, "it's all right."

She turned and found his eyes full of such a conflict of feeling that she could not at once discern his thoughts. Anne had come to stand just behind him, but her gaze was only for Darcy as he drew her hand close. "I- I am sorry," she mumbled, dropping her eyes sorrowfully. A spark of fear and mortification grew in her. She had shamed Darcy in public by acting a hostile, impudent shrew. Of course Wickham deserved to be told off, but not by herself, who ought to have behaved as a lady! Dread spread over her. What must Darcy think?

He squeezed her hand, a gesture none but she could have noted. She looked up again to a tender, if fleeting, smile. "Do not be sorry, Elizabeth," he murmured quietly. With one more press to her fingers, he gently guided her to stand next to Anne and moved to address himself to Wickham.

A crowd had begun to gather now. The two militia officers who had been flirting with Kitty and Lydia quickly crossed the street and stood ready to obey Colonel Fitzwilliam's command. Kitty and Lydia, unfortunately, trailed just behind with rather unbecoming interest. Elizabeth peered behind them with trepidation. At least Mary and Georgiana were not at hand. Georgie ought not be near Wickham, especially not now!

"Wickham," Darcy's voice was cold and unbending, "What do you mean by imposing yourself on a young lady of my family, and in the middle of the street? Have you no decency or honour left in you?"

Wickham sneered and tried to jerk away from Fitzwilliam, but unsuccessfully. Richard wrenched one arm behind his back and with his other hand gripped Wickham by the tendons of his neck and clamped down, hard. Wickham cringed, his knees crumpling in pain as he tried to cower away. "*Answer!*" Fitzwilliam hissed.

"I thought she was someone else!" he sniveled, the pain in his body causing him to momentarily forget that he still held dangerous information.

Darcy had not forgotten. He could take no chances that Wickham would utter Georgiana's name under Richard's duress. He flicked his eyes to his cousin, who relented with the intuition of a brother.

Another glance over his shoulder assured him that Elizabeth had already taken action to preserve the situation. She was firmly ushering her sisters and Anne into her aunt's house, and mercifully, Bingley and Jane had appeared from nowhere. Bingley took up station behind Darcy, while Jane grimly followed her sisters into their aunt's abode with the intent of keeping them under wraps. Elizabeth, however, returned to stand staunchly at his shoulder.

Despite everything, he could not but feel a swell of triumph. *This* was the astounding woman he would be privileged to spend his life with, who would fight loyally at his side and lie sweetly in his arms! He leveled a challenging glare at Wickham, whose widened eyes testified that he, too, stood in awe of the spirit of Elizabeth Bennet.

Darcy stepped closer, lowering his voice so that his words might be kept between only them. "*What have you done with miss King?*" he rasped.

Wickham threw back his shoulders as best he could under the colonel's grip. "What do I want with that nasty, freckled thing? A dowry of ten thousand? I can have all of that and more, without being shackled to a silly wife. You'll be only too happy to pay up to keep me from telling what I know."

Fitzwilliam shook Wickham until his teeth rattled. "Where is she, then?" he demanded.

Wickham blinked, trying to recover somewhat. "Probably in London, or on her way to Brighton with her uncle! He got an 'anonymous' tip that someone wished to abscond with his niece. I knew if she disappeared you would take after her and try to save her from me. You are so predictable, Darcy! I only lament that you came back so quickly."

Darcy drew back fractionally, satisfied that the innocent young lady, at least, was unharmed. Now to prevent any possibility that it might ever happen again.

"George Wickham," Colonel Fitzwilliam pronounced, "you are a deserter from His Majesty's Militia. I hereby place you under arrest."

Wickham jerked but Fitzwilliam held firm. He began to panic. A tribunal meant certain doom. *Damn that Elizabeth Bennet!* If she had not distracted him so, he would have been long gone! Fury took over where shrewdness had once prevailed. "You are no better than I!" he lashed out at Fitzwilliam. "What are you but a poor second son, a penniless whelp, totally dependent on *that* parsimonious snob for everything! You cannot even afford to marry without his leave!"

Fitzwilliam collared Wickham roughly, his face taking on a dangerous hue. "Guard your words well, sir! I may be all that stands between you and the gallows!"

Wickham spun to glare recklessly at his persecutor. "Do you think I don't know about you, Richard? That I don't see the way you look at her, the way you pine your miserable existence away waiting for someone you can never have? Aye, Darcy is too thick, but you and I are the same, *Richard!* You can lock me up, but it won't help y-" Wickham's taunting was finally cut short when Fitzwilliam slammed his head against the brick of the Philips' residence. He sagged, senseless.

Richard let him fall to the walk, straightening his coat and glancing self-consciously at his cousin... and beyond him. Georgiana had just exited a nearby tea shop with Mary Bennet and had stopped in open-mouthed horror at the scene unfolding before her. Darcy had not yet perceived her, but Elizabeth followed his ashen gaze immediately. She whirled and quickly beckoned both girls to follow her into her aunt's house.

Darcy was only dimly aware of what had taken place behind him. He blanched at Wickham's words, his eyes boring questioningly into his cousin. Richard dropped his head in defeat, waving for the gathering crowd of militia officers to collect the downed deserter.

Chaos reigned for some minutes. Word was sent for Colonel Forster. Wickham was dragged away, staggering and muddily conscious. Local gentlemen who had stepped away from the scene to shield their ladies began to brave the streets once more. The town's residents slowly resumed their business, with many a surreptitious eye cast toward the worthy gentleman of Derbyshire and his heroic cousin, both of whom had cut such a dashing figure in detaining the pariah of the week.

Fitzwilliam dared to meet Darcy's even gaze, but could not hold it for long. He looked away, collecting his fallen hat from the mud and brushing ineffectually at it. Bingley clapped Darcy on the shoulder. "Fitz, I'm going to see to the ladies." He glanced awkwardly at the colonel and slipped inside the house just as Mr Philips emerged.

"Mr Darcy! What has happened? I heard a man attacked the lady in the street! Oh, my gracious, my poor wife is in hysterics!"

Darcy sighed. "All is well, sir. Is Miss de Bourgh very much shaken up?"

The man arched his brows over his spectacles. "Miss de Bourgh? Why, I believe she is well. It is your sister, Miss Darcy, who appears most distressed."

Darcy closed his eyes. *Not now!* Wickham, that blasted deviant, had broken his beloved sister's heart. What a shock it must have given her to see him just now! Heedless of Mr Philips, who was beginning to jabber excitedly to a blank-faced Fitzwilliam, Darcy moved toward the door of the house. Elizabeth intercepted him as he was reaching for the handle, slipping outside to him and pulling the door closed behind herself.

"Georgiana?" he questioned brusquely.

Elizabeth put a hand on his arm. "She is well enough, only a little rattled.

Miss de Bourgh and my sister Mary are attending her. Jane," she cast a grateful look over her shoulder, "is fighting the good fight to contain my younger sisters until Mr Bingley can make arrangements for us all to travel homeward."

Darcy heaved, the tension beginning to leave him. "But… Georgiana? And Anne?" he asked again, numbly. Elizabeth did not answer. He followed the direction of her gaze and discovered his cousin leaning against the house, his hand wearily covering his eyes. Fitzwilliam's mouth twisted in an agonized scowl. Though still mystified at the sudden source of his cousin's disturbance, instinctively he started to pull away from Elizabeth to go to him. In trial and storm, Richard had always been there to comfort him, however exasperating his methods might have been. He could do no less!

Elizabeth, however, tightened a staying hand on his forearm. He looked back at her and she shook her head. "Go to Georgiana," she urged. It was more of a command, really. Nodding slowly, he acquiesced, darting one last look over his shoulder.

He found Georgiana and Anne with their arms about each other's shoulders. He did not know which to expect to be the most overwrought, but quickly found that Anne had come through her ordeal with rather more philosophical bemusement than he had expected. He had witnessed the entire episode from down the street, beginning with Anne and Elizabeth's easy familiarity and right up to Elizabeth's glorious assault on all things George Wickham. He had anticipated that sheltered and tender Anne would have been mortified beyond words, horrified into a stupor by Wickham's audacious attack, but she offered him a comforting smile as he approached.

Georgiana, on the other hand, had her face hidden in her handkerchief. She had never been one given to fashionable hysteria, and with a questioning look at Anne, he took his place to Georgiana's left in a seat Mary Bennet vacated for him. Georgiana clenched his hand, but would not lower her shield.

"Georgie," he inquired softly, "are you well?"

She nodded mutely, the lace bobbing and tickling over her nose.

Anne cleared her throat. "Mrs Philips offered us some refreshments, William. I believe I will take advantage of her hospitality."

He watched her go, then turned back. "Georgiana, will you speak to me?"

She shook her head. Dimly he became aware that she was not crying- not exactly. She seemed only distressed, perhaps ashamed and embarrassed.

He bent close to her ear to murmur low encouragement. "I never heard him say your name, Georgie, nor could anyone else have but possibly Elizabeth or Anne. Richard clubbed him pretty hard. I do not think he will be speaking anything of coherence for the rest of the day."

She drew a shuddering breath, but made no other reaction. He was thoroughly baffled. She had never, even after the escapade with Wickham, hidden her face so determinedly from him. He cast his troubled gaze about the room and it landed on Jane Bennet, who apparently had been observing them with interest. Acknowledging his silent plea, she came to sit with Georgiana as well. By a subtle shake of her head, the sage Miss Bennet advised him not to press his sister just now.

Hanging his head, he resigned himself to his meek position as Hand Holder.

~

Elizabeth casually assumed a posture on the walkway outside her aunt's home, about an arm's length from the colonel. She did not speak to him, but she did smile and wave at some of the town's passers-by. A few darted nervous glances her way, but her open friendliness and general sterling reputation in the community encouraged a wave of support that she hoped would flood over all of the innocent ladies touched by the potential scandal.

Fitzwilliam still did not move. She avoided looking directly at him. That would have been Darcy's style, but some innate sense whispered to her to offer the colonel silent comradeship without requiring anything of him.

At last he spoke. "Are you well, Miss Elizabeth? And my cousin Anne?"

"Quite well, sir. Thank you for asking."

He was silent once more, gazing thoughtfully across the street at no object in particular.

"How long have you been in love with Georgiana?" she at last questioned in a low voice.

He shot her a convicted glare. "It is not what you think."

She arched a brow. "And just what do I think?"

He returned his gaze to the nothingness across the street. "You must think I would take advantage of my position as her guardian. You must be horrified that I, a man twice her age, would even think of her."

She shrugged. "The age difference is not unheard of. My aunt and uncle Gardiner share a similar such difference, and I cannot find it within me to criticize their union. As to your guardianship, I have it on the very best authority that none could look after their charge more perfectly."

He squinted curiously at her, pressing his lips. At last he began to articulate his feelings. "You asked me once if war was not terrible."

She nodded.

"I have been three tours of duty overseas. Truly, Miss Bennet, there is no more horrifying device known to mortal man. The cruelty, the blood... the brutal squandering, Miss Bennet. I could never describe to a lady what my eyes have seen, but the nightmares... they are known to every man who wears a uniform. I cannot lay down my head without seeing my brothers dying, hearing the screams of men and horses... such a bloody, senseless waste of life!"

Elizabeth closed her eyes.

Fitzwilliam swallowed and continued. "We cope as best we can, because our loved ones back at home depend on our protection. I shall not venture to philosophize on the imperial dogma- I have seen the good and also the harm. Mine is to do my duty and serve my men."

Elizabeth nodded in understanding, taking a supportive half step closer to him.

He sighed. "Georgiana has always been to me the epitome of everything sweet and fine. Since she was born, and then when she was a few years old and lost her mother- I have been close to her for her entire life, Miss Bennet. I watched her grow from adorable child to shy youngster to graceful young woman, and I have never felt but admiration and brotherly affection- that is, until this summer."

He paused, biting his lip and shaking his head. "I never wanted to kill anyone more in my life! The violence I abhor on the battlefield, the necessary evil of my duty, all of that honed to a single point for me when Darcy sent me that express from Ramsgate. I would have gladly spilled the scoundrel's guts, coldly defiled my hands with another man's blood, if only to spare what was good and right in my world from the pain and ruination of what the truly wicked would devise.

"Everything clarified for me on that trip south. My life has meaning and purpose if I can spend it protecting that which I love. I would gladly lay it at my cousin's feet to preserve her purity and innocence! It is not like the passion Darcy feels for you, Miss Bennet. Forgive me if I cause you any discomfort!" he interjected upon noticing Elizabeth's vivid blush. "I imagine that emotion would arise if I gave it rein, but I cannot allow it. I am her guardian! It is shameful that I should harbour thoughts of her. I will be an old man while the bloom of youth is still fresh on her! She deserves better, Miss Bennet."

"Better than a man who would sacrifice his happiness for her sake?" she challenged.

He eyed her carefully. "Better than one with no future or prospects, who bears unspeakable scars both in body and in spirit. She is sweetness and perfection, and I would have her give her heart to one who is worthy of her."

"I suspect she may have already done so."

He closed his eyes again. "Do not tell Darcy," he implored. "The subject is closed and I shall not pursue it. She is too young to even consider such matters. Let us not speak of it again."

Elizabeth drew a ragged breath. "As you wish, sir."

"And, Miss Bennet," he opened his eyes, the bright, cheerful expression she had grown accustomed to returning faintly. "I would thank you for your kindness. You will make the finest Mistress that Pemberley has ever known."

~

Darcy fleetingly thought to arrange for a carriage to take their entire party back to Netherfield after their ordeal in the street, but quickly thought better of it. Making such provisions would publicly declare that their party felt shame and humiliation after the incident. Better, he decided, to hold their heads high.

With that in mind, he left Georgiana in Jane and Mary's capable hands and approached Mr and Mrs Philips, both of whom shrank slightly with the honour of such a man's condescension. Mrs Philips was only a slightly more practical version of her sister, and Darcy cringed at having to depend upon her prudence to keep up his family's good name. "Mrs Philips," he greeted her cordially, "your hospitality is quite unrivaled, as always. I have greatly appreciated each opportunity to partake of your home's elegant welcome."

Mrs Philips blinked, glancing uncertainly toward her husband. Such, from a man accustomed to the finest circles, was high praise indeed! Mrs Philips drew herself a little straighter and preened a little.

It had not been her wish to welcome all of these girls into her house after that shocking display in the street. Her niece Elizabeth, however, had given her no option. Before she had been able to object, the entire party had been received and served refreshments. She had always rather taken her sister Fanny's part in her belief that Elizabeth was far too outspoken and direct, but her staff were another matter. They had leapt at the prospect of being of service to a young lady who had always been kind to them, and who even now stood poised to become one of the finest ladies in all of England. Who knew what avenues for their own advancement lay open through her?

Mr Philips found his voice before his wife did. "Most civil of you, Mr Darcy. We were all very horrified yesterday when it became known that Mr Wickham, whom we have received in this house, had taken advantage of a local girl in such a way. Poor Miss King! I wonder what became of her?"

"Miss King?" Darcy inquired, with deliberate confusion. "Why, Miss

King is known to be traveling with her uncle. Mr Wickham has in the past preyed on young ladies, as he attempted to do with my noble cousin, but that particular lady, at least, is safe." There. Thanks now to Mrs Philips and her ilk, Mary King would be vindicated through the town, and Anne viewed with sympathy.

"Do you know," Philips leaned close with an uncomfortable glance at his wife, "that Wickham fellow owes most of the shopkeepers money."

Darcy sighed and nodded. "I have already begun arrangements to purchase this debts. Wickham was my father's ward, thus it is mine to take responsibility."

Philips' eyes widened. "That is right good of you, sir! Is... is Miss Darcy well?"

"Well enough, I thank you. She, like myself, suffers from grave disappointment in our childhood friend."

"Oh, I see," he nodded. He stood in mock relaxation for a moment until his wife was temporarily diverted by a question from one of the maids. "I hear," he whispered to Darcy, "that he takes up with... you know... Some of the *lesser* ladies of the town."

Darcy pressed his lips thin but made no reply to that comment. No doubt Wickham had not been lodging alone. He'd had access to funds and incentive to lie low, so a young companion of some sort would certainly have served him well. He hoped the girl, whoever she was, would have the sense to go through Wickham's belongings once she had word of his capture.

Though it cost him every last shred of his peace of mind, Darcy remained to make polite conversation with the Philipses, and even extended an invitation to Pemberley after Christmas, should the wedding plans not interfere. His being roiled with both anticipation and dread. Come what may, he would make absolutely certain that Elizabeth was his wife well before the end of the year! A quick calculation on the length of time for the banns.... Oh, hang the banns! All he was really waiting for was Elizabeth's father, and then he intended to carry her off as soon as may be.

His dream of Elizabeth at Pemberley for Christmas was possible, only just, if Mr Bennet continued in his rapid recovery. Elizabeth would be his, and without delay, if he had a say in the matter! He would not look forward to a flood of visitors- particularly not these visitors- quite so soon, but Pemberley was large and his people were loyal. There were plenty of places Elizabeth would need to become acquainted with, and it was easy to get lost!

Just before the walking party were to set out again from Meryton, he found a moment to draw near Anne. "Are you well?" he whispered.

She turned laughing eyes on him. "Why would I not be?"

"Well, I… I only wondered," he offered lamely.

"At seven and twenty, I am rather on the shelf, William. Title, fortune and all, there are plenty of others in the *ton* more alluring than I, and I have never yet had my presentation. I long ago relinquished any thought of marriage. What need do I have? I have Rosings, and any man pursuing me is likely to be more interested in my property than in myself. You must know what that is like. I would not subject myself to a knave just to have the distinction of the marriage estate. I had always intended to leave it to your second son, or maybe to Richard's children if he should have any."

"Then…" his brow furrowed, utterly astounded, "you are not… overcome, with all that has occurred?"

Anne actually laughed. "I may never have another kiss me quite so expertly as your Mr Wickham, William! Say what you will about the man, he has his momentary charms. I have spent twelve years feigning serious illness. I intend to live, now, William. Oh, do not look so shocked! I shall not behave immodestly, but I will not allow one incident to overshadow the happiness I intend to enjoy from here on out. Perhaps one day I may, after all, marry, but it shall no longer be a pall hanging over my life. At present all of your friends seem to be spoken for, so I shall have to shift for myself."

He took her hand, smiling gently and thinking that even Anne's brief acquaintance with Elizabeth had brought a sparkle to her that had never been there before. Elizabeth and Fitzwilliam had just entered the room, and Anne's eyes went immediately to the young lady. "You have done extremely well, William. I had expected you to select an entirely different sort, but you surprised me! You could not have chosen a better bride. I predict many years of joy for you both."

He grinned like the boy she remembered so long ago. "I hope so."

Thirty-Four

The Netherfield party, with the exception of Darcy, retreated to that house directly upon arriving at Longbourn. Darcy closeted himself in the Longbourn library to apprise Mr Gardiner of all that had taken place, as it was within his rights to have a thorough explanation.

"Are Miss Darcy and Miss de Bourgh well?" Gardiner inquired.

"Miss de Bourgh is. My sister, I believe, is still somewhat shaken, but she assured me as they departed that I would see her well by the time I returned. I wonder, however, that you do not ask how Miss Elizabeth fared?"

Gardiner offered a sly grin. "I know her better than that, perhaps. She seemed well enough when they came in. Did she ever tell you about that fellow who was trying to pay court to Jane when she was but fifteen?"

Darcy's mouth tugged to the side. "Mrs Bennet made mention once that Miss Bennet had received some very pretty poetry from a gentleman."

Gardiner laughed. "Far from pretty! The girls were staying with us at the time. The fellow was a perfect eel- another Mr Collins, I should say. Jane felt obliged to receive his attentions because of her mother, but even at thirteen Lizzy would have none of it. She made a point of telling him all manner of unflattering stories about her younger sisters, playing the pianoforte rather more poorly-and *loudly*- than usual, and once she even went so far as to purposely trip over the man's feet and spill hot tea all over his lap. He did not return!"

Darcy could not help a loud, hearty laugh, a sound which startled the ladies outside the library.

"Lizzy!" Mrs Bennet snapped. "You are a terrible influence on that gentleman! Why, he was so perfectly respectable and dignified until he started spending so much time around you!"

Elizabeth exchanged smiles with her aunt. "You are quite right, Mama."

~

At last a very tired Fitzwilliam Darcy bid his beloved a good afternoon, with the intentions of spending the rest of the day in his bed. Elizabeth had ferreted out a secluded nook in the hallway where they could have a moment of privacy. It occurred briefly to him that Elizabeth owned a perfectly good bed upstairs, but even as alluring as that sounded, he was too tired for his passions to overcome his good sense in disallowing the fantasy.

She wound her arms around his neck and allowed him to kiss her gently. "Elizabeth," he murmured, "please tell me it will not be long before I can remain always with you!"

She arched a brow. "Unless you wish to continue scandalizing the neighbourhood, I think it best we get the nuptials over with quickly and remove our shocking presence from the vicinity. I do hope there is not a town *too* near Pemberley!"

He chuckled, brushing a joyful kiss into her crown of curls. "Not as near, but we have a good many more tenants. You will have to earn their loyalty early if we are to keep up the Darcy family name!"

"I shall endeavour to do so, but it is the Master's affections which shall preoccupy me."

"Then you shall be assured of success on all counts," he verified with another kiss. "Elizabeth, I must go, because I may soon find myself far too relaxed and fatigued to remain on my horse all the way back to Netherfield. At present, I am trying not to wonder if Longbourn boasts any additional guest quarters."

"It does not," she gave a firm push to his chest with a playful smirk. "William, there is one last thing before you go."

He quirked a knowing expression at her. "Richard?"

"How did you know?"

"Never mind. What wisdom have you to impart regarding my dear cousin?"

"None. Leave him alone, William. I beg you would not question him about Wickham's words. If he needs to speak of it to you, he will, but I expect it will not be for years, if ever."

He sighed. "I wondered if that might not be the case. Georgiana's reaction was rather peculiar as well." He shook his muddled head to clear it. "If you wish it, it shall be so. I will say nothing- at least, not unless I have cause."

"Thank you, my love." She raised herself up on her toes to kiss his very surprised face.

He froze. "What did you just call me?" he quavered, his voice hushed.

"You heard me," she whispered in his ear, pressing another kiss to his cheek.

"No, most assuredly I did not! I beg you would repeat yourself."

She raised a cheeky grin to his eyes. "You will have to work to earn another such endearment, William! Before you should attempt to do so, however, I am of the opinion that you must first see to the needs of one I care for very much."

He drew back reluctantly. "I will tell Georgiana of your concern."

That impish smile he so adored graced her features once more. "I was speaking of you, William! Go get some rest, my love!"

He drew her into his arms, furtively glancing down the conspicuously empty hall. "I am at your command, my Elizabeth."

~

Worn out and nearly overwrought, Elizabeth withdrew to her father's room for the remainder of the afternoon. She tucked herself neatly into her double-knitted blanket and hovered near as Mrs Cooper spooned broth for her father. He was not what one might call alert, but he was becoming steadily more responsive. He was swallowing the nourishment offered on his own now, and his eyes opened more frequently. He still seemed only vaguely aware of his surroundings.

Elizabeth could not help but wonder at the singular consciousness which had roused him briefly the night before, but Mrs Cooper did not think the incident so remarkable. That opinion, Elizabeth thought privately, might change if Mrs Cooper had been told *all* the details of Mr Bennet's wakefulness the previous night! She watched him closely as they helped him to lie back on his pillows. There was a brief eye contact, a flash of recognition, and a smile, and Mr Bennet slipped once more into peaceful dreams.

There was a soft tap on the door and her uncle's face appeared. "Lizzy, there is a young man here to see you."

She pursed her lips in an attempt at annoyance. "Not Mr Darcy? It had better not be he!"

"No, I think we can safely guarantee *that* young man is curled up sound asleep somewhere. This lad claims to have been sent by Mr Bingley to speak with you about your farm. I told him to wait for you in the library."

"Oh! I had not expected this so soon. I had hoped that father…."

"Your father has confidence in your abilities, Lizzy. I thought I would stay in the room with you, but you can make this decision. You need the practice, after all." Her uncle's eyes sparkled with encouragement.

Elizabeth found the young man waiting nervously, crumpling a stained cap in work-hardened hands. He was young, perhaps her own age, but he had been head of his family already some while. He rose smartly and greeted her with every respect.

The interview was over quickly. She was impressed with his desire to care for his family- two sisters, he claimed, with a third employed at Netherfield. He also announced proudly to her that he had just become engaged to marry one of the other maids from that estate, who had recently inherited a generous dowry from an unknown uncle. "We won'n be needin' char'ty through the win'ner, Miss," he assured her. "We're well 'nough set up to start. All we ask 's a chance."

"And you shall have it," she smiled. "The Brown family are set to depart for Derbyshire in a few more days. You may take up residence as soon as may be."

The young man's face glowed. "Thank ye, Miss!"

He took his leave and Elizabeth was treated to a broad wink from her uncle. She took his arm as he affectionately tugged her out of the library. He fixed her with a toying look, his eyes holding hers until she began to laugh. "What!" she finally demanded.

"You will make a fine Mistress," he winked. "I always knew you were cut out for more than a parson's wife."

Elizabeth sighed with a twinge of pride. Just a twinge. "I hope I can prove myself worthy. I wish very much to honour and please my h- Mr Darcy."

"In that, my dear, you cannot fail. The gentleman seems determined to be pleased! He is quite obstinate, I daresay- almost as much so as a certain relation of mine," he winked.

She grinned. "Yes, I suspect our future together shall not be boring!"

～

What Elizabeth had looked forward to as a restful evening proved to be somewhat less so. Scarcely an hour after the young farmer's call, the bell was rung again. As it was growing rather late, the family were surprised to be receiving any callers. This past week, however, had taught even Mrs Bennet a new equanimity respecting the extraordinary.

Charlotte Lucas, shivering and wet from a fresh rainfall, was shown bashfully into the drawing room to be surrounded by a bevy of curious faces. "Charlotte?" Jane ventured wonderingly.

Charlotte blanched for a moment, then turned as her dear friend entered the room behind her. "Charlotte, darling!" Elizabeth enthused. "What brings you at this hour?"

"My mother desired my removal," she mumbled, shuffling her feet on the rug.

Mrs Bennet's eyes shifted between the two young women suspiciously. It was she, who had spent so many years contriving to marry her girls well, who first surmised the cause of the rift in the Lucas household. "Oh, dear me, you have gone and withdrawn your acceptance of Mr Collins!" she ejaculated. "And in this house! Oh, what will the neighbours say!" She wrung her hands in exaggerated worry.

Elizabeth drew a long sigh as Charlotte's gaze sank. "Of course, Charlotte, you are welcome here!" She shot a long stare at her mother, catching her aunt's amused expression as she did so. "*We* shall be most pleased to receive you."

Charlotte wearily returned her friend's smile. "Thank you, Lizzy. I shall not intrude long on your generosity...."

"Nonsense, Charlotte. We shall discuss everything in the morning." Elizabeth firmly dragged her friend upstairs and made arrangements for a hot bath to warm her. Mary volunteered to share her smaller room, and at last the tired family lay down to rest for the night.

"I know my mother is dreadfully disappointed." Charlotte set her cup down on her saucer and watched as Elizabeth arranged her father's pillows.

"Mine would be," Elizabeth sighed reluctantly. "I am curious, though; what led you on to do it? I always thought you rather practical regarding marriage, and this seems very contrary even to your own advice to me a few days ago."

Charlotte nibbled a bit of her biscuit thoughtfully. "I suppose I could not bring myself to marry a man I could not respect," she admitted at last. "Oh, I never had any great admiration for your cousin, you understand, but when he so easily betrayed your family and forced me to do the same, why, I knew I could never live under his rule. I would come to despise him- if I have not already done so- and I could not imagine knowing him as I now do and going through with the marriage. He is and will always be utterly subject to the whims of Lady Catherine, or another just as corrupt and domineering, and I would be subject to his. No, Lizzy, practical as I have always been, it was something I just could not do. I know it was foolish, and I have disgraced myself and my family, but… I just could not marry him."

"It took courage to refuse him Charlotte. You should be proud of yourself, as I am of you."

"You say so, Lizzy, but now I am virtually homeless! My parents are ashamed of me and I shall never marry another, for who would be willing to have me? I attracted little enough attention before, and now! No, there is none who would have me."

Mrs Cooper, sitting in the corner with her knitting, cleared her throat gently. The girls both looked to her. "Not all are quite so choosy, Miss. Some young man of modest means would be right pleased to meet with a practical lady of sense. Not all are in a position to care so much about a broken engagement."

Charlotte offered a wan smile to the woman who had overheard so many private conversations of late. "That is very kind of you to say, Mrs Cooper, but such gentlemen are extraordinarily rare." Mrs Cooper just lifted her eyebrows and returned to her work.

"You could come to Pemberley…" Elizabeth suggested hesitantly. Darcy had proven more generous than she might have ever hoped, but taking a fallen woman into his home, particularly to be in company with his sister, might be too much to ask.

Charlotte sighed. "Miss de Bourgh promised me a place with her. How ironic that I could live in that very man's parish, and in the wondrous Rosings he praises unceasingly! I think, though, that he may be rather disappointed in the near future. Miss de Bourgh told me something of her plans, and I gather that she has been in no way impressed with Mr Collins' performance of his parochial duties."

Elizabeth laughed. "I quite believe it! Anne de Bourgh is one acquaintance I shall try not to anger. I am dying to know all that occurred yesterday afternoon."

"Oh, Lizzy, you would have found it so highly amusing! My poor father was most distressed, as Lady Catherine blamed him for the entire 'inhospitable' county. I think she thinks all of Hertfordshire is set against her! She returned from Netherfield alone when Mr Darcy refused to satisfy her, fuming and raging about both her brother and her daughter. No one understood most of what she said, but Mr Collins flew into a panic to arrange their return to Kent. I think it may be some while before Mr Bingley sees his carriage again! It was when he almost forgot to bid me his farewells and my father said something about the Mr Collins' return for the wedding arrangements that I spoke up. My mama started to cry and tell me I was a shameful daughter. I think Papa is more distressed about losing Lady Catherine's intimacy than mine."

Elizabeth sighed. Such a frantic muddle it had all become! Poor dear Charlotte. Elizabeth hated that her friend had been made to suffer for her loyalty and dignity. She took Charlotte's hand firmly. "One way or another, Charlotte, you shall be cared for. I will not allow you to pay such a price for standing up to Lady Catherine and her lackey!"

"I thank you, Lizzy. I was so looking forward to managing my own home, but I shall be content. I believe I have done rightly. Is your mother still very vexed?"

"Oh, Mama! She thinks you quite foolish, so be prepared for a scolding and some very snide remarks, but she seems satisfied at least that she shall not have to yield Longbourn to you one day." Both girls broke into giggles.

A moment later they could hear from downstairs that a caller had arrived. As it was still early, Elizabeth did not expect it to be Mr Darcy. Her suspicions were confirmed when Dr Cooper, the younger, came up to them. His eyes immediately went to the young ladies and then to his mother.

Smiling, Elizabeth excused herself. Charlotte was somewhat less prompt in her response, but followed her friend dutifully. The doctor shyly bowed them out of the room before closing the door to examine Mr Bennet.

When he had finished his examination of his patient, he descended the stairs once more and presented himself uncomfortably at the entrance to the drawing room, where nearly everyone save Kitty and Lydia had gathered. Elizabeth rose to speak with him, but it became apparent rather quickly that his mission was not a medical one. He softly asked permission to speak with Miss Lucas... alone. Charlotte, embarrassed and seeking to hide anywhere but in his presence, eventually relented.

Elizabeth ushered the blushing pair into the library, then turned smugly about, crossing her arms and finding her aunt standing near. "A doctor's wife! Do you know, I think it will be just the thing for her."

Mrs Gardiner only smiled and rolled her eyes.

~

On the third day after their arrival, the Earl of Matlock and his Lady took their leave. They generously paid a call at Longbourn before setting back out for London with their son, the colonel, in tow. Colonel Fitzwilliam had remained long enough to coach his old comrade, Colonel Forster, in the disposition of one former Lieutenant George Wickham, deserter to His Majesty's armed forces. With a few favours called in, Wickham was spared a tribunal and the gallows, and was soon made to see the merit in a long voyage to Australia.

Elizabeth was sorry to see the Fitzwilliam family leave, but they all assured her they would return rather shortly to celebrate her nuptials. "Good heavens, we may as well remain here, for I declare you shall be wed before the month is out. That boy will not wait a moment longer than necessary!" the Countess was heard to lament. "I do hope you have some success at reining him in, my dear. You still have to come be fitted for your wardrobe in London! How you have time to get married now, I shall never fathom!"

Elizabeth had made what assurances were in her power to soothe her future aunt, enjoying her glimpses at the earl's unsuccessful battle with his own amusement. He stood just behind his wife, and his cheeks were suspiciously bright with mirth.

Darcy and Bingley had arrived with them, as it had already become their habit to spend the larger part of their days with their betrotheds. It was fortunate that Mr Bennet's burgeoning recovery still required some measure of deference from his family, if proper decorum were to be observed. Had such not been the case, the gentlemen would scarcely have had a chance to see their beloveds, as Mrs Bennet would undoubtedly have had the girls frantically about their wedding plans. As it was, that lady could hardly sit quietly for more than a moment, eager as she was to be about the business of matrimony.

Each day Darcy would hopefully inquire about Mr Bennet's health, anticipating the day when the father would be well enough to consent to his daughter's marriage. He intended to pay a visit to the vicarage the very moment the man had given his blessing! On this day, as the Fitzwilliam carriage drew out of sight, Elizabeth offered him a knowing smile and a small wink.

His eyebrows rose hesitantly. "Your father?"

"He finally read the Times, which Jane forgot to check before leaving with him. I am to understand that a few days ago there was a rather interesting entry." She quirked him a playful smile. "He tells me that if I do not bring you to him, he shall come down the stairs himself. I do think he means it!"

Darcy closed his eyes. The announcement! He had nearly forgotten about it in the flurry of the last days, and as he had rushed off every morning to see Elizabeth without bothering with his own morning paper, he had not seen it himself. Nary a word of it had been mentioned by the magnanimous Mr Gardiner, but it was clear that it had not passed unnoticed by the family. What explanation would the justifiably offended father demand for all of his actions of late?

His stomach fluttering, Darcy followed where she led, back to that familiar little room. Mr Bennet was sitting up in his bed, his white hair tousled and his dressing robe still in evidence. Darcy swallowed. All of the times he had rehearsed the day he would ask a man for his daughter's hand, he had somehow never pictured himself accosting that man in his sickbed, with an incriminating announcement already printed in the man's newspaper. It felt like robbery somehow, to come to a man who had very little opportunity or strength with which to object.

He bowed in the entryway. "Mr Bennet. I am very glad to see you so greatly improved."

Mr Bennet raised his glasses from a bedside table, where they had rested upon his book. "Mr Darcy! Why, I thought you had left the country last week for London. Very good of you to come back to check on an old man who cannot remain astride his horse."

"I… yes sir," Darcy shifted uncomfortably, glancing at Elizabeth. She had said Mr Bennet expected to see him! The man he spoke to now seemed to have no knowledge or recollection of any of the recent events. That was worrisome, certainly, but it might also spare him an awkward explanation about their last encounter.

Mr Bennet lowered his glasses again, glancing between Mr Darcy and his daughter. "Was there something in particular you wished to discuss, Mr Darcy? I recall you had that question about our hardy wheat variety. I should think it would do very well even in your climate. I can provide you with some seed to sample."

"No, indeed, I had something of a rather more personal nature to discuss." Darcy glanced once more at Elizabeth, unable to stop himself. She seemed not at all inclined to come to his rescue. Instead, she was simply gazing at her father, her curly head tilted curiously to the side.

"Ah, you must have heard about that tenant of mine who has been so dependent upon charity. The talk of the village, I am afraid. I do hope the good people at Netherfield have not been put to any inconvenience. Longbourn may be modest, but we can see the family through the winter."

"No, sir, that was not at all what I came to speak to you of." Darcy sighed, pressing his lips together and blinking in frustration. Elizabeth had been apprising him of her father's progress, and he was quite sure that Mr Bennet had been informed about the Brown family, among many other matters! Perhaps his memory suffered more greatly than any could have suspected.

"Indeed?" Mr Bennet gestured to the chair with which Darcy had already become familiar. "Take a seat, Mr Darcy. I shall be eager to hear what I can do for you."

Darcy took the seat, watching in some dismay as Elizabeth moved past him to exit the room. It was right and proper for her to go, of course, but he could not feel at all satisfied about addressing himself to a man in Mr Bennet's condition. He suddenly wished that Elizabeth might make some plausible excuse for the conversation to be delayed a few more days.

"Lizzy, close the door, please," Mr Bennet called. Elizabeth stepped outside and began to draw the door closed after herself when her father corrected her. "No, I meant for you to remain, Elizabeth! You are managing most of the household affairs just now, if I am not mistaken, and you ought to hear whatever this man's concerns are."

Elizabeth slid a cautious look to Darcy over her shoulder, and did as her father asked. She moved by Darcy again to take the chair opposite him, near her father.

"Now, Mr Darcy, how may I be of service?"

Darcy clenched his fingers into a fist, then forcibly relaxed them. Best to have this over and done with! "Mr Bennet, I wish to marry your daughter."

Mr Bennet merely gazed expectantly at him, as if Darcy had just announced he was about to go hunting but had not declared which field he intended to plunder.

Darcy blinked. Had the man not heard? "I… I love her, Mr Bennet, and I have the means to care for her extremely well. She shall want for nothing, I assure you. I can provide you with whatever assurance you require. I only ask your blessing, sir."

Mr Bennet remained quiet, his face wearing a kindly puzzled look. Darcy could feel himself growing red. He looked to Elizabeth, who was narrowing her eyes slightly, then back to Mr Bennet's face.

At last the man spoke. "Mr Darcy, I have an abundance of daughters. Pray, which of them did you wish to claim? I had thought you a rather sensible man, so it cannot be Lydia. Though your purse is deep, I should think you would prefer a wife of some economy, so it cannot be Kitty. I expect you would not wish to compete with your friend, so it cannot be Jane. And Lizzy! No, far too stubborn for your taste, I declare. Mary it is! She is rather more respectable, but quite as silly as Kitty and Lydia in her way. Still, I do not think she will give you any trouble, so long as you curtail her playing in public. Of course, Mr Darcy, you may take her as soon as you please."

Darcy's face drained of all colour. Mr Bennet smiled, contented with the result of their discussion, and reached again for his glasses and book.

"Mr Bennet, there…" Darcy's voice cracked. "There has been some sort of mistake! It is Miss Elizabeth I wish to marry!"

Mr Bennet's eyebrows rose above the rim of his spectacles. "Lizzy? Surely not! She is tolerable, I daresay, but you will never have a moment's peace, Mr Darcy! She will argue with every decision you make, steal all of the newest books from your library, use up an entire week's allotment of candles in one night, and will ruin the hem on every gown you buy her."

Elizabeth's head bowed, but by the roundness of her cheeks, Darcy could tell she was chuckling rather than hiding in shame at her father's remarks. Perhaps Mr Bennet was not so pitiable as he had been allowing himself to believe.

"All of these would be nothing, I assure you, Mr Bennet. I love Miss Elizabeth, and I shall marry no other." Darcy's voice still warbled, but by the end of his short statement his voice had grown a precious little in firmness.

"Do I understand you correctly that you would *share* your *library*? My good man, do be sensible! Surely there is some more handsome girl in London who would not cause you such worry and distress- one who might not thwart your authority at every turn! A man in your position clearly requires a much more docile wife!"

Darcy stared incredulously at Mr Bennet. The older gentleman smirked back at him. If his sudden intuition were correct, Mr Bennet had the most peculiar means of protecting his daughter that Darcy had ever seen. Intimidating hopeful men by insulting his daughter was not a tactic Darcy would have chosen, but it was effective in one regard- it crystallized his resolve. So devious was his method, in fact, that Darcy catalogued Mr Bennet's pleasant perversity as a likely means of screening future suitors for Georgiana.

"Mr Bennet, sir," Darcy cleared his throat and spoke in such terms as he might have used with his aunt. "I may have spoken carelessly and rather unwisely on a number of occasions, but I have long considered Miss Bennet to be the handsomest woman of my acquaintance. I greatly admire her lively intellect and her generous heart, as well as her independent nature. I quite look forward to sharing my library, along with any other meagre possession I might claim, because truly, sir, *she* is my treasure. I should be content with no other woman, sir, and if it is your intention to refuse your blessing, I shall haunt Netherfield Hall until next spring when Miss Bennet reaches her majority. You would be most welcome to attend the wedding, should you be so inclined, but Miss Elizabeth and I will marry with or without your blessing, and not one day later than May the twenty-second!"

From the corner of his eye, he watched Elizabeth give a start. "You know my birthday, sir?"

He sidled a sly grin at her. "I paid very close attention to all of your conversations, Miss Elizabeth." She treated him to a gentle laugh and one of her bewitching smiles.

Mr Bennet was chuckling and began to wipe his spectacles on the bedsheet. "Quite so. Well, well, Mr Darcy, you may marry my Lizzy, if you think you can handle her. I wondered what it would take to bring you to the point! If you defend my girl so ably before the *ton* as you just did to her cantankerous old Papa, I expect you shall do quite well together."

Darcy took a great breath and shook his head in relieved confusion. "I hope you do not think, Mr Bennet, that I ever truly disdained your daughter."

Mr Bennet replaced his glasses once more. "No! I believe that much was plain the other day. That was quite an interesting discussion we were having. Where did we leave off? Oh! Yes, I believe we were discussing that fabulous Berkshire boar you had recently acquired. Fascinating discipline, swine husbandry."

Darcy narrowed his eyes suspiciously. He glanced quickly at Elizabeth, whose cheeks had suddenly flushed to a most becoming rosy hue. Mr Bennet's head injury had been of such a nature that it was impossible for an observer to know what the man remembered and what he did not, but Darcy's frame suddenly tingled with embarrassment. Evidently Mr Bennet remembered quite a lot of what had taken place since their cold morning ride!

As if in confirmation, Mr Bennet's cheeks pulled into a wide grin. "I anticipate, Mr Darcy, that you are planning to wed sooner rather than later."

Darcy closed his eyes and swallowed. "Yes, soon indeed, sir." He pulled a document from his breast pocket and flinched a little when he saw Elizabeth's eyes widen in shock. "If you will forgive me, sir, I had taken the liberty of having a special license drawn up." He frowned, sorry to be confronting the injured father with such plans to quickly spirit his daughter away, but Mr Bennet deserved to know the entire truth. "I thought, sir, it might simplify matters, so that the wedding date could be chosen with respect to your recovery, and still...."

"And still be soon enough to suit the eager groom, you mean," Mr Bennet finished with a calculating smile. "Do not forget, young man, I was once such a groom myself." He fixed Darcy with an enigmatic stare which the younger man could not quite decipher.

Darcy looked down, folding and re-folding the document awkwardly. "I fear that, upon reflection, you may have cause to believe I sought to overrule your authority in your own household concerning more than one matter during these past several days. I assure you, sir, that was never my intention."

Mr Bennet frowned, pulled at his spectacles, and gazed long at the earnest young man before him. "Mr Darcy, as you have been frank with me, so I will be with you. I have no desire to part with my daughter so quickly, and I was most surprised to discover her... revised opinion of you. I have, however, witnessed ample evidence to the proof of her affections, and I have faith in her good sense.

"Furthermore, I have not been wholly unaware of your actions to preserve the good names of my family as well as yours. I believe you to be an honourable fellow, sir, and you may come as near to deserving my Lizzy as I imagine any man might be able to. If, in addition to these things, you have also contrived a means to spare me months of agonizing shopping and dissertations on lace and satin, I shall suffer you to take her from me at your convenience. My one condition is that I be granted the right to visit her- and that marvelous library of which I have heard so much- whenever the fancy strikes me."

Darcy was by now offering his future father-in-law a toothy grin and trading elated glances with his fiancée. "Truly, sir?" He asked in a near whisper, as though he could not believe his ears. "We may marry so soon?"

"I give you until December the fifteenth, Mr Darcy, not one day longer, else I shall not be held responsible for what elaborate arrangements my wife might impose upon you. I, personally, would rather not find out."

"That... that is only eight days from today!" Darcy nearly leapt out of his chair in his burst of pleasure and shock. "How can it possibly be contrived so quickly? And... if you will forgive me, sir, can you possibly be well enough?"

"Well enough to manage my affairs without the help of my Lizzy? Certainly not, but if I am not mistaken, she has suddenly become rather useless around here. Her thoughts are elsewhere. The sooner you get the affair over and done with, the sooner I can send Mary or Kitty to live with you and set to work training Lydia. My youngest daughter also has quite a sharp mind, if one can only divert it from her thoughts of officers. She may make a suitable replacement for you about Longbourn, Lizzy." He smiled at Elizabeth and she clasped a loving hand over his.

"And now, if you will be so good, sir, I believe there is another eager young man waiting below. Do send him up on your way out." Mr Bennet winked at his blushing daughter and picked up his book, ignoring Darcy completely.

The couple exchanged half-laughing shrugs of resignation, and rose to go. As Darcy was holding the door open for Elizabeth, Mr Bennet called their attention back. "Lizzy! Do be sure to close the door when you tell your mother of your wedding date. I am still recovering from a head injury, after all."

Thirty-Five

The following week brought much improvement in Mr Bennet's strength, as well as an event much dreaded by Caroline Bingley.

She stood between her brother and sister, a wooden smile fixed upon her face, as the Netherfield party welcomed their host of tenants. Charles beamed hugely, greeting each family with his accustomed graciousness and making each feel welcomed in his ballroom. It was to be a relaxed affair, an event which would grant the local families a special evening of recognition without causing the discomfort which usually comes with mingling stations.

Caroline swelled a little with pride as she observed each guest's impressions of her arrangements. She could host a soirée to make any Londoner envious, but this evening of understated hospitality had been challenging for her. Though the concept was still foreign to her, she complimented herself that somehow she had managed to achieve a rustic kind of elegance.

She had even gone so far as to provide nosegays and shoe roses for the young people in attendance, sparking high praise for the Master's sister among the guests. None need know that suggestion had truly come from Mrs Nichols, nor would Caroline care to know whether that lady had received her inspiration from observing the annual events held at a nearby estate.

Charles at one point turned to her with a highly satisfied expression, and she knew she had managed to redeem herself somewhat. Still not fully able to relinquish her desire to impress Darcy, her eyes trained steadily on him until he accidentally turned his head. He caught her look, offered a small bow, and returned his gaze unflinchingly to the door. The next guests to enter were the Bennet family, who had been invited because their complement of daughters boasted among them the future Mistress of Netherfield. Charles had also managed to obtain a special license, so a joint wedding of the sisters was planned. Jane would take up her mantle in a mere three more days. This would be the last event at which Caroline would preside in this house, and the realization was bittersweet.

Caroline's eyes remained on Darcy, trying to discern any play of emotions across his granite features. No flicker of anything beyond his usual civility emerged until he found the one he was waiting for. His stiff countenance finally melted when Elizabeth Bennet drew near and allowed the footman to take her wrap. Darcy could not bound to her side eagerly enough, and as the couple exchanged tender greetings, Caroline at last surrendered. Nothing would ever tear the besotted Darcy from his Elizabeth. She would do better to turn her attentions elsewhere.

Swallowing her pride, Caroline presented herself before the couple just as they had been about to slink away from the crowd at the door. "Miss Elizabeth and Mr Darcy, I do not believe I have taken the opportunity to properly congratulate you on your engagement. May I heartily wish you both every joy?" Her eyes were cast down, but she meant what she said.

It was with great astonishment that she saw Elizabeth's hand reaching to cover her own. Her gaze flashed up in awe. "Thank you, Miss Bingley," the other young lady replied gently. "As we are to be sisters soon, would you do me the honour of calling me Elizabeth?"

Caroline blanched somewhat. She shifted her gaze to Darcy, finding his expression composed and neutral. A glance back to Elizabeth showed the other's manner to be everything sincere and welcoming.

Elizabeth smiled, not discouraged by Caroline's reluctant silence. "May I also compliment you on your gracious arrangements for this evening? I shall be sure to report back to our Mrs Hill, as I am certain she might like to adopt some of your ideas. Jane, I believe, is very inspired at what you have accomplished this evening."

Caroline took a deep breath and squared her shoulders. "Yes, well... I am quite sure that you will have much to discover much about entertaining as Mrs Darcy. Should you ever find yourself in need of advice, I would be most pleased to oblige... Elizabeth."

Elizabeth's eyes sparkled with something akin to mischief as Darcy took her arm and firmly directed her toward the refreshments. Caroline drew a long breath. The mortifying confrontation was over and done with, and with any luck she might still be welcomed into the Darcys' homes. She would have need of the connection if she were to meet with eligible men!

Darcy placed his hand low on Elizabeth's back as he guided her away. Elizabeth darted him an amused glance, and his cheeks dimpled as he returned her smile. No words were needed to convey their thoughts. Caroline would always be Caroline, but she was no more than a benign trial at worst. Elizabeth, in truth, began to hope for much more genial relations than had previously existed between them.

Darcy had just helped his future bride to a drink when the young lady was approached by his smiling cousin. Colonel Fitzwilliam, returned already for their wedding three days hence, was flanked by both of his female cousins. That fact did not deter him from soliciting Elizabeth's hand for the first set. Bingley had apparently arranged for a lively evening of country dancing, much to Darcy's chagrin. Lacking the formality and order of a proper ball, a swirling, raucous evening of barely organized cavorting with Bingley's farmers was everything dreadful to him.

Elizabeth glanced furtively at her betrothed with a wicked gleam in her eye. "I apologize, Colonel, but I find myself engaged for the entire evening. Mr Darcy had requested the honour some days ago to redeem himself on the dance floor. I expect it will take him many attempts to get it right."

Richard burst into laughter, punching his cousin in the shoulder. "It just may! You shall be forgiven for keeping your fiancée all to yourself this once, Cousin, but you cannot hide forever. One of these days, you will have to dance with someone else again!" The music struck up a sprightly melody at that moment, and with a bow, the colonel released Georgiana and extended his arm to Anne. He had never truly expected to win Elizabeth's company, but it had been worth the trip across the ballroom to witness the reddening of his cousin's face.

Darcy turned to his love with a relieved grin. "I believe I am in your debt. How shall I begin to repay you?" He held his hand out to her, intending to invite her to the floor.

Elizabeth caught Georgiana's look over his shoulder and her eyes twinkled. "Before I consent to dance with you, William, I must know that you have improved somewhat in civility since our last endeavour. Is there some other lady present upon whom you might practice?"

Darcy's eyes narrowed slyly. "One handsome enough to tempt me? There are only two women in the room it would not be a punishment for me to stand up with. As you have denied me your hand for the first set, I shall inquire of the other." He turned to his sister with a wide grin, flashing his rarely seen brilliant teeth. "Georgie, may I have the honour?"

Georgiana flushed in pleasure. Her brother had expressly forbidden her to dance with any but himself, Charles, or Richard, but she was giddy at the chance to experience one of her first social events. This casual evening of entertainment was a perfect opportunity to set her at her ease, and she intended to relish every moment. Her cheeks pinked as William took her arm and led her to the floor.

Elizabeth found her way to her father, who had perched himself near the refreshments and in full view of the dance floor. He raised a glass to his lips, chuckling at the expense of the young couples in the room. At the moment, his primary diversion was a rosy-cheeked Charlotte Lucas, who had accompanied the Bennet family, and her shy young doctor. The couple had nearly patched things up with Charlotte's family, but that young lady had determined to remain with the Bennets until her marriage. Charlotte had been a welcome draught of common sense in a house full of romantic excitement.

"How are you feeling, Papa?" Elizabeth drew a chair near him, her eyes finding the tall, dark-haired Adonis on the dance floor just as that gentleman happened to be craning his neck in search of her.

Mr Bennet studied his daughter. "I would answer you if you truly seemed interested in my reply."

"You know I am, Papa!" Caught, Elizabeth steered her gaze firmly back to her father. "I am not certain it was wise for you to come tonight. You must take care not to tire yourself! Remember, Mr Darcy offered his coach to take you home early."

"How very generous. A true hardship to him, I am sure," her father gibed. "However, I believe I shall have to deny the good fellow the honour of escorting myself and my *daughter* home early." The last bit was spoken with a pointed gleam in his eye. "At present I am deriving too much enjoyment from watching him look for you. At any moment, that raw-boned lad next in line is going to tread upon his toes if he is not careful! I confess, however, I would find your Mr Darcy far more entertaining had Mr Collins and Lady Catherine seen fit to remain in the area."

"You are cruel, Papa!"

"Cruel! I am not the one who refused to stand up with the poor man again! Have a heart, Lizzy. If you do not rescue him immediately the dance ends, I predict your mother will attempt to draw him into a conversation on wedding lace. No man should be subjected to such a fate." He shuddered.

Elizabeth laughed. "Mr Darcy has found the perfect method of appeasing Mama. He lets her have her head, and then makes himself scarce."

"I could have taught him that strategy long ago." Mr Bennet raised his glass, savouring the light drink- the first he had been allowed in some while. "Ah, here he comes, Lizzy. If you can convince him to it, I shall keep Miss Darcy company on the wall. We, neither of us, ought to be out in public at present, correct? She shall be quite comfortable here, and I shall be spared the trouble of conversing with Mr Hurst, who is at present also in search of a seat near the refreshments."

Elizabeth glanced in the direction he indicated, shaking her head. "I believe Georgiana and Mary were going to perform together shortly. They ought to be withdrawing at any moment to make ready."

Mr Bennet lowered his glass, his eyes wide. "Mr Darcy! Did you make some mention of offering your carriage in case I should feel poorly?"

Darcy, who had in the past few days come to take very little of what Mr Bennet said at face value, peered quizzically at his future father-in-law. Elizabeth's answering smirk decided it. "Only after I have danced with Miss Elizabeth, sir," he smiled, releasing his sister and drawing his fiancée toward the floor. He was rewarded with a sweetly arched brow from his bride-to-be and a hearty chortle from her father.

Darcy dipped his head lower, his eyes lingering on those delicious chocolate spirals framing her pretty face. *Three more days, and I shall know what those curls feel like between my fingers!* He shook himself slightly. He would never get through the night, let alone three more days, if he allowed thoughts like that! *Deep breath!*

"Mr Bingley just informed me," he leaned near in a whisper, "that the next is to be a waltz. I am most eager to claim your hand for that dance, but I believe it will be all I will be able to manage for the night!"

"The waltz! I have never danced it, William. Is it very challenging?"

"It will not be so for you. For me, it will be the most exquisite torment imaginable, but I shall bear it if I must." He angled a suggestive smile down at her.

"Mr Darcy! Your manners have not improved after all!"

The musicians lifted their bows and Darcy slipped a hand about her waist, tugging her scandalously close to himself. Both of their breaths caught. "Allow me to make amends," he pleaded, offering his leading hand. "I find you exceedingly handsome and devastatingly tempting. I am utterly enchanted by your fine eyes and your light, pleasing figure."

"Oh!" Elizabeth choked back a mock affronted cry. "Do I detect another insult you are putting to rights?"

"Not at all. Come, my Lizzy, I want to see your cheeks flushed and those eyes brightened by the exercise." He tightened his arm around her and led her in a spinning, breathless interlude to the music. Elizabeth's heart was pattering wildly. *No one* she decided *should ever dance this unless they are betrothed, at the very least!* Her gaze locked on his compelling dark eyes. How they avoided colliding with the other couples, Elizabeth could not fathom. All she could focus on was the man who had captured her entire heart, and the feelings playing across his face as he held her.

Colonel Fitzwilliam, again partnering with the cousin he had barely known before, gave a curt nod in their direction. Anne smiled indulgently as she took in William and Elizabeth's enraptured inattentiveness to their surroundings. "It is a good thing," she whispered to her cousin, "that the wedding is not far off!"

~

Happy for all of Mrs Bennet's maternal feelings was the day she got rid of her two most deserving daughters. She sat beside her relatives in the family pew, all aflutter with excitement and pride in the fine matches her girls were making. Everyone turned as the rear doors of the church were opened to admit Mr Bennet with his two favourite daughters on his arms. His steps were slow, but his smile was incandescent.

Though Mr Bennet would sorely regret the loss of any sensible conversation to be had at Longbourn, there was no greater gift a father could ask than to know his daughters would be cherished and adored. That, he decided as he looked at each of his eldest girls, was never again to be a worry for them, at least. They both fairly glowed in radiant happiness. Jane was resplendent in soft pink, drawing sighs from around the church, but it was Elizabeth, in her sage green, who took the breath of a certain gentleman away.

Mr Bennet, chuckling a little, kept a close eye on Darcy as he walked his girls down the long aisle. Bingley fairly vibrated in elation at his friend's side, but Darcy was the very picture of one who has beheld his first masterpiece. His face was awash in speechless wonder, as though he were afraid it was all a dream and any movement might wake him from it. He had to be prompted twice to take Elizabeth's hand, so intent was he on staring at her face and catching the reassurances she mouthed silently to him. Once he had taken her hand, Mr Bennet was quite certain that Elizabeth would never get it back again.

Mr Bennet withdrew, his fatherly duties for these two daughters, at least, ended forever. He blinked away the unshed tears, obstinately determining to seek his amusement at the young grooms' expense. Darcy spent the entire ceremony in a daze, he observed with a merciless grin. Bingley looked ready to jump out of his tailcoat. His girls, however, he observed with unapologetic pride. They were everything gracious and lovely, smiling encouragement to the young men who so hopefully and fervently swore their devotion.

Darcy did not once crack a smile until the vicar announced Elizabeth to be his bride. At that pronouncement, the man's face underwent the most dramatic shift imaginable! He exceeded even Bingley in his boyish enthusiasm as he swept his new wife into his arms and fairly scandalized the entire congregation. The town of Meryton whispered for weeks afterward that Miss Elizabeth Bennet must have bewitched that taciturn man from Derbyshire to cause him to commit such a breach of propriety.

Laughing heartily- one of only a handful of voices in the congregation to do so- Mr Bennet peered across the aisle. That young sister of Mr Darcy's, as well as the colonel and Miss de Bourgh, clapped in glee and laughed merrily at Darcy's expense as he ushered his bride out of the church. Mr Bennet released a conflicted sigh. Oh, yes, he was delighted for his girl, beyond a doubt. Christmas this year, however, would not be the same without her... and neither would any other day.

Epilogue

Fitzwilliam Darcy was worried. Elizabeth was nowhere to be found, though he had already sought her in all of her usual haunts. He clutched his letter more tightly in his gloved fist as he barged through the library door once more. Her usual chair, by the fire, was quite empty.

"Do you want to send the footmen out, sir?" Mrs Reynolds caught up to him, wringing her hands in her apron. She, like every other person at Pemberley, had fallen at once head over heels in love with the young Mistress, and was most vexed that the young lady had once again slipped from her watchful gaze.

Darcy clenched his jaw. "When did you speak with her last?"

"Just after luncheon, sir. The Mistress was well, she just said she wanted a little air."

"In her condition! What is she thinking of? And you did not send someone with her?"

"Why yes, she took Miss Darcy when they called on that new family in the cottage, but they said they didn't need any other attendant. Miss Darcy returned over an hour ago, sir, and said as far as she knew, Mrs Darcy had gone to her bath!"

"She has not, and her maid has not seen her return." Darcy's fist tightened again, crumpling the innocent letter between his fingers. "She was not in the conservatory, and it is far too cold yet for her to be walking out." His mind played through any other possible options. "Have the stables been checked?" he finally inquired.

"No," Mrs Reynolds shook her head. "Mrs Darcy seldom…." She never got a chance to finish her sentence. Mr Darcy had spun about and raced out the door, in search once again of his free-spirited young wife.

Mrs Reynolds chuckled a little and shook her head. The only one who really worried for the Mistress' safety was her husband, who would have been fretting over her had she been only as far away as the next room. Mrs Darcy was quite a capable young woman, Mrs Reynolds assured herself. An ideal Mistress she was, after the pattern of Lady Anne herself, but with far more boundless energy. She was exactly what the young Master had been needing all along. Wiping her hands on her apron, she hummed a little tune and set back to her duties.

Darcy had set out for the stables at a run. He only took a deep breath when he at last spotted his wife's figure, still svelte despite her third month of pregnancy, silhouetted against the light filtering through the end of the barn. "Elizabeth!"

She turned from the horse she was petting, one of his many wedding gifts to her, with an impish smile. "Oh, dear, have I set the house into an uproar again?"

"The house! Forget the house, what about me?"

"Come closer, William, and I will apologize properly," she grinned.

He approached, still trying to look stern. "Elizabeth, you ought not be tiring yourself just now. And in this weather! It is going to snow very hard this evening, Elizabeth. It is not like that 'light winter' you were having in Hertfordshire. Even an April snow in Derbyshire is something you should not be caught out in!"

"How fortunate for me, then, that I have such a wise and devoted protector!" She shot a pert look up at him and unbuttoned the front of his coat so she could wriggle her way under the warm folds, forcing him to put his arms about her. *Dastardly woman!* he thought with an inward smile. She somehow always managed to put him right where she wanted him, which… was usually rather pleasant.

"Elizabeth, you must take this more seriously," he arched a firm brow at her, frowning a little. It was his last ploy, and it was doomed to fail.

"Oh, I am *very* serious." She turned her face up to his and deliberately knocked his hat to the ground, weaving her fingers through his hair and tugging his towering frame down to her level. "There. Now, I shall be quite warm, William!"

"I ought to scold you and send you indoors like the wayward woman you are!" he thinned his lips and cocked a hint of a smile at her.

"But you will not. You are going to tell me what is in that letter in your hand. Now then, when shall we be attending your cousins' wedding?"

"What?" he shook his head in astonishment. "I never… How do you do it?"

"Oh, it is rather simple, William. Richard has been calling on Anne ever since we wed, and it cannot have taken all of that time to settle Lady Catherine in the dower house."

"Indeed it can! I thought we would require an armed escort there for a while!"

"Ah, but the colonel was rather persuasive, was he not? I am surprised at you, not seeing how he managed to wheedle into even your aunt's good graces at last during that undertaking. Poor Anne never stood a chance against such charm!"

"Well, however much *you* may have suspected it, *I* did not! I thought there was some... attachment... in another quarter. You remember, the one that I am not to speak of."

"The colonel is a gentleman, William! To imply that he would form designs on a girl who is not out, and his own ward! Perfectly shocking." She blithely flicked some snow from his coat.

"Indeed. And I am to expect that this ward of his is not displeased?"

"Not at all. It was she who was encouraging his attentions to Anne, I believe. She is young, William, but she is mature enough to know it. She very selflessly wanted to see her dear cousin happily retired and settled before he was injured in the army. As for Richard's interests, well, Anne and Georgiana do have many qualities in common, after all, and I think he found much in her to admire as well. It is almost like she and Georgiana are sisters, rather than just cousins."

Darcy stared at her penetratingly. He had never divulged that particular secret, not even to Elizabeth, but it seemed she had her ways. "*How do you do it?*" he dared to ask again.

"Do what, William?" she arched her brows innocently. "I have not yet the clairvoyance to determine their wedding date. Have you any intention of telling me?"

"No indeed!" he tucked the crumpled letter back into his coat. "I insist on having some secrets, after all."

"It won't work," she insisted with a grin. "Just like when you gave me Persephone here," she stroked the mare's nose again. "You cannot surprise me, William!"

"I did surprise you at least once, I take comfort in that."

"That is true! I think I have never been so shocked in my life! I had no idea then that you possessed a very proper streak of recklessness. If, however, a proposal of love is to be the nature of your surprises, William, I invite you to continue to try."

"Indeed, I shall." He laughed out loud and bent to scoop her up in his arms.

Elizabeth squealed in delight, wrapping her own arms around his neck. "William, you must put me down! After all, you might drop me and heaven knows, we can have no risks to my health right now!"

"Not likely. I am bundling you in my arms and taking you directly to bed, Mrs Darcy."

"William! What will everyone say?"

"What they have been saying since you came here- that you are the best thing to ever happen to me." He lifted her a little closer for a sweet kiss.

"Flattery will avail you nothing, sir."

"No, but this usually does." He pressed her lips in a deeper kiss, encouraging her to welcome his tender caresses. His generous Elizabeth never denied him! They remained so for several delicious, speechless moments. At length, he was forced of necessity to set her feet again on the ground, but he was unwilling to relinquish her quite yet. He backed her against a wall, cupping her face in his hands and continuing his passionate ministrations.

Eventually she pressed her hand to his chest. "William, do not forget that Charles and Jane expected to arrive later today," she reminded him softly.

"They are not here yet, and I intend to make the most of our privacy," he murmured into her cheek.

"And I have not had a letter from my father in nearly ten days." She arched her neck, shivering as his lips traveled down her jaw.

"You cannot mean...." He ceased his attentions to her milky skin, drawing back in mild alarm.

"He did make you promise to welcome him at any time he saw fit! I know Mama has been badgering him to bring her here. She is most anxious to see the prize I have captured."

"Oh, so it truly is Pemberley you desired, and not myself." He quirked an eyebrow at his saucy little wife.

"Of course it is, but I have found the Master of Pemberley to be rather engaging as well, particularly when he steps in to rescue me from a dreadful fate! Now, were you going to save me from this approaching snow storm?"

"Indeed, and it seems I must hurry, for I believe I detect some frost bite... here... and here...." He indicated the endangered places of her person with his warm lips. "In fact, Mrs Darcy, I do not think I can be at all easy until I have inspected every... little... part of you."

"Far be it from me to reject such noble aid," she whispered, tilting her head to the side and closing her eyes in rapturous enjoyment.

"Come, then." He wrapped her in his arms once more, lifting her easily and beginning the march to the house. "If I am to face dangerous elements and wild beasts..."

"William!" she cried in mock offence.

"... I require a little fortification," he continued firmly. "It is your duty, my dear lady, to render such succour- for the good of the estate."

She laced her fingers around his shoulders, tipping her head back playfully. At last she offered a resigned sigh. "The things I put up with to be Mistress of Pemberley!"

"A hardship, to be sure," he agreed. "Sadly for you, the Master is rather particular, and will accept no substitutes."

"He *is* a most trying fellow! If only he would speak once in a while, so one might determine his true sentiments!"

"I should have thought them rather obvious," he grinned, quickening his pace toward the house. "He is quite violently in love, utterly bewitched body and soul, and is happiest when in the arms of his dearest, loveliest Elizabeth."

"Then he shall find his feelings returned with equal fervour." She pressed a distracting kiss to his temple, nearly causing him to stumble as he carried her. She whispered low into his ear, "You will be gratified to know, my love, that I intend to keep you *exceedingly* happy for all of our days."

His eyes lit. "That sounds intriguing."

She toyed with a wavy lock of his hair. "Oh, it will be!"

Darcy stumbled through the door of the house as his butler opened it, refusing still to release his wife. He nearly raced up the stairs with her, ignoring the fatigue in his arms until he had her all alone.

Gerald Perkins, the butler of Pemberley for the last thirty years, turned stoically away as Mrs Reynolds paused before him, her shocked gaze following the disappearing figures of the hatless Master and his Mistress. Her wide eyes rose to her towering associate.

"Estate business," Perkins explained, with a faint twinkle in his eye.

Mrs Reynolds shook her head. "Hush, or word will start out that the Master is a rash, heedless sort!"

"No," Perkins asserted. "I think the Master eminently wise and sensible."

Mrs Reynolds smiled, a happy tear touching her eye. "As do I."

Fine

ABOUT THE AUTHOR

Nicole Clarkston is the pen name of a very bashful writer who will not allow any of her family or friends to read what she writes. She grew up in Idaho on horseback, and if she could have figured out how to read a book at the same time, she would have. She initially pursued a degree in foreign languages and education, and then lost patience with it, switched her major, and changed schools. She now resides in Oregon with her husband of 15 years, 3 homeschooled kids, and a very worthless degree in Poultry Science (don't ask).

Nicole discovered Jane Austen rather by guilt in her early thirties- how does any book worm really live that long without a little P&P? She has never looked back. A year or so later, during a major house renovation project (undertaken when her husband unsuspectingly left town for a few days) she discovered Elizabeth Gaskell and fell completely in love.

She published her first book, a *North & South* variation titled *No Such Thing As Luck*, in 2015. *Rumours & Recklessness* is Nicole's second published book. She has since published *Northern Rain*, another North & South variation, and is currently working on both another *Pride and Prejudice* variation and a third *North & South* story.

Printed in Great Britain
by Amazon